zero over berlin
joh sasaki

translated by
hiroko yoda with matt alt

VERTICAL.

Published by Vertical, Inc., New York

Zero Over Berlin was originally published
in Japanese as *Berurin Hiko Shirei* by Shinchosha, Tokyo, 1988.

ISBN 1-932234-09-8

Manufactured in the United States of America

First American Edition

Vertical, Inc.
257 Park Avenue South, 8th Floor
New York, NY 10010
www.vertical-inc.com

Foreword

A chance meeting with an elderly engineer triggered my interest in the flight of the Type Zero Carrier Fighter.

At the time, I was fascinated by sixties-era F-1 racing. I was making the rounds interviewing people who had worked as part of the Honda racing team back then. I had something of a connection to Honda myself, fueling all the more my interest in auto racing and the industry that surrounded it.

Meeting Toshihiko Asano changed all that. He was the director of research and development at Honda. Talking to him dramatically shifted my interest from cars to aircraft. He had played a central role in Honda's first F-1 project, and had also overseen the development of the firm's new engine technology. But years earlier, as an engineering officer during World War II, he had developed and improved engines for aircraft at the Imperial Naval Aviation Technology Development Center in Yokosuka.

At our second meeting, he happened to tell me a story that had nothing to do with F-1 racing. It was a strange and fascinating tale from his past, the facts of which he had painstakingly pieced together over the course of his years living and working in Europe. In the many times that I visited him since that fateful conversation, the questions and mysteries surrounding his story were all that we talked about.

When Mr. Asano succumbed to stomach cancer in 1985, he left me a wealth of materials that he had gathered over the course of his investigation. I spent years poring through the notes, letters, and copies of official documents dedicated to answering the question he had carried with him for a lifetime.

The mystery that had so fascinated Mr. Asano dealt with an Imperial Japanese Navy Type Zero Carrier Fighter. One of the aircraft, it was said, had flown from Japan to Germany during World War II. No official records of any such flight exist. Military aviation experts shake their heads in disbelief when told the story. But the older he got, the deeper Mr. Asano's conviction grew. In 1940, he said, at least one Zero fighter must have landed at a Luftwaffe airbase just outside of Berlin. Not only that, he continued; the pilot must have been Japanese, too.

And as it turns out, Mr. Asano was absolutely right.

Part One

CHAPTER 1

The old man said:

"I've seen a Zero fighter. In Berlin, right in front of my eyes." It was July 1964. Toshihiko Asano was in Mainen, a town near the Nurburgring racing circuit.

"I saw the Zero. When it came to Berlin," repeated the elderly German as the two stood in the lobby of what passed as the local hotel.

It was the year of Honda's debut in the World F-1 Grand Prix series. It was the very first time they had designed and sent not just an engine, but an entire race car, the RA271, to the Grand Prix. It was a historic moment not only for Honda, but for the entire Japanese automotive industry.

Honda's machine may not have won the race, but the spectacle of the Far East's first effort had won the hearts of both spectators and participants alike. In fact, Honda had garnered even more attention than the Brabham or Ferrari teams. German fans seemed to have high hopes for the Japanese. Perhaps this was driven by the Honda team's already respectable record in world motorcycle races. Or, perhaps, it had been the article in *Auto Motor Und Sport*, the German motorsports magazine, that so captivated the racing fans.

The article had been titled "A Mysterious People." It focused on Honda's debut in the F-1 race, and it was extremely favorable. At the time, there weren't any German cars entered in the race. Perhaps because of this, German fans seemed to have pinned the hope for snatching victory from the British squarely upon the Japanese.

One aspect of the article surprised Asano and his teammates. It reported that the Honda development team included engineers who had worked on the famed Japanese Zero fighter during the war. This referred to team director Yoshio Nakamura and to Asano himself, both of whom had been involved in the Zero project. Engineer Shoichi Sano, who didn't make the trip to Germany for the race, could have been included as well. All three had worked on engines for Japanese military aircraft, including the Zero, during the war in the Pacific.

When Asano and the rest of the Honda team had been interviewed a month earlier in the Netherlands, they had disclosed their backgrounds without hesitation. The look of respect on the reporters' faces at the words

"Zero fighter" had been unmistakable.

"The Zero fighter? You built the Zero fighter?" they had asked in amazement.

Asano and Nakamura patiently explained that they had worked on only one part of the famous aircraft. Once the reporters had gotten the idea in their heads, though, there was no clearing the misconception. Undoubtedly, the organizers of the race had demanded a bit of sensationalism from the reporters. Whatever the case, when the articles finally hit the newsstands, they practically claimed that Asano and Nakamura had built the Zero fighter with their own hands.

From the moment Asano and his teammates arrived at Nurburgring, they were mobbed by spectators and reporters who, enthused by the article, begged to shake hands with the people who had designed the legendary Zero fighter. At first, Asano frantically denied the claim, but after a while, he gave up. In truth, he wasn't particularly upset about being recognized as an engineer who'd worked on the Zero fighter project. In any event, it was hardly stretching the truth.

One night, an old man by the name of Klausen came to visit Asano.

"Are you a member of the Honda F-1 racing team?" he asked in English. "Are you Mr. Nakamura? Or Mr. Asano?" Klausen was a red-faced man with thinning hair. His breath smelled of alcohol. Perhaps he had had a beer.

"I am Asano. How can I help you?" replied Asano in English. Was this another racing fan obsessed with Asano's role in the Zero project?

"I saw an article that said you built the Zero fighter."

A-ha, thought Asano.

"No, I didn't 'build' it," said Asano with a smile. "I did a little work on the engine, that's all."

The old man continued on as if he hadn't heard Asano's response.

"My name is Klausen. I run an auto-repair shop in a town about a hundred miles from here," he said, and pointed to the magazine clipping in his hand. "I saw the article and I had to come here, but it took me a little longer than expected. By the time I made it here to Nurburgring, the race was already over and I didn't get to see your machine. So I asked around where the Japanese team was staying, and came to find you."

"You did?" asked Asano, touched at finding a fan so far from home. "So you like Honda's car? But your own country is building such wonderful machines, like Porsche..."

"I'm interested in Honda's motorcycles because of my job," said Klausen. "But, to be honest, I wanted to see what kind of a machine the Zero fighter engineers came up with. Is it anything like Dr. Heinkel's race car?"

"Thank you for the comparison, but it was a total failure. It crashed in the middle of the race. The car has already been removed to a transport truck."

"Crashed?!" cried Klausen. "So you can't show it to me?"

"Unfortunately, no, Mr. Klausen," replied Asano.

The old man shook his head in disappointment. "I heard it was beautiful. The papers said you used a 12-cylinder engine. Is that true?"

"Yes. We developed our own 60-degree V-12 engine."

"Twelve cylinders?" exclaimed Klausen. "That's like an aircraft! The Daimler-Benz 601A, it was the same kind of engine. Did you get the idea from them?"

The question took Asano by surprise. He knew about the DB601A, the engine of the Messerschmitt Me109 fighter (during the war, the aircraft was known as the Bf109, as the company's name was not "Messerschmitt" but "Bayerische Flugzeugwerke"), but it hadn't influenced his work on the F-1 project. In fact, the resemblance hadn't even occurred to him. But there was no denying that the huge engine that they had selected was similar to those used in airplanes. Honda's RA271 could well be called an F-1 machine built around an aircraft engine.

"You seem to know your way around engines," said Asano.

"I told you. It's my job."

Suddenly the old man tottered. Asano grabbed hold of him.

"I'm sorry," gasped the old man. "Just let me sit down for a moment. I've got a bad leg." Asano eased the old man onto a nearby sofa and sat down beside him. The old man withdrew a handkerchief from a pocket and began wiping his forehead.

"It's from the war. I got hit on the line, defending Berlin. It doesn't hurt, but it doesn't have any strength, either."

"So you fought in the war," said Asano.

"I was an officer in the Luftwaffe at the end of the war. Too old even back then, though."

"Luftwaffe? Were you a pilot?" asked Asano.

Part One

"No. I was ground crew. Maintenance. So I've seen my share of aircraft. Biplanes, low-slung monoplane fighters, reconnaissance planes, bombers, you name it. I love the things."

"The Germans had their share of impressive designs," said Asano. "We learned a lot from studying your aircraft."

"I saw all sorts of aircraft in my day, but the Zero fighter was something else. Very beautiful," said the old man. "It looked like...like a sixteen-year-old girl. A petite one, an athlete."

Asano grinned.

"You sound like you've actually seen a Zero fighter with your own eyes."

"That's right. I have," replied the old man. "With my own eyes."

"A Zero fighter?" asked a shocked Asano. "Where?"

"In Berlin. At Gatow, the airfield." The old man laboriously removed a photograph from the pocket of his jacket. It was very old. The edges were worn and tattered. Asano took the photograph and studied it for a moment.

It showed a single-seat aircraft surrounded by several men. Asano immediately recognized it as a Type Zero Carrier Fighter. How many times had he seen it? There was absolutely no question about it. Judging from the cowling and exhaust pipes, it appeared to be a Model 11.

Two men stood in front of a wing.

One of them appeared to be a German officer. He wore a long coat and carried what appeared to be a cane. He was a big man, apparently in his fifties, perhaps even older. It wasn't difficult to guess that he was someone important, a high-ranking officer. He even looked a little familiar, thought Asano. Like someone he'd seen quite often, long ago.

The other person was a young man in a flight suit. He looked rather Asian. He wore a white scarf around his neck. The older man was smiling, but the face of the young man was stern and rigid.

Several men stood behind the Zero. They appeared to be soldiers, perhaps ground crew.

The old man pointed to the photo and said, "That's me in the back. This picture was taken the day the Zero arrived in Berlin."

"A Zero fighter flew to Berlin? This is the first I've heard of it," said Asano.

Klausen nodded emphatically. "Of course it did. I saw it with my

7

own eyes!"

"When was this?"

"The day the Zero landed in Berlin? It was during the war."

"Yes, but when, exactly?" Asano asked. Klausen's breath still reeked of beer. "When exactly did the Zero come to Berlin?"

Just then, a young mechanic on the Honda team called Asano's name. The crew was going to have dinner, he said. It was time to discuss the race and have a debriefing about what had happened.

Something bothered Asano. Still, he returned the photograph to the old man. "Mr. Klausen, I beg your pardon, but I must have dinner with my teammates. I thank you for your support."

"It was a beautiful aircraft," repeated the old man. "As beautiful as a young lady. And you're the one who built it..."

The old man took Asano's hand in a firm grip. He shook it for a very long time.

"I'll be cheering for you," said Klausen. "If the Japanese are behind it, I know it'll be a great machine. It's only a matter of time before you win."

When Asano reached the dining table, he told Nakamura about the old man. Nakamura had been attached to the Army Aviation Technology Development Center during the war. He had been an engine specialist. If the conversation turned to aircraft during the war, he'd keep talking all night.

"I'm sorry I'm late," said Asano. "An old man, a fan of Japan, showed up. He was very supportive. A Luftwaffe officer during the war. And he said that he'd seen a Zero fighter."

"A German?" Nakamura asked back, surprised. "He saw a Zero fighter?"

"That's what he said. At an airfield near Berlin, during the war. He even had a photograph."

"Uh-uh," said Nakamura, shaking his head. "There weren't any Zero fighters in Germany during the war. He made it up."

He's probably right, thought Asano.

Asano realized what had been bothering him. There was no way the story about the Zero in Berlin could have been true. Asano had been part of the Naval Aviation Technology Development Center, and he hadn't heard anything about it. There hadn't been any announcement to the effect, nor

Part One

had there been so much as a rumor. And he'd never seen any mention of it in the official reports and articles that appeared after the war.

Yet—what to make of the picture?

So did the enigma take root in Toshihiko Asano's mind.

CHAPTER 2

To be honest, when I first heard the story, I wasn't sure what was so mysterious or interesting about it.

I wasn't really interested in aircraft, and I didn't have much of a clue about the fine points of World War II. As a kid I hadn't spent time memorizing the names of cars and planes and gobbling up war movies; rather, I played journalist and enjoyed creating my own newspapers.

After hearing Asano's story, I had another look at him. He was an old man: black-rimmed glasses, hunched shoulders, and a bad posture. His skin was mottled and pale. From the beginning I'd sensed that he suffered from some kind of illness, some internal disease.

My subdued reaction to the tale seemed to disappoint Mr. Asano. He reached for his cigarettes on the table and slid one from the package.

We were in Honda's headquarters. The room was comfortable, with thick wall-to-wall carpeting. The entire floor had been converted into a sort of lounge for retired executives. We were the only ones there that afternoon. The only interruption came from the secretary, who occasionally brought us fresh tea.

Mr. Asano exhaled a long cloud of smoke towards the ceiling.

"Do you think Kłausen was lying?" I asked. "Even with the picture?"

Asano shook his head. "I don't know. But there's no question that the photograph was real. That was a Zero fighter in the picture."

"But they say that no Zero ever flew to Germany."

"That's right. I looked into it at length myself. I gathered all the documents and materials I could find, and went to the trouble of asking people who'd know. But I couldn't turn up any official record."

"Are you absolutely sure the picture was taken in Germany?" I asked. "It could have been shot in Japan, when a German officer was visiting."

"That occurred to me as well. But then I remembered the name of the officer who was standing in front of the Zero fighter," said Asano.

"Who was it?"

"Hermann Goering. Commander of the Luftwaffe, Reich Marshal of the Greater German Reich. He never came to Japan."

Part One

I ran through the story again in my head.

"So you're saying that no Zero fighter is supposed to have flown to Germany. Yet one was photographed somewhere in the country. Which means that one of those statements has to be false. Either a Zero did fly to Germany, or the photo is a fake."

"That's right. It has to be one or the other."

Just off the top of my head, I suggested: "Perhaps it's a composite shot, some kind of trick."

"No. It can't be," said Asano firmly. "Why would Klausen have gone through all the trouble of making and showing me a fake photo? What could he have possibly gotten out of it—the satisfaction of tricking a naïve Japanese? Is that what you think? I've gone over that day a thousand times in my head. I don't think the man was lying, and I don't think the photo was a trick."

The idea of Klausen being some kind of con man leapt to mind, but I kept my mouth shut.

"I'm not an expert about this sort of thing, so it's tough for me to tell what, exactly, is strange about the story," I said. "There may not be any official record of a Zero flying to Germany, but that doesn't mean that it couldn't have happened. Right? If the photograph exists, isn't that the proof right there? Maybe the records were lost."

"Yes, but remember what it was like during the war. The Navy deployed the first Type Zero Carrier Fighters in the summer of 1940. By that time, World War II had already broken out in Europe. That fall, Germany, Italy, and Japan formed their alliance. The following year, in June, the Soviets and the Germans declared war on each other. And in December, the war in the Pacific began. So when, and how, could a Zero fighter have flown from Japan to Germany? If it had been before the war, most likely the plane would have traveled over the Soviet Union. But when you consider the political tension between Japan and the U.S.S.R. once the war was on, it just wouldn't have been feasible. Assuming the flight took place after the Axis powers allied, the southern route across the British colony of India would have been severed as well. I don't think the RAF would have given permission for a cutting-edge Japanese fighter plane to make an overflight."

Mr. Asano continued to summarize the international situation at the time for me. I had some idea about some of what he was talking about, but truth be told, I lacked the big picture. What's more, I knew next to nothing about India or the Middle East. But after hearing Mr. Asano's explanation, I was finally able to piece together a picture of the geopolitics of the era.

"So you're saying that there's no way that a Zero fighter could have made it to Germany during the war," I said.

"Exactly. If a Zero had flown to Germany then, you can bet that it would have been public knowledge even during the war. We're talking about a flight between Japan and Germany. It may not have been as sensational as the feat of the *Kamikaze*, but it would have been something, for sure. Why didn't anybody hear about it?"

Mr. Asano's voice was taking on the tone of a teacher speaking to a slow student.

"Have you ever heard of an aircraft called the A-26?" asked Asano. "It's a twin-engine land-based aircraft. Two prototypes were produced during the war."

"No. I don't know much about aircraft," I replied.

"The first was developed at Tokyo University's aviation research facility. In the spring of 1944, it broke the world record for the longest non-stop flight. This was during the war, so the record was unofficial. But I heard that it flew over 16,000 kilometers. It was big news back when I was working as a Navy officer."

Mr. Asano peered into my eyes intently, as if trying to gauge my reaction. He continued. "The second A-26 prototype left for Berlin in the summer of 1943. It never made it. It took off from Singapore and avoided British-controlled India and headed over the sea for the German army base in Crimea. But it disappeared without a trace. No radio transmission, nothing. The purpose of the flight was to establish an air route between Germany and Japan. The land route had been cut off ever since war had been declared between Germany and the Soviet Union. The only contact was sporadic, using submarines. Japan must have had high hopes for the A-26."

Asano went on to tell me about the flight of another aircraft, the Italian SM82 transport plane. The aircraft took off from the Crimean peninsula, flew over Baotou, China, and finally landed at the Fussa airfield in Tokyo—a 13,000 kilometer flight without a stop to refuel. The Japanese military had been inspired by the flight. They devoted themselves to establishing safe air routes to their European allies.

"Did the disappearance of the A-26 make the news in Japan at the time?" I asked.

"No. The flight was top-secret. The only people who heard anything were people like me, who were working in the aviation industry, and even then it was just rumor. The mission and the plane's disappearance were never reported publicly."

"So that means it's possible that there aren't any records for the Zero fighter's flight, either," I said.

"Well, yes and no," replied Asano. He seemed to be searching for the right words. "The mission could have been planned and executed in total secrecy. From that standpoint, sure, it's possible that no official records exist. But everyone involved in the flight of the A-26 came forward after the war. So, you see, there's no way that even a top-secret mission can disappear without a trace. When you look at it that way, the answer is no."

"It's been thirty-eight years since the war ended. Maybe the records were thrown away, or people forgot about it," I suggested.

"You think a Zero did fly to Germany?" he asked.

"I understand how difficult the flight must have been from a political and military standpoint, but it doesn't sound impossible."

"I agree," said Asano, nodding vigorously. "In fact, you can't help thinking it must have been possible. During the war, a Zero fighter flew to Germany, and a few people even saw it. I don't know who was at the controls, what route it took, or when exactly it happened. But the fact is, a Zero fighter overcame countless obstacles and made it all the way to Berlin. It makes more sense to me to think that it did happen."

"But somehow the records all disappeared," I said.

"That's right. It should have been pretty big news in the military, but nobody heard a thing. Doesn't that strike you as odd?" And then Asano added, "As a writer, doesn't this interest you at all? Is the musty old story worth investigating and writing about?"

"Well, sure," I said somewhat cautiously. I knew Asano was trying to persuade me. "Yes, the story's a little strange."

"All the notes and material I've collected are at my home in Atsugi. Why don't you stop by one of these days? We can talk more about it then."

"Is there any way to corroborate Klausen's story?" I asked.

"How about a letter from East Berlin?" asked Asano. "It says something about a Japanese pilot who participated in the defense of Berlin at the end of the war. It said the Japanese pilot was an officer who…arrived in Berlin in a Zero fighter."

That was the moment I finally found myself drawn into the story. At the time, of course, I didn't know I would write a book about it. But I sniffed something interesting, and something was telling me to take the old man seriously.

Even if I didn't uncover anything intriguing enough to justify writing about at his house, I figured that if I could learn more about World War II and aviation technology, it wouldn't be a waste of time. I promised Asano that I would drop by on the following Saturday. That was 1983, early in the winter.

CHAPTER 3

Ten years passed since Toshihiko Asano's conversation with Herr Klausen in the summer of 1964.

Honda had suspended their first F-1 project at the end of the 1968 racing season, transferring most of the engineering team to consumer automobile development projects. Asano spent some time working on engines for compact cars. After developing a new air-cooled 1300cc engine, he left the research and development branch. He had just been promoted to vice president of operations for Honda Belgium. He was 56 years old.

Two years later, Asano had finally adjusted to working in a new land. He also managed to get some time off here and there to take small trips. Asano resolved to devote his free time and spare money to investigating the question of the Zero fighter. Who knew? Maybe he could manage to corroborate the old German's story. By 1974, Asano was devoting whatever time he could to his quiet little quest.

After poring over the extensive official records and research materials dealing with the Type Zero Carrier Fighter, Asano sent a letter to the readers' column of the British aviation magazine *Air International*:

> *I'm looking for any information about a Japanese A6M Type Zero ("ZEKE") fighter that flew to Europe during World War II. I am interested in records, photographs, stories, and anything else you may have. I was an engineer who worked on aircraft engines during the war. My job focused on making improvements to the Zero fighter's engine.*
>
> *Toshihiko Asano*

Asano's letter was published but there was no response for some time.

He made two weekend visits to West Germany. Needless to say, he spent both trips trying to track down Klausen's whereabouts. The only clue Asano had was Klausen's comment that he ran an auto repair shop in some town a hundred or so miles from Mainen. Asano thought this could mean Dusseldorf or Frankfurt, but he wasn't able to track the man down. He placed personal ads in the newspapers of both cities to no avail. Klausen appeared to have been over sixty when Asano met him in the lobby of the inn; perhaps the gentleman had already passed away.

Sometime after his two visits to the Rhineland, Asano received a letter from the U.S. It was from a retired U.S. Air Force colonel living in Phoenix, Arizona. He wanted to hear the full story behind Asano's request.

He called himself an amateur aviation historian. While he hadn't heard of anything pertaining to Asano's question specifically, he was very interested in seeing copies of any materials Asano had to back up the story. Asano replied that he hadn't managed to confirm anything himself as of yet.

Three months after Asano's request had been published in the periodical, he received another letter, this time from England. It was postmarked "Aldershot." The man who sent it said he used to belong to the Royal Air Force.

To a friend I haven't yet had the pleasure of meeting, Mr. Asano:

I read your request for information in Air International *with great interest. It brought back more than a few old memories, and so now I find myself writing to you. I was assigned to a RAF base in Iraq as a cook from 1940 to 1942. During this time, we were attacked twice by Iraqi forces.*

The second of these attacks was large and employed more than a fair number of ground forces. The first, however, had been quite small and carried out by air. There were very few injuries, so the attack isn't particularly well documented. However, I remember that the airplanes that carried out the attack featured red circles on their wings. Just a few aircraft, made of steel, monoplane fighters with a low-slung wing design. They were in formation when they appeared over our airfield.

Some time later, I saw a photograph of a Type Zero fighter and was convinced that it was the aircraft that had attacked our base. My colleagues, however, denied it. In fact, there is no record of a Japanese aircraft ever attacking a British military base in Iraq. I had written it off as a misunderstanding, but I just can't get those bright red circles out of my mind. I don't know if my story matches the type of information that you are looking for, but I couldn't get your request out of my mind, either. Please let me know if there is any way that I can assist you.

Sincerely,
Robert Partridge

Part One

Asano immediately wrote a letter thanking the man and asking for more details.

He received a reply two weeks later, but it didn't contain more details than the original letter. Asano wrote back again, asking the man if he would be willing to meet in London. You're welcome anytime, came the reply, Aldershot happens to be only thirty miles from London. Five weeks later, Asano made arrangements to meet the former RAF cook during a business trip to London.

Partridge turned out to be a sixty-year-old man with puffy, red eyes. He was thin and slightly stooped. He arrived at the meeting wearing a worn leather hunting cap and a thick tweed jacket. He said that he had worked as a cook and a truck driver after the war. He had taken his pension and currently lived in his hometown, Aldershot. Though he didn't appear to be highly educated, his English sounded curiously middle class.

Asano offered to buy Partridge a drink at the pub in which they had met.

"I'd like a Scotch," said Partridge. "My body takes to Scotch more than ale in weather like this."

Asano placed an order for two Scotches. The drinks arrived. Asano took a sip. "Do you know aircraft very well?" he asked.

"Not as well as cooking," replied Partridge. "I wasn't a pilot, but I was stationed at an airbase. I know as much about aircraft as kids do about rock musicians these days. I don't know how to fly one, of course. And don't ask me about aerodynamics."

"Do you read *Air International* regularly?"

"From time to time. I don't buy them. I borrow them from the library on occasion. I happened across your letter quite by accident."

Partridge raised his glass to his lips. Asano noticed that his eyes were already bloodshot. He appeared to have started drinking prior to their meeting.

"Can you swear that it was a Zero fighter that you saw?" asked Asano.

"I didn't say that," said Partridge, shaking his head. "After the fact, I thought it could have been a Zero fighter. I first saw a picture of a Zero fighter in 1944, '45. Maybe after the war. I don't remember exactly."

"You said you saw the rising sun marking on the wings?"

"It was an airplane with red circles painted on the wings," replied Partridge.

"Did you think the planes might have been Japanese, at the time?" asked Asano.

"No. Not at all. I didn't even know what kind of markings the Japanese used back then. When was H.M.S. Prince of Wales sunk? That's when our countries declared war on each other."

"December 1941," said Asano.

"That's right! The attack on our base happened a year before that, towards the end of 1940. We were in Iraq. We never dreamed the Japanese would attack us."

"You wrote that you'd seen aircraft attacking in formation. How many planes, exactly, were there?" asked Asano.

"Well... I don't recall exactly. I think there were maybe just two planes. But the soldiers on the watchtower reported seeing three. Everyone who saw it happen tells it differently. That's why I said 'a few planes' in the letter. But come to think of it, it happened so early in the morning that there weren't all that many witnesses. Maybe four or five who saw the whole thing."

Asano took another sip of Scotch. "Could you tell me everything that you remember, from the very beginning?"

Partridge nodded and raised his empty glass. Asano ordered another Scotch for him.

It happened at the Musalla Airbase, in a suburb of Baghdad. One of the RAF's stations in Iraq, Musalla was under the command of the No. 70 RAF Bomber Squadron at Hinaidi Airbase, with six Vickers Victoria twin-engine biplane bombers.

The day of the attack, there were no alerts or travel restrictions at Musalla. Relations between England and Iraq were increasingly tense, but no one expected any sort of imminent military action. That being said, the day before, a young officer newly stationed at Musalla had stirred up some kind of trouble in Baghdad, and there had been all sorts of trouble trying to get him out of Iraqi police custody. The RAF officers were keeping a wary eye on the movement of the Iraqi military forces. The morning of the attack, Partridge left his barracks and walked to the mess to begin preparing breakfast. He thought he heard the roar of a large aircraft in the distance and looked to the sky. It was just after dawn. The sound seemed to be coming from the direction of the sun, which was still low on the horizon. It sounded unfamiliar. He was only an enlisted man, but Partridge knew the distinctive sound of every aircraft in the RAF. This was an engine Partridge had not heard before. Still, he couldn't see the plane.

Partridge continued on to the mess, keeping a nervous eye on the sky to the east. It wasn't time for the courier plane to arrive yet. He glanced at the observation tower. The man on watch was scanning the sky to the east with a pair of binoculars. Perhaps he had caught sight of the plane's shadow.

The roar of the incoming aircraft's engine grew steadily louder. Finally it sounded as if it had reached the airfield.

Suddenly, the staccato cracking of machine guns filled the air. Partridge saw smoke rising from the hardstand where the bombers were parked. A series of small explosions wracked the six Victorias, spraying shrapnel from their metal hides far into the air. The sound reached a crescendo as a single small aircraft flew overhead, incredibly low, and peeled upwards into the sky. Partridge saw that the wing wasn't marked with the triangle the Iraqis used. It was a red circle.

A split second later, the second fighter came in fast, strafing what remained of the Victorias. The bombers shook with the force of the machine-gun fire raking their bodies. Some pitched forward on their noses; others slumped to the side and came to rest on a single wing. Suddenly there was a tremendous explosion from the midst of the shattered aircraft.

Gathering his senses, Partridge made a dash for the mess. The air raid siren filled the air as the guard in the watchtower belatedly realized what was going on. Soldiers and pilots stumbled from the barracks, scattering for their positions at the base.

Partridge made it all the way to the mess before he realized, through his panic, that he really should have been heading to the air raid shelter instead. He spun and ran for the shelter, next to his barracks, and leapt in headfirst.

"We're under attack!" somebody shouted.

"Air raid!" shouted somebody else.

The air was filled with panic. An officer waved his handgun desperately, impotently, at the air. More than a few soldiers were still in their underwear. A truck slammed into the sandbags in front of the shelter, rode up for a moment, and tipped over onto its side. One of the aircraft cut a wide turn at the edge of the base and came in for another run from the east. It was going for the hangars on the north side of the base. A short burst from the aircraft's machine guns perforated several of the rooftops. The anti-aircraft cannon next to the runway roared. The fighter was flying so low that it seemed as if its belly would scrape the tops of the buildings.

There was an explosion as the base's fuel depot took a direct hit. The main tank and oil drums began going up one after another. Every time one of them blew up, a gust of scorching wind buffeted the base. Partridge pulled his head down as low as it could go behind the sandbags.

It had all happened so quickly. There hadn't been any warning of the attack. It ended just as suddenly. The aircraft disappeared into the westward sky and didn't return.

It must have been a full thirty seconds before the soldiers finally gathered their wits and climbed out of the shelter. The men began trying to put out the fires, but the Victorias had burned nearly beyond recognition.

"The base went to full alert for some time after the attack," said Partridge, "but we never counterattacked against the Iraqis. That decision must have come from very high up. I'm sure a formal protest must have been filed with the Iraqi government. But the Iraqi Army didn't make a single move against us until sometime the following April. Everybody chalked the first attack up to the work of some kind of splinter group in the Iraqi forces." As Partridge finished his story, he raised his Scotch and drained it in a single gulp.

"Are you sure it was the Iraqis?" asked Asano.

"Well, if it wasn't, who else? There might have been Germans in the area, but not one of the witnesses reported seeing iron crosses on the planes."

"What makes you think there were Germans in the area?"

"The Luftwaffe gave air support to the Iraqi forces during their big attack the following April."

Asano wasn't all that familiar with the history of the Middle East during the war. "Why was the relationship between Iraq and England so tense?" he asked. "Hadn't Iraq already won independence by then?"

"The Iraqis had gotten their independence in '32, but we still kept a lot of forces there," replied Partridge. "The Iraqi royals supported us, but the nationalists were calling for our total withdrawal. Some of the more extreme factions in the Iraqi Army even advocated a coup d'etat. It was a

Part One

tense time. I think it was after that first air attack, we deployed a brigade of Indian troops to Basra in anticipation of the outbreak of hostilities."

"So Germany must have been backing the Iraqis," said Asano.

"They tried. But then one of the Iraqi units went renegade in April of '41. They surrounded the British Embassy and dissolved the parliament. Their ground forces attacked our base as well. The RAF bomber squadrons were scrambled. A wing of Luftwaffe fighters was dispatched, but didn't make it in time. The Indian troops moved in on Baghdad and crushed the rebellion first."

"So that's what happened," said Asano. So the Germans could have carried out the first attack, he thought. "Do you remember the type of aircraft that attacked your base?"

"I know one thing for sure. They weren't German," said Partridge. "The other pilots who saw them attacking couldn't figure out what they were. But we all agreed that they were monoplane fighters with low-slung wings."

Partridge ordered another Scotch. Asano ruminated over the story for a while.

Iraq. 1940. The military forces on edge. The RAF base in Iraq. The early morning air raid. A pair of unidentified fighter aircraft. Red circles on the wings. The possibility of a German attack...

At the time, Asano didn't realize just how important this piece of information would prove to be. In fact, he was actually somewhat doubtful. He had hoped to hear about Zero fighters—that's why he had made the journey all the way here. But were these fighters really Japanese? It actually made more sense to think that they were Iraqi planes. The red circle that he saw could have been a false memory. A drunken hallucination...

Asano stood up. "Thanks for your time. You were a great help," he said, shaking Partridge's hand.

"No need to thank me. But if you really think I was helpful, how about buying me a few more drinks?"

Asano handed the bartender enough to cover two more Scotches, then left the pub.

CHAPTER 4

About a month after meeting Partridge, Asano received another letter in the mail. This time it was from an engineer who lived in East Berlin, capital then of the German Democratic Republic.

Dear Sir:

Several days ago, I happened to read your request in Air International, *and it brought back quite a few memories.*

I was only fifteen years old at the end of the war, but I had been put to work at the Rechlin Flight Testing Center northwest of Berlin. I recall that just before the end of the war, a Luftwaffe field officer escorted a new pilot to our airfield. He was Japanese. He wore a military uniform the likes of which I'd never seen before, and he wore an insignia identifying him as a captain. He struck me as someone who must have led quite a distinguished military career, as he wore a Knight's Cross to the Iron Cross on his lapel. I was told that he had been assigned to our composite fighter squadron. This was in April of 1945, the height of the defense of Berlin.

I had the chance to speak with him briefly on one occasion. I don't remember his name, but he said that he was an officer in the Japanese Navy. He also said that he had flown a Type Zero fighter all the way to Berlin.

That's all I can tell you. I hope this helps you in your quest for information about Zero fighters in Europe.

Sincerely,
Fritz Hartman

Asano read the letter over and over again. On the surface, it was just another piece of ambiguous information, no different from Partridge's story. Partridge had only seen a red circle on the wing of an unidentified airplane, while Hartman vaguely described meeting a man who identified himself as a Zero pilot.

Asano wasn't surprised to hear that there were Japanese naval officers stationed in Berlin, even ones who had piloted aircraft. But to have made it to Berlin in a Zero fighter was another matter altogether. Common sense dictated that there must have been many different ways to make it from Tokyo to Berlin at the time without flying a death-defying mission. And why should a Japanese officer join the Luftwaffe? Why did he fight for them? Honestly, Asano felt more doubt than excitement regarding the information in the letter.

Asano wrote a reply asking for more details about the situation. Hartman's next letter turned out to be even more intriguing than the first.

All I remember is that the Japanese pilot arrived at Rechlin in early April of 1945. The last time I saw him was April 26th.

The reason that I remember the date so clearly is that it's the same day that Hanna Reitsch flew in. Do you know Hanna Reitsch? She was a captain in the Luftwaffe and a famous test pilot. She broke all sorts of flight records in gliders, and also happened to be one of the heartthrobs of German boys at the time. At any rate, this was the day that she flew in from Munich with Luftwaffe General Greim.

They said that they were on a dangerous mission to the Berlin Reich Chancellery. Hanna and the general switched into a two-seat FW190 fighter and headed to Gatow airfield in Berlin. Later on, I heard that another person had been piloting the plane, so Hanna had to crouch down and ride in the aft part of the fuselage.

Twenty fighters took off to escort and protect Hanna on her mission. The Japanese pilot was one of them. He flew a single-seat version of the FW190.

One of the pilots who made it back told me the following story.

It was only a twenty-minute flight to Gatow, but the formation began taking heavy fire from Soviet fighters as they approached. Roughly half of the German fighters had been shot down by the time they reached Gatow. Hanna's plane had been hit but made a safe landing at the airfield. Some of the surviving escorts landed there as well.

Hanna and the general first attempted to make it into downtown Berlin by car, but most of the roads were damaged beyond being passable. They decided that it would be safer to take an aircraft and make an emergency landing on Unter den Linden Avenue instead. Hanna and the general took a Fieseler Stortch courier plane and headed into Berlin that evening, escorted by the remaining fighters. The Stortch took heavy anti-aircraft fire, but somehow made it to Unter den Linden in one piece. Once the fighters confirmed that Hanna had landed safely, they headed back to

Rechlin.

The Japanese man wasn't among the pilots that made it back. Nobody saw him get hit, but these were the hours just before Hitler's suicide. It's a virtual certainty that his plane was shot down by Soviet forces as he made his way back to the airfield.

I was only fifteen years old. Before I had been inducted into the Hitler Youth, I was a little boy who loved nothing more than aircraft and stories about pilots. That's the reason I remember this story so clearly. (I heard it from a pilot who made it back, and it spread like wildfire among the people working at the airfield.) We spent the day excitedly discussing Hanna Reitsch's incredible bravery and flying skills. Berlin may have been about to fall, but she never flinched at flying into the middle of the city to complete her mission. It was a foolish end to a foolish war, but I can't deny that I was moved by Hanna's flight that day.

To be honest, I paid very little attention to the Japanese pilot. I thought of him as just another volunteer from an allied nation or colony. That's probably why I forgot his name even after speaking with him.

Reaching back into my hazy memories, I recall that while he introduced himself as a Japanese, he didn't look particularly Asian to me. He wasn't all that short. He had dark hair, dark brown eyes, and was quite reserved. His features seemed almost Spanish to me. And his German was fluent.

That's all I remember at the moment. But given a little time, perhaps I'll be able to recall some further details. For some reason, I find myself enjoying my attempts to remember this Japanese pilot. I hope that I can be of more assistance in the future.

Sincerely,
Fritz Hartman

Asano made up his mind to go to East Berlin even before he finished the letter. He wanted to meet this Hartman face to face, to hear the story straight from the horse's mouth. Perhaps Asano's questions would help Hartman clarify things and dislodge dusty old memories from the far reaches of his synapses.

Asano cast an eye towards his calendar. The 1974 Christmas holiday was only three weeks away.

CHAPTER 5

Toshihiko Asano passed through the checkpoint at Friedrichstrasse station and into East Berlin on December 22, 1974.

He removed a piece of paper from the pocket of his jacket and confirmed the address of the hotel that Hartman had given him. It was the Unter den Linten Hotel, near the Brandenburg Gate. They had made plans to meet in the lobby on the first floor. Asano had been told that the hotel was a ten-minute walk from the station.

An hour later, Asano and Hartman shook hands in a lobby full of tourists from West Germany. Hartman was a slender middle-aged man with a gaunt face, high forehead, and glasses worn over thoughtful blue eyes. His voice was quiet and deep. He spoke English with a thick German accent. He introduced himself as an engineer, but Asano thought he looked more like a professor or a doctor.

It was almost lunchtime. Asano asked Hartman if he wouldn't mind getting a bite to eat. Hartman readily agreed. The two headed to the hotel's restaurant and shared a toast of Bulgarian wine before placing their orders.

The two chatted about engineering for a while. Then, Asano asked:

"Do you really think the Japanese pilot flew a Zero? Is it true that a Zero fighter made it to Berlin during the war?"

"It wouldn't be something you hear every day," said Hartman, nodding slowly. "But it wouldn't have been impossible. I believed the man. That's probably why I wasn't very surprised at the time."

"Did he tell you when, exactly, he arrived in Berlin?"

"I asked him once. He told me four or five years previous."

"That would be 1940 or '41," said Asano thoughtfully. "But why?" Hartmann shook his head.

"I suppose you still can't remember his name," said Asano.

"It's difficult to remember foreign names the first time you hear them. Especially Asian ones," replied Hartman. "Hans Joachim Willaperht."

"Come again?"

"The name of an acquaintance. An electrical engineer, like myself. But when he was posted to North Korea, nobody could remember his name. They called him 'Han' instead."

As the two continued their dinner, Hartman pieced together what he was able from thirty-year-old memories. Hartman discussed not only his own first-hand knowledge, but also the talk and rumors that had been circulating on the base at the time.

The composite fighter group stationed at Rechlin had consisted of salvaged aircraft and pilots who had escaped the destruction of their bases. The British and American troops had already pushed the Western front to the Elbe; the Soviets on the east surrounded the opposite side of Berlin. Very few operational Luftwaffe bases remained within German borders.

The pilot's Japanese nationality had been a concern ever since his arrival at Rechlin. The base commander considered ordering him to fly to Salzburg in what had once been Austria. If the pilot had been a German, he would have been expected to fight no matter how hopeless the situation. But there was no reason for a foreigner to give his life in defense of the motherland.

The base commander told the pilot:

"It's only a matter of time before Berlin falls. There's no reason for you to keep fighting. Salzburg is still safe. Why don't you go there and wait for us Germans to surrender?"

The Japanese pilot replied:

"Sir. I volunteered to remain behind as an advisor to the Luftwaffe. I've trained and sent countless young men into combat as a flight instructor. My responsibility is to the skies over Germany. I appreciate your concern, but I respectfully decline orders to fly to Salzburg."

Within days of being assigned to Rechlin, the Japanese claimed five Soviet fighters. The head of maintenance tried to paint the kills on the tail of the FW190, but the pilot refused. He said it was pointless. From then on, he never spoke of his victories again.

One afternoon, Hartman took a break from his work placing sandbags and approached the Japanese pilot. The man stood by the hangar, an oddity, a foreigner with a Knight's Cross to the Iron Cross on his lapel. It was more than enough to pique the young Hartman's curiosity.

"How many kills have you gotten?" began Hartman.

"Probably 22 or 23," replied the Japanese.

Hartman couldn't believe it. He'd expected so many more. "Then why..." said Hartman, casting a glance at the Knight's Cross to the Iron Cross.

Part One

The pilot looked down and flicked the decoration on his lapel. "It's only a token of respect. It doesn't have anything to do with the number of planes I shot down."

Disappointed, Hartman searched for something else to say. Finally, he managed:

"Where did you learn how to fly a Focke-Wulf? How many hours do you have on it?"

"Standel," replied the Japanese pilot. There was a flight school there. "I was there as a teacher rather than as a student, though."

"You mean you were an instructor at the base in Standel?"

"That's right. An instructor and an advisor to the Luftwaffe."

"But why did you get assigned to combat?"

"It was time for me to change jobs," said the pilot, smiling wistfully. "I didn't want to help create suicide squadrons."

"You mean the Raptors?"

"Yes. They were rushed through training at Standel and in Prague. They crashed their planes into American bombers. The brass is obsessed with the idea of turning out another squadron of them. There isn't any work for an instructor like me anymore."

"What do you mean?" blurted the boy. "It's all flying."

"No!" said the pilot, fixing the boy with a stern gaze. "I teach students how to fly. How to take off, fly through the air, and then land. Not how to take off and die in the sky!"

Taken aback by the vehemence of the response, Hartman timidly changed the subject. "Have you ever flown a Zero fighter? I heard you're good."

The anger seemed to drain from the pilot's face. He looked up toward the sky, as if remembering something from his distant past. The beginnings of a smile played across his lips. The pilot suddenly seemed gentle, almost happy, for a moment. Still looking off into the distance, he replied:

"I flew a Zero to Berlin."

"Really?" asked Hartman. "When?"

"About four years ago."

"Really? I didn't know! What happened to the Zero? Where is it?"

"I don't know," replied the Japanese, slowly shaking his head. "I don't know what happened to it. It may have been scrapped, or destroyed in the bombing."

Hartman peppered the pilot with the kinds of questions any German boy of the time would have asked. How fast can a Zero fly? What are its armaments? How does it handle? Is it a better plane than the P-38? How about the FW190? The pilot patiently answered each question in turn.

Suddenly, the pilot cut in with a question of his own. "Do you want to be a fighter pilot?"

Hartman nodded. The man gazed sadly at the sky and shook his head. Perhaps he thought it was a childish dream, or perhaps he was thinking about the tragic end that combat pilots inevitably met. The young Hartman couldn't understand the look on the pilot's face. But now the boy's break was over; it was time to return to his work, preparing the sandbags. It was the first and last time he ever spoke to the Japanese pilot.

Soon after Hartman's conversation, Hanna Reitsch and General Greim arrived at Rechlin airbase. Hanna was supposed to proceed to Gatow immediately, escorted by a squadron of fighters for protection. The base kicked into high gear to prepare for the flights.

Hartman was working on the side of the runway when the Japanese pilot approached him, carrying a bundle. He tossed it over to the boy, who opened it to reveal a pair of aviator's goggles and a chocolate-colored flight helmet. They weren't German. They looked well worn. What did it mean? Was the pilot giving them to him?

When Hartman looked up, the pilot was already walking towards his fighter. Hartman watched as the man snapped a salute towards the aircraft, climbed the ladder into his Focke-Wulf, and took off for his sortie. He never returned.

Asano finished the last of the wine in his glass. The story was far richer than he had expected. He knew it was absolutely true. It couldn't be a lie. One thing was certain: the Japanese pilot existed. He had been an officer in the Japanese navy and had flown a Luftwaffe fighter on the front lines just before the fall of Berlin. He hadn't scored an exorbitant number of kills, yet was a decorated ace pilot who sported a Knight's Cross to the Iron Cross. This had been a Japanese man who had led a singularly interesting life, thought Asano.

But the most important piece of information still remained hazy. Did he really fly a Zero fighter from Japan to Berlin? Was such a flight even possible? If it had occurred, when did it happen, and why?

At the end of their meal together, Asano tried asking Hartman more questions in a futile attempt to dislodge further details from the man's memory. Finally, Asano said: "Do you still have the helmet? Would you mind if I took a look at it? There should be a name written inside of it. If I learn the name, I'll be able to find something out about the man."

"Unfortunately..." Hartman shook his head with regret, his voice trailing off for a moment. "I looked for it. But I couldn't find it. I had been using it as a winter hat. And I know I had it until I was at least 24 or 25 years old."

"So it's been lost?"

"It seems so," said Hartman. "I don't remember throwing it away, though."

Asano could barely conceal his disappointment. The flight helmet was the missing link, incontrovertible proof that a Zero fighter pilot had been in Berlin. Asano couldn't believe such a priceless treasure had been lost. No matter how interesting Hartman's story had been, without evidence, it wouldn't help Asano unravel the mystery.

Shortly thereafter, Asano thanked Hartman and stood up to leave. His trip to Berlin had occasioned nothing more than his listening to a man reminiscence for two hours. Asano wondered if the story had been worth the expense. Perhaps it was too early to tell. Whatever the case, Asano planned to spend the rest of the week sightseeing in Berlin with his wife. At the very least, the lunch with Hartman had provided him with an interesting tale to tell about the trip.

"I had a wonderful time," said Hartman. "Would you mind if I asked you a question myself?"

"Certainly," replied Asano.

"Why are you so interested in this Zero fighter that flew to Germany and its pilot? What brings you all the way from Belgium just to hear me reminisce?"

Asano thought for a moment. "Improving the Type Zero Carrier Fighter's engine was my first job as an engineer. Our group developed the model 21 engine with a two-stage supercharger, based on the Nakajima Sakae 12. I spent upwards of ten hours a day on the engine. I listened to its cry, stroked its body. I've worked on all sorts of engine projects since then, but I've never forgotten the Zero's model 21. It was like a dream. It was the pride of my youth."

Hartman stood quietly, studying Asano's face.

"Our defeat took all that away," continued Asano. "But as a former aircraft designer, the fate of the Zero fighter is unspeakably important to me."

"When did you work on the Zero's engine?" asked Hartman.

"I worked on the Sakae engine between 1940 and 1941," said Asano. Almost immediately upon saying the words, old memories began flooding his mind. Asano remembered a man in the electronics branch of the Aviation Technology Development Center who was building two special pieces of radio equipment. He seemed to remember him being a technological officer. Hadn't his name been Morita? Asano remembered chatting with him in the mess. He had said something then. Something like, "The next radio I make has to be something that'll impress the Germans. I'm going to hand-pick the parts for two special ones." Why had he mentioned Germans? And why two radios? Two radios. Now Asano remembered that two Type Zero fighters had been specially transported to the flight-testing area. A month later they had been assigned to the 14th Air Corps. It wasn't common for used equipment, particularly aircraft that had been tested so extensively, to be sent into combat.

It was an epiphany. But why here and now? These were ancient memories, minor details. Was this some kind of sixth sense telling Asano to take heed?

Asano paid the check for both of them, and said goodbye to Hartman outside the hotel.

Ever since that meeting, Asano began to undertake research that required a high degree of patience. He wasn't a professional researcher. Nor could he devote himself full time to his historical studies. It was painstaking and inefficient work. He gathered enough documents to fill an entire bookshelf in his library. Still the core of the mystery eluded him.

Asano's health was failing. As he worried about the progress of his illness, he began to wish for someone to help him with the legwork. Someone who could lock himself into a library for hours on end. Someone who could track down leads regardless of the distance or time involved. Someone fearless enough to conduct interviews without hesitation. Someone experienced in hunting down and gathering information. A journalist, perhaps. If only he could find the right person, thought Asano, he'd finally be able to fill in the blanks, to resolve the question once and for all.

As luck would have it, that's exactly when Asano happened to meet a young writer who was researching sixties-era F-1 racing.

Part Two

CHAPTER 1

September 26, 1940. General Ernst Udet, Chief of the Luftwaffe Technical Office, arrived at the Führer's new official residence near Berlin's Brandenburg Gate at two minutes to four in the afternoon. Hitler's invasion of the British Isles, code-named Operation Sea Lion, had been postponed indefinitely. But the Luftwaffe's bombing campaign continued in the face of heavy losses. It was the height of the broad-daylight raids that would come to be known as the fourth phase of the Battle of Britain: the Blitz.

The orders had come suddenly, but Udet already had some idea as to why the Führer had called him. There were probably questions that needed answering about the aircraft to be used in the bombing campaign. Or perhaps the Führer was interested in the progress of the development of the He177 long-range bomber. Whatever the case, Udet knew, the meeting would not be a comfortable one.

From the moment Udet had begun to voice his doubts about the air campaign, he had joined the ranks of officers who had become a magnet for Hitler's criticism. Why aren't we winning? What are our shortcomings? Where are our new long-range dive bombers? When will the new heavy fighters be completed? What about the deployment of the new strike bombers? Why aren't the new high-precision bombing sights ready yet? For a man like Udet, who loved nothing more than sketching portraits and flying aerobatics, the pressure was almost too much to bear.

Udet often thought about telling the truth in response to these questions. The He177 was plagued by technical problems, and there was no way to predict when if ever it would be ready for combat use. The twin-engine Messerschmitt Bf110 fighter was overweight and no match for the nimble single-engine British Spitfires. As for the Bf109, it barely had the range to make the flight from France to London. In all honesty, Germany's absolute lack of strategic sense when it came to air combat had doomed Operation Eagle from the very beginning. If the Führer really wanted to gain air supremacy over the skies of England, he would need to form all-new air squadrons equipped with long-range fighters and bombers. But Udet also knew he could never bring himself to say any of this.

Luftwaffe Field Marshal Milch was already there when Udet

entered the Führer's office. Milch stood in front of a map table that was set beneath a portrait of the Führer on the left wall. Milch flashed a perfunctory smile. Udet returned the greeting with a smile of his own. Milch had risen to become one of Hitler's closest advisers, but for some reason had never managed to gain Goering's trust. In fact, he was already losing influence among the officer, personnel, and technical corps. Field Marshal or not, his reputation was sliding fast.

Udet noticed that the map atop the table was that of Eastern Europe. When had it been switched? Until recently, it had shown a portion of the British Isles. Perhaps the rumors about the Führer losing interest in the invasion of Britain were true. Or perhaps he actually believed that all he had to do at this point was sit back and wait for Churchill's surrender.

Hitler entered his office. Udet and Milch came to attention and saluted. Hitler rounded his luxurious wooden desk and studied each of Udet and Milch's faces in turn. His complexion looked good. The hint of a smile was upon his lips. It was the expression that the Führer wore when he had had one of his occasional epiphanies. He must have had some sort of revelation about a bold new campaign today. It would undoubtedly throw the officers into utter turmoil.

Hitler spoke.

"I summoned Lieutenant Commander Galland of the 2nd Fighter Wing here yesterday. Two days ago, he shot down his fortieth aircraft over Britain. I awarded him the Knight's Cross with Oakleaves. He's only the third to ever have received one, I believe?"

"That is true, mein Führer. He is the third. The third recipient after Dietrich and Moelders," answered Milch.

Hitler nodded. "He is a great pilot. He has bravery, courage, and unparalleled skill. And even more, he is a true patriot. It was an honor to give an award to an officer like him."

Galland must have made one hell of a favorable impression, thought Udet. Udet recalled the rumor he had heard several days ago at the State Ministry of Aviation. When Reich Marshal Goering had inspected the front line in early September, he had asked Galland what, if anything, he needed. Galland had offhandedly replied that he wanted some Spitfires for his squadron. Udet suspected Galland hadn't repeated the same joke at his award ceremony.

"I spoke with him at length," continued Hitler. "I asked him why the operation was taking so long and going so badly, in spite of Goering's assurances that it would take no more than four days. His explanation of the problems we have been facing was quite persuasive. As an officer on the front lines, his words have weight. Let me tell you that many of his points echoed those you have brought to my attention. One of them involved the ambiguity surrounding the role of the Luftwaffe's fighter squadrons. Another was about their equipment and technology.

"He feared that he would be seen as a coward, but still he spoke up. Up to now, the fighter squadrons have been relegated to a secondary role in the Luftwaffe. Their duties have been patrolling specific areas, maintaining air supremacy over the front lines, and supporting ground operations. The invasion of Britain marks the very first time the fighter squadrons have been deployed offensively. The pilots are straining under the responsibility that has been placed upon them. If I had heard this from anyone else, I would not have taken it seriously. But I would never dismiss an ace like him, recipient of an Knight's Cross to the Iron Cross, as a coward. I have taken his words to heart."

According to Hitler, Galland said that the Bf109s assigned to his fighter squadrons were simply not suitable for strategic operations. They were capable of no more than eighty minutes of flight time, restricting their operational radius to roughly 120 miles. In short, they were incapable of sustained air-to-air combat over the skies of Britain. Thirty minutes were required to take off from the airbases in France, cross the straits of Dover, and reach southern England. This meant that the Bf109s were restricted to merely twenty minutes of combat time by the time they reached London or Portsmouth. There was simply no way to defend the bomber squadrons while evading anti-aircraft fire and the radar network. Air combat over the skies of Britain was too much responsibility for the Bf109s to bear.

"He asked me something," said Hitler, pausing as he looked into the faces of the two officers. Udet stood at perfect attention, waiting for the Führer to continue. Could Galland possibly have brought his Spitfires up again?

"He asked me," repeated Hitler, "to dispatch new strike fighters to his squadrons as quickly as possible. What he really wants is an aircraft with sustained flight capability. An aircraft with extended flight range. I promised him that I would deliver. I would send him fighters with a longer range than that of the Messerschmitts. He is the pride of the entire

Luftwaffe. It is not that he does not believe in victory, or lacks fighting spirit. What he needs is a new fighter that can fly for long distances as soon as possible. So I promised him."

Udet and Milch stood in silence. The Führer was in high spirits. He should not be interrupted.

"General," said Hitler, fixing Udet with a stare. "Have we done anything to increase the flight range of the Bf109s yet?"

"It's under discussion, mein Führer," answered Udet cautiously. "The E type has already been deployed to the 2nd and 3rd Wings. It can be equipped with a detachable auxiliary fuel tank. But..."

"But, what?"

"Even on these aircraft, we have been mounting small bombs instead of the fuel tanks. The Bf109s are being used as bombers in the attack on London."

"I'm aware of that," said Hitler, frowning for the first time. "It may do for the moment, but that makeshift approach won't work forever. I assume that we need to develop a new type of aircraft."

"As you are undoubtedly already aware, Kurt Tank has begun designing a new single-seat fighter with an air-cooled radial engine," said Udet. "It should be ready for combat in six months or so."

"What is its range?"

"According to preliminary test data, more than 500 miles, mein Führer."

"That's still not enough to hit all of England. Can we develop a fighter capable enough to satisfy a pilot like Lieutenant Commander Galland? A fighter as powerful in the air as the Spitfire, yet with a superior flight time and operational range?"

"It's entirely possible with our country's prowess in aviation technology," interrupted Milch suddenly. "Until now, our military didn't prioritize operational range when designing new fighters. But you are talking about a fundamentally new type of aircraft. I estimate that it will take two years to complete it."

Udet cast a glance at Milch out of the corner of his eye. He knew Milch didn't have a clue about the current state of the aviation industry. Every engineer, every factory worker, was completely exhausted from the constant demands placed upon them. At the beginning of the year, for example, they had been producing only twenty-five Bf109s a month. Udet was already demanding that the companies increase their production to three hundred and fifty aircraft per month. Asking them to develop a new fighter on top of the increased workload was insane.

"Mein Führer," began Udet. "Our domestic aircraft production facilities are at full capacity. Heinkel and Messerschmitt are already at work developing a new type of high-speed aircraft that does not require a propeller. I don't see any room for developing another completely new fighter at this time."

This time, it was Milch who cast the sideward glance at Udet. Udet ignored it.

Hitler must have noticed the tension between the two. He waved his hand in front of his chest as if to calm them.

"Fine, fine. I'm aware of that," said the Führer. "But I think you already know about the upcoming ceremony. Our country, Italy and Japan will forge the strongest military alliance ever known to man. An axis of power that will cross all of Europe and extend into Asia. The Japanese government doesn't want it to be perceived thus, but it will be a true alliance between the militaries of our nations. Tomorrow we will form an indomitable union, not only politically and militarily, but industrially and technologically as well. It is the inauguration of a new federation of chosen nations, nations dedicated to eradicating Bolshevism, nations whose rightful and honorable ambitions have been crushed by the British and Americans until now."

Hitler took a document holder from the top of his desk and handed it to Udet.

"On the eve of signing the pact, I receive a report like this from Intelligence Chief Canaris. Our agents have gathered information about a new type of fighter developed by the Japanese navy. Are you aware of this, General Udet?"

"I read a synopsis a week ago," replied Udet. "According to the report, a squadron comprised of these new fighters achieved a decisive victory on the Japanese front line on the Chinese mainland September 13th, wresting total control of the skies over China from the Nationalists."

"September 13th," said Hitler with a trace of sarcasm in his voice. "On roughly the same date, our Luftwaffe was humiliated in the skies over London, indefinitely postponing Operation Sea Lion. That was September 15th."

"I'm afraid so, mein Führer. We did manage to terrorize the city of London with our first operation on the fifteenth, but our forces took heavy losses as well," said Udet.

"Because our forces were not given the appropriate equipment at the necessary time and place," said Hitler. "As Chief of the Technical Office, your role in the whole fiasco can hardly be downplayed. Wouldn't you agree, General Udet?"

Udet snapped his heels as he stood at attention again.

"It is as you say, mein Führer."

"Take a look at today's report. It's full of data on the new Japanese fighter. It confirms the assumptions of the report on the September 13th attack: this aircraft is capable of flying unheard-of distances. They predict that the range could easily exceed that of the Messerschmitt Bf109 by three or four times. And it's capable enough to wipe out the entire Chinese air force in a single day."

Udet glanced over the statistics and commentary in the report. It came from the Abwehr bureaus in Tokyo and Shanghai, and contained data about the aircraft's performance down to the tiniest detail. The report also contained a full map of China as well. It appeared that Intelligence Chief Canaris had some good men working for him in Asia.

"A lightweight aircraft," said Udet thoughtfully as he paged through the report. "So it was developed as a carrier-based fighter."

The data that most impressed Udet concerned the aircraft's effective flight range: between 1,000 and 1,300 nautical miles, or 1,800 to 2,300 kilometers. A fighter with such capabilities would certainly put the whole of Great Britain within range of German bases on the French coastline, but the figures were difficult to believe. They were almost beyond common sense.

After reading through the entire report, Udet raised his head and said:

"The Chinese forces weren't flying Spitfires. They were using Russian I-15s and I-16s, with some American Curtiss fighters in the mix. It's difficult to compare these results with the situation facing our Luftwaffe."

"I see," said Hitler. "You aren't convinced by the data?"

"It is difficult to believe," said Udet, shaking his head. Milch reached out for the report. Udet handed it over. "I believe you're already aware of the level of Japanese industrial technology, mein Führer. The Japanese didn't have a single steelworks or even a steam engine only half a century ago. They boast of their aircraft as having been produced in Japan, but in reality they were assisted heavily by Junkers and Heinkel."

"They may be nothing more than aping monkeys, but miracles are always possible. Perhaps they have managed to refine our technology into a better aircraft. Have you heard of a company by the name of Mitsubishi?" asked Hitler.

"A manufacturer of ships and military aircraft," answered Udet. "They must have received some technical support from Junkers when they designed this aircraft."

"What you're telling me is that this Zero fighter could be considered a brother to the Stuka," said Hitler. "Could this be the fighter that Galland is looking for?"

"What do you mean, mein Führer?" asked Udet, frowning. "Are you saying that you want to provide Galland with these aircraft?"

"Not Galland. The entire Luftwaffe! Didn't you just say that Messerschmitt and Heinkel are too busy to design a new aircraft right now?"

"I didn't mean that, exactly, mein Führer," said Udet. "What I am trying to say is that they are in the middle of developing a new type of aircraft that will revolutionize air combat as we know it. If only we had a little more time!"

"You will have it. You have it as we speak. They should focus all of their efforts on developing these high-speed aircraft. But we have an urgent need for long-range fighters. Urgent!"

"Do you wish to import this aircraft from Japan, then?" asked a confused Udet. Can he possibly be serious? "Are you planning to have blockade runners bring large numbers of them here?"

"I have a better idea. Why don't we produce them domestically?" asked Hitler. "All we would need is a submarine to bring the design plans here."

Udet, shocked into silence, said nothing. Hitler peered into Udet's eyes with amusement. He seemed to be enjoying Udet's reaction.

Licensed production of a Japanese naval fighter.

It was an extraordinary measure. But whether it could be carried out in reality was another question. Which factories had the excess production capability to handle it? How many engineers could be spared for the job? How would the materials be gathered in Germany? Who would oversee the production? Did he plan to invite the Japanese designers here as well? Cooperative production wasn't easy even when there wasn't a war going on. No matter how Udet looked at it, the whole idea felt spur-of-the-moment, half-baked.

Hitler glanced at Milch. "You said it would take two years to develop a new fighter."

"Yes, that is what would be required, mein Führer," answered Milch.

"If the aircraft design already existed, though, how long would it take to produce and deploy?"

"Roughly a year, I believe," replied Milch casually. "It would depend on the number that must be produced, but if you mean forming just a single Geshwader wing from these aircraft, one year would be more than enough."

"You have six months, Field Marshal Milch. Any longer than that and the effort is worthless."

Udet hesitated, then said, "We should first test this fighter to see if it truly lives up to the claims. We should not rush to any conclusions."

"Test it. Let Galland test it! If anyone should judge the capabilities of the aircraft, it should be him," said Hitler.

"But where? Should we send Galland to Japan?" asked Udet.

"We can't afford to send him to the Far East right now. He will have to test it here in Germany."

"So we will bring one of the aircraft here," said Udet.

"As quickly as possible," agreed Hitler.

Maybe just one aircraft, thought Udet. It wouldn't be asking too much to bring one on board a blockade runner. Just six months ago, Heinkel had sent three He117s to Japan.

"The decision to produce it or not would be based on the test results, I assume," said Udet.

"A splendid idea," said Hitler. "I shall trust Lieutenant Commander Galland's decision on the matter. The whole project could be scrapped, depending on the results. But in the meantime, it may be worth discussing plans to produce it. That is my final word on the matter. Are there any questions?"

"Just one, mein Führer," said Udet. "I heard that the Japanese navy has been dead set against signing the Tripartite Pact. Do you think they will agree to license one of their aircraft to us for production?"

Hitler finally raised his voice. "Just what are you afraid of, general? What is on your mind?"

"Mein Führer!" cried Udet, shaken. "My intention wasn't to dampen your enthusiasm. I was merely thinking aloud."

"If you think that someone in Japan will try to hinder our plans, use Matsuoka. Isn't he their minister of foreign affairs now? I remember him bragging about his political connections. He would climb the Brandenburg Gate stark naked on his hands and knees if he knew it was a request from me. And what about Oshima? The former ambassador. The last I heard, he was at Ribbentrop's beck and call. So what is the problem, General Udet?"

Milch stepped forward.

"Mein Führer," he said. "We can raise the matter with the Japanese as soon as the Tripartite Pact is signed tomorrow. I don't expect any significant opposition to licensing the aircraft from the Japanese. But we should ask them to send a fighter for testing. We can't ask for it for free, so let us prepare to purchase one of the aircraft."

There was no way Udet could simply let Milch take charge of the plan. Udet needed to manage the situation himself. Whatever the case might be, Udet was Chief of the Technical Office. He was personally in charge of procurement and supply for the Luftwaffe. Udet was a World War I flying ace. There was no way he could let the responsibility for military technological development and supply fall to a former manager from Lufthansa. He stepped forward.

"We should purchase two. One for testing, and one to be disassembled for further study," said Udet. "I propose taking charge of drawing up plans for production myself."

"Please do, General Udet," said Hitler, jovial once again. "I place you in charge of the technical and practical sides of the matter. If you need any political assistance, Field Marshal Milch will lend a hand. Isn't that so, Field Marshal Milch?"

Milch cast another glance at Udet. "It will be so," he said in a tone not quite as happy as that of his Führer. "I look forward to hearing Galland's opinion of the fighter."

CHAPTER 2

Once they had reached the anteroom outside of Hitler's office, Milch turned to Udet.

"Two fighters is a bit much, don't you think?"

"I should think we'll need at least that many if we're discussing licensing them for production," answered Udet.

"Maybe so. But how are you going to get them here? Perhaps I spoke a bit too hastily when I suggested purchasing the fighter. It won't be easy."

"All we need is an armed freighter, or a blockade runner."

"Oh, is that all?" asked Milch, his voice dripping with sarcasm. "Once the Tripartite Pact has been signed, the British will undoubtedly tighten their naval blockade. Are you planning to send a Japanese ship with such important cargo through the Straits of Malacca? Too bad you didn't do it earlier. You might have actually pulled it off."

"So we'll have them flown over land. The distance from Tokyo to Berlin is about fifteen or sixteen thousand kilometers. The report said the aircraft have an incredible range. They'll be here in a week or so," Udet replied.

Milch practically sneered at Udet. "Listen. The state of affairs will drastically change tomorrow. The entire world knows that this alliance isn't political lip service. Roosevelt will be furious. The alliance is a brilliant diplomatic coup for the Führer; it'll keep America out of the war. But the Japanese, on the other hand..."

"What about the Japanese?" asked Udet.

"Joining the Axis puts the Japanese on thin ice. They'll become official enemies of the British. England and Japan have enjoyed something of a balance of power up until today. The alliance will throw it off. When that happens, it's only a matter of time before tensions flare and war breaks out between them in China. I suspect the British fleet in Singapore will go to full alert as soon as the alliance becomes public news. Now, do you still think that a Japanese military aircraft can make it over India?"

Udet said nothing as Milch continued his tirade.

"I suspect you know that it's impossible to make it overland through Russia as well," said Milch. "The Führer is concerned about the future of the Far East. The question now isn't whether we will go to war against the Soviet Union. The question is when. I seriously hope you aren't considering sending the aircraft over Russian territory."

The utter precariousness of the situation finally began to dawn on Udet. It would not be an easy task. It wasn't the kind of thing he could hand over to his subordinates and simply forget about. He had been cornered.

Udet cursed his own carelessness. He never should have taken responsibility. Now he had put himself in the line of fire. What he should have done is let some grandstander take the reins while he stood behind in the shadows, watching and waiting. If Milch wanted the credit, he should have let him take it. Even if he was only a former manager of Lufthansa.

"I have a meeting at the Foreign Ministry after this," said Milch. "I will tell Ribbentrop of the Führer's wishes. I assume you will take charge of executing the plan."

Udet reluctantly nodded. "Yes, I accept the responsibility," he said quietly. "Let us arrange a meeting with the Japanese ambassador tomorrow. Besides Kurusu, perhaps we should have the Imperial Japanese Navy's attaché attend as well."

"An excellent idea. I'll make the arrangements by this afternoon," said Milch.

Udet stood silently for some time after Milch left the anteroom. He had already made up his mind to get out at the first chance that presented itself. He fervently hoped for some setback that would cancel the entire project.

The following afternoon, Udet flew to East Prussia for a meeting with Reich Marshal Hermann Goering. Goering was hosting a party in honor of Galland, who had just received his Knight's Cross to the Iron Cross, at his hunting estate there. At the same time, Hitler, Ribbentrop, Foreign Minister Ciano from Italy, and Ambassador Kurusu from Japan were signing the Tripartite Pact in Berlin.

The lodge of the national hunting preserve was located in a well-tended forest. Built from hewn logs, it featured broad eaves and a thatched roof. It was mating season for the deer. Udet watched as a group of them ran through a copse of trees behind the lodge.

Goering, clad in a hunting outfit of green suede, arrived to greet Udet.

"Make it short, Ernst," said the Reich Marshal, giving Udet a friendly pat on the back. "Galland bagged an enormous deer, a buck with a beautiful rack of antlers. He didn't use the machine guns on his Bf109 to get it, either." Goering chuckled, amused by his own joke. Goering's pants were caked with dried blood. Udet assumed he must have helped Galland dress his kill. Or perhaps he had slit the throat of the fallen deer himself with his hunting knife. Goering also held the title of Reich Master of the Hunt. His devotion to the sport was legendary throughout the Nazi party.

In front of a comfortable fireplace in the living room of the lodge, Udet reported the events of the meeting with the Führer the previous day. Udet dropped all pretense of formality when talking with the Reich Marshal. In fact, the two were quite alike. They had both served as biplane pilots during the First World War, and enjoyed playing as hard as they worked.

Accepting a glass of German Mosel wine from Goering, Udet spoke frankly about the Führer's wild plan. Goering had received the same report on the Zero's flight performance from the Abwehr, but hadn't had a chance to read it yet. Now he summoned the folder to be brought to him. Receiving it, he began to quickly skim the contents.

"If these results are true, perhaps this isn't necessarily a bad thing," said Goering. "If the Luftwaffe had possession of these fighters three months ago, perhaps Churchill would be living in New Zealand by now. We certainly wouldn't be having endless discussions about the fact that our Messerschmitts can only fight for twenty minutes over the skies of London."

Udet stared in shock. "Did Galland say that?" he asked Goering.

"No. We haven't discussed the war. We've only talked about hunting, women, and drinking. This is such a beautiful preserve. We don't need that kind of...unromantic talk here."

"Would you prefer I didn't discuss this here?"

"No, it's actually quite an amusing little plan. So very much like the Führer. The Japanese ambassador must have been totally taken by surprise."

"Indeed. It must be a sensitive issue. We are asking them to sell their top-secret new fighter to us, after all," said Udet.

"But they have no choice. They have to agree," said Goering. "I know their navy was against the Tripartite Pact. Now they won't be able to reject a request from an ally."

"So you're definitely considering licensing the Type Zeros for production?" asked Udet.

"It's an order from the Führer. Who am I to criticize it? Let's just get the technical specifications from Japan and compare them against the Abwehr's report. If they look promising, we can proceed with the plan to purchase the fighters under a conditional contract. But I don't want this to delay Messerschmitt's work on the high-speed fighter, either. Will you be able to coordinate these projects separately?"

"I'm not planning to move any engineers from the high-speed fighter project to work on this matter," said Udet.

"Then everything depends on the results of the flight testing, I guess."

"We also need to discuss exactly how to bring the aircraft to Germany."

Udet relayed what Milch had told him yesterday. It would be difficult to use a freighter. It would be too hazardous to try flying the fighters over Russia. Taking the southern route risked the possibility of an encounter with the RAF. Udet laid out just how difficult it would be to actually get the fighters even if Germany did go through with the purchase.

"I agree. Going through Russia is out of the question," said Goering. "There's nothing to do but try the southern route, Ernst. If those fighters manage to break through the RAF's defenses, I think they'll be more than worthy enough for production. And if the fighters can't do it, we probably shouldn't even bother flight-testing them anyway. Am I wrong?"

"But we're only going to purchase two fighters. Are two fighters enough to make it over India?"

"That's their problem. I don't care how many aircraft Japan actually dispatches. We'll just buy the ones that land safely in Germany."

Udet began thinking about how he would suggest the plan to the Japanese. Suddenly, Goering said:

"There must be a pilot like Galland in Japan, too. They must have some kind of ace over there. If he manages to bring one of these Type Zeros to Berlin, I'll award him the Knight's Cross to the Iron Cross. I'll even invite him here and let him take a big buck! I don't care about nationality or background; I respect anyone who's a good pilot. Let's ask the Japanese to send their best."

Udet nodded, lost in thought. Breaking through the RAF's defenses would definitely certify the plane's worthiness for production. Damn right. *And that way, even if the plane never actually makes it, it won't be my fault. Even if it never makes it, never gets tested, never gets produced, I won't be open to criticism from the Führer.*

Udet smiled at his old companion. The Reich Marshal broke out in a broad grin and chuckled in satisfaction.

Udet raised his wine glass and drained it in a single gulp.

CHAPTER 3

Junzo Yamawaki, secretary to the Ministry of the Navy, reported to the Office of the Imperial Japanese Naval Attaché in Berlin at precisely eleven o'clock the following morning.

The Attaché's Office was a stylish, ivy-covered two-story brick house located near Berlin's Breslauer Platz. The Imperial Navy had moved from Bayerische Platz to the new location two years earlier. Up until then, the Attaché had occupied a single floor of a nondescript building. But the completion of the new Japanese Embassy three years earlier had spurred them to purchase the sprawling new house. The official reason had been the increasing importance of Japan's relationship with Germany. But keeping up with the Army and the Ministry of Foreign Affairs had played no small part in the decision.

Yamawaki glanced at his wristwatch as he passed through the reception hall and took the stairs to the second floor.

He was a legal advisor to the Imperial Navy, a civil servant with a level of authority equivalent to a lieutenant junior grade. He had graduated from the law school at Tokyo Imperial University, and had also studied international law and geopolitics for three years at Princeton in the United States. He had recently turned thirty and was known throughout the navy as a dashing man about town. Yamawaki had been dispatched to Germany at the beginning of September to meet with Rear Admiral Tadao Yokoi, who had just been posted to Berlin himself, and to gauge the European reaction to the signing of the Tripartite Pact.

The Japanese expatriate population in Berlin could hardly contain their excitement at the signing of the Tripartite Pact. Yamawaki himself still bore a hangover from the previous night's official festivities. He had met a tall German girl from the Ministry of Foreign Affairs, and they had adjourned to her appartement until two in the morning. Perhaps the night could be thought of as a sort of Japanese-German alliance on the civilian level, thought Yamawaki. If word of his fling ever made it into the official report, the head of the Imperial Navy would have Yamawaki's head on a silver platter. "Deviation from official policy" was no laughing matter.

Yamawaki checked the time again before knocking on the door to Rear Admiral Yokoi's office. Yokoi had called for the meeting at the party

Part Two

last night. When Yamawaki had asked why, Yokoi said that he wasn't sure himself, other than that it was at the request of Ambassador Kurusu. It all seemed very important and urgent.

Yamawaki heard a voice beckon from inside the room. He opened the door, the effort causing him to wince from the pain still shooting through his head.

Rear Admiral Yokoi, in full uniform, glanced up at Yamawaki. "You certainly did seem to enjoy yourself last night," he said. "Your eyes are still bloodshot."

"I got a little carried away, I suppose," said Yamawaki. "The party last night was something else. It was like a festival, or the cherry blossom viewing parties in Tokyo in the spring."

The office was a well-lit corner room on the second floor. Yokoi's desk was set in front of a large bay window. A huge globe sat on the right side of the desk, while a scale model of the battleship *Mikasa* occupied the left. An enormous portrait of the Emperor stared down on the room from its position high on one luxuriously papered wall. A small table and chairs for guests were set against the wall opposite the Emperor's stern gaze. Yamawaki set his leather case on the tabletop.

"It was a day for the history books. You can hardly be faulted for having a bit too much fun," said Rear Admiral Yokoi a bit too brightly.

This was Yokoi's second tour of duty as an officer in Berlin. His unabashedly pro-German attitude was no secret within the navy. Perhaps his spirits had been buoyed by his chance to participate in signing the pact that he had so long yearned for. In any event, he and Yamawaki had rubbed each other the wrong way from day one.

"I saw an army officer carrying on like a drunken maniac with a German soldier. Someday, he said, we should divide the United States between Japan and Germany. According to his fantasy, the area east of the Rockies would be German territory, while the rest would be Japan's. I think he may even have been serious," remarked Yamawaki cynically.

"The world is full of ignorant people. Perhaps especially our army. They haven't seen much of the outside world," said Yokoi.

"Some Japanese are still ignorant even after having lived in America for a long time. Our foreign minister is a prime example."

Yokoi's tiny, round eyes drilled into Yamawaki.

"I'd advise watching your mouth when you're outside of naval facilities. Unfortunately, these days it isn't as easy for all of us to speak our minds as freely as you do."

"I'll do that," said Yamawaki. "Can I trouble you for a cup of coffee? My head hurts all the more for remembering the stupidity spewing from that army officer last night."

"I'll have a cup brought in."

Just then, Japanese Ambassador to Germany Saburo Kurusu strode into the room. He had arrived in Berlin in January that year to work on the Tripartite Pact. Unlike his pro-German predecessor, Ambassador Hiroshi Oshima, he was recognized as a diplomat with an open-minded and international worldview. Ironically enough, however, the changing politics of the last few months had led him to become one of the signers on the Tripartite Pact. Since arriving in Berlin, Yamawaki had met him several times, including at the previous night's party. The two nodded a silent greeting in each other's direction.

Rear Admiral Yokoi turned to Ambassador Kurusu. "Would you like some coffee? Yamawaki here had a bit too much to drink last night and needs a little time to regain his composure."

"Yes, thank you," replied Kurusu, sitting down at the table with Yamawaki. "You should be taking it easy today. I apologize for calling you in."

"What's the problem?" asked Yokoi. "The long-awaited pact is finally signed. You could have taken the day off yourself."

"I plan to do just that after passing this task along to you. Ciano invited me to his cottage on Lake Como. I'm thinking to take my wife there."

Yamawaki suddenly recalled Kurusu's wife at the party. She was a white woman and an adroit hostess who had seen her share of official parties. Yamawaki had seen the high-ranking Nazi officers—who loathed even the hint of mixing between the races—eyeing the ambassador and his wife unpleasantly throughout the affair.

The coffee arrived. Kurusu waited for the receptionist to leave before turning to Yokoi.

"Rear admiral. Do you know anything about the new fighter the navy has just deployed? I hear it is code-named 'Type Zero.'"

"Type Zero?" asked Yokoi back. "You mean the one we just deployed recently?"

Part Two

He must mean the Type Zero Carrier Fighter, thought Yamawaki. Yokoi seemed to hesitate. Was he allowed to discuss the highly confidential subject with anyone, even the ambassador?

Kurusu broke the silence. "I don't know much about it, myself. But it's actually the entire reason I called this meeting. Just before the ceremony yesterday, Ribbentrop told me that he wanted to discuss it with us as soon as possible."

"'Discuss'? Discuss what? The navy hasn't made a single public comment about that aircraft yet. It's still highly confidential."

"Well, he seemed fairly well informed about the subject. He knows that the aircraft is being built by Mitsubishi Heavy Industries in Nagoya. He even knew its engine capacity, its weapons, its top speed, things like that. Did that air corps in China, the one that succeeded so admirably the other day, actually use this aircraft? I hadn't been aware of that. Ribbentrop called it 'the most exciting development in the history of the Japanese aviation industry.'"

"So, what did Ribbentrop want? What did he say about the fighters?" asked Yokoi.

Kurusu took a sip of coffee. "He wishes us to cooperate and allow the Germans a license to produce these new fighters," he answered slowly.

"The Germans want to develop our navy fighters here in their own country?" repeated Yokoi, as if in shock at Kurusu's words.

Yamawaki sat up straight in his chair. What a wonderful subject for the morning after a party. As effective as a sauna for killing a hangover. What next? Hitler taking the Imperial Princess as his adopted daughter?

"Precisely," said Kurusu. His expression was serious. "He said it would be the first large-scale co-production between Japan and Germany after the ratification of the Tripartite Pact."

"And what did you say?"

"I have no idea about this aircraft. I told Ribbentrop that I would pass his words to the naval attaché. No sooner had I said that than he requested a meeting. We will meet at Luftwaffe Headquarters at two o'clock this afternoon. They wish to buy several aircraft first, for testing, before finalizing the contract."

"Hold it, please. So everything's already decided?"

"It certainly sounds like it. He said some high-ranking German officers would be present at the meeting. General Udet, Chief of the Luftwaffe

Technical Office, and one or two others."

"Even if the Germans are requesting full cooperation, I don't think we need to make an immediate response. This aircraft is a secret weapon. And as you are undoubtedly already aware, more than a few people in the navy are reluctant to forge any closer of a relationship with Germany."

Listening to Kurusu and Yokoi talk, Yamawaki imagined the faces of the military officials who had been against the Tripartite Pact. Would they give permission to have their beloved aircraft produced in Germany so easily? Then again, Mitsubishi would probably see the whole affair as nothing more than another business opportunity.

"There's no way the higher-ups will go along with this. I wouldn't expect a favorable answer from them." The strain in Yokoi's voice was unmistakable.

"Minister Ribbentrop tells me that this is a direct request from the Führer. I heard he has taken a very personal interest in seeing the plans for developing the aircraft."

"I don't care whose request it is. The Imperial Navy has its own policies. Signing the Tripartite Pact is one thing. Cooperative development of weapon systems is something else altogether."

"I'm afraid they don't seem to see things that way, rear admiral. I made the same point to Ribbentrop, but we signed the Tripartite Pact yesterday."

"Are you saying this was decided under the pact? I find that difficult to believe."

"Not specifically. But military cooperation among the Axis nations is a fundamental part of the pact. And I hope you haven't forgotten the other documents that were exchanged in addition to the pact."

"Are you talking about the secret articles? What does that have to do with this?"

Kurusu withdrew a folder from his leather bag. He opened it and began to read.

"To aid Japan in the establishment of a new order in Eastern Asia where she must fully prepare to face any crisis, Germany will provide as much industrial, technological, and material support to Japan as feasible."

Kurusu looked up and continued. "This is from a letter to our Minister of Foreign Affairs from the German ambassador to Japan. Germany is promising to fully cooperate with Japan regarding military technology. But the obligation can be interpreted to extend both ways. Which means that Japan cannot easily deny a request for technological cooperation, or any kind of support, for that matter. The Tripartite Pact has been signed. The Germans are requesting assistance in the form of new Japanese fighters for their country. To establish, to borrow Ribbentrop's words, large-scale co-production between Japan and Germany."

Yokoi glanced at Yamawaki. Yokoi seemed to be searching for some sign from him. Yamawaki nodded. Kurusu was right. There was no other way to interpret the secret articles to the pact. The Imperial Navy had fully agreed to the content of the secret articles, which were inseparable from the pact itself.

"Looking back," said Kurusu, "Germany has provided us with no small amount of technological assistance themselves, from weapons to industrial equipment. In fact, I don't think it's any exaggeration to say that a rejection of the Germans' request would constitute not only a violation of the pact, but of the loyalty and trust that has been built between our two countries. And don't forget that we may need their assistance in developing new weapons ourselves in the not-so-distant future. So, I say, we cannot simply dismiss this request."

This'll cause quite a stir in Tokyo, thought Yamawaki. And another huge dispute within the navy, to be sure. The army and the foreign ministry would likely cooperate to pressure the navy. The rightists would jump in on the act, too. "Why are you dragging your feet about cooperating with the German Reich? Are you traitors?" Yamawaki could almost hear the angry shouts of the rightists.

Yokoi thought for a moment, then exhaled loudly through his nose. "Did you say the meeting would be held at two o'clock? Fine. Let's go. I'd like to have Yamawaki accompany us as well."

Kurusu breathed a quiet sigh of relief.

CHAPTER 4

Seven men sat around the large oval table that dominated the room.

General Udet, Chief of the Luftwaffe Technical Office, sat in the host's chair, flanked on either side by his adjutant and assistant. Ambassador Kurusu sat across the table from Udet. Rear Admiral Tadao Yokoi sat to Kurusu's right, while Secretary Junzo Yamawaki sat on Kurusu's left. A young civilian, hired as an interpreter by the Germans, sat next to Yamawaki.

Udet ground his cigarette into an ashtray and began to speak.

"Our countries signed the Tripartite Pact only just yesterday. At today's meeting, we'd like to have an open and frank discussion about several topics. What do you say, Mr. Ambassador?"

"We have no objections, General," answered Kurusu. "To be honest, we are completely exhausted from the discussions leading up to the signing of the Tripartite Pact. We too would welcome an open and frank discussion."

"Wonderful," nodded Udet in satisfaction. "Major Graf, would you explain to these gentlemen exactly why we are interested in the new fighters of the Imperial Japanese Navy?"

Graf stood up. He wore the coveted Knight's Cross to the Iron Cross, which signified that he had survived fierce combat on at least three occasions. As a major in the Luftwaffe, he must have seen his share of dogfights. The skin over nearly half of his face was scarred from a burn and stretched as tight as a drum over the bones. His nose had lost much of its shape. Yamawaki had a difficult time looking directly at the major. He noticed that Graf seemed to make the other Japanese nervous as well.

Major Graf began to talk, air hissing from a corner of his ruined mouth with every word. Graf described, at considerable length, the current situation facing the Luftwaffe, beginning with the recent raids on England. Just as Udet had promised, the major spoke unflinchingly, even about the difficulties plaguing the Luftwaffe. Yamawaki had expected head-on talks with the Germans, but even then, he was shocked to hear a major discuss the Luftwaffe's problems so openly. Ally or no, he suspected that no officer of the Imperial Navy would be as frank regarding any mistakes and miscalculations in the Japanese war strategy.

Part Two

Are we really this important to the Germans? thought Yamawaki. *Then again, perhaps they wouldn't have spoken this openly before the pact.*

Yamawaki had spent only three weeks in Berlin. It was still difficult for him to reach any conclusions about the way Germans thought and acted.

Major Graf had also brought reports about the Type Zero Carrier Fighter. Yamawaki was shocked once again. The reports were far more detailed than anything he had seen, but what he did know about the capabilities of the fighter matched the German report precisely.

After Major Graf finished his briefing, Udet spoke again.

"I hope that you won't try to deny that these fighters exist, gentlemen. Rear Admiral Yokoi?"

Yamawaki glanced at Yokoi. *Now that the Germans have managed to get their hands on such detailed information, there's no way he can play innocent. At this point, feigning ignorance about the fighters would do nothing but anger them.*

Yokoi hesitated for a moment. Finally, he said:

"You must be talking about the Type Zero Carrier Fighters that we first deployed this summer. Your report is complete, and I have nothing to add or amend. Instead, I would like to ask you a question myself."

"Please."

"How did the Abwehr obtain this information? The fighter hasn't been introduced publicly. Most Japanese are totally unaware of its existence."

Udet laughed. "Unaware they may be, but the fighters were built in a huge factory, sent to bases, and flown in the sky. You can't keep a secret forever. And we have 'helpers,' shall we say, in Tokyo and Shanghai. We even have confederates and spies in the protectorate in Chungking. An area you bombed repeatedly, I believe."

"I take my hat off to you," said Yokoi. "Please continue."

Udet stood up and began to outline his plan. His voice took on a theatrical tone, almost as if he were imitating Hitler. Germany wanted to procure two or three Zero fighters for their combat squadrons. If the fighters' performance lived up to expectations, Germany would like to proceed with licensing and producing the aircraft. Factories and engineers would shift their focus to its production. Udet said he even planned to take personal charge and ensure the supply of materials and machine tools.

Udet continued to elaborate on the ambitious plan. If the licensed production proved successful, he said, Germany and Japan would make an enormous step towards developing totally new weapons cooperatively.

At the words, Yamawaki recalled his fellow officers admitting that some of their equipment was in desperate need of improvement. Several types of electronic and optical devices leapt to mind, including radar, radios, and precision rangefinders, and some large weapons.

Udet took his chair again. Graf spoke, this time remaining seated.

"The general may have gotten slightly ahead of himself. As we haven't seen the actual aircraft yet, I insist that we test it first to confirm that its capabilities match the report. Once we have the results in hand, we can begin discussing plans for production."

The Japanese delegation nodded in agreement. Graf continued:

"As such, we would request that you dispatch two fighters for testing. The Luftwaffe will purchase them. The place of delivery will be Berlin. The contract will be fulfilled when the two fighters actually arrive."

"When would you like them to be delivered?" asked Yokoi.

"By November 15th."

"That's impossible," Yokoi said. "We must first supply the Imperial Navy itself with these aircraft. We won't have any spare planes before then."

"When will they be available?"

"We need at least four months. Delivery can be no earlier than the end of January of next year."

"If that's the case, the plans for production are meaningless."

"We need three months to build the aircraft. And we need time for the delivery, too."

Udet cut in.

"Nonsense! Rear admiral, we don't have time to waste haggling over minor details like a pair of merchants. Need I remind you that Japan and Germany signed a historic pact yesterday? The Führer expects an immediate response! If necessary, we will have a letter sent directly from the Führer to your leader. Or would you prefer that we take this matter up with Foreign Minister Matsuoka?"

"This isn't about politics, general," Yokoi replied. "My answer is based on technical considerations. But that being said, I'm afraid that changing the date of the deployment of the aircraft falls outside of my jurisdiction. I simply don't have the ability to authorize it. It's something that needs to be decided at a higher level."

Both parties sat in silence.

Yamawaki pictured the reactions of his top bosses. Former Prime and Navy Minister Mitsumasa Yonai, Admiral Isoroku Yamamoto, and Vice Admiral Shigeyoshi Inoue would definitely reject granting the license to Germany. They were staunch opponents of the Tripartite Pact. They had even suffered terrorist attacks from right-wingers and Army extremists because of their views. There was no way they would support this.

On the other hand, Minister of the Navy Koshiro Oikawa's reaction was not hard to predict either. "Well, we accepted the Tripartite Pact, after all," he'd say, caving into the German demand without a moment's thought. The Naval General Staff would put their full weight behind the proposal as well. With Hitler's personal missive and Minister Matsuoka's poking his nose in, the Navy's decision was as good as made for them; the "high-level decision" referred to was something of a foregone conclusion.

"I will contact Japan and pass your request along at once," said Kurusu. "We will then wait for a response from headquarters. Can you give us any leeway over the date of delivery?"

Udet and Graf looked at each other. Udet nodded, somewhat reluctantly.

"We hope the aircraft can be delivered by the fifteenth of the month after next," said Graf. "But if that turns out to be impossible, we will request a full explanation as to why, and a timetable for the delivery. Our request may be rescinded if we do not receive favorable answers to our questions."

Yamawaki broke in, knowing that he had to participate in some way to secure future promotion. "As you know, the Type Zero Carrier Fighter is the Imperial Navy's highest secret. We cannot have these meetings or negotiations go public. I hope that you understand our situation and treat this matter with the same level of caution that we do."

"Of course," Udet answered. "We shall minimize the number of participants, and keep as few records as possible. We have no issue with treating this matter as highly confidential."

"We would like to confirm something else," said Kurusu. "We cannot rely on shipping to ensure safe delivery of such important cargo. May we expect the German government to support negotiations with the Russians to ensure a route over their territory?"

"NO!" cried Udet. "You will not take the Russian route! Absolutely not!"

CHAPTER 5

Taking their leave of Kurusu, Yokoi and Yamawaki shared a car back to the Naval Office. Yokoi barely spoke during the ride. He sat with his arms crossed and his eyes fixed on the back of the chauffeur's head. Yamawaki pondered Udet's last words. What did they mean? "You will not take the Russian route! Absolutely not!" His tone could mean only one thing.

Yokoi finally spoke to Yamawaki as the two entered the rear admiral's office.

"When are you leaving for Japan?" Yokoi asked.

Yamawaki peered through the window at the houses outside for a moment. "In three or four days. I enjoyed watching the Germans; they seem to be thriving even during wartime. I even had a chance to see Hitler up close."

The atmosphere in Berlin had surprised Yamawaki. He had heard much about the tragedies that Germany had suffered in the early 30's. And with the war effort kicking into high gear, Yawamaki expected a dismal city, with food and power shortages. Instead he found Berlin to be a bright and brilliant place. Yamawaki experienced two British air raids during his stay, but he noticed the attacks barely left a mark on the daily lives of the civilian population. The public transportation system functioned smoothly. Government and private offices remained open. People freely went to operas, sang at beer halls, picnicked in the park. Unlike Tokyo, the streets were full of cars, and the women donned the latest fashions. It was quite easy to understand why some Japanese officers had become enamored with the Third Reich and supported the Tripartite Pact.

Yokoi sat down behind his desk. Leaning back in his chair, he silently stroked his chin with his right hand. His expression was as puckered as if he'd eaten a sour pickle.

A long moment passed. Finally, Yokoi broke out of his reverie.

"Can you leave sooner and discuss this with Minister Oikawa directly? I feel terrible about informing him by telegram."

"That's no problem at all," answered Yamawaki. *I have to give him a detailed report anyway.*

"Do you think the Navy will approve it?"

"I think so. Do they have a choice?" Yamawaki explained that, legally speaking, the production plans were a matter for discussion between Mitsubishi Heavy Industries and the German factories alone. Mitsubishi was obliged to provide all of the aircraft promised to the Imperial Navy, but nothing prohibited them from signing a new contract to license the fighters to another party. Nobody had even considered the possibility when the Imperial Navy and Mitsubishi signed their agreement. It was a good-faith contract. The Navy could not legally hinder Mitsubishi in any way.

"But that being said," said Yamawaki. "The question of how we're going to deliver the aircraft is a tough one. We can't use submarines, for obvious reasons. If we can't fly over Russia, we'll have to either punch through central Asia or fly across India. But I'm not totally clear about the capabilities of this aircraft. Could it make it over Burma and India without landing once?"

"I've heard the fighter has incredible range, but that distance... It seems too much to ask."

"If that's so, we'll need to arrange an airfield for refueling somewhere in India," said Yamawaki.

"What are you talking about? India is a British colony," said Yokoi. "Besides, the British are stationed in Hong Kong, too. There's a British fleet in Singapore. The RAF is stationed in Iraq. The southern route is out of the question."

"What about central Asia, then?"

"Are there any airfields there? We don't even have complete maps of the region."

"There is a commercial flight route between central Asia and Moscow."

"If we are to avoid Russian territory," said Yokoi, "the planes will have to fly over a huge desert and a mountain range to make it to Turkey."

"Yes. There's no question it won't be easy," said Yamawaki.

Yokoi stood up, walked over to the globe near his desk, and gave it a spin. He waited for it to come to a stop.

"Why was General Udet set against the Russian route, I wonder? Germany and Russia have signed a non-aggression pact. They may not be allies, but they certainly aren't enemies."

"I respectfully disagree," said Yamawaki. "I believe that war between the two is imminent."

Part Two

"What—Germany declaring war against Russia? Impossible."

"Who was it who said 'the state of affairs in Europe is complex and full of intrigue'? Nobody in Japan predicted that Germany and Russia would sign that treaty in the first place."

"Are you saying their relations are breaking down now?"

"Based on what I've seen and heard, I predict there will be a falling out within a year. No. More like nine months."

"A bold opinion, Yamawaki. I suspect the other officers would call you insane."

"The Imperial Navy pays me for my 'bold opinions.' In any event, declaring war against Russia is suicide. If it happens, mark my words: Nazi Germany will fall."

Yokoi's eyes began to search the room. He appeared worried that Yamawaki's comments may have been overheard.

"You're talking about the fate of a country. Don't be so flippant."

"I can't help but speak my mind, especially about this."

"Watch your mouth. All the military liaisons in Berlin have been hinting that Hitler may be shifting his focus from England to Eastern Europe. But I don't think Germany will go to war with the Soviets."

Yamawaki gripped his bag a bit more tightly, as if to leave.

"Well, I assume you'll be the one handling the Germans' request, then," he said.

"I want this to stay totally confidential," replied Yokoi. "I want to involve the minimum number of people possible. Who's going to handle this in Tokyo? Whoever they put in charge, I think we should use a code word for this."

"Like what?"

"How about 'eagle' or 'hawk'? Something like, 'We sent two eagles.'"

"Eagles? Anyone can tell that refers to military aircraft."

"It doesn't really matter what word we use. Pick a different one, then."

"How about 'ibis'? A nice native feel. Too elegant?"

"No, that's fine," agreed Yokoi. "The code word is a secondary issue anyway. We'll go with 'ibis.' So, speaking of the ibis, I want you to investigate the feasibility of delivery by air and report the conclusion to me at once. If they say it's impossible, that's fine. I just want to be able to tell them something concrete. At any rate, the situation may well change by the time you reach Tokyo."

"I'll leave Berlin tomorrow. I'll head straight for Tokyo."

"Have a safe trip. Don't make any references to this matter in your written correspondence."

Yamawaki bowed and left Yokoi's office.

CHAPTER 6

Yamawaki made his way back to Japan from Berlin via Siberia, stopping briefly in Dalian, China. At roughly the same time, a lone navy aircraft touched down in Shanghai. It had originated from the Chinese city of Hankow. The Type 96 transport carried ten pilots from the 12th Air Corps of the Second Joint Air Corps of the IJN, stationed in Hankow. Among the pilots were a Lieutenant Keiichi Ando and a Flight Sergeant Kyohei Inui.

Lieutenant Ando and Sergeant Inui piloted the number one and two planes in their squadron. Three days earlier, they had participated in a particularly vicious bombing of the Chinese airbase at Tai Ping Si in Chengdu. The campaign had been quite successful, they had been granted a special R&R leave, and they had decided to fly to Kunda airbase and spend some time in Shanghai.

Most of the pilots switched to civilian clothes and headed straight for the Japanese restaurants, such as the famed Tongo or the Tsukinoya, in Shanghai's Hongkou quarter. Ando and Inui remained in uniform, however, and crossed Garden Bridge into the British-U.S. protectorate. Their first stop was the closest public bath house, located near Park Hotel on Nanking Road, where they cleaned themselves up. Ando hit on the idea of going to see the Filipino jazz band that would be playing at the Jockey Club Hotel that night.

Officers and N.C.O.s led completely separate lives within the military. In Japan's navy air corps, officers and N.C.O.s not only slept and ate separately, but were served different meals in flight as well. The places that they visited after hours were just as clearly segregated.

According to custom, then, it was almost unthinkable for a lieutenant such as Ando to spend his leave with an N.C.O like Inui. As such, they had to find hangouts that other naval officers didn't frequent.

The incident occurred as they walked east on Nanking Road from the nearby racetrack. It was after dark, but the street was illuminated by the glow of lampposts and countless neon signs. It might well have been the most crowded place in the city.

A couple stepped out from a restaurant. The man was Japanese and appeared to be about fifty; he wore a mustache, a white suit, and a soft hat. The woman at his side was a young Caucasian in a lavender dress. Ando and Inui had decided to grab a bite of Cantonese food before heading to the Jockey Club Hotel when they spotted the couple. The man met Ando's gaze. He looked over Ando's uniform with a sneer. He raised his hand in some sort of a signal, and a car that had been parked on the side of the street began moving towards him.

Without warning, the sound of a gunshot echoed through the air.

Ando and Inui instinctively turned in the direction of the sound. Someone screamed. The crowd pushed, leaving an empty space around the scene. In the middle stood the man with the mustache, now hunched over and clutching his shoulder. A young Chinese man, clad in shabby black clothes, pointed a gun directly at him.

The young man pulled the trigger—nothing but a tiny click. Staggering, the Japanese man reached into his jacket and pulled out a gun of his own. The young man squeezed the trigger of his gun again and again. Each time it clicked dry. He stepped back, still holding the gun straight in front of him, then suddenly, lowering his aim, spun and dashed into the crowd.

Holding his good arm straight out, the Japanese drew a bead on the young man. Someone shrieked in terror. The crowd jostled to get out of the way.

Ando dove at the Japanese and knocked his arm as the gun fired. A streetlamp shattered, spraying shards of glass across the street.

The man pushed Ando away, hard, and took aim again. Ando grabbed the man's wrist and twisted it.

"Let go!" the man shouted. "You idiot!"

The young assassin had disappeared into the throng. Members of the crowd studied Ando and the Japanese man from a distance. Ando released his grip.

The man's face was red with anger. He spun to glare at the people who had gathered to watch. The frightened crowd recoiled as he swung his gun in their direction.

Ando looked for Inui and found him with the Caucasian woman, who was squatting in the street, breathing raggedly. She was too frightened even to speak. Inui's hand was placed gently on the woman's back. She seemed not to be hurt.

"What were you thinking?" screamed the man. "He was a guerilla, anti-Japanese!"

"Look at this crowd," said Ando. "You would have hit an innocent bystander. You might have killed someone."

"I guess it's all right to kill a Japanese, huh? Why did you help him?"

"I wasn't trying to help him. How's your shoulder?"

Suddenly remembering that he'd been hit, the man put his hand over the wound. A bloodstain was slowly spreading across his white suit.

"It's nothing." Perhaps he was used to being shot. "But you! You're going to pay for this."

"You'd better see a doctor."

"Give me your name."

"Lieutenant Ando. 12th Air Corps."

"And him?" he asked, pointing at Inui.

"Sergeant Inui. He's in the 12th with me."

"Where are you staying? At Suikosha?"

"Probably. For now, we're thinking to catch a show at the Jockey Club Hotel. We'll be there until midnight."

"I'm going to make you pay for this."

"I don't get it. What do you mean, 'pay'?"

Suddenly, the man turned around. "Tatiana? Are you all right?" he asked the woman.

The Caucasian woman sobbed and tried to stand. Inui helped to pull her to her feet.

The man jerked his chin towards the car. She walked over unsteadily and climbed into the back seat. The man turned to follow. Suddenly, Ando asked:

"And what's your name?"

"My name...? I can't say it in a place like this, you fool!"

"You have an attitude problem, sir. Those aren't Shanghai-style manners."

"I work at Broadway Mansion. I hope you know what that means."

The man got in and slammed the door behind him. The car jerked forward and started proceeding down Nanking Road, bathed in the glow of the streetlights and signs.

The crowd began to disperse. Several of the bystanders launched into animated discussions of the incident they'd just witnessed.

"Lieutenant! Are you all right?" asked Inui.

"I'm all right. And you?"

"It was over before I even realized what was going on. What did he mean by 'Broadway Mansion'?"

"I'm not sure." The man had left his soft hat behind on the road. A Chinese boy picked it up and darted back into the crowd. Ando stared at the spot where the boy had been just a moment ago.

"Maybe it's home to some special business?" Ando said.

"You mean opium?"

"I guess he was trying to tell us he's part of some shady gang. That'd explain why he was targeted."

Two hours after the incident, Ando and Inui were enjoying after-dinner drinks at the Jockey Club Hotel. The club there was small but renowned for its high-quality music. Indeed, the audience consisted mostly of music lovers rather than singles on the prowl. The club played dance and standards early in the evening, jazz and blues later at night. Caucasian singers often dropped by after finishing their own sets at other clubs. Sometimes they even sang with the band. The club was like an oasis for white people in Shanghai during the war. When Ando and Inui arrived, the Filipino band was in the middle of a swing jazz number.

A moment later, two Japanese dressed in civilian clothes entered the room. One was old, the other young. They paused at the entrance, looked around for a moment, and headed straight for Ando and Inui's table. A waiter couldn't make it out of the way in time, and a tray full of glasses and bottles crashed on the floor.

"We're police. With the consulate," said the older of the two when they reached Ando. "Are you Lieutenant Ando?"

Ando's head jerked up.

"The band's still playing. Are you deaf?"

"Maybe. I don't hear music," said the man, flashing a cynical smile. "You must be Lieutenant Ando."

Some of the other customers turned around for a look at Ando. They didn't frown at him, but it was more than obvious that they were annoyed.

There was no choice. Ando stood up and headed for the exit, trailed by Inui and the two men.

As soon as they were outside, the lieutenant turned to face the detectives. "I'm the man you're looking for. Better have a damn good reason for interrupting my evening."

"A Japanese was shot on Nanking Road today," said the older detective. "You're aware of that, aren't you."

"Yes. I happened to be there."

"The victim told us you helped the Chinese attacker to escape. Said he tried to return fire, you stopped him. Army Military Police wants to know what happened."

"Stopped him? Look, you've got the wrong picture, but I'm not in the mood right now to tell you what happened. I'll be available tomorrow morning. I just got in from Hankow, and my nerves are still shot from front-line duty."

"We would like you to come with us right now, if at all possible."

"Do I have a choice? If you can wait until tomorrow, I'd be more than happy to replay the whole scene for you. Complete with sound effects."

"Unfortunately for you, lieutenant, this isn't a game," the man said grimacing. "Army troops are poised on the Garden Bridge as we speak. They're just waiting for the signal. They'll support the Military Police's search for anti-Japanese forces hiding out in the British-U.S. protectorate. They're ready to cross the bridge any time now. You see, it's not exactly a laughing matter."

"Are you saying we're about to invade the protectorate?" Ando asked back in shock.

"That's precisely what I'm saying. It's a security issue for the 30,000 Japanese stationed here. We can't allow them to be exposed to any more danger."

"Sending over those troops will just escalate the conflict. Anything could happen after that."

"We didn't start this. The anti-Japanese terrorist who shot one of us did."

Ando recalled a similar incident that had happened in May. A Japanese man had been wounded in an armed robbery. The man happened to be a plainclothes M.P., and the Imperial Army had tried to send troops to search the protectorate then, too. But the Navy's marine troops had intervened. They had squared off at the Garden Bridge, and that time, the Army had backed down. History repeating itself, thought Ando.

"And that must be Sergeant Inui. We'd like him to join us as well," the man said, fixing Inui with a steely gaze.

While Ando and Inui spoke with the two policemen, a naval marine commander stood on the north side of the Garden Bridge, locked in heated debate with a commander from the Thirteenth Army.

The Navy had dispatched two troops of marines as soon as they had heard the news from the Japanese Consulate. The troops were headed by Commander Kazuhiro Matsukura, one of the staff officers for the naval expeditionary force in China. It was rare for Matsukura to command troops personally. He had been ordered to stop the Army from entering the British-U.S. Protectorate.

The old joint protectorate in Henan of Suzhou, widely known as the "British-U.S. Protectorate," was a special area that had been set up to protect British, American, and Italian interests in the area. Needless to say, Japanese forces could not and did not set foot in the protectorate on a whim. This had turned the protectorate into a haven for the anti-Japanese movement and the main depot of supplies for Chiang Kai-Shek's forces. The Army had long desired to oust the anti-Japanese movement from the area and saw the shooting incident as the perfect excuse to take action. Whatever the reasoning, however, England and the U.S. would definitely see the Japanese Army's incursion as a serious breach. The state of international affairs being as sensitive as they were, allowing the army to run wild in the protectorate was out of the question. Shigetaro Shimada, commander in chief of the expeditionary fleet in China, had ordered Matsukura and the marines to stop the army from crossing the bridge—at any cost.

The Thirteenth Army's unit, commanded by Lieutenant Colonel Chikayoshi Natsuumi, stood locked in a standoff with the marines. The situation was tense. At the scene was Major General Hidenari Nose of the Thirteen Army, its chief staff officer. Three trucks filled with soldiers had been parked so as to block the intersection to the north of the bridge. The frontmost truck sported a light machine gun on its roof. A pair of cars sat parked in front of the trucks. Major General Nose stepped out of one car. The other car remained closed and silent, its dark windows hiding any sign of activity within.

Seeing the deadlock between Commander Matsukura of the Navy and Lieutenant Colonel Natsuumi of the Army, Major General Nose had finally decided to intervene.

"This concerns the security of all Japanese stationed here. You must let us through," the general said to Matsukura.

Part Two

"I'm sorry, sir, but we cannot allow you to pass, and I beg you not to ask again. I'm here under strict orders from the commander in chief," replied Matsukura, polite but firm.

"I'm fully aware of the treaty," said the general. His high-pitched voice perfectly suited his small frame. "The Navy is responsible for all matters pertaining to the British-U.S. Protectorate. I'm fully aware of that. That is why we were forced to stand down last time. But what is the purpose of an army if it would stand idle when a compatriot has been assailed? If you continue to block our way, we'll have no choice but to resort to force."

"We have similar orders, sir," replied Matsukura calmly.

Civilians watched the standoff between the Japanese military forces with bated breath. Rickshaws and cars had stopped approaching the north side of the bridge. Others were undoubtedly taking detours to avoid the area entirely. The Shanghai Municipal Police Force had already cordoned off the south side of the bridge. Not a single car or pedestrian was crossing it from the side of the British-U.S. Protectorate.

"This is going nowhere," said Nose, glancing at his wristwatch.

Major General Nose looked directly into Lieutenant Colonel Natsuumi's eyes for a moment. Then he turned away. The headlights of the trucks were on. There was a loud clicking sound as one of the soldiers cocked the machine gun.

Commander Matsukura quickly spun around and gave a signal to the marines. His soldiers split into two groups. One lined up against the west side of the bridge, while the other stood in front of the nearby Soviet Consulate. The rapid footsteps of the soldiers echoed through the air.

Alarmed, the civilian bystanders who had gathered to watch began to back away from the military forces. Within moments, the crowd had dispersed, leaving only the Japanese troops in the street on the north side of the bridge.

Major General Nose looked at Commander Matsukura.

"I have no choice but to give the order to advance."

"I have no choice but to give the order to block your advance, sir," countered Matsukura.

"We're on the same side. Are we really going to have to shoot at each other?"

"It seems that way, sir."

Then there was silence. The commanders glared fiercely at one another. The troops on both sides stood at attention, waiting for orders. Nobody moved an inch. A pin drop would have sounded like a hand grenade.

Suddenly, the sound of an approaching engine broke the silence. A car crossed the bridge from the side of the British-U.S. Protectorate, stopping just behind the marines. Four men stepped out of the car. Two wore navy uniforms. The other two wore suits. It was Lieutenant Ando, Flight Sergeant Inui, and the two detectives from the consulate.

The appearance of the four men drew a commotion on the opposite side of the intersection as well. The door of the mysterious black sedan parked in front of the Army trucks opened. An officer stepped from the car and made his way through the silent intersection. His collar bore a military police insignia.

The officer stopped directly in front of Matsukura. The M.P. was a slender man. He didn't appear to have any eyebrows—was it due to a nervous condition? simply a trick of the light?—and his face looked completely pale. He looked at Ando, who was standing behind Matsukura, and spoke.

"I am Major Shibusawa, a military police officer stationed here in Shanghai. You are Lieutenant Ando from the 12th Air Corps, correct?"

"Yes," replied Ando, stepping forward. "I seem to have become quite a popular man in Shanghai lately."

The two men's voices echoed through the silent intersection as clearly as if they had been using bullhorns.

"I would like to discuss the incident you were involved in earlier this evening. A Japanese man was shot by a Chinese. Will you come with me, Lieutenant Ando? Flight Sergeant Inui, I would like you to join us as well," said Major Shibusawa.

"If this is voluntary, I'd rather not come tonight," answered Ando. "But I suppose I don't have a choice."

Just then, a naval serviceman sprinted from the direction of the Japanese consulate on the west side of the bridge. He appeared to be an orderly. All eyes were upon him.

As soon as he reached Matsukura, the soldier made a report in a loud voice.

"Sir. There is activity among the American warships. Armed sailors appear to be preparing to make a landing."

At this the area fell silent again. Ando and Shibusawa stared at Commander Matsukura and Major General Nose. Matsukura turned to face Nose.

"Do you want to involve U.S. forces in this, sir?" he asked calmly.

Nose glared at Matsukura. He seemed to be struggling to control himself. His cheeks were trembling with humiliation.

"We'll fall back," said the general hoarsely. "But rest assured that this is the last time the Army will be under the Navy's thumb."

Dismissing Lieutenant Colonel Natsuumi, he turned and stomped angrily across the intersection.

Shibusawa turned to Ando and said, "Lieutenant Ando. Sergeant Inui. You two must come with me."

Ando and Inui looked at each other, sighed, and shook their heads.

Exhaling heavily, Matsukura ordered the marines to stand down.

Sounds of life gradually began to return to the streets.

CHAPTER 7

Junzo Yamawaki arrived in Tokyo on the evening of October 8th. He had flown to Vienna from Berlin, taken the train to Moscow and then switched to the Trans-Siberian Express, which took him to Dalian, Manchuria. A specially chartered navy aircraft awaited his arrival. Yamawaki boarded the Type 96 Attack Bomber, flew to Haneda Airport in Tokyo, and proceeded directly to the Ministry of the Navy. The brick building was located downtown, in Kasumigaseki. Yamawaki headed for the second floor and opened the door to an office. He hadn't even had time to freshen up from his journey.

He gave a detailed report to Lieutenant Commander Seishiro Ohnuki, adjutant to the Ministry of the Navy. A telegram informing of the German request had already been sent to the ministry from Berlin, but the finer details of the conversation with the Luftwaffe required a report in person. Ohnuki listened intently, nodding occasionally, without interrupting or raising any questions.

Ohnuki was a tall man, thin, with thinning hair and rimless glasses. He wore a winter uniform with a bright white adjutant's sash. He didn't appear particularly aggressive but had stood his ground against the rightist extremists who visited the ministry on a daily basis to complain about the navy's cool attitude towards the Tripartite Pact. In fact, Ohnuki had a reputation throughout the navy of being far tougher than he looked.

During the army uprising four years earlier, when Ohnuki was serving under Naval Captain Seishiro Sato, he had led a unit of marines from Yokosuka to defend the ministry building. If the Army troops had managed to occupy the Imperial Palace as intended, by all accounts Ohnuki would have been the one to lead the marines in to rescue the Emperor. It went without saying that Ohnuki was regarded highly by his fellow naval staff officers. He was known for his cautious stance regarding the Tripartite Pact.

After listening to the complete report, Ohnuki finally spoke to Yamawaki.

"We have already made our reply. The Navy will send two Type Zero Carrier Fighters to Germany."

Yamawaki's eyes widened. He stared at Ohnuki.

Ohnuki continued, "We have decided to send them as quickly as possible. We have already spoken with Minister Matsuoka and General Tojo. But, since you've been on top of this from the very beginning, would you handle the execution of the project? Admiral Oikawa quite specifically requested that you participate."

As it happened, none of the senior adjutants or Secretary Shume Sugita were present. Yamawaki and Ohnuki were the only ones in the dark, high-ceilinged room.

"So you've already talked to the Minister of Foreign Affairs and the Minister of the Army?" asked Yamawaki in confusion.

"That's correct. Matsuoka wants to present the aircraft to Hitler as a gift to commemorate the signing of the Tripartite Pact. They say Minister-General Tojo is drooling at the prospect of developing new weapons with Germany. The Navy doesn't have much say in this matter. The ministers, for their part, seem to feel that giving Germany whatever they want will get us something in return, someday. At any rate, I hear that both of them are firmly behind the plan."

"But within the Navy…" Yamawaki seemed to be searching for the appropriate words. He couldn't believe the Navy had moved so quickly. "Was there any dissent at all?"

Yamawaki wondered if the navy he knew had changed in the month he was away. Even if they were to agree to the German demand, Yamawaki had expected at least a good ten days or so of debate and argument.

"That's a good question," said Ohnuki, leaning over his desk towards Yamawaki and lowering his voice conspiratorially. "Only a handful of people in the navy and the government even know about the request at all. Minister-Admiral Oikawa doesn't want to publicize it; he thinks it'll only serve to polarize the Imperial Navy all the more. We've finally managed to pull ourselves together. An extended debate over this could send us back to square one. We're already on the bus."

Wouldn't do to miss the bus, I guess, thought Yamawaki, pondering the changes that had taken place over the preceding few years. The Navy had originally taken a firm stand against antagonizing the U.S. and Britain with the Tripartite Pact. But the war had been going so well for Germany that there was no choice but to rethink that strategy. It wouldn't do to miss out on the inevitable distribution of captured territory after the end of the war. So the IJN had swallowed their humiliation at being left out of the loop regarding Germany's non-aggression pact with the Soviet Union, and agreed to the Tripartite Pact. At any rate, now that they had signed the pact, the Japanese fleet had to prepare for the possibility of fighting the United States. According to studies undertaken at the Naval University in May, however, war against the United States would inevitably result in Japan's total defeat. In spite of this, the navy had turned into one of the staunchest supporters of the Tripartite Pact. Yamawaki forced these dark thoughts out of his mind. The navy couldn't possibly have sunk this low. Or had they?

"We completed our discussions with Mitsubishi Heavy Industries before you arrived," said Ohnuki. "I don't know much about business, but I heard that Mitsubishi will receive royalties once Germany begins manufacturing the Type Zero. Some set amount of money for every aircraft produced. One of Mitsubishi's directors told me that once the royalties start coming in, they'll be able to reduce the price of the aircraft for the navy as well. So this isn't such a bad thing for us, either."

Yamawaki said nothing. Ohnuki continued:

"We'll be moving out of these quarters tomorrow. Did you know that a room's been set aside for Military P.R. activities on the first floor of Military Aviation Headquarters?"

Yamawaki shook his head.

"I have reserved that room. That will be our office for this project, effective tomorrow. Let's proceed in total secrecy. I don't want anyone bothering us."

"What, exactly, would you like me to do?" asked Yamawaki.

"I'd like you to handle the details regarding negotiations with Mitsubishi, and communications between the two governments. Also, choice of flight route and the selection of pilots. Nothing more."

"I'm just a specialist in international law. I'm not a diplomat or a manager. Do you really want me to handle this?"

"Oh, it won't be all that difficult. I have faith in you, Yamawaki. You're a civilian officer, so you can be impartial. That makes you the perfect man for the job."

"You mentioned selecting the flight path," said Yamawaki. "But what 'flight path' is there? Planning one would be nearly impossible, even for an expert."

"Don't give up before you've even started! There's a report on the capabilities of the Type Zero Carrier Fighter right there. Why don't you take it home and read it? Understood?"

Yamawaki had been cornered. Everything had been decided before he arrived, it seemed. Yamawaki could hardly feel good about accepting such a project. He nodded resignedly, took the documents and his suitcase, turned, and walked towards the door. Just as he placed his hand on the door-knob, Ohnuki called his name again. Yamawaki turned around slowly.

"You know Vice Admiral Inoue, I take it," said Ohnuki.

"Vice Admiral Shigeyoshi Inoue?" asked Yamawaki. Inoue had been dead set against signing the Tripartite Pact. Yamawaki had never spoken with the man directly.

"What about him?"

"He was ordered to take charge of Military Aviation Headquarters on October 1st. He started working there as of yesterday, the 7th. To be sure, he was supposed to take direct charge of anything related to Type Zero Carrier Fighters, but..." Ohnuki trailed off for a moment, having difficulty choosing the right words. "The vice admiral doesn't know anything about this. And we're going to keep it that way until we get a formal contract for co-production from the Germans. The only ones in the loop on this one are you, me, and the Minister of the Navy. Just the three of us. I hope you know how to keep a secret."

"You can count on me," said Yamawaki, taking out a handkerchief. The room wasn't particularly hot, but he could feel the sweat beading on his forehead. The fatigue from the long journey was catching up with him.

I guess this is my punishment for enjoying myself a bit too much with those European dames, thought Yamawaki. No sooner had he arrived in Tokyo than he had been assigned the near impossible task of transporting the Type Zero aircraft to Germany. Yamawaki had expected the plan to be scrapped due to the difficulty of getting the aircraft to Berlin. There was no problem dispatching the planes from Tokyo, of course. Yet what were the chances of them actually making it...?

So this will be the first big failure of my career, thought Yamawaki, steeling himself for the inevitable.

CHAPTER 8

The very next day, Junzo Yamawaki and Lieutenant Commander Ohnuki began working in a cramped room located in a corner on the first floor of Military Aviation Headquarters. Ohnuki had already prepared a large map of Asia, and they unrolled it over two tables that had been pulled together to accommodate it. The enormous map stretched from China in the East to Turkey in the West. It even included Palestine. Yamawaki and Ohnuki also placed a locking cabinet on one side of the room, each of them taking a key. They installed a special phone line in the room as well, with a secret number that was not listed in the Naval Ministry's phone book. They instructed the operator that it was to be used only as their personal, direct phone line.

The two began by studying the capabilities of the Type Zero Carrier Fighter. One of the aircraft had made a confirmed flight of 1,800 kilometers during the bombing campaign in Chungking the previous month. According to the Naval Aviation Technology Development Center, the aircraft was capable of flying for 2,600 kilometers at cruising speed if equipped with drop tanks. The officer in charge at the development center, however, said that the actual limit in real-world conditions would be about 2,000 kilometers.

The Type Zero Carrier Fighter used 92-octane aviation fuel. U.S. military aircraft required 100-octane, but one of the advantages of the Type Zero was that its engine could operate even with poor-quality fuel. 92-octane was easy to acquire even outside of industrially advanced nations. That meant that fuel would be readily available even on the southern route.

The officer in charge also said that the Type Zero required a runway of at least 200 meters for take off. The aircraft had been developed as a carrier fighter, and in fact this distance was fairly short. Aircraft carrier landings required the use of a tail hook to bring the aircraft to a halt. As such, the Type Zero also featured reinforced landing gear, stronger than those of land-based planes, so as to withstand the stress of being repeatedly yanked to a stop on the carrier deck. This meant that it could land even on poorly maintained airfields.

The information was enough to allow Yamawaki and Ohnuki to begin preparing the flight plan. They began to plot a route across the

Part Two

Eurasian continent with refueling stops spaced at a distance of 2,000 kilometers.

The best first stop outside of Japan appeared to be Hanoi. On the 23rd of the previous month, the Japanese Army had advanced into the northern part of French Indochina, while the navy had established a base on the outskirts of Hanoi. The army's advance had been negotiated with the French ambassador to take place within specific boundaries and without fighting. But Tominaga, the Army officer who had planned the operation, forged orders from the General Staff Office and led his troops in a forceful military takeover of the entire area. Fed up with the situation, the navy's support vessels had left as soon as the army troops had disembarked. The operation had been unprecedented in its sheer chaos. The Emperor had been so upset upon hearing the report that he had ordered severe punishment for Tominaga; the story was so famous that Yamawaki had heard it all the way out in Berlin. The Japanese advance into Indochina had been the immediate reason for the American embargo on steel exports to Japan.

But now that the Japanese Army had established a firm position in Indochina, they were in an excellent position to cut off Chang Kai-Shek's supply lines once and for all. The 14th Naval Air Corps had quickly established a base there as well, in the Hanoi suburb of Gia Lam.

Thus making it as far as Hanoi would present no problems for the Zero fighters. But after Hanoi, the aircraft would have to pass through Burma and India, both British colonies, and Iraq, a stronghold of the Royal Air Force. There was no way around any of the countries. The map measured over 6,000 kilometers from Hanoi to the Iraq-Turkey border. The aircraft would require at least three stops to refuel along the way.

Yamawaki and Ohnuki also discussed the possibility of flying from Yichang base in China to Afghanistan. But that would require crossing either the peaks of Tibet or the desert of Takla Makan. As Rear Admiral Yokoi had said in Berlin, that route cut through an enormous blank patch in the Japanese maps. It would be impossible to plan for refueling stops there. If we were to take this route, thought Yamawaki, we'd probably stand a better chance disassembling the aircraft and transporting them by camel!

"I'm starting to envy the *Kamikaze*," said an exhausted Yamawaki, referring to the prototype aircraft that had made a historic flight from Tokyo to London in 1937. "The *Kamikaze* didn't have to hide! It wasn't even a civilian plane, either. They used a modified Army Ki-15!"

"Well, then, shall we ask the British government for permission?" asked Ohnuki sarcastically. "Perhaps we can preface it by saying, 'We're very excited at the prospect of delivering these new fighters to your enemy. Would you mind helping out?' Maybe if we bow low enough, the British royal family will take pity upon us."

"They'd probably tell us they'd be happy to provide a base," said Yamawaki. "Of course, the next day, the Zero would have a British pilot at the controls. And I doubt it would continue on to Berlin. London would be a better bet."

There was only one solution.

RAF or no RAF, the Zero fighters would have to take the southern route through India and Iraq. Yamawaki and Ohnuki would somehow have to prepare secret refueling stops along the way. There was no other way to get the aircraft west.

"I'm warning you," said Yamawaki to Ohnuki. "If the planes run into the RAF over British territory, we aren't going to be able to settle things with just an apology. It could start a war between Japan and England."

"We'll avoid confrontations, then," said Ohnuki. "At all costs. Even if it means the pilots deliberately crash their aircraft in India or somewhere. To be honest, I'd rather not leave any kind of proof at all behind."

"Well, they'll have an easier time over Iran," said Yamawaki. "I'm going to the Ministry of Foreign Affairs tomorrow. They might have some ideas about making it through the region."

"I'll go to the Ministry of the Army and try to dig up information about India," said Ohnuki.

Two days later, Ohnuki told Yamawaki that he had discovered a ray of hope for their project.

The Japanese Army had some spies in Malaya and India supporting the Indian independence movement. One of them was Captain Ryojiro Shibata. He had been sent to Delhi as a special press correspondent, and he happened to have some very interesting information. One of the feudal lords in Rajasthan, western India, had begun secretly supporting the anti-British movement and had lately been very receptive to Japanese requests.

His name was Gaj Singh. He could trace the roots of his royal family back a thousand years. He was thirty-nine years old and owned a vast area of land on the western edge of Rajasthan. He was known as the thirty-seventh Maharaja of the kingdom of Kamanipur. He had studied in England, was known for being a liberal landlord, and had earned the trust and admiration of his sharecroppers. He took an active hand in managing his assets and owned several spinning factories, mines, a bank, and a railroad company. He had a palace in the Thar Desert, and had spent more than the total net worth of the Dutch or Flemish royal families in decorating it.

Gaj Singh also had a private army equipped with modern weapons. They were well trained, not only for guarding his palace and lands, but for standing on the front lines in their anticipated war for independence. Many of the soldiers had prior military experience or had been directly trained by Singh himself. They were dedicated troops, as capable as the grunts in any other regular army. If the war for independence finally began, each of the men would train and command a squad of soldiers on their own. Singh trained some two hundred young men in weapons and intelligence gathering at his facility every year. The graduates were then dispatched to secret posts throughout India.

Singh had been a major supporter of Chandra Bose, leader of the radical Indian National Congress, since 1928. He had donated nearly 100,000 pounds to Bose's movement and remained a staunch supporter during Bose's exile in Berlin from 1933 to 1936.

Immediately after the signing of the Tripartite Pact, Singh traveled to Delhi to meet Captain Shibata, whose acquaintance he had made some time earlier. Their discussion centered on the position of the Indian independence movement in the event of a war between Britain and Japan. Singh made it clear that his private military had grown large enough to organize a regiment of friendly forces if the time came. In addition to a large number of small arms, Singh's forces had access to a light armored car, several machine guns, and two airplanes. Moreover, Singh had also built an armory, complete with a repair shop, and a private airfield on his property.

A private airfield! Yamawaki looked at the map. Singh's territory was located in western India, roughly four thousand kilometers from Hanoi.

"We'll need another airfield en route," said Yamawaki. "It'll have to be somewhere in eastern India. Maybe in Bengal."

"This is great news. Yesterday we didn't have a single friendly spot across those six thousand kilometers. Now we just need three more airfields. Three," repeated Ohnuki, his eyes glued to the map.

"It's good news to be sure. But what did you say to the Ministry of the Army?"

"I just told them what they wanted to hear. I said I was conducting research to create a safe air route between Japan and Germany. That we're at the point where we're mapping potential refueling stops along the way. The minute they heard 'Germany,' they opened right up."

"Should we hope the Indian anti-British movement will provide a refueling stop in Bengal as well?"

"Yes. And it looks like we can use the same strategy in Iraq. Precisely because the British Empire is so vast and powerful, I suspect we'll find more than a few people who are against them."

CHAPTER 9

On Tuesday, a week after Yamawaki and Ohnuki had sequestered themselves in their cramped office at Military Aviation Headquarters, they received a response from the Ministry of the Navy's personnel division.

In the name of Minister-Admiral Oikawa, Yamawaki and Ohnuki had requested the name of a fighter pilot who would be up to the task of piloting the minister's personal courier service. Their criteria specified only the cream of the crop. Transport and bomber pilots were excluded. Indeed, the request specifically narrowed the pool down to pilots of single-seat fighters.

Military Aviation Headquarters would undoubtedly balk at sending such an experienced pilot over to fly a courier plane. They would rather not spare a single one of their best men. In fact, there was a good chance that the Navy would go ahead and recommend someone who was fairly inexperienced. They would need to scrutinize the response very carefully.

"What do you think?" said Ohnuki, handing a document to Yamawaki. "It says he shot down six planes in China with a Type 96 Carrier Fighter. He was injured and reassigned to Tateyama."

Yamawaki gave the report a quick read.

Lieutenant Tetsuro Toda, graduate of the forty-eighth marine class.

Born Chiba 1906. Served with the Kasumi-ga-ura, Saeki, and Omura Air Corps. Went to sea aboard the aircraft carrier *Soryu*. Joined the 13th Air Corps stationed in central China in 1935, where he mainly piloted the Type 96 Carrier Fighter. Credited with six confirmed enemy aircraft kills and four additional unconfirmed kills. Received a citation for carrying out his orders with valor in combat operations in Nanking in 1937. Lost control of his aircraft during takeoff, collided with the aircraft behind him, and was severely injured in early 1938. Accepted orders to return to Japan for recuperation. Made a complete recovery and accepted assignment to the Tateyama Air Corps.

"What do they mean by 'four additional unconfirmed kills'?" asked Yamawaki.

"He said he shot them down, but his wingman didn't see it," answered Ohnuki.

"Is this usual? Do they usually include unconfirmed kills?"

"Well, it's better to have a larger number in the report than a smaller one."

"It sounds like cheating."

"Well. Let's meet him," said Ohnuki. "Are you up for a trip to Tateyama?"

Lieutenant Tetsuro Toda was a broad-shouldered man with a thick neck and closely cropped hair. He looked like a martial artist. He was only of average height, but his powerful physique made him appear much larger than his actual size.

Yamawaki and Ohnuki caught up with Toda after he had just completed a training run. Yamawaki noticed a momentary flash of contempt on Toda's face when Ohnuki introduced himself as a lieutenant commander. Toda was undoubtedly the type of flyer who dismissively referred to officers at the ministry as "bricks."

"I have something sensitive to discuss," said Ohnuki. "Can you keep a secret?"

"I'm a Japanese man, lieutenant commander," replied Toda. "If you ask me to keep a secret, I'll take it to my grave."

The three men walked into a nearby hangar. They took seats in wooden chairs around a table normally used by maintenance men. The air in the hangar was cold and smelled strongly of oil. A biplane, apparently a Type 93 trainer, sat open for maintenance. The runway and a windsock could be seen through the large entrance to the hangar.

"This isn't official yet," said Ohnuki, searching for the appropriate words. He continued cautiously. "We are discussing a plan at the ministry to fly Type Zero Carrier Fighters to Germany. We're here today to see if you will accept the mission."

Lieutenant Toda removed his flight helmet and crossed his legs.

Ohnuki gave Toda a brief summary of the plan, leaving out the purpose of the mission, the reason why the Germans wanted the aircraft to be flown to Berlin. Ohnuki maintained the cover story that the Type Zeros were being used to secure an air route between Japan and Germany. Toda showed no visible interest in the plan. In fact, he appeared quite negative by the middle of Ohnuki's explanation. Several times he exhaled audibly through his nose in frustration and irritation.

"So what do you think, lieutenant?" asked Ohnuki. "Do you think we can make it to Berlin?"

"Total amateurs," Toda spat out, shaking his head. "It's impossible, lieutenant commander. You say the Type Zero can fly 2,000 kilometers. But that's assuming it flies at constant speed, without deviation. In a combat situation, the aircraft will use three or four times the normal amount of fuel. And you've got to leave extra for flying around thunderclouds and sandstorms. Only an armchair pilot would draft a flight plan based on a 2,000 kilometer range."

"We are aware of these considerations," said Yamawaki. "But the Naval Aviation Technology Development Center gave us that figure. Doesn't that mean anything to you?"

"No. I have to disagree. A 2,000 kilometer range is impossible without extra fuel. But you can't base the plan on using drop tanks. What are you going to do if a Spitfire shows up? If you don't want to fight, you've got to run. The only way to run is to drop the tanks. You've got to pretend as if the tanks aren't even there." Toda continued with a hypothetical example. "Let's say we encounter an RAF squadron just after takeoff," he said. The drop tanks would have to be detached at once to lighten the aircraft. That would reduce the amount of fuel to just the 470 liters in the Zero's fuselage and wing tanks. The plane would need to be operated at full throttle for roughly thirty minutes to escape the enemy aircraft, during which time it'd consume three to four times the amount of fuel used in cruising flight. Somewhere in the range of 180 to 250 liters. You'd be left with anywhere from 220 to 290 liters, allowing the plane to fly a maximum of seven or eight hundred kilometers. There wouldn't be any way to make it to a refueling stop 2,000 kilometers distant."

Ohnuki looked pale. He asked, "So, what else do you think is impossible about the plan?"

"Well, the Type Zero is a single-seat fighter," said Toda.

"So?" asked Ohnuki.

"As you know, you can't fly a fighter by instruments alone. You can either fly while watching the ground, or by using the Beaufort wind scale, or by flying in the company of a long-range scout. Your plan calls for two Type Zero Carrier Fighters to fly across Asia, so you've got to fly during the day to keep an eye on the landscape. Just think about how insane it is to fly during the day through an area controlled by the RAF. And we're talking totally unfamiliar terrain in Iraq and India. It's not some cakewalk over the Yangtze River. And this is ten-thousand-plus kilometers. I don't think there's anyone in the Imperial Navy capable of pulling something like that off!"

"Anything else that'll keep the plan from succeeding?" prompted Ohnuki.

"Two planes, that's a problem," replied Toda.

"Why?"

"Look. A naval flight unit consists of three aircraft. That's how we fly, three planes in formation, at all times. We form a triangle, with the leader at the front, the second in command on the left, and the third on the right. It's the superior formation for both offense and defense. With only two planes, we won't even be able to protect ourselves."

"So you think we stand a chance if we use three planes instead," said Ohnuki.

"Well, I, ah..." stammered Toda before regaining his composure. "You're talking about penetrating RAF-controlled territory. If you're using Type Zeros, you'll need a larger formation. I'm talking three flights."

"Nine planes," said Ohnuki, almost to himself.

"I'm not saying nine makes it possible!" interrupted Toda. "Even if nine planes manage to break through Burma and India, they'll have one hell of a flight ahead of them. You can send out an entire squadron and I don't know if any of them will make it to Berlin. We're not talking about the flight of the *Kamikaze* here. We're talking about combat-fitted aircraft. And now that the Tripartite Pact's been signed, the RAF isn't going to turn a blind eye when we fly through the area."

"So you're saying the plan is impossible," said Ohnuki.

"That's exactly what I'm saying, lieutenant commander. I'm an Imperial Navy man. If ordered to do so, I would make the flight. But if I were asked what the chances for success were, I'd honestly have to answer: zero. It's stupid to lose brand new carrier fighters on a plan that we've established is impossible from the start. And by the way," said Toda, "I'm talking as someone who's shot down more than ten enemy aircraft."

"Only six confirmed," corrected Ohnuki.

"That's right, six confirmed," said Toda, "But I'm not playing a game here. I'm talking about the number of planes I actually shot down. And make no mistake about it, I've shot down more than ten."

"Fine, fine," said Ohnuki. "Please continue."

Part Two

"Understand something. I'm talking from the standpoint of someone who's bested more than ten enemy pilots. I hope you realize I'm not being timid here when I tell you your flight plan is doomed to failure. You've got your head in the clouds. Let me tell you something: there isn't a single naval aviator who'll tell you otherwise. I guarantee it."

Ohnuki looked even more pale. "Let me ask you something, lieutenant."

"What is it?" asked Toda.

"Why were you cited for valor in Nanking? How did someone as cautious as you achieve such an honor? It must have been quite dangerous. Yet you came through with flying colors."

Toda seemed blithely unaware of the sarcasm behind Ohnuki's question. He even smiled when he answered.

"Oh, that was nothing," said Toda. "It wasn't a big deal. I flew low over the city to scare the hell out of the chinks who were hiding in the castle. I think I killed thirty, maybe even fifty, with every pass. My group strafed the castle grounds more times than I could count."

"You're saying…" said Ohnuki, swallowing uncomfortably. "These were Chinese soldiers, right?"

"I don't know. I wasn't looking that closely. Maybe some farmers. Hell, there were probably women and children in there too. The Army was on a roll, back then. The reputation of the Navy was at stake, so we went in and did what we needed to do. Must've been hell on earth down there. You know, that was the same day we bombed the USS Panay," said Toda patronizingly.

Yamawaki noticed that Ohnuki's fists were clenched tightly on his lap. His knuckles were bone white. It occurred to Yamawaki that this would be a good time to break off the conversation. Toda's remarks were bordering on insubordination, and Ohnuki's replies were becoming increasingly angry and cynical. Toda said he thought the plan was impossible. There was no need to select him as a pilot. It was time to end the discussion.

"Thank you for your…opinions, lieutenant," said Yamawaki. "I guess our plan has some holes in it." Yamawaki could practically feel Ohnuki's eyes drilling into him, wondering just what the hell Yamawaki was up to. Yamawaki ignored him and added, "I guess it's time to go back to square one."

"That's okay," smiled Toda blithely. "If you have any technical questions, feel free to drop by and ask me. Anytime."

"As we said at the beginning, please don't share the details of this conversation with anybody," said Yamawaki.

"I know, I know. Even if I did, nobody would take me seriously."

Ohnuki barely spoke during the ride back to the Ministry of the Navy.

CHAPTER 10

On Friday, three days after meeting with Lieutenant Toda, Yamawaki and Ohnuki visited the headquarters of United Petroleum in Otemachi, Tokyo. The Ministry of Foreign Affairs had arranged the visit. Through the Ministry's Asia division, Yamawaki formally requested United Petroleum's assistance in locating refueling stops along their flight route. The ministry reported a favorable response. For the past few years, United Petroleum had been developing several oil fields in the Persian Gulf region alongside British and American concerns. They hadn't had much success with their test wells in Iran, but they had discovered one oil deposit in the desert in Al-Hasa. It was quite possible that United Petroleum had better information about the Gulf than the Ministry of Foreign Affairs.

The person who handled Ohnuki and Yamawaki's request was a young man. He wore a fashionable, custom-tailored suit. Even though he was meeting with two men from the military, he kept his attitude perfectly neutral, neither humble nor arrogant. He projected an air of importance and charisma. Yamawaki could tell the young man was a member of the financial elite from the moment he set eyes on him.

His name was Yasuda. He appeared to be about the same age as Yamawaki. He wore black horn-rim glasses. He said he had just returned from Tehran a month ago, and his skin showed it: he was so tanned from the desert sun, he almost looked like someone from an island in the South Pacific. He sported a short mustache, which he explained was common in the Middle East. In fact, he said, a young man from Japan wouldn't be treated as an adult there without one.

Yasuda spread a large-scale map out in a reception area adjacent to the executive meeting room. The single-color map showed the region south of the Persian Gulf to the Gulf of Oman as well as the Iranian steppes. The map was marked in English. Apparently it had been made in England or the United States.

"As you know, thanks largely to British and American capital," began Yasuda in impeccable language, "test wells and oil fields are being developed all over the Persian Gulf region. In particular, the Anglo-Iranian Oil Company of Great Britain has secured a large share of oil rights in Iran. They have begun large-scale development along the northern and northeastern shores of the Persian Gulf. The most successful development to date has been the oil fields, refinery, and export center in the city of Abadan. Thanks to protection from the Royal Navy, the British have managed to create a spectacularly well-equipped export center there."

Yasuda watched the two guest's faces as if gauging their reactions. Yamawaki nodded. Yasuda continued:

"Great Britain and the United States have deep connections to the governments and tribal leaders of the Persian Gulf. They have explored every possible angle for extending and maximizing their profits in the region. They are well aware that the Persian Gulf is poised to become a massive export center, capable of satisfying most of the world's oil needs. At the moment, no one is sure of the exact amount of oil in the Gulf region. But new oil fields continue to be discovered. The entire Gulf area—that includes Oman, Iran, Basra in Iraq, and Kuwait, which just ratified their first constitution last year, and Saudi Arabia, where the Americans have invested massive quantities of capital—each and every one of these countries is a possible source of oil. It isn't difficult to understand the attention American and European investors have been paying to the region. Modern industry depends on oil to survive. Oil also happens to be the lifeblood of the military, and securing oil supply lines is critical. Wouldn't you agree, lieutenant commander?"

"Completely," answered Ohnuki.

Yasuda explained that the Japanese had been a bit late in exploring the Gulf's possibilities. American and European investors had already secured rights to the areas with the highest potential. There was very little room for latecomers. Some Japanese investors had given up on land-based sites altogether and were focusing on acquiring ocean-drilling rights instead. Ocean drilling promised somewhat lower profits due to the added cost of complicated extraction techniques, but still appeared to be a worthwhile investment opportunity in light of projected future oil prices.

"That being said," continued Yasuda, "there are some areas that the Americans and British have abandoned as nonviable. We have acquired land rights to several of these areas and continued the digging and exploration process ourselves. This is one of them."

Yasuda pointed to an area close to the Strait of Hormuz in southern Iran. Here the peninsula of Oman thrust into the curve of the Persian Gulf like the tip of a knife. There was a town called Bandar Abbas there.

"Our dig," said Yasuda, "is some 150 kilometers to the east of the town of Bandar Abbas. Somewhat removed from the caravan route. The Americans acquired rights to the area in 1935 and had been attempting to develop it ever since, but they abandoned their claim last year. At that point we acquired the rights for ourselves and have been sinking test wells. We're planning to give it another two months. Geographically, it's at a delicate point. It happens to be the farthest east of any of the potential oil sites in the Persian Gulf. There is a good chance that no oil fields exist beyond this point."

Yasuda explained that the oil camp, located forty kilometers inland, was almost totally isolated. The closest thing to an actual road in the area was a nearby route for camel caravans. The first thing the Americans had done upon arriving in these barren lands was to build a simple runway to allow for delivery of supplies by air. They had abandoned their claim to the area last August. United Petroleum took over their camp and runway and dispatched about twenty Japanese men to begin working there. There was not another living soul within fifty kilometers of them. And of course, there wasn't any RAF presence, either. The closest town, Minab, a hub for several caravan routes, was some sixty kilometers distant.

The runway was roughly 1,000 meters long. It had been built to accommodate an American Douglas twin-engine transport and seemed out of place in such a desolate locale. Now it was used only twice a month for flights chartered by United Petroleum out of Abadan. The site didn't have any maintenance facilities, but it could provide fuel and a rest area.

Yamawaki made a visual estimate of the distance on the map. 1,600 kilometers from southern Rajasthan in India to the oil camp. From there it'd only be 1,600 or 1,700 kilometers to Baghdad. Maybe 2,000 kilometers if they had to refuel in the Kurdish region to the north of Baghdad instead. The camp looked perfect for an intermediate refueling stop.

"Does this place meet your needs?" asked Yasuda. "What do you think?"

"It appears ideal. Wonderful," said Ohnuki, nodding.

"Would you like to use it, then?"

"I think so."

"Do we need to negotiate for landing rights with Iran? After all, ours will be foreign planes," asked Yamawaki.

"There are only two government officials in Minab. If anyone complains, just give them some money," said Yasuda. "This isn't an Iranian runway. It's one of the assets of United Petroleum. There's nothing to worry about."

Yamawaki's eyes widened a bit at the man's condescension. Did he act this arrogantly when he was in Iran too?

Yasuda seemed to notice Yamawaki's discomfiture, and hastened to continue:

"Did you know that Germany and Japan are Iran's first and second largest trading partners? The Soviet Union used to be number one, but Germany and Japan quickly overcame their lead. Railroads, roadways, towns and cities, buildings, spinning factories, and machine tools... German engineers have scattered throughout Iran to assist in their technological development. Reza Shah is extremely supportive of the Axis idea. With the signing of the Tripartite Pact, Iran will undoubtedly be interested in strengthening ties to our country as well. They will be extremely accommodating. It won't matter if you ask permission before or after the fact."

Ohnuki spoke again. "What about the British capital invested in oil development? Doesn't the Shah—"

"This is our moment to kick the British out of Iran once and for all, lieutenant commander," interrupted Yasuda. "England will fall to the Germans, will it not? We just signed a pact with Germany. This is the time to cement our position. Germany and Japan are poised to assume custodianship of Iran in England's place. Our greatest fear as industrialists is the threat of having our investment in the region seized by enemy forces. We could wake up one day and be ordered out of the country. I ask that you send a fleet to the Persian Gulf as soon as possible. All you would need are a few cruisers and some marines: only as many as England and the United States have already committed to the region to protect their own interests. The area is as strategically important to Japan as the Yangtze River. Are you going to sit back and let the West reap the fruits?"

Ohnuki coughed uncomfortably. "You said you planned to continue sinking test wells for the next two months. That means the runway will be available for the next two months at least, correct?"

"Exactly. Until the beginning of December," answered Yasuda. "If we fail to locate an oil field by then, we will have to leave. Without workmen to clear it, the runway will be buried beneath the dunes before long."

United Petroleum's runway appeared quite useful for the mission.

Part Two

Yamawaki and Ohnuki decided to discuss the matter further at their office. The two thanked Yasuda for his time and stood up to leave.

That's two potential refueling stops along the 6,000 kilometer stretch. It seemed impossible at first. Now the ball's rolling, though. Yamawaki prayed that they would be able to locate stops in eastern India and Iraq.

There was also the matter of the pilot. They needed pilots skilled enough to complete such a long-distance mission. Men who could think on their feet, who were flexible enough to deal with unforeseen crises. The question as to whether such pilots actually existed remained up in the air. Perhaps the real problem was, the better the pilots, the harder it was bound to be to convince their commanding officers to let go of them. It wouldn't be easy to get them to agree to surrender their best men to such a farfetched mission. Yamawaki couldn't wait to receive the answer to their second request for a pilot.

CHAPTER 11

Roughly when Yamawaki and Ohnuki were visiting to United Petroleum in Tokyo, Rear Admiral Tadao Yokoi spoke again to Major Graf at the Luftwaffe headquarters in Berlin. It was three weeks after the signing of the Tripartite Pact.

This marked the third meeting between the two since the official request. As Udet and Kurusu were busy attending to other matters, Graf and Yokoi met alone.

Yokoi knew the meeting would be a difficult one. While the Japanese government had said they were willing to accommodate the German request, there had been no progress. In fact, Yokoi had just received an update by telegram the day before the meeting: *Having difficulties securing air route*. He couldn't even give the Germans a rough timetable for dispatching the aircraft. Breaking this news to Graf was the only purpose for this third meeting of theirs.

"It's been three weeks, Rear Admiral Yokoi," said Graf. "Are you aware that we're fighting a war at the moment? Time is of the essence. We cannot tolerate a slow response."

"I apologize for the inconvenience," said Yokoi, lowering his head. Yokoi outranked Graf but, given the situation, was having to play the supplicant role. It was frustrating.

"I can't make any promises. But I suspect that our government will contact us shortly with a clear plan for transporting the aircraft."

"What makes you think so?" asked Graf.

"I know the man in charge in Tokyo. He's been putting everything he has behind it. I will send another telegram to Tokyo telling them that Major Graf is displeased with the current pace of the process."

"Please do," said Graf icily. "As we requested at the outset, if delivery is delayed, we will need an exact explanation as to why and an updated schedule. We haven't heard anything concrete from your government yet. What is taking them so long?"

"The air route. The problem is securing the air route, major," Yokoi said. He tried not to stare at the burns on Graf's face. "They have mobilized the government's resources. They are working around the clock on the question of how to break through the more difficult areas, namely India and

Iraq."

"Difficult?" asked Graf without changing the expression on his face. "We're not asking you to fly over England. This is simply the case of finding a single route across open country! I hope you aren't telling me that the Japanese government hasn't built any kind of relationship with friendly elements in India and the Middle East yet. What about unofficial relationships with those outside of government and the ruling families there?"

"You aren't the first to point out my nation's lack of diplomatic panache, major."

Graf looked down for a moment, clasping his hands on his desktop without speaking. An uncomfortable silence ensued. The meeting had lasted all of three minutes, but for what? He could have cancelled with a simple phone call. It was pointless to continue the discussion any further.

Graf raised his scarred face. "Rear admiral. Do you have time to accompany me to Tempelhof Airport?"

Yokoi looked confused. "Yes, but what for?"

Graf began gathering a sheaf of documents together atop his desk. "A high-ranking Iraqi officer is leaving for Vienna today. I can introduce him to you if you are interested."

"Are you saying he will help us with our current project?"

"I'm saying you should talk to him and see. He may be Iraqi military, but he's more than a little upset about Britain—they've never stopped treating Iraq as colonial territory. I overheard him criticizing the Hashemite Kingdom, puppet regime of the British. He may be willing to help."

"What is his name?"

"Colonel Mohammed Hussein," answered Graf.

In the car to Templehof, Graf briefed Yokoi on Hussein's background. According to Graf, Hussein was born into a well-respected family in southern Iraq. He attended a military academy in Istanbul and graduated in 1913, the year before World War I broke out.

During that war, the great powers of Germany, England, France, Italy and Russia swarmed the Middle East, each eager to claim a piece of the Arab world for themselves. The Ottoman Empire allied with Germany and declared war against Russia, England, and France. As a young officer in the Arab division of the Ottoman Army, Hussein fought the Russians on the front line in the Caucasus. During the battle, he was hit by a fragment from an exploding artillery shell and was severely injured in his leg.

Hussein first became acquainted with the Arab Nationalist movement while recuperating from his wounds. Shortly thereafter, he became deeply involved with a group of officers within the Arab division who shared his sentiments. Hussein turned against the Ottomans once and for all after the Empire executed scores of intellectuals in a crackdown on the Arab Nationalists during 1915 and 1916. Two of his uncles had been killed in the purge.

In June of 1916, the Sharif of Mecca declared the independence of all Arab people from the Ottoman Empire. Leading a group of Arab soldiers, Hussein defected from the Ottoman Empire and joined the British-Indian army which was marching north from Basra. Fierce Ottoman attacks had halted the British advance, but they were starting to regroup around the time Hussein and his troops joined them. By December, they had pushed all the way to northern Iraq. Hussein and his soldiers served as the right wing of the advancing forces and were the first to arrive in Baghdad for its liberation in March of 1917.

That fall, Kurdish soldiers within the Ottoman Army began to revolt as well. The weakened Turks began to lose their grip on the battle raging in northern Iraq. Hussein gathered and reorganized fellow Arab Nationalist soldiers into a new unit. Joining the Arab Army of Prince Faisal, he led an assault on Damascus. In September of 1918, Hussein's forces participated in the attack on Dara in Syria, cutting off the retreat of the Fourth Turkish Army. Three days later, after having lost some half of his eighty-man troop in the fierce fighting, Hussein received a personal commendation from Prince Faisal. Hussein was nothing if not a role model for his fellow officers in the Arab Army.

"Why would an officer who fought alongside the British turn against them now?" asked Yokoi.

"He was never particularly favored by the British. He's an Arab. And an Iraqi. He wasn't eager to see Ottoman control substituted by British rule—granted, through the Hashemites."

"I recall having heard that Iraqi royalty favor the British."

"The King of Iraq was selected by Churchill himself. He's actually a Saudi. Iraq doesn't need him. Or at least it's safe to say that Hussein certainly thinks so."

"You're saying that Germany supports this Hussein?"

"We will upon request. Perhaps that is the reason he is visiting

Berlin. I wouldn't know. I'm not directly involved."

"Are they discussing some sort of treaty, some sort of agreement? Or perhaps military support?"

"I don't know," answered Graf curtly.

Colonel Mohammed Hussein was a sturdy military man with a dark complexion and a splendid moustache. He appeared to be in his mid-forties, with dark hair, dark eyes, and chiseled features. He stood roughly six feet tall, about Graf's height. He wore a suit.

In the interest of secrecy, Yokoi and Hussein met in the office of a Lufthansa manager to keep out of public view. The runway could clearly be seen outside the window in the room. It was just the three of them: Yokoi, Hussein, and Graf. No interpreters, and no guards.

After brief introductions, Hussein spoke first.

"Rear admiral, I congratulate you on the signing of the Tripartite Pact. The time is ripe to roll back British and French colonialism."

As Yokoi thanked him, Hussein stared directly into his eyes, flashing a fearless smile all the while.

"It is the twilight of the British Empire," continued Hussein. "England is about to lose control of Africa, the Middle East, and India. They are reckoning with nearly every nationalist movement the world has to offer. And they are also facing a spectacular defeat at the hands of your country as well. Thanks to the Tripartite Pact, they have the Strait of Malacca to worry about as well as the Strait of Dover."

Hussein expressed his strong stance against British colonialism and praised the coming new world order with Germany and Japan at the center. According to Hussein, the Tripartite Pact signaled the liberation of the occupied tribes, a new hope for the oppressed peoples of the world. Hussein held forth for more than ten minutes. *He's certainly eloquent for a soldier,* thought Yokoi. *When the time comes, he could well be the next leader of Iraq.*

When Hussein finished his speech, his cheeks were flushed. There were even beads of sweat on his forehead. Now he grabbed Yokoi by both shoulders and began to shake him. "Please! Please attack Singapore! Sweep the British Royal Army out of the East. Send the British fleet to the bottom of the Strait of Malacca! If you do, India will rise. So will Iraq! Once the battle begins in India and Iraq, Britain will fall before long. There is no way for them to maintain a war on three fronts. They will have to surrender. Which will necessitate a total withdrawal from all of Asia. The British will go back to their own puny isles, and their government will sign a peace treaty with the glorious Führer of the German Reich. You will do that for us, won't you, Rear Admiral Yokoi?"

The admiral coughed uncomfortably. He wished Foreign Minister Matsuoka or Minister-General Tojo were here in his place.

Lowering his voice, Hussein asked, "Is there anything I can do to help you?"

Yokoi stole a glance at Graf from the corner of his eye. Well, Graf did introduce us, thought Yokoi, I suppose there's no need to keep secrets here.

"Actually, we are attempting to send a courier flight between Japan and Germany. To do so, we need to find refueling locations in the Middle East. We are having a hard time securing them due to the presence of the RAF."

"You mean you're looking for airfields?"

"Precisely. We need airfields to refuel our courier aircraft."

"A courier flight between Tokyo and Berlin?"

Yokoi nodded. Graf looked at Hussein and nodded in agreement as well.

Hussein appeared to think for a moment.

"Can I contact you directly from now on?" he asked suddenly. "May I contact you through the Japanese Embassy in Baghdad?"

"You can use the Germany Embassy," cut in Graf. "Contact me through the German Embassy, that would be quicker."

"I shall get back to you about this matter tomorrow," said Hussein. "Do you have any special requests?"

"This project must not become known to the RAF. That is my only special request for the time being," answered Yokoi.

CHAPTER 12

The selection of pilots was bogged down. Yamawaki and Ohnuki had requested the name of another pilot from Personnel, offering the same yardstick as before: highly skilled pilots with experience flying fighters. But if the search turned up more pilots like Tesuro Toda, they planned to relax the criteria to include bomber and even transport pilots. Nearly anyone would be preferable to Toda.

"That son of a bitch," said Ohnuki. "There's no way he shot down six planes. Ten to one, he's counting the kills of his wingmen for himself."

Yamawaki and Ohnuki received two dossiers the following Wednesday. At first glance, it appeared that these were problem pilots. It was obvious the Navy was trying to get rid of them. But upon closer inspection, Yamawaki became more and more convinced that Personnel had given them a pair of diamonds in the rough.

They were an officer and an N.C.O., both with experience piloting Type Zero Carrier Fighters in central China. Comparing their dossiers to Toda's was like night and day. Yamawaki handed the folders to Ohnuki.

"So there are pilots out there who are better than Toda," said Yamawaki.

"Who do we have this time? These guys are about to get drummed out of the service."

"One's an officer. Lieutenant Keiichi Ando. He used to be with the 12th Air Corps. The other was with the 12th as well. Flight Sergeant Kyohei Inui. They were among the first pilots to fly the Type Zero."

"They were? And they've been grounded? That's a waste." Ohnuki paged through the dossiers as he spoke. "Lieutenant Keiichi Ando. Graduated with the 60th class. Then he's, what, thirty years old?"

"If you read the whole thing, you'll see why HQ is trying to get rid of them," said Yamawaki. "What's interesting is that Ando and Inui were in the same squadron as Toda. For a while, anyway."

Ohnuki peered at the documents again.

Keiichi Ando, the eldest child of Naval Officer Keisuke Ando, was born in 1910 during his father's tour as a naval liaison in Washington, D.C. His mother was an American woman born into a middle-class family in Richmond, Virginia.

Naval officers required an official permit from the Ministry of the Navy to get married. They were reluctant to issue one in Ando Sr.'s case. Impatient, he and his bride held a small ceremony with several close friends as witnesses and began living together. The ministry finally relented and granted a permit when Ando's wife became pregnant.

Ando was ordered back to Japan when his son was two years old. A lieutenant then, he returned with his family, and they had a daughter, Mariko, one year later. When Keiichi turned six, Ando was promoted to lieutenant commander. He was assigned to the Office of the Imperial Naval Attaché in Washington, D.C., for a second time. The whole family moved back to America. The following year, Ando was ordered back to Japan once again. This time, his wife and two children remained in the American capital. There wasn't any explanation in the report as to why.

Keiichi attended a private school in the city. His mother took ill and passed away when he was thirteen. Only then did Keiichi and Mariko return to Japan.

After graduating from secondary school in Yokohama, Keiichi renounced his American citizenship and enrolled in the 60th training class of the Naval Academy. Upon graduation, he joined the Kasumi-ga-ura Air Corps, was rotated to the Tateyama Air Corps, and was eventually assigned to the aircraft carrier *Hiryu*. In 1934, Ando's father died when a Type 90 Flying Boat crashed en route to Saipan.

The following year, Keiichi Ando was promoted to lieutenant junior grade and was ordered to attend flight school in Germany. It was the same year the Luftwaffe dropped any pretense of adhering to the Treaty of Versailles. Ando left Japan in December. He began six months of intensive training at the Luftwaffe's flight school at Braunschweig the following January. He trained with a Heinkel He51: basic flight and landing techniques, formation flying, dogfighting, and night flying.

In 1937, Ando received his first combat assignment as a pilot, to Kunda Base in Shanghai. He flew a Type 96 Carrier Fighter in the 13th Air Corps of the Second Joint Air Corps, where he participated in air operations over Nanking. Over the next two years, before being transferred out of the 13th, he was credited with fifteen enemy aircraft kills.

His dossier contained a footnote here. Ando had been ordered before a military court of inquiry to face charges of insubordination. During the bombing of Nanking Castle, the lead aircraft had strafed a group of people who appeared to be soldiers. The other aircraft followed their leader and strafed the area again. Ando, however, did not open fire. Upon returning to base, Ando's flight leader asked him why he hadn't used his machine guns. He responded that his weapons had malfunctioned. His head of maintenance corroborated the claim. However, in light of Ando's criticism of Imperial Army activities in Nanking, the base commander felt compelled to report his misgivings about Ando's loyalty in his file. As it turned out, Ando's flight leader had been none other than Toda.

The base commander also appeared displeased with Ando's refusal to open fire on pilots who had bailed out of their aircraft with parachutes. According to the Imperial Naval Air Corps Rules of Engagement, killing enemy pilots was as important as shooting down aircraft. Ando's flight leader reported that Ando never shot at pilots who had bailed out of their aircraft. Ando, for his part, maintained that he simply hadn't seen them.

In 1938, Ando was cited for engaging an American Curtiss Hawk III without official orders. According to the footnote, on October 20th of that year, Ando, leading a flight of four Japanese fighters, encountered six Chinese aircraft over Anqing, southwest of Nanking. The Chinese squadron may have consisted of former U.S. servicemen with "the Flying Tigers," an American volunteer corps. Ando and the enemy flight leader crossed paths and immediately entered a one-on-one aerial duel. Aircraft on both sides ascended to keep watch over their respective leaders. The dogfight lasted for close to fifteen minutes. Ando maintained the upper hand and scored several direct hits on the enemy aircraft. Finally, his opponent waved a white flag from his cockpit, whereupon Ando immediately broke off his attack.

Rumors of the incident raced through the base the following day. Ando was summoned before the base commander. He and his fellow pilots steadfastly denied the rumors. Still, talk of Ando having arranged a duel with an American continued to circulate around the base.

In December of 1938, Ando was promoted to lieutenant. The same month, he was reassigned to the Bihoro Air Corps in Hokkaido. (As a sort of punishment, thought Yamawaki.) He was transferred to the Yokosuka Air Corps in December of 1939.

The following year, Ando scored a lucky break when he was assigned to pilot an aircraft known as the Model 12 Experimental Carrier Fighter. Proving his skills as a superior pilot behind the controls of the

Model 12, Ando earned an assignment to the 12th Air Corps. Ando's tests of the Model 12 proved so remarkable that the fighter was rushed into deployment with the 12th before its official unveiling. Ando moved to Hankow Base in China, where he flew in a new squadron formed exclusively of the prototype aircraft. Shortly thereafter, the Naval Air Corps officially adopted the Model 12 Experimental Carrier Fighter as their main combat aircraft, rechristening it the Type Zero Carrier Fighter.

On September 13th of the same year, Ando shot down an additional three Chinese fighters, increasing his career total to 18 kills. On October 4th, he participated in the fierce attack on Tai Ping Si Base, located in Chengdu on the upper part of the Yangtze river. While their wingmen covered them in the air, Ando and three other pilots made emergency landings on the tarmac at Tai Ping Si, destroyed several enemy aircraft on the ground, took off again, and returned to base unharmed.

On October 7th, Ando found himself subject to a military police investigation into an incident involving a Japanese man being shot on the streets of Shanghai.

On October 12th, Ando returned to Japan and remained grounded pending further orders at Yokosuka base.

Ohnuki looked up from the dossier.

"Talk about someone who has a problem with authority. He could be as hard to deal with as Toda."

"But the man's record speaks for itself," said Yamawaki. He looked into Ohnuki's eyes, searching for some sign of agreement. "I mean, that landing at Tai Ping Si is almost beyond comprehension. Read the dossier. It looks like he just went in and out of an enemy base without a single scratch."

"Is that bravery, or stupidity?"

"There's only one way to find out. We have nothing to lose by meeting him."

"Will he follow orders, is the question."

"If you want pilots with a bubbly personality, you might go ask the Salvation Army. We're not looking for a charm school graduate here. We're looking for someone who can get the job done. The best part is that he's got plenty of flight time on the Type Zero."

"What do you think that last investigation means?" asked Ohnuki. "The most recent one? He must have really screwed up to get transferred back home like that."

"Minister Oikawa received a report from the head of military police. It said that Ando saw a terrorist attacking a Japanese in Shanghai, but helped the shooter escape."

"Are you serious?" Ohnuki was shocked.

"My reading of the report didn't give me the feeling that he actively helped the assailant. But the man who was targeted happened to be a very important man."

"Who?"

"Former Army Colonel Kaoru Tatsumi."

"Ah, that right-wing nut of the Imperial Way faction? He left the army in, what, 1936?"

"And went off to China to work for the biggest of the right-wing bosses, Kodama, as his man in Shanghai."

"So, it was Ando's bad luck to get on Tatsumi's wrong side, and he got grounded..." said Ohnuki thoughtfully.

"And we're probably just another stroke of bad luck for poor Lieutenant Ando," Yamawaki noted.

"Perhaps so," said Ohnuki, nodding several times. "It seems we've found one of our pilots. I wonder who the other one will be."

CHAPTER 13

Flight Sergeant Kyohei Inui was born in Hamamatsu in 1911. He joined the Navy's marine force at Yokosuka Base in 1932, trained as a maintenance engineer, and completed training in the same year. In January of 1933, he received his first assignment as a maintenance man for the Tateyama Air Corps.

Inui's aptitude with machinery owed largely to the fact that his family ran an automobile repair shop. In the Tateyama Air Corps, his specialty was fighter engine repairs. In 1936, Inui applied to marine flight school and was accepted as a pilot and trained with the 34th Class. He graduated in 1937 and joined the Saeki Air Corps. Later, he transferred to the 13th Air Corps of the Second Joint Air Corps at Kunda Base in Shanghai, where he piloted a Type 96 Carrier Fighter.

Inui served in the same squadron as Ando. Inui had also flown on the day of Ando's private duel with the Curtiss Hawk III in 1938. Inui was officially credited with eight kills. His score was second only to Ando's in the 13th Air Corps.

In December of 1938, Inui was transferred to the Bihoro Air Corps in Hokkaido; in December 1939, to the Yokosuka Air Corps. In July, 1940, he received orders to report to the 12th Air Corps in China as a fighter pilot. In September of the same year, he flew as Ando's lead wingman in the bombing campaign over Chungking, where he earned two more kills. He was cited for valor by base commander Takijiro Onishi and promoted to Flight Sergeant First Class of the Naval Air Corps.

Inui participated in several additional attacks against Chinese forces along the Yangtze River. On October 4, 1940, he was part of the attack on Tai Ping Si Base, landing on the enemy tarmac alongside Ando and destroying several aircraft on the ground.

On October 7th, Inui was investigated by the military police while on furlough in Shanghai. On the 12th, he was ordered back to Japan. He remained grounded in Yokosuka awaiting further orders.

"What a great combination," said Ohnuki with admiration. "Now we have a top pilot in Ando, and Inui's a good pilot who's a mechanic to boot. And they seem to be better at working as a team than almost any other pair of pilots."

Yamawaki smiled. "They also have the distinction of having been kicked out of the Air Corps twice together. Talk about problem cases."

"I thought we were saying personality didn't matter."

"The lieutenant we met yesterday was out of the question. But these two feel like they could be a real handful, too. I think we need to interview them. Can I ask you to involve yourself, lieutenant commander?"

"Certainly. Time is an issue, so I'm thinking to choose these two. But maybe I ought not to decide on the basis of documents…"

"I looked through the list from Personnel. You know, several people from the 60th Class happen to be posted right here in our building. Perhaps you could ask them about Lieutenant Ando," suggested Yamawaki.

"Do you recommend anyone in particular?"

"Lieutenant Mitsuyoshi Segawa, for starters," said Yamawaki. "I know him. He's with Fleet Central Command, Second Division. I can arrange a meeting, if you'd like."

"Please do," said Ohnuki. "As soon as possible."

CHAPTER 14

Ohnuki and Yamawaki could not possibly have invited Lieutenant Segawa to their own room at Military Aviation Headquarters, so they met in the officer's mess in the courtyard of the Ministry of the Navy instead. It was still half an hour before lunchtime. The mess was still fairly empty, but it was close enough to lunch to sit and talk without attracting undue attention.

The trio took an isolated table in the back of the room and ordered tea. Segawa was a bright and friendly career military man. He was also quite overweight, and his uniform was stretched tightly over his body. His pale hands were as smooth as a child's.

"What? Ando's back in Yokosuka again?" asked Segawa, brimming with curiosity. "What'd he do this time?"

One thing was clear from Segawa's reaction: Ando had a reputation among his classmates. Yamawaki wondered just what kind of opinion Segawa had of Ando. He stared intently at Segawa's pasty white face. Yamawaki saw no hint of contempt or dislike. At the very least, Yamawaki could tell Segawa wasn't pleased with Ando's treatment.

"He got mixed up in an unfortunate incident in Shanghai," answered Ohnuki. "It wasn't his fault, but he didn't exactly ingratiate himself with the military police. Did you hear about the standoff between the Army and Navy over the bridge to the protectorate?"

"In May?" asked Segawa.

"No, there was another one, earlier this month. The Army backed down again, but they needed a scapegoat to save face. Someone had to pay. So the Navy kicked Ando and a flight sergeant out of China. I heard they barely had time to pack."

Yamawaki told Segawa everything he knew about the incident in Shanghai. Even now, Yamawaki didn't really understand why Ando and Inui had to be kicked out of the Air Corps. Neither of them had any connection to the Japanese man who was shot, nor were they involved in the standoff between the Army and the Navy. Neither bore any responsibility whatsoever for either of the incidents. The only thing Yamawaki could imagine was that the 12th Air Corps must have been itching for a chance to get rid of the two. If that was the case, it was quite clear why they had recommended the pair to Yamawaki and Ohnuki.

"What kind of man is Ando?" asked Ohnuki. "We'd like you to be as honest as possible."

Segawa appeared to select his words carefully. "He's known for being the rebellious type, I'll tell you that."

"Rebellious?"

"Maybe it would be better to say he's strong-willed. He's not one to conceal his thoughts. Maybe it's his American half, maybe his American education. He's totally direct and straightforward. At the academy, he wouldn't accept anything he saw as illogical."

"Such as?"

Segawa pressed his hand to his forehead as if that would draw out old memories. "There was one time when an instructor was shouting us down, forcing this one-sided theory down our throats. He said any student who didn't accept what he was saying was free to leave. Nobody really thought they could get up and go, but Ando did just that. A couple more students followed him. Eventually the whole class was cancelled."

"What was the issue exactly?"

"Looking back, it seems so stupid. The instructor treated Admiral Togo like a god. He kept repeating Togo's comment, 'One gun that scores a hit a hundred times out of a hundred is worth a hundred guns that score only once in a hundred.' Several students disagreed. The instructor blew his top."

Shocked, Yamawaki mumbled, "'One gun that...'? Even an elementary school student can see through that math. The Navy's still teaching stuff like that?"

"I suppose some instructors simply don't base their lessons on logic. I don't know what happened to that particular one, though."

"I've got to admit I'm a little surprised," said Ohnuki. "I expected Ando to be an old-fashioned military man. I pictured him as something of a samurai, to be honest. But he seems to be quite a practical man."

Segawa nodded in agreement. "He's very practical and logical. And very stubborn. I'd say my little anecdote pretty much says all I have to say about him. He doesn't suffer fools gladly."

"Do you think he's too stubborn? Can he work as part of a team?" asked Yamawaki.

"Oh, no, he's a team player. He was respected by his classmates. He had close friends. And he never ordered anyone around. He had the knack of persuading them without falling back on rank or title."

Yamawaki remembered what he had read in Ando's dossier. The incident where his guns "malfunctioned" in Nanking probably stayed as low profile as it did because he convinced his maintenance man to cover for him. His wingmen undoubtedly covered for him about the "duel" episode with the American pilot. It appeared that Ando was not the sort of trouble-maker that his record suggested he was. Superiors who hated him had it in for him, but more than a few people had rooted for him, too.

Segawa told Yamawaki and Ohnuki the names of several of Ando's close friends from the academy. Yamawaki hadn't heard of any of them, but Ohnuki knew a few of the names.

Segawa added that Ando had been quite popular with the ladies as well. When the 60th class traveled to Australia for navigational training, they had been invited to stay with families in Melbourne. Each family hosted several students. According to a classmate who shared a home with him, Ando immediately made friends with the eighteen-year-old daughter of the family and proceeded, once, to "disappear" for several hours after lunch.

"Some people were jealous," laughed Segawa. "They said he only got lucky because of his mixed blood. He may have been popular with the ladies, but he never joined in on our locker-room banter about them. Even after going to sea with the fleet, I heard he never visited brothels like the others did. Old-fashioned in that way, I guess. Some of his shipmates dis-liked him for it."

Segawa told Ohnuki and Yamawaki about another incident involv-ing Ando. After they graduated, the students were divided into two groups and sent to special training classes in gunnery, torpedoes, radios, naviga-tion, and flight testing with the Kasumi-ga-ura Air Corps. The students spent several weeks in each class, and at the end of the training period, were allowed to choose their own specialty. On the day of the initial flight apti-tude test, the flight instructor climbed down from the Type 3 Trainer and turned to Ando.

"You've flown an aircraft before, right?" he asked.

Just like everyone else, of course, it had been Ando's first flight. The moment the other students heard the instructor's question, however, they knew Ando would be flying with the Corps. In fact, Ando had wanted to fly with Kasumi-ga-ura from the very beginning. His wish came true.

"So he's a born flyer," commented Ohnuki quietly.

"Maybe I'm just being proud of a former classmate," said Segawa. "But I did really look up to him."

"In what way?"

"He was just—one hell of a guy. That doesn't mean everyone loved him. He had his own way of doing things, that's for sure."

"I can imagine."

"You know, he got it from his father."

"What do you mean?"

"Well, the Navy never really liked his marrying an American. He may have been promoted anyway, but it must have been a weight around his neck until the end. They made him pay for it, that's for sure, with the worst possible assignments. I had the chance to see his record at headquarters. They sent him out to sea in the oldest, most run down ships in the fleet. Ando's father died in an accident while Ando was serving on *Hiryu*."

"I heard it was a flying boat."

"Do you know what his mission was?"

"No."

"He was laying the groundwork for a facility of 'comfort women' for officers in Saipan. He was being made to pimp women, like some kind of flunkey. I don't know if Ando knows, though."

It was almost lunchtime. Officers began entering the mess. Servants busily worked the tables. It was about time for Yamawaki and Ohnuki to move to their own table. The three of them stood up.

"I have one last question," said Ohnuki. "Let's say you're commanding a very difficult and important mission, and you need a top-notch pilot. You hear Ando's been selected. Would you be happy, or would you want him replaced?"

Segawa tilted his head slightly. He spoke softly, as if to himself. "The more important the mission, the more I'd want Ando on the roster."

Segawa stood up, bowed, and headed towards the separate dining area for the higher-ups.

Ohnuki watched Segawa's back as he walked away.

"Well, Ando's in," he said quietly.

CHAPTER 15

Imperial Army Intelligence Officer Ryojiro Shibata halted in the middle of the crowd. He was in a street bazaar near the Red Fort in Old Delhi. The intermingling scents of spices, food, body odor, and animals filled the air. He could hear the voices of dealers, voices arguing, voices laughing, voices begging. A baby cried somewhere. He heard the lowing of cows and the crowing of roosters. The bells of bicycles, the sound of a coppersmith's hammer, the sound of pots clattering, the sound of knives chopping. It was like a whole different India compared to the upscale street scene in New Delhi. Shibata silently cursed himself for having brought his jacket. He wiped his forehead with a hemp handkerchief. Suddenly he stopped and looked over his shoulder.

In the year and a month since Shibata had been posted in Delhi as a special press correspondent, he had become more than capable of distinguishing one Indian face from another. He'd know it if he saw the same face twice.

It appeared that nobody had attempted to hide or look in a different direction when Shibata turned around. There weren't any Caucasian faces in the crowd, either. It appeared that he wasn't being followed.

Shibata waded further into the crowd.

It was the middle of October. Three weeks had passed since he had received news of the signing of the Tripartite Pact in Berlin. Shibata reported to Tokyo that he had established contact with the feudal lord Gaj Singh roughly ten days earlier. He had absolutely no idea what kind of waves his report made at headquarters.

Which is why he had been utterly shocked to receive the coded telegram two days ago. It was from the Eighth Section, Army Division of the Imperial General Headquarters.

INTERESTED IN MOVEMENT OF MAHARAJA STOP CONTINUE YOUR CONTACT STOP TOP PRIORITY STOP SECURE REFUELING LOCATION FOR SMALL AIRPLANE IN BENGAL OR ASSAM STOP PREPARE 2000 LITERS 92 OCTANE AVIATION FUEL AND 100 LITERS TEXACO AIRCRAFT OIL 120 STOP

Part Two

Apparently, the Army or the Imperial General Headquarters needed a forward air base in eastern India at once. Japanese forces had advanced into the northern reaches of French Indochina one month earlier. Could they be planning a push from Indochina into Malaya, Burma, and even India? Fine, we've signed an alliance with Germany and Italy, thought Shibata, but that really is biting off more than we can chew! It was true that the anti-British movement continued to grow in Asia, and that it was increasingly difficult for the British Empire to protect its borders while keeping a thumb on its colonial subjects at the same time. Even then, Shibata felt that it was far too early for Japan to be securing refueling bases in India. First they needed to suck those anti-British and Indian independence movements into the framework of the Greater East Asian Co-Prosperity Sphere. That would take at least another two or three years of hard work, not only on the part of agents like Shibata, but on all levels including the civilian.

Whatever the case, thought Shibata, the international situation was changing, and it was changing fast. *After all, even a trickling brook could change direction and turn into a roaring waterfall. I shouldn't worry so much. I shouldn't worry about the overall picture. There must be something going on behind the scenes, beyond my imagination. That's why they want the refueling base.*

Shibata pushed deeper into the bazaar, elbowing his way through the throng. He walked into a cheap eatery with a white eagle painted on its storefront sign.

Ryojiro Shibata was a thirty-one-year-old captain of the army. After graduating from the academy, he served in a regiment for three years but realized early on that he wasn't suited to battlefield duty. He had been elated to receive orders to report to the General Staff Office for training as an intelligence officer.

Shibata was sent to the Tokyo Foreign Language School for special training in conversational English and Malay. He was being groomed to become an asset for the realization of a Greater East Asian Co-Prosperity Sphere. He had been born in Taipei and had lived in Bangkok from age 8 to 12. Living in Southeast Asia would present no problems for him, and perhaps that was why the General Staff Office selected him.

One day, Shibata asked his commanding officer why he had been recruited for intelligence.

"You look more Malayan or Javanese than Japanese, Shibata," he was told. "Get a suntan and you're a shoo-in for a native!"

Shibata's first posting was to Singapore. As a first lieutenant working in the attaché's office, he had a room in the officers' quarters. He spent two years gathering information about the anti-British movement among the Indian population there. He then returned to Japan but was soon dispatched to New Delhi, a year ago, in September of 1939. This time, he did not wear a military uniform. His mission was to work abroad as a "special correspondent." He was promoted to captain. When he arrived, England had just declared war on Germany. Without bothering to consult the Indian Parliament, Viceroy Linlithgow declared war on behalf of India as well. In effect, India had declared war on Germany without any input from its people. Indian anger towards their colonial masters was reaching a head.

Shibata sipped his lukewarm tea. A young Indian man approached him.

"Where are the birds?"

"Not in the sky," answered Shibata. "Perhaps they're behind a boddhi tree."

"Please come with me," said the young man.

Shibata followed him through a maze of alleys. Presently they arrived at a warehouse. It was almost totally silent; Shibata couldn't hear the bazaar at all. Several men unloaded baskets of grain from a horse-drawn wagon. They cast a dubious eye at Shibata's hemp jacket and pants as they worked. One of the warehouse doors stood wide open. Shibata followed the young man in. It was dark and cool inside, but the two walked through and out the back of the warehouse and took a small staircase leading to the roof.

A huge parasol stood on one corner. An elderly man in a turban sat in the shade beneath it. It was the Sikh grain merchant Pritam Singh. He appeared to be looking over documents for his business.

Upon seeing Shibata, Singh offered a friendly wave and ordered the guide to go back downstairs.

"I apologize for making you come all the way out here," said Singh.

Perhaps it was due to his amazing white beard, or the sharp look in his eyes that belied his age of sixty years, but Singh looked more like a n ascetic or a wise man than he did a merchant.

"Every once in a while, it's nice to meet someplace like this instead of some hotel or country club," said Shibata, looking out over the jumble of

Old Delhi houses from the rooftop. He could see a part of the Red Fort wall to his right. "I've never been this far into Old Delhi before."

Singh offered a chair and Shibata took a seat.

Singh leaned towards Shibata. "How can I help you?"

Shibata leaned in towards Singh as well. "You promised me help before. I wasn't planning to ask so quickly, but the fact is that I do need it now. I need your assistance with the Indian independence movement."

"Ah! So finally I have the chance to return your favor. Tell me, what do you need?"

"I would like you to find an airfield in either Bengal or Assam that's safe from RAF attacks."

Pritam Singh's eyes gleamed.

"By when?"

"As soon as possible," said Shibata. "I need to report their availability as soon as possible."

"May I ask what this is for? I hope this isn't some kind of preparation for a Japanese invasion."

"I wasn't informed as to the purpose. But I strongly doubt that is the case... In fact, I guarantee that it's not."

"Airfield, airfield..." mumbled Singh. "An unexpected request."

Singh sat up straight in his chair and turned his gaze to the streets of Old Delhi. Shibata looked around. It was an ancient city, built by the Mughal emperor Shah Jahan. It had been the center of a dynasty that had lasted for three hundred years. In 1858, however, right when Japan was in turmoil over whether to open its shores to foreign influences, the empire was destroyed by a greedy European nation. British military forces held a tribunal in the royal chamber of the Red Fort, expelling Bahadur Shah the Second from the city. Shibata felt sadness mixed with anger as he looked out over Old Delhi.

"Mr. Shibata," said Singh. "I've kept a very close eye on Japan over the last half century. I've watched the changes you've gone through with respect and awe. It's been fascinating to watch Japan grow into a worthy opponent of the great European powers and into the true leader of Asia. And while I don't support the Japanese expansion into Korea and Manchuria, I still pray for the continued prosperity of your country. I must repeat, I cannot support what Japan is doing to China. I'm sure you've heard the story of the old man in China? Do you remember what he said?"

Shibata knew the story well. He remained silent.

"He said, 'If you Japanese think the Indians will welcome you with open arms, you're deluding yourselves. If you try to assume England's role, India will fight you with everything they have. Just remember that.' More than a few Indians have worried that Japan may prove even more greedy and cruel than the European conquerors. And now they have China to prove it."

"I think you already know that Japan doesn't have any military or political ambitions for India," said Shibata. "We firmly believe in the principles of the Greater East Asian Co-Prosperity Sphere. I don't deny that our military may assist in helping the Indians liberate themselves from England in the future. I promise you that we won't ignore the voice of the people of India when we do so. There's absolutely no need to worry."

"But—" said Singh.

Shibata interrupted him. "About China. Let me assure you that more than a few Japanese deeply regret what happened there. I admit that our military forces have done some terrible things, possibly atrocious things, that Japan simply cannot justify, internationally or otherwise. But I promise you that the situation in China will improve. We aren't that stupid, or arrogant. We will learn from our mistakes." *Did I go too far? Am I convincing him?* "Sir, I beg you, please believe me. If what I'm saying were untrue, Japan wouldn't have offered its unconditional support to the Indian independence movement."

Shibata was referring to an incident two months in the past. Four Indian independence activists had just escaped from a prison in Hong Kong. They asked the Twenty-First Imperial Japanese Army in Guangdong for protection. They requested help in smuggling themselves back into India via Singapore, to continue their campaign against the British. Army Headquarters, Eighth Section received a report, accepted their request, and set a plan in motion. First, they moved the four to Shanghai and placed them aboard a Japanese cargo freighter bound for Singapore. Eighth Section also arranged for money and guns for the group. They even told them to feel free to contact the Japanese Embassy and the Army Attaché Office anytime they needed help.

Two of the four activists stayed in Singapore. The other two headed for India, by land. They traveled through Calcutta to Delhi, where they met Singh and told him everything about their experience. The four were the most ambitious of the anti-British activists working in Southeast Asia.

Singh immediately contacted Shibata to thank the Japanese Army for their support. Singh also told Shibata that three other important activists planned to escape from the Hong Kong prison as well. Shibata sent a cable to Tokyo requesting that full support be given them. After Shibata contacted Tokyo, Singh told him that he'd like to return the favor sometime, calling it his responsibility.

Shibata and Singh sat in silence for quite some time. The seats had been dried by the wind, and Shibata was beginning to feel a little cold. Singh turned to face Shibata again.

"This airfield is not for an advance force."

"Absolutely not," answered Shibata without hesitation. "I'm sure it has a military purpose, but I assure you that it has nothing to do with preparing for an invasion."

"What is it, then?"

"This is a complete guess, but I suspect our government is attempting to establish an air route to link Japan with the East India independence movement. Perhaps they're planning to start airlifting necessary supplies for them. Tokyo only requests a small airstrip, enough for a small plane to land, refuel, and take off. Just a simple runway would do."

Singh stroked his beard in thought.

"All right, Mr. Shibata," said Singh, as if he'd finally made up his mind. "Would you go to Calcutta?"

"When?" asked Shibata. *Looks like I did it.*

"Tomorrow. I'll contact my friends in Calcutta immediately. There is a large organization for Muslims there. They may be able to assist you."

"Will our use of the airfield come with any conditions?"

"No. I won't ask anything. As a favor to you."

"I'm at a loss for words. I deeply appreciate your kindness."

Singh sat, his eyes fixed on Shibata, not a hint of a smile on his face. It was a cold, penetrating stare. Shibata prayed that his government wouldn't betray Singh. There was no question that this man was a powerful fixer of the independence movement.

CHAPTER 16

The day after meeting with Lieutenant Segawa, Yamawaki and Ohnuki traveled to Yokosuka in an official vehicle belonging to the Ministry of the Navy. They were told that Lieutenant Ando and Flight Sergeant Inui had been grounded in Yokosuka and were awaiting further orders. Yamawaki and Ohnuki contacted the Military Aviation Headquarters to find out exactly where the two were. They were at the Yokosuka Air Wing Headquarters. It was fortunate for Yamawaki and Ohnuki that Ando and Inui had not received any new orders yet. They could talk to the two pilots alone without involving any higher-ranking officers.

Ando and Inui were out when Yamawaki and Ohnuki arrived.

"I believe Lieutenant Ando is in Yokohama," said the orderly on duty. "I don't think the sergeant is with him, but he should be in Yokohama too."

"Do you have any idea where they might be in Yokohama?" asked Ohnuki.

"Maybe 'Blue Max'? It's a bar in Motomachi. I heard they go there a lot. Other than that, I really don't know."

"Let's check this out," said Yamawaki to Ohnuki.

Blue Max was located on the first floor of a stone building that faced a canal in Motomachi, Yokohama. A waiter showed them into the bar. The two men looked around. The bar had a high ceiling and a refined atmosphere. It was still early in the evening and only ten or so tables were filled. A good third of the customers were Caucasian.

There was an open space in the middle of the room, apparently a dance floor. Just beyond the dance floor, a band was playing a jazz number. The musicians' outfits didn't match. Perhaps they hadn't actually been hired to play.

Ohnuki told the waiter that they were looking for Naval Lieutenant Ando. The waiter pointed at the stage.

"Which one?" Ohnuki asked in shock. "He's playing right now?"

"He's the trumpeter," answered the waiter.

"Would you mind telling him that Ohnuki, from the Ministry of the Navy, is here and wants to talk to him?"

Immediately after the waiter left, Ohnuki turned to Yamawaki and asked in a hush, "Do you know anything about music?"

"I enjoyed the opera in Berlin," said Yamawaki. "Why?"

"What is this? Is this jazz?"

"Yes. The title of this song is 'St. Louis Blues.'"

"What in the world is this place? A dance hall? A café?" asked Ohnuki, looking around.

"Well, they're serving alcohol, so it isn't a café. And I don't see any waitresses here, either."

"But it's illegal to serve alcohol and have a band play!"

"The band doesn't seem to be official, and I don't see any dance girls. But if this place is what you think it is, it'll be shut down within a month."

Yamawaki stared at the man playing the trumpet. He was obviously of mixed blood. His hair was dark and slightly wavy. His white sleeves were rolled up on his arms. He looked hollow and dark, and didn't particularly seem to be enjoying himself. If anything, he seemed to be playing to purge some pain.

Yamawaki and Ohnuki stood near the counter and waited for the music to end. When it did, Yamawaki began to applaud. Ohnuki glared at Yamawaki.

"It was a great number," said Yamawaki defensively.

"We're on duty," replied Ohnuki dryly.

The waiter approached Ando and whispered something in his ear. Ando looked towards the counter. He seemed to notice Ohnuki's uniform and frowned. He placed his trumpet on the piano, picked up his jacket, and walked towards the counter.

"I am Lieutenant Commander Ohnuki. This is Yamawaki, secretary to the Ministry of the Navy."

Ando looked at them. His expression was one of boredom.

"Can we talk for a moment?" said Ohnuki.

"I'm afraid I don't feel much like talking at the moment, sir," replied Ando, in a far from polite tone. "I guess I don't mind listening, though."

"You're just as the report described you."

"I don't know how it describes me, but I'm glad you have something on me already. That saves me some breath. Base commander Takijiro Onishi cited me for a second time two weeks ago in Hankow. I was reassigned from his Air Corps only five days later. Now I've been ordered to stay in Yokosuka for the rest of my life."

Ando stopped the waiter and ordered a beer. When the mug arrived, Ando downed half of it in a single gulp.

He looks so jaded, cynical, thought Yamawaki. *Sunken cheeks and dull eyes. Born in 1910... That makes him around thirty now. He looks much older. Is this what the front lines do to you?*

"Is alcohol really necessary?" Ohnuki complained. "I have something serious to discuss."

"I'm not on duty, sir," said Ando, not bothering to face Ohnuki. He placed an elbow casually atop the bar. "Why don't you join me?"

"Not a happy drinker, are we?"

"You've got that right, sir. As I'm sure you already know, I've had my share of trouble with my commanding officers. I've been rotated through plenty of different air corps. Each reassignment gave me plenty of time to brush up on my drinking skills."

"Eighteen kills. That's nothing to sneeze at. So why are you constantly getting in trouble with your commanders? Why did you duel with the American? If you did?"

"Only the pilots were in the air, sir. It's just like my wingmen said."

"And your refusal to strafe Nanking Castle?"

"Before I answer that, I have a question for you myself, sir. How much is known about the attack on Nanking here in Japan? Do you know what our troops did there, sir?"

"I've heard rumors."

Ando took another swig of beer. "Fortunately, my guns were malfunctioning that day. Then my sights went out. Seems I was firing in a totally different direction."

"Did you manage to shoot down eighteen enemy aircraft with malfunctioning guns and sights?"

"There's nothing to explain, sir. You can court-martial me if you want. But you won't get anything new, sir."

"I guess you aren't much of a team player, Ando."

"Have you ever fought on the front lines, sir?"

"I've never fought on an actual battlefield, no."

"I was there in China since 1937," said Ando, somewhat thoughtfully. "I've been praised as a model Imperial soldier. So I wouldn't say that

I'm not a team player."

"We have a mission for you," Yamawaki spoke up suddenly. "How do you feel about flying again?"

"Where am I being assigned?"

"To a special courier corps serving directly under Minister Oikawa."

"Never heard of it. Is this something new?"

"That's the cover story."

"Cover story?" asked Ando. "So what's the real mission? Bombing another beautiful and historic city? Firebombing some more farmers, women, and children? Turning another city with two thousand years of history into smoking rubble?"

Ohnuki frowned. Ando was openly criticizing the military command, accusing the "bricks" like Ohnuki. Ando's comments were far more seriously insubordinate, and condescending, than Toda's.

Ando turned to look straight into Ohnuki's eyes. "What's the city? Kyoto? Kure? Nagasaki? I'm more than happy to join the campaign, sir."

Suddenly, almost reflexively, Ohnuki balled a fist and smashed Ando in the side of his face. Ando's head recoiled as he staggered back from the impact.

Yamawaki shouted in surprise. Time froze for a moment. Yamawaki couldn't believe what he saw. The music ground to a halt. Blue Max was silent. The customers stared at the three of them.

Ando turned, slowly, to face Ohnuki again. His upper lip was cracked and bleeding. Ohnuki hadn't pulled his punch. Ando spat blood onto the floor, and his mouth twisted into a cynical sneer.

"I'll pretend I didn't hear the garbage spewing out of your mouth just now, lieutenant," said Ohnuki. "Go to the bathroom and sober yourself up."

"Why?" Ando had lost none of his attitude. "You want an insubordinate pilot for the minister's own courier service?"

"Don't worry. You'll never have to talk to the minister. You can be as arrogant as you like. All we want are top-notch pilots."

"If I called myself the best fighter pilot in the navy, would you still think I'm being arrogant, sir?"

"You won't hear me disagree on that point, lieutenant. I came here to find the best the Imperial Navy has to offer."

The two stared silently at one another for some time. Ando was obviously considering what Ohnuki had just told him. Perhaps he wondered just how far he could trust Ohnuki. For his part, Ohnuki stoically endured Ando's stare.

Finally, Ando's gaze softened. He seemed to have come to a decision.

"Tell me about it, sir."

The tension had been deflated. Yamawaki began to hear the sounds of conversations, ice clinking in glasses, and the beginnings of the bass player hesitantly launching into a new number.

"I need to have two Type Zero Carrier Fighters flown to a remote location," said Ohnuki without any trace of anger. "A very remote location."

"I wish you had said that from the beginning. That's the perfect mission for me. Where am I taking them? The Philippines? Saipan?"

"Berlin."

Another long silence. There was no change in Ando's expression. He simply stared into Ohnuki's eyes. Finally, Ando spoke again.

"That's too far to fly nonstop."

"How about refueling every 2,000 kilometers?"

"Positive. I assume you want me to refuel in Lingxi, Irkutsk, Omsk, and Moscow?"

Ohnuki looked at Yamawaki.

"No," Yamawaki said. "You will stop in Hanoi, Eastern India, Rajasthan, Bandar Abbas, and Iraq."

Ando blinked slowly.

"Have you cleared this flight plan with the British government?"

"Uh-uh," said Ohnuki, shaking his head. "And that's why we need you."

"That's a flight directly through a region controlled by the RAF."

"Do you think it's too much for a Type Zero Carrier Fighter to handle?"

"I can't take responsibility for this causing Britain to declare war on Japan."

"You are absolutely prohibited from engaging in combat. You are to run at the first hint of trouble. Lose any aircraft following you and head for the next airfield. When you're flying 2,000 kilometers, you can't spare any fuel on dogfights. Correct?"

"You said two fighters. Am I flying them one at a time?"

"No. Both go at once."

"Have you settled on the other pilot yet?"

"Not yet. But I think you have some idea of who we have in mind."

Ando allowed himself to smile. Yamawaki realized it was the first time he had seen Ando smile the entire visit. It was an earnest smile, a boyish smile, the kind Yamawaki hadn't expected from someone with Ando's attitude. Drawn in by the man's personality, Yamawaki found it difficult not to smile himself.

"Sir," said Ando. "I'd like to recommend a certain flight sergeant by the name of Kyohei Inui."

"Where is he?" asked Ohnuki.

"Nearby. Inui and I have been pretty down since we had our wings clipped. To be honest, I was nearly convinced we'd never fly again."

Yamawaki and Ohnuki exchanged glances. Ando was everything they'd expected him to be. Arrogant but self-confident. A pilot through and through. He was indeed the one they'd been looking for.

CHAPTER 17

The three men headed for the warehouse row of Yokohama's Customs Office in the government car. It was just after five in the afternoon, and the work of loading and unloading crates had ended for the day. There was no sign of life on the road, and it looked much wider than usual. There weren't any streetlamps, and all of the windows were dark. Before long, the entire area would be pitch dark.

Ando signaled the chauffer to stop. They were already deep within the warehouse area, surrounded by brick buildings with identical facades. They had stopped under a roof extending over the loading area for one of the buildings.

"He's here? What's he doing in a place like this?" asked Ohnuki dubiously.

"You'll see soon enough," answered Ando.

The three stepped out of the car and stood in the darkness of the warehouse district. Ohnuki lit a cigarette. Ando leaned casually on the car's hood, his arms crossed on his chest. It seemed they would have to wait. Yamawaki removed a small tin box from his pocket, opened it, and popped several mints into his mouth.

Presently they heard what sounded like a swarm of bees off in the distance. Soon it developed into the sound of an engine running at full throttle.

Yamawaki and Ohnuki looked in the direction of the noise. It came from beyond the row of warehouses, from the direction of Osanbashi bridge. Suddenly a light pierced the darkness from around the corner. It looked like the headlamp of a motorcycle. A second headlamp appeared behind the first. The two motorcycles seemed to be racing. Ohnuki, Yamawaki, and Ando moved closer to the wall of the warehouse.

Suddenly the squeal of rubber on pavement echoed between the buildings. The lead mototcycle, inclined at a dangerous angle, slid sideways until the rider skillfully leveled the bike and screeched to a perfect stop in front of the three. The trailing motorbike slowed down and stopped just behind the first.

The lead rider wore a flight helmet and goggles. His leather jacket appeared quite old and well worn. The white scarf thrown over his neck appeared to be the type issued to fighter pilots. He raised his goggles and smiled at Ando.

"What happened, sir? I thought you were at Blue Max," said the rider.

"I came here looking for you," said Ando. "But after seeing you stop your machine like that, these people might not want to talk to you anymore."

"I didn't expect to see a uniform—and sash—out here." The rider cut his engine and stepped off the motorcycle.

So this is Sergeant Inui! thought Yamawaki, looking the man over. His skin was tanned, his face mightily intrepid. In contrast to Ando's disillusioned air, ambition seemed to rise from every molecule of Inui's masculine frame. His jacket seemed practically bursting at the seams trying to hold it all in.

"Inui," Ando introduced him.

Ohnuki stared at the sergeant, evaluating the man. Ando had passed the test. Now it was Inui's turn.

"Inui," said Ando, "this is Lieutenant Commander Ohnuki, who's with the Ministry of the Navy. He came all the way down here looking for us."

Inui's face clouded for a moment. "I thought it was over."

"What are you doing here?" asked Ohnuki.

"Racing," said Inui, without even bothering to salute. "High speed racing."

"Just for fun?"

"Nobody pays me for it."

"You know you're wasting precious gasoline?"

Yamawaki stepped forward. Running interference for Ohnuki was one of his duties. It was increasingly evident that this evening of music and motorcycles was totally foreign to Ohnuki's realm of experience. Ohnuki's stick-to-the-rules attitude was far more common among Army men than in the Navy. Perhaps that accounted for his success at the ministry.

"I'm Yamawaki, secretary to the Ministry of the Navy. We're here tonight to discuss a very sensitive mission. Do you have some time to spare for us?"

Inui looked at Yamawaki and Ohnuki with barely disguised contempt. He didn't say a word, but the smirk on his face told the whole story.

"Inui. This is serious," said Ando reproachfully. "Don't judge people by their rank."

Inui nodded. He signaled to the man on the second motorcycle to leave. The other rider kick-started his bike, turned it around, and rode away.

Inui turned back to Ohnuki, a sardonic smile still on his face. He slowly removed his gloves. Yamawaki began to worry about the situation. Inui seemed so recalcitrant, so self-destructive, that he seemed almost hell-bent on receiving further punishment. Outside of Ando, Yamawaki had never encountered such an insubordinate soldier. Ando's case could partly be explained by alcohol. But Inui acted like a man who was convinced that his career with the Navy was already over.

"I want you to listen to me very carefully, sergeant," said Ohnuki, his voice steely. "I understand you've had issues with your commanding officers. I understand you saw and heard things in China that made you question the military. But I didn't come here to listen to your complaints or to debate official policy. I'm not here to speak for the government or the navy, so just get that out of your head right now."

Inui shrugged. Ohnuki continued:

"I'm here with a mission for you. If you prefer, I can look for another pilot. But if you let this opportunity pass, you'll regret it for the rest of your life. So act like a man and pull yourself together. If not, I'll take you on man-to-man first."

"He's serious, Inui," came Ando's voice from behind Ohnuki. "The lieutenant commander introduced me to his fist earlier this evening. Must say it was quite an impressive greeting. Enough to make me change my mind a little about the bricks."

"Sir?" said Inui, his eyes widening in shock. "Is that why you've been so quiet?"

"Let's just say I owe him one. Just listen to the man, okay? I should tell you, too, that I'm the one who suggested he see you."

Inui's face brightened. "You mean we can fly again?"

"Type Zero Carrier Fighters," replied Ohnuki.

Inui turned to face Ohnuki. "I'll do it, lieutenant commander. If it means getting in the air again, I don't care if you demote me. Where are we going? Manchuria? Indochina?"

"Farther afield, I'm afraid. Quite dangerous."

"Well, don't keep me hanging. Come on, I'm happy to fly to the

North Pole if I have to."

"Berlin."

"Where?"

"Ber-lin," repeated Ohnuki.

Inui turned to Ando. "Is that possible?"

"Yeah, it'll take days," replied Ando.

"What's so dangerous about Berlin?" asked Inui.

"The RAF will be waiting for us along the way," said Ando.

Inui suddenly stood at attention, clicked his heels, and saluted Ohnuki.

"Lieutenant Commander Ohnuki. I humbly request assignment to this mission."

Ohnuki looked completely bewildered. Meeting Toda had left him totally unprepared for this. If Toda was the average navy pilot, what in the world was up with these two?

"You're going to accept the mission without hearing about the route?" Ohnuki croaked.

"Sir," asked a perplexed Inui, "is that a problem?"

"No," said Ohnuki, shaking his head. "No, but there's a lot to explain. Spare me your time."

CHAPTER 18

The two pilots remained silent after listening to Ohnuki's presentation. Yamawaki studied their faces but couldn't detect any sign of emotion. Did they think the mission was impossible? Or did they think it was a cakewalk? Yamawaki couldn't tell one way or the other.

The four men sat in a restaurant overlooking the harbor. They had taken the table farthest from the other customers. Only a short while ago they could see the wharf from the windows. Now it was pitch dark outside, and the only thing visible was their reflection in the glass. Occasionally a boat horn sounded from the darkness.

Under the dim yellow light of the restaurant's lamps, Ohnuki had described the plan to fly the Zero fighters to Germany. Yamawaki was surprised that Ohnuki spared no detail, not even the true purpose and background of the flight. Usually, that sort of information was considered something pilots didn't need to know to do their jobs.

Finally, Ohnuki turned to Ando.

"So. What do you think? Is it feasible?"

It was the exact same question he had asked Toda several days ago.

"Yes," said Ando, sitting a little more upright in his chair. "It isn't impossible. Pointless, yes, but not impossible. It's a stupid plan."

"What do you mean?"

"Even if Hitler equips the Luftwaffe with the Type Zero Carrier Fighter, it won't change a thing. Hitler can't beat the British. No way, sir. From what I've been reading in the papers, Hitler's supposed to have invaded England a while ago. The operation's been postponed again and again. How long's he planning to wait? Sir."

"It's been postponed indefinitely."

"Right. Producing Zeros in Germany, that's actually good, creative thinking. It still won't change a thing. The Luftwaffe may gain control of the air over England for a while, but that will only serve to drag the U.S. into the war. If things go that way, Germany's fate is sealed. They'll have to retreat to the Rhine."

"Are you telling me you won't accept the mission because it's pointless?"

"No, I'll fly the mission, sir. I just wanted you to know that it's

pointless. And I want you to know that I'm not doing this for you. No matter how serious you are about this mission's end goal, you'll never convince
me to do it for that."

"Then why are you flying the mission?"

"Because I'm a pilot. If I get the chance to fly somewhere far away,
I'll volunteer every time."

"You won't have to volunteer for this. You're being ordered to. The
Imperial Navy isn't looking for self-centered pilots. We need servicemen
who'll remain true to their mission."

"The Zeros aren't going anywhere unless I decide to take this one,
lieutenant commander. As they say, you can lead a horse to water, but you
can't make it drink."

Ohnuki smiled wryly. "I have to hand it to you, Ando. You're right.
But it's too bad I can't describe you as a good serviceman."

"Fair enough," nodded Ando in agreement. "I'm a pilot before I'm
a soldier, sir."

"With an old-fashioned set of values."

"I admit it, sir. I'm an old-fashioned pilot. Neither a simple aviator,
nor even your regular fighter pilot. Do you know the difference between
someone who flies a plane and someone who's a pilot? I'm a pilot. I'm
descended from men of old who piloted their ships to a faraway land,
America."

"Why did you join the military, Ando?"

"I didn't, really. I simply took the shortest path to becoming a pilot.
In our hellish age, it seemed like a decent enough option."

The more he listened, the more Yamawaki was impressed by
Ando's candor, his lack of interest in awing anyone. Perhaps he did overdo
the arrogance, but Yamawaki realized it was simply a byproduct of Ando's
self-confidence. At the same time, it was easy to see how Ando rubbed most
of his superiors the wrong way. The Imperial Navy didn't have much room
for officers who questioned the status quo these days.

Now Ohnuki looked at Inui. "How about you? Still happy to take
the mission, after hearing the details?"

"Is there some reason I shouldn't be happy, sir?"

"All right," Ohnuki nodded. "It was a dumb question."

"If you had said the plan was impossible," said Yamawaki to Ando,
"we would have had to go back to square one. I'll cable Berlin tomorrow.

When can you leave?"

"When will the aircraft be available?" asked Ando.

"One week from now," answered Yamawaki. "Mitsubishi Heavy Industries is providing two aircraft. They were supposed to go to the regular forces next month, but we requisitioned them. We'll get them fresh off the Suzuka assembly line."

Ohnuki had already coordinated the production of the aircraft with Mitsubishi executives before Yamawaki had even returned from Berlin. He had Mitsubishi remove the serial numbers from all the various components of the aircraft. And while the Type Zeros still featured their trademark shiny gray coloration with rising sun markings on the wings, Ohnuki told Mitsubishi not to paint any factory information on the planes. That way, in the event of a crash, the RAF would learn less about production capabilities and deployment status from the wreckage.

"We'll leave four weeks after receiving the aircraft, then," said Ando. "We need to familiarize ourselves further with the handling and range of the Zero. The more familiar we are with the planes, the more we'll be able to reduce fuel consumption. Ideally we'd like to increase the range to at least 3,000 kilometers. I think the Zero can do it. Do we have the time?"

Yamawaki's mind immediately turned to the calendar. It was October 24th. It would take a week to get the aircraft from Mitsubishi. Four weeks after that meant departing on November 28th. Supposing it would take ten days to make the flight to Berlin, the aircraft could be handed over to the Germans on or about December 8th. That would be three weeks late by Major Graf's timetable.

"Lieutenant..." began Yamawaki, but thought the better. This pilot wasn't interested in playing games. If he said he needed four weeks for familiarization, that was probably true. Besides, it would take some more time to arrange the refueling stops in eastern India and Iraq.

"What?" asked Ando.

"Nothing. The schedule is acceptable," said Yamawaki. "Four weeks of training after delivery of the aircraft. The departure date will be set for the end of November, with arrival in Berlin to occur sometime around December 8th."

Ohnuki added, "You'll receive official orders tomorrow." Ando and Inui's eyes brightened.

Part Two

Ohnuki continued. "You'll be assigned to the Naval Aviation Technology Development Center, Experimental Flight Division. There you'll work on long-distance flying techniques for the Type Zero Carrier Fighter. After four weeks, you will receive orders to transfer to northern Indochina. That will serve as your order to fly to Berlin. Any questions?"

"What about that Minister of the Navy's courier stuff?" asked Ando.

"You can forget about it," laughed Ohnuki. "That was a cover story for Personnel. It'll continue to be the cover story, but that's nothing for you to worry about."

"This project is code-named 'Ibis'," added Yamawaki. "Use it whenever referring to the mission, to help maintain confidentiality."

"Ibis?" asked Inui.

"The name of a bird. A beautiful Japanese bird," said Yamawaki.

"An endangered species," added Ando. "The perfect name for us."

When Ohnuki rose, Ando and Inui immediately stood up as well. Inui saluted sharply.

"I apologize for my poor attitude earlier this evening, sir," said Inui.

It was a show of etiquette Yamawaki wouldn't even have imagined an hour earlier. Ohnuki nodded in satisfaction.

Yamawaki stifled a shout of joy. He wanted to laugh out loud, grab the two men, shake them by the shoulders.

Ohnuki and Yamawaki split from Ando and Inui and walked to their car. Once they were out of earshot, Yamawaki couldn't contain himself any longer. He started laughing.

"What's wrong?" asked Ohnuki.

"Lieutenant commander, you're a born player," answered Yamawaki. The two laughed over the events of the evening, again and again, on the ride back to headquarters.

CHAPTER 19

Ryotaro Shibata arrived in Calcutta by train on the evening of October 24th. He checked in at the Taj Capital Hotel on Chowringhee Street. Pritam Singh had selected the hotel for him. The lobby appeared to have a British influence, and the majority of the customers were white. He was likely the only Asian guest in the hotel that day. The Indian concierge scrutinized Shibata's passport during check-in. Shibata was mildly surprised to find a message already waiting for him. It was from Singh. It said that a chauffeur would arrive the next morning to show Shibata around Calcutta. It also instructed Shibata to use the same code phrase as before.

The next morning, a Sikh, wearing a large turban, arrived at the hotel by car. When Shibata asked where he was going, the Sikh handed him an envelope. It contained a first-class train ticket for the railway that ran from Sealdah station out to Eastern Bengal. Shibata needed to board a train bound for Darjeeling and switch to a branch line along the way. The name of the destination station sounded somewhat familiar to Shibata. It was a small town located halfway down the Jamuna River.

The Sikh glanced into the rear-view mirror constantly during the drive and took a circuitous route to the station to avoid being followed. The man didn't say a single thing to Shibata after hearing the password. He remained silent as Shibata got out of the car at the station.

Shibata regretted not bringing any luggage. He carried his wallet in his vest pocket but hadn't brought a single change of clothes. He had left everything in his hotel room. He knew where he was headed, but he didn't have a clue as to how long he might have to be there. He belatedly realized that going to Eastern Bengal meant this wasn't going to be a day trip.

Perhaps Pritam Singh had arranged things this way on purpose to deceive British intelligence. But Shibata wished that he had been given a bit more information. He'd taken extra care when he boarded the train at New Delhi.

Shibata shared his compartment with an Indian mother and child. They greeted each other at the beginning of the trip, but otherwise sat in silence. For some time after the train started, Shibata waited for someone to contact him. No one appeared save for the conductor, however. Hopefully someone would be waiting for him at his destination.

Part Two

After they passed the houses of Calcutta, the scenery unfolded into the vast expanse of the Ganges River delta. The land looked deep green, fertile. Shibata watched palm trees and paddy fields stream past the window, then a river. Here and there he saw smoke rising from what appeared to be villages. Occasionally, he spotted children who stood along the tracks waving to the train as it sped past.

Once the train crossed the Ganges River, a waiter appeared at the compartment. After taking orders from Shibata and the woman and child, he spread a white tablecloth across the compartment's small table. Less than five minutes later, he whisked in trays bearing their meals.

The first stop after the meal just happened to be the station where Shibata needed to change trains. It was already three o'clock by the time he arrived at the terminal of Sirajganj. He stepped off the train just as he had boarded: empty-handed.

Shibata glanced around the open area in front of the station. He had not been given any instructions or directions. Someone had to be there to meet him. A British Army truck sat parked in front of a colonial-style white building across the traffic circle. Perhaps a British base was nearby. For the first time, Shibata began to worry. Could there really be a safe airfield this close to British military presence?

Had Singh misunderstood Shibata's request? Had some details been misconstrued along the way? Shibata turned his back to the truck and studied his surroundings.

Just when the other passengers were done clearing out of the station, a truck that had been parked off to the side of the building began to move. It wound its way around the traffic circle and stopped in front of Shibata. A man climbed down from the driver's seat. He appeared to be around thirty years old and didn't wear a turban. Shibata had sat down on a bench to wait. The man approached him and bowed.

"Are you Mr. Shibata?"

"Yes. And you?"

"My name is Das. Where are the birds?"

"Not in the sky," answered Shibata. "Perhaps behind a boddhi tree."

"Our friend in Delhi asked me to take care of you."

The man's English was impeccable. His eyes were bright and inquisitive. Shibata thought he might be a teacher. He had heard that more than a few members of the radical independence movement were teachers or civil servants. Perhaps this man even lectured his students on the subject. The shirt he wore looked crude, but apart from that, he was a clean, well-groomed man.

"How long will it take?" asked Shibata.

"To the airfield? It's no more than five minutes from here."

"The British appear to have some sort of base here."

"It's quite small. There's only one platoon garrisoned there."

"At that airfield?"

"No, at the port. It's on the opposite side."

"Is there a hotel here? Perhaps I should go there first."

"Our friend in Delhi asked me to take care of you. Please allow me to offer my colleague's house."

"Thank you," said Shibata, climbing into the passenger's seat of the truck.

Some five hundred meters later, they had already left the city limits. The truck continued into a wide expanse of fertile-looking paddy fields. What appeared to be orange trees lined both sides of the road. They weren't quite thick enough to shade the truck from the scorching Indian sun.

"How is Calcutta?" asked Das.

"What do you mean?"

"The leaders in Calcutta cannot make a move at the moment. British intelligence is on full alert right now."

"Why is that?"

"A famous leader of the independence movement has been imprisoned in Calcutta. British high officials are convinced someone will try to break him out. Things are very sensitive right now."

"Are you talking about Chandra Bose?"

"You know of him?"

"Of course I do," said Shibata. "I watched the events of July 3rd with great interest."

Chandra Bose was one of the leaders of the Indian National Congress. He had been born into a well-to-do family in Calcutta and had graduated from Cambridge University. He returned to India at the age of 24. Almost immediately, he became involved with the Indian National Congress and its anti-British activities as part of the Indian independence movement. In 1922, he joined a radical splinter group and its party organ, *The Swarajya*.

Part Two

Soon his well-reasoned arguments began to persuade not just the members of the Indian National Congress, but also average Indian citizens. Before long, Bose was elected mayor of Calcutta. The Maharaja that Shibata had met from Rajasthan was a staunch supporter.

Bose had been jailed on numerous occasions for his activities against the British. In 1933, Bose was deported. He spent his exile in Berlin, returning to India in 1936. Upon his return he spent yet another year in detention.

In 1938, Bose was elected as chairman of the Indian National Congress. However, Bose and Gandhi fought almost constantly. Despite winning his reelection campaign by a landslide, Bose was removed from his position the very next year. Shortly after Bose's departure from the Indian National Congress and hot on the heels of England's declaration of war on Germany, the Viceroy of India declared war on the Third Reich.

Bose knew that Indian resentment against the British was coming to a head. He began a campaign for nationwide support that summer. He ordered groups under his command to destroy British statues and memorials anywhere they could be found. Indians saw the statues of British admirals and generals that dotted their lands as nothing more than symbols of British colonialism—in other words, monuments to atrocity and tyranny. Bose chose these statues as his targets. He gave his order in June, and the campaign against the statues was to begin on July 3rd.

But the British Criminal Investigation Department (C.I.D.) caught wind of Bose's plan and arrested him a day before the plot was to be carried out. Shibata had heard that Bose was being held at Presidency Prison in Calcutta.

"It's been three months," said Shibata to Das. "Have they set a release date yet? He's an incredible leader."

"We are under martial law," replied Das. "It's preposterous. Even worse than the Rowlatt Act. Now they can arrest people based on things they've said or written in the past. With the new law, he'll probably be in prison until the end of the war."

"I assume that means..."

"That's right!" interrupted Das cried. "Of course we're plotting his escape. But the C.I.D. keeps an eye on everyone who's a Bose supporter. I suspect you couldn't contact any, correct?"

Shibata reconsidered his impression of the Sikh driver. He had appeared unfriendly; apparently, he had just been nervous.

Their truck crossed over a small river. A sandbar had formed in the middle of the current. The rice paddies Shibata had seen earlier were replaced by tropical scrub brush. Shortly after crossing the river, a rolling, grassy field swung into view on their left. The land on either side of the road had been leveled. The shrubbery gave way to palm trees.

Shibata saw four poles standing in the middle of the field. It didn't appear to be farmland. In fact, the way the poles were arranged, it looked more like a football field. Shibata could also see what appeared to be a two-story Georgian-style house. Several barn-like structures stood behind the house.

"I take it a lot of British live around here," said Shibata, looking over the field. "We can't let them catch wind of our activities."

"We are aware of the need for secrecy," said Das. "You needn't worry about the British."

"But this looks like a perfect football field. The British must play here. Don't they?"

"It is a polo field. More precisely, the remains of a polo field. This used to be a country club. The field over there used to be a golf course."

Shibata glanced at his watch. More than five minutes had passed since leaving the station. Das' airfield had to be nearby. The number of British buildings in the area worried Shibata.

"I hope the airfield isn't anywhere near here."

"You're looking at it," answered Das, guiding their truck off the road and onto the grass. The truck lurched as it went over a ditch. "This is your airfield."

"What? But you said this was a British country club!"

"The villagers spent a lot of time building this place, but the British seem to have grown tired of it."

The truck drove for another fifty meters into the grass and came to a stop. Das opened his door and got out of the truck. Shibata stepped out from his side.

The grass was sparse and uneven. The field was in poor condition, but the ground was surprisingly firm. There weren't any rocks or gravel.

"That building over there is a club house," said Das, pointing. "It isn't being used. The buildings behind it were once used as stables."

"You're telling me there isn't anyone using this place?" asked

Shibata skeptically.

"I assure you that that is the case. The villagers still clean the area up twice a year to keep it in shape, but the Brits haven't come for going on five years now. My friends and I play football here occasionally. That's about it."

"How long is the field? It has to be long enough for a plane to land."

"The distance between the sets of poles is about 200 meters. There's more grass beyond that. I should say it's around 450 meters, altogether."

Shibata walked on the grass.

400 meters or so. Is that long enough for a small plane to land? The pilot will have to avoid those shrubs. So the usable length is probably two-thirds of that. Can an airplane land and take off on a grass field? Shibata remembered the airfield on the army base in Tachikawa. *That wasn't grass. Are we going to have to clear and level the area?*

"Quite some time ago, a single-engine British aircraft made a landing here on the polo field," said Das, as if he'd read Shibata's mind. "Some general flew in from Dhaka to see a game."

Das assured Shibata that the area was more than suitable as a refueling stop for a small airplane. He said he would arrange a deal for the fuel with the depot in town. There was no worry; the owner of the fuel depot was a member of Das' organization as well. Das couldn't promise to find a trustworthy mechanic, but the town had a garage for repairing cars. If necessary, perhaps the pilot could find tools there. In addition, the clubhouse could be used to rest in, and the stables for hiding the aircraft. Unless the planes flew directly over the nearby town, they wouldn't be noticed. Das even offered to arrange some men to stay and assist with everything from landing to takeoff, provided they had prior notice.

Shibata and Das climbed back into the truck and made a slow circle around the polo field and surrounding area. It was just as Das had said. The field did seem suitable for a small plane. *They aren't looking for firemen and a canteen, now, are they?* It looked good enough to contact Tokyo. The question of the British Indian army presence in the town still bothered him, however.

"Have them fly in from upstream of the Janas River," instructed Das. "Nobody will notice them flying in. If anything happens, we'll close down the bridge. That would buy half a day, more than enough time to escape."

Das drove back onto the road.

"Let me show you around town," he continued. "I want you to see the size and morale of the British force here for yourself. Once we're done, I'll take you to a private house where my colleagues have gathered."

"What is it? A meeting?" asked Shibata.

"We want to hear what you have to say about the Tripartite Pact and the future of Asia."

"I'm not really in a position to expound our policies, Das."

"That's fine. Just talk about how the Japanese military sees Asia, especially India. We just want to hear the honest truth."

Das looked into Shibata's eyes. Shibata didn't sense any malice.

"We're isolated out here in the countryside," continued Das. "We're desperate for information about the outside world. We're at war. Where are things heading?"

It was the following afternoon by the time Shibata made it back to his room at the Taj Capital Hotel in Calcutta. The suitcase he had left in his room appeared to have been opened by someone. It wasn't a thief; the fifty-pound notes he had stashed inside were untouched. It had to be British Intelligence. They were paying extra attention to Calcutta, and Shibata prayed that Chandra Bose would make a successful escape from Presidency Prison before the Japanese aircraft were due.

CHAPTER 20

That Monday evening, a man approached Yamawaki in the circular driveway in front of the Ministry of the Navy. It was Sugita, a secretary. He had been an upperclassman when Yamawaki was at Tokyo Imperial University, and had spent three years studying abroad, at Oxford. Sugita didn't like the meals in the officers' mess, so he often headed to the restaurant at the Tokyo Club for lunch instead. Sugita's desk sat next to Yamawaki's in the office pool.

"What have you been up to these days?" asked Sugita. "I heard you've locked yourself away somewhere with Lieutenant Commander Ohnuki."

"That's right. We're handling some sensitive documents."

It was close to the end of the day at the Naval Ministry. Uniformed officers walked past the two. Sugita and Yamawaki began ambling together.

"Rumor around the office has it there's some sort of new top-secret project going on," said Sugita.

"I don't think so," answered Yamawaki. "Minister Oikawa gave us permission to drop our other projects and focus on what we're doing, that's all."

"What kind of work is this?"

"Consequences of signing the Tripartite Pact. We're researching the impact it'll have on England, the United States, and other countries."

"Sounds like a job for the Ministry of Foreign Affairs."

"I've been in contact with them."

"How about the Ministry of the Army?"

Yamawaki paused for a moment at that particular question. *Does he know about the project?*

"I've been contacting the related ministries, yes," answered Yamawaki guardedly.

"What's this I hear about the private courier flights for the minister?" pressed Sugita, still unsatisfied. "I heard you requested the names of pilots from Personnel."

"The minister wants his own pilots, who'll fly anywhere and any time he wants."

"Oh. By the way," said Sugita, stopping suddenly when the two reached the front gate. "Vice Admiral Inoue was looking for you a few days ago. Sounded like he wanted to hear about the German reaction to the signing."

Yamawaki stopped too. "I already turned in my report to Minister Oikawa."

"Looks like the vice admiral read it. I think that's why he's looking for you."

"Do you think I should go and see him?"

"I don't think that's necessary. But if he shows up again, I'll give you a call. Where are you working?"

"I'm moving around from room to room, and I'm out of the building a lot. So please just ask the operator."

"I understand." Sugita still appeared unsatisfied, but with that he turned and walked off down Sakurada Street in the direction of Toranomon Gate.

Small wonder Sugita was suspicious. A colleague with whom he had long shared a room had suddenly left without specific orders. It was only natural that he suspected Yamawaki was working on a secret project. It was even possible that Sugita had already gotten wind of it.

Yamawaki knew he would face still more questions in the future. *I'd better coordinate my story with Ohnuki. And I'll just leave Inoue alone for now. Explaining what's going on in Berlin to him won't accomplish anything. I don't think it'd have any major impact on his decision-making ability, at any rate. Unless he orders me into his office, I'll let sleeping dogs lie.*

Yamawaki headed down Sakurada Street and turned onto a side street in the direction of Gaisen Street.

CHAPTER 21

Just as Ohnuki had promised, the two Type Zero Carrier Fighters arrived seven days later. They had been delivered straight from the Mitsubishi Heavy Industries aircraft factory in Nagoya. Although originally slated for deployment with the 13th Air Corps, Mitsubishi had re-assigned the aircraft to Minister-Admiral Oikawa's project. Undoubtedly, the prospect of licensed production in Germany had played a prominent role in their decision. Mitsubishi now had to run around-the-clock shifts to ensure that the 13th Air Corps would get their pair of the state-of-the-art aircraft as well.

The two fighters were transported to Yokosuka via Suzuka airfield. The aircraft were officially designated as A6M2 Type Zero Carrier Fighters, Model 11. Unlike the Experimental Carrier Fighter Model 12, the Model 11 featured a Nakajima Sakae 12 engine, rather than the Mitsubishi Zuisei. These were the exact type of aircraft Ando and Inui had flown in China.

The bodies were painted a shiny gray, with black cowlings. The main wings and sides of the fuselage featured large rising sun markings. Unlike regular production aircraft, however, the only visible designation was the "Type Zero Carrier Fighter" lettering stenciled on the rear of the planes. The serial number and date of manufacture had been left off. The rudder of each plane bore a provisional number, "11" and "12" respectively.

Ohnuki and Yamawaki made sure they were at Yokosuka Air Corps on the day of delivery. They had already arranged to set aside some hangar space. It was the first time Yamawaki had laid eyes on the cutting-edge fighters.

Ohnuki, Yamawaki, Ando, and Inui gathered around the freshly delivered Zero fighters. The aircraft were so new that they could practically smell the freshly applied paint. The propellers, cowlings, cockpit glass, and wings shone brilliantly in the autumn sunlight.

Yamawaki wasn't particularly knowledgeable about aircraft and, aside from the occasional ride in a transport, hadn't spent much time in or around them. But even he could tell that these fighters were a breed apart. They didn't have the wooden patchwork look of a biplane or the lump-of-steel construction of the average military aircraft. They were sleek and sharp. *Beautiful*, thought Yamawaki. *It's hard to believe these planes were responsible for the success in Chungking. They managed to down more than double their own number of enemy planes.*

The group remained silent for quite some time. Ando stared at the fighters with a soft look in his eyes. Inui prowled around the aircraft, inspecting various parts and components. Ohnuki and Yamawaki made a slow counterclockwise circle around the planes. The sight of the two aircraft gleaming in the afternoon sunlight was one they would never forget.

"They're beautiful," said Yamawaki, entranced. "I expected something bulky, something weapon-like. But they're beautiful. They look almost fragile."

"Perhaps the design is what appeals to the Germans," noted Ohnuki thoughtfully.

"Think they can make it to Berlin?"

"That's a question for the pilots."

Yamawaki looked at Ando. Ando had walked up to a wingtip and was gently stroking it with one hand. He looked as if he were dreaming.

Suddenly realizing that Yamawaki was watching him, Ando drew back his hand and blushed.

"Yes?"

"Can these beautiful planes really make it to Berlin?" asked Yamawaki. He knew the question was meaningless. He knew the answer already.

"I'll only guarantee that one or the other will," answered Ando, the soft smile still on his face.

"But you said it wasn't impossible the other day."

"It isn't. There's a chance that both of them will make it. We'll do our best, but there are a lot of hurdles. You know that better than we do."

Yamawaki couldn't but recall the flight route. The jungles of Indochina. The Shan highlands. The Patkai mountains between Southeast Asia and India. The Ganges, spreading across the delta like the mesh of a net. The vast expanse of desert and badlands beyond Rajasthan. The list went on. Ando and Inui didn't just have political and military obstacles ahead of them, Yamawaki knew. The path to Berlin would be physically arduous as well. Yamawaki had planned the route himself, and Lieutenant Toda had told them in no uncertain terms just how insane such a flight path would be.

"If everything goes well, both planes will make it," said Ando. "But it's a very long flight. One of the planes could break down and require a crash landing."

"But, lieutenant, I clearly remember you saying that this was your mission, that it was...pointless, but not impossible."

"I haven't changed my mind. You told us you wanted to transport two planes. I said that it wouldn't be impossible and that we would do it. We will leave for Berlin on these two planes. We'll use every trick in the book to get them out west. But I suggest bracing yourself for the eventuality that only one will arrive."

"We're contractually obligated to deliver two planes to the Germans!"

"Mr. Yamawaki, we're not hopping from base to base with the Naval Air Corps," cut in Inui. "We won't have access to any spare parts. The airfields we'll be using won't even have decent workshops. It means these two planes'll have to serve as warehouses for each other."

"Warehouses? What do you mean?"

"I mean that, it worst comes to worst, we'll have to cannibalize one of the planes to repair the other one, or take the working parts from both to build a whole new plane. They may have been manufactured on the same day in the same factory, but that doesn't mean they're equally good. There are always differences. The inferior of the two will act as a flying parts warehouse for the better one. Parts may start wearing out somewhere in Iran or Iraq. If that happens, it's better to take one apart to fix the other than risk losing them both."

"Yamawaki," interrupted Ohnuki. "If one of the planes gets to Berlin, I'll see the contract as being 90% fulfilled. One fighter should be enough for flight testing, and they can still take it apart for their own research. They won't complain."

Ando walked behind the left wing of the fighter in front of him. He put a foot on the wing, hoisted himself up to the fuselage, and slid into the cockpit.

Ohnuki looked up at Ando. "There's still something we need to discuss. When will you be back?"

"Just let us circle around," said Ando. "It'll only take twenty minutes or so."

Ando tightened the strap of his flight helmet, put on his goggles, and signaled the ground crew. A young maintenance man turned a crank at the bottom of the cowl. The propeller began to spin. The exhaust pipe spat black smoke for a moment. Ohnuki and Yamawaki backed away from the plane.

Inui's Zero fighter roared to life as well. The pilots began adjusting their engines. It was as though the two planes were trying to coordinate their breathing. Soon the sound of the engines' rotation took on the same pitch. Ando and Inui looked at each other and nodded. They signaled the maintenance men to remove the wheel blocks. Ando's fighter began to roll forward, followed by Inui's.

Ohnuki and Yamawaki watched the scene intently. The two Type Zeros increased their speed, accelerated down the runway, and leapt smoothly into the air without even the hint of weight. They looked to Ohnuki and Yamawaki like giant birds spreading their wings and gliding over a valley.

The two fighters made a broad right turn after clearing the runway, gained altitude, and headed towards the Miura peninsula to the east. Ohnuki and Yamawaki stood in silence, watching the planes recede on the horizon.

The pilots returned half an hour later.

As the four stood in front of the fighters once again, Yamawaki briefed Ando and Inui on the airfields along the route. There hadn't been any major progress in the previous week. The Army was still negotiating for airfields in Eastern Bengal and Rajasthan. Iraq was still under negotiation as well, through extra-diplomatic channels. Iran was a sure thing, thanks to the cooperation of United Petroleum. The Turkish airfield was secure; Ando and Inui had been cleared to use an army base outside of Ankara. The next stop after Ankara would be a Japanese ally, Italy. An Italian Air Force officer stationed in Japan had arranged for the Zero fighters to stop in Rome.

Yamawaki promised Ando and Inui that he would take care of all necessary preparations within the next four weeks. The negotiations with India and Iraq would be concluded by then. Detailed maps of Indochina, the Persian Gulf, and Asia Minor had been requested and would be ready in a week at the latest. Ando and Inui could focus their full attention on familiarizing themselves with their brand-new Zeros and training themselves for the long flight.

"I want you to phone in a report twice a week," said Ohnuki, giving Ando the number for their separate office line at the Military Aviation

Headquarters. They decided to talk at five in the afternoon every Monday and Thursday, unless the pilots were still conducting exercises at that time. Because Ando would be using an Air Corps office phone, they needed to use codes. They decided on "planes" for the Type Zeros, "Hanoi" for Berlin, "Takao" for Iraq, "Kanoya" for western India, and "Saeki" for eastern India. That way, anyone who happened to overhear Ando would think he was simply discussing his transfer to the 14th Air Corps.

Just before leaving, Ohnuki turned to Ando.

"Do you have any requests, maintenance-wise? Gauges, uniforms, weapons, anything at all? I'd like to help in any way I can."

Ando tilted his head and thought for a while.

"I'd like you to change the radios," he answered determinedly.

"The radios?"

"I know, from experience in China, that the Type 96 Sora 1 series are useless. We had a name for them over there: ballast."

"Is a radio absolutely necessary? The bombing campaign there was successful without them, right?"

"If functional radios didn't exist, I wouldn't request them. But pilots in other countries are provided with radios. I would like a pair. If they work, we'll definitely use them."

"So, they are necessary."

"In this day and age, yes."

"I'll try to arrange something. But the Sora 1 radios are the best we have in this country. Do you know where we can find better ones?"

"In Germany. England. The Americans probably have better ones, too."

"Understood," Ohnuki waved his hand. "I'll make sure to find you a usable radio before you leave. Anything else?"

"Compressed oxygen cylinders and masks. We'll need to fly at high altitudes in case of emergencies."

"Will they understand that? Is that standard equipment?"

"Yes. At any rate, we'd like all of this two weeks before departure. We'll need to test the radios, too."

Ando had made himself clear. Ohnuki promised to get him the oxygen tanks and radios.

CHAPTER 22

That night, Ando went to Blue Max in Motomachi. It was just after seven o'clock. The bar was filled with customers and quite hot. The dance floor was filled with couples, their foreheads shiny with sweat.

It was Thursday, October 31st. All dance halls in Japan had to shut down at midnight. Blue Max was one of them.

Blue Max had started as a piano bar for foreign sailors. The owner didn't hire bands or showgirls, deciding instead to throw the stage open to anyone who wanted to play or dance. As such, Blue Max didn't fit the legal description of a dance hall, but the Military Police didn't care about such details. Blue Max played foreign music and was filled with men and women dancing cheek to cheek, which made it a dance hall in spirit if not in letter. And according to regulations, it was illegal for such halls to serve alcoholic beverages of any kind. The Military Police knew that Blue Max was serving alcohol. When the order was finally issued, it wasn't open for discussion; the owner was simply told to shut his place down.

Starting the year before, posters saying *Live Frugally, Japan* had begun popping up all over the city. Music and dancing certainly didn't conform to the definition of "frugal." Without a doubt, the government was trying to clamp down on Western influences. That summer, music teachers had been forced to abandon the foreign "do-re-mi" for the "ha-ni-ho" scales of the Japanese language. Japan was changing, and the changes seemed to be driven by a small minority, a group without any appreciation for the beauty of music, full of hatred for any kind of worldly pleasure. But their dark ideas were spreading through the country.

Ando shook his head, as though to clear his mind. *If this is our last chance to play and dance freely, we'd better go out with a bang. Live this night to the fullest. Because after this, it's time to kiss it all goodbye.*

Ando had promised his sister Mariko, who was working at a hospital in Yokohama, to meet at Blue Max that evening. He had only seen her once since returning to Yokosuka three weeks ago.

The dance number ended and the couples began moving back to their seats. One of the couples caught Ando's eye: a white man in a sailor's uniform and a woman in a red dress. It was Mariko. She turned toward the sailor and flashed an innocent smile at him. Her cheeks were flushed.

Perhaps she was a little tired. When she spotted Ando, her eyes gleamed with obvious joy.

Mariko was a tall and expressive woman. Like Ando she was of mixed blood, but her face looked more Asian than his. She had a high forehead and light brown eyes. Her attractively small nose was a typical one for a Japanese, but she had a large mouth that made people mistake her for a big talker. Her teeth were beautifully white and even (she was proud of them). She had tied her wavy black hair up in a knot.

"Sorry I came a little early," said Mariko as she approached Ando, taking both of his hands in her own. Her palms were moist with sweat. "You've put on some weight. You're looking good!"

"Last time we met I'd just gotten back from the front. I must've looked a bit rough," agreed Ando, squeezing his sister's hands. "You look pretty tonight. Nobody would guess you're a nurse."

"Really? How do you like the dress?" asked Mariko, with a little twirl. Ando remembered it as one that he had bought in the Joint Protectorate in Shanghai two years ago. Made of Chinese silk.

"I gave that to you, didn't I?"

"Yup. You said you bought it at a shop called Madam something-or-other in Shanghai. This is only the second time I've worn it."

"Was the size okay?"

"I had it altered a little to bring in the waist. But other than that, it was perfect. And you're looking nice in your suit tonight, Keiichi." As she said this, Mariko reached and fixed Ando's tie.

"It's getting hard to find a reason to wear one these days."

"Looks like you're not the only one who thinks so. The other customers seem to think tonight's their last chance, too. These days, you get looks if you wear anything except that five-button national uniform."

"Remember that song that went, 'I'm in my blue suit, I've got a spring in my step'? That was a big hit. Feels like ages ago."

"That was only three years ago! Keiichi, would you believe people are giving me a hard time about my hair? They think I had it permed!"

Several of Ando's acquaintances dropped by to chat. Some shared his passion for music, while others were simply regulars. The customers seemed to have had quite a bit to drink already. Ando looked out over a sea of reddening eyes. It appeared everyone was trying their damndest to get liquored up and to get in the mood to hit the dance floor.

The women looked flashier and more beautiful than ever. They all seemed to be wearing their best dresses. Their necklaces and earrings seemed to glitter a lot more than usual. Tonight could well be their last chance to dress up. More than a few were probably wearing every shiny thing they owned. Gazing at the crowd, Ando remembered the new law regulating the production and sale of items deemed "extravagant" by the government. It had taken effect just before his transfer to Hankow earlier that year.

Ando and Mariko sat facing one another. They shared their table with an elderly couple. The four spoke for a while. It turned out that the old man was a former sailor and that his wife loved to dance. They said they were devastated about Blue Max closing down and couldn't miss their last chance to see the place.

"Where's your next mission?" Mariko asked Ando.

"Europe," replied Ando, ignoring Ohnuki's gag order.

"Europe?" Mariko's eyes narrowed. "There's a war going on over there."

"That's right. I'm being transferred from one battlefield to another. From China to Europe. On the bright side, they're sending me to Berlin."

"Are you going as a fighter pilot?"

"No. Just as a transport pilot. I'm not going to the front." *Well, that's close enough that Mariko won't get mad at me afterwards. And I can tell Ohnuki I kept the most important part a secret.* "It's top-secret."

"Is it going to be dangerous?"

"Like any military flight, I guess."

"But Berlin is so far away. How far is it from Tokyo?"

"I'm not going on foot. Don't worry."

"When are you leaving?"

"End of next month."

"When are you coming back?"

"No idea. Haven't been told anything about coming back."

A waiter came over. Ando ordered a Scotch and soda.

"Are you playing tonight?" asked the waiter. "There's only a few hours left."

"If I feel like it," said Ando. The waiter left. "So how about you? How's life?"

"Me?" Mariko looked up. "I'm okay."

"How's work?"

"Same old, same old. It's backbreaking—we've got too many responsibilities. We're always short-staffed."

"Do you still like being a nurse?"

"It's all I know how to do. I can't switch jobs now. Anyway, I hope it doesn't sound like I don't like what I'm doing."

"You've been doing this for a while. How old are you now?"

"Twenty-seven."

"Can't be easy being single at your age."

"I know. That's what everyone tells me. But what can I do? I can't get married to myself."

The music reached a crescendo. It was too loud to talk. Mariko raised her cocktail glass and took a sip. The bright smile from just a few minutes ago had vanished from her face.

Ando sat up a little straighter.

"What happened with the doctor?" he blurted out. The question had been on the tip of his tongue the entire evening. He hadn't dared ask three weeks ago. He could tell the man was still on her mind. But she didn't reply. She just looked down and shook her head slightly.

Ando waited a minute longer, hoping she might say something. But she didn't. It was clear she didn't want to talk about it.

Ando regretted having asked her the question. As worried as he was, he had no right acting like an inquisitor. He was talking about her relationship, for God's sake. He could have softened the question—no, avoided it altogether. A waiter placed a glass in front of Ando, who snatched it and downed the drink.

An acquaintance of Ando's who worked at an importing firm took the table next to theirs. The firm dealt with lauan wood from the South Pacific. He was close to forty and an avid fan of the nightlife. Ando introduced him to Mariko.

"I'm happy to hear that this lovely lady is your sister," said the man. "I was just wondering how I could get to know her. May I dance with her?"

Ando spread his hands to say, *That's up to her!*

The smile returned to Mariko's face. She seemed to be trying to shake off Ando's question.

"Sure. I'll dance."

Extending her hand towards the man, Mariko stood up. He took it, and the two walked towards the dance floor.

Just after Mariko left, a woman approached Ando's table. She was a singer, a friend of Ando's. He called her Yuki but he didn't know if it was her real name or a stage name. She looked about the same age as him; a boyish haircut topped a small face with decidedly feline eyes. She wore a gold china-doll dress.

"When did you get back to Japan? I didn't know you were here," she said, slurring her words a little. Same old Yuki.

"Just a little while ago," Ando replied, casually.

"How was Shanghai? I hear dance halls are huge over there!"

"I don't know for how long, though," said Ando, pointing at the chair where Mariko had been sitting. "I bet the dance halls in Hongkou'll get caught up in the war too. Could be shut down any day."

Yuki sat on the chair and crossed her legs, exposing her pale white thighs.

"Think I can find a job in the joint protectorate?"

"I don't know. I'm not in the entertainment industry."

"Don't be cold."

"I get that a lot."

"How many girls have told you that, I wonder?"

"More than a hundred."

"I believe you."

"I wasn't lying."

"Did you have someone back in Shanghai?"

"When? This time, or last time?"

"Both times."

"The Army brass in Hongkou are crazy about dancers and singers. Some become their mistresses. No room for me."

"But the Japanese Protectorate wasn't the only place you hung out, was it? What about the Joint Protectorate? How did you like the White Russian girls?"

"Couldn't tell you. I was there to fight a war, not to screw."

"But you went to Shanghai, didn't you? Shanghai. Sounds so charming. Romantic."

"How about Nanking? And don't forget Chungking."

"You really know how to bring a girl down! Come on, tell me about the women in Shanghai. I heard they've got some serious luxuries. While here we can't even get a perm! Don't tell me you didn't touch women over there."

"Will you please stop talking about this when my sister comes back?"

Yuki snorted and took a cigarette from her bag. She lit it, inhaled deeply, and exhaled a cloud of smoke as she scanned the dance floor.

"The band got so excited when she showed up," remarked Yuki.

"Bet they were disappointed to find out she was my sister."

"Nobody wants trouble with the famous Ando," laughed Yuki.

"Smart move." Ando sipped his Scotch. "Looks to me like someone didn't get it, though."

"Huh?"

The music ended and the crowd burst into applause. The customers were whistling, hooting, and cheering. Even Ando started clapping.

Blue Max was different that night. Most of the customers were regulars. Very few knew anything of each other outside of the place, but that night, everyone was an old friend, united in a solidarity that only people enjoying themselves for one last time can feel. Like partners in crime, sharing a secret.

The party was at full swing, maybe a little too full. The excitement of the crowd drove the band to play all the harder, spurring the customers to party even harder.

That night at Blue Max, every man was a player. Every woman was a knockout. The excitement in the room was palpable.

Ando's friends persuaded him to pick up his trumpet and take the stage. He played two swing numbers with the band, his horn alternating between passionate and sad, perfectly suited for the final night of Blue Max. As he ended his songs, several women, Yuki among them, grabbed for Ando and showered him with kisses. Yuki still hanging on one arm, Ando dragged himself back to the table where Mariko waited for him.

CHAPTER 23

At nine in the evening, Blue Max remained packed to capacity and no one showed any sign of leaving. Rather, customers kept pouring in. The waiters brought out some cheap chairs from their room in the back, but there were simply too many people to serve. Dozens of people stood talking and drinking. It was as crowded as a train during rush hour. The entrance door was kept open for ventilation. Some of the customers had stepped outside for a breath of fresh air.

Yamawaki appeared at the entrance. He searched the faces of the crowd, looking for one in particular. Ando noticed and signaled Yamawaki to come over. Yamawaki twisted and angled through the dense crowd.

"Looking for me?" asked Ando. "What could possibly be so important that you've come to catch me here again?"

"I'm not on duty," replied Yamawaki. He studied Mariko out of the corner of his eye. "I liked the look of the place when I visited last time."

"Well, this is the last day it's going to be open. Did you know that?"

"I heard every dance hall in Tokyo is going hard tonight. I came to enjoy the scene for one last time."

"Things are getting pretty tense these days."

"We may both be at war, but things are so different in Berlin."

Noticing that Yamawaki couldn't keep his eyes off of Mariko, Ando introduced the two.

"This is my younger sister, Mariko."

"Hi. Junzo Yamawaki. I work at the Ministry of the Navy. Lately I've been working with your brother," said Yamawaki, bowing slightly.

Mariko immediately stood up and bowed. "Thank you for looking after my brother," she said.

"He's handling my next mission," Ando told Mariko. "He just returned from Berlin." *I hope she won't let on that I told her about the mission.*

"It's nice to meet you," said Mariko, bowing slightly again.

"The pleasure's all mine," replied Yamawaki.

Yamawaki and Mariko continued to look at each other. There was surprise in Yamawaki's eyes, like he'd seen something amazing for the first time. Mariko noticed the look on his face and wondered why.

Part Two

"M-Miss Ando, do you come here often?" stammered Yamawaki.

"No, this is my first time." Mariko smiled modestly. "My brother told me all about this place, but he never did invite me here. So tonight's my first, and I guess last time."

"This is my second time. I first met your brother here, a week ago."

"Here? You didn't meet him at the base?"

"No. I was told that he'd be here. Playing the trumpet."

"Ah. It's his hobby. He even took his trumpet with him to the front."

"Do you like dancing, Miss Ando?"

"Yes I do. How about yourself, Mr. Yamawaki?"

"I'm not very good at it, but I'm working on it," said Yamawaki, now studying Ando from the corner of his eye. "This is silly, just standing here. Would you mind dancing with me?"

Mariko shot Ando a glance. She seemed to be begging for his permission. It appeared the interest was mutual.

Ando nodded. Then, he said to Yamawaki:

"Let me buy you a drink. What'll you have?"

"Whatever you're having, lieutenant."

Yamawaki extended a hand towards Mariko, who took it. They smiled at each other and walked toward the dance floor.

Man oh man. Ando wasn't surprised Yamawaki could be dapper. But he didn't expect Mariko to agree to dance with him so quickly. Ando felt a stir in himself that he hadn't when the man from the trading house had asked Mariko to dance. He somehow couldn't believe Mariko had accepted Yamawaki's request without hesitation.

Yuki came up to Ando again.

"Your sister's Miss Popular tonight," she said, wrapping an arm around Ando's neck.

"I dunno. You're flashier than her. Everyone loved your number."

"Think I might do well in Shanghai?"

"Still thinking about that?"

"What's left for me in Yokohama? Idiot soldiers and jealous old hags. I don't want to become a street performer. I'm going to Shanghai."

"If you can blind yourself to the reality unfolding outside of it, the joint protectorate can be a fun place."

"What do you really think about the war? Are things going to get worse? Or are we nearing the end?"

"Don't ask me. But I don't see any sign of things letting up in China."

"Everybody says we'll be fighting the United States and England next."

"That's very possible."

"Maybe I shouldn't have fallen in love with a fighter pilot."

Ando looked at Yuki. She was serious.

"Look," she said, "I just don't want to end up with the short end of the stick. I've got a sax player who thinks he's God's gift to women, a factory owner who spends money like it's water, and a fighter pilot who's cold as a cucumber. Go on, tell me: who should I pick?"

"I'd say forget the fighter pilot."

Yuki turned away from Ando and sat down in Mariko's chair.

"You see, that's what I think, too. Don't you worry, I'll go to Shanghai all by myself. But if you happen to go back to China, we might run into each other."

Ando commandeered a waiter and ordered two Scotches with soda. Yuki smiled at Ando and pleaded with her eyes. He added a martini to the order.

After a while, Yamawaki and Mariko returned to the table. Both of them were breathing hard. Sweat beaded on Yawamaki's forehead.

"I heard you told Miss Ando that you were flying to Berlin," said Yamawaki. He didn't sound particularly angry. Perhaps it was because he was civilian staff.

"I didn't tell her any of the details," replied Ando.

"Just don't talk about it again. I'm asking you two not to. Please."

"Anyway, Mr. Yamawaki," said Mariko, changing the subject. "I'd love to hear about your trip to Berlin. Did you see an opera there? Wagner or Verdi?"

Ando and Yuki stood up and gave their chairs to Yamawaki and Mariko.

Yuki took Ando's hand and led him to the dance floor. Blue Max wasn't a large place, so customers took turns using the chairs to avoid squabbles. Ando and Yuki first danced a waltz, then a fox trot.

An hour later, the owner of Blue Max took the floor to thank his customers for their support. He had just turned fifty, he said, and he used to work in a hotel before opening the bar. He had also lived in Singapore for a while.

"If I ever get another shot at running this kind of business," he said, "it'll be another bar with the same name. I don't know when and where it'll pop up, but I firmly believe that it will. In fact, I'm under the impression that it has to happen. I look forward to seeing you all again then."

The waiters handed out clean glasses and poured champagne for all. The owner announced that it was on the house, to thunderous cheers from the patrons, and proposed a toast to everyone's health on this, the last night of Blue Max. The crowd applauded. Some of the customers had brought noisemakers and began setting them off.

The band began playing again. It was a jitterbug, and the customers started returning to the dance floor. One couple appeared semi-pro at least, and people moved away to give them more room. Entranced, other dancers stopped and began cheering them on halfway through the song. The party was in full swing.

Suddenly, a clamor sounded from across the room. The music stopped, squealing to an end like a deflating balloon.

Ando looked up in shock. The couple on the dance floor stopped dancing and stared at the entrance. Those at the tables broke off their conversations and looked one and all in the same direction.

It was a group of five or six, casting long shadows in the light of the doorway. Two were men in khaki-colored national uniforms. The rest were middle-aged women wearing very conservative clothing. One woman wore a white sash. Ando couldn't make out the words written on it.

The party-crashers surveyed the scene with evident contempt. The dance floor emptied as the couples returned to their tables. No one said a word.

An old man in national uniform, complete with gaiters, strode to the center of the now-empty dance floor. It was easy to tell from his bearing and posture that he was a retired military officer. He frowned and shook his head with emotion.

The rest of the group followed him to the floor, their footsteps echoing through the silent bar. A clean-shaven young man who appeared to be freshly discharged from military service looked around and leered. He held a wooden sword in his hand.

The woman with the sash was plump, with a dark-colored sweater and a long skirt. She appeared to be around forty years old. The light illuminated her sash. It read:

National Moral Mobilization Committee

The owner walked up to the old man in gaiters.

"It was my understanding that our permit extended until midnight."

"The neighbors are complaining about the ruckus." The old man sounded arrogant and unrelenting.

"Tonight's our last night, so we're a bit more crowded than usual. I'll make sure the door stays closed to keep in the noise."

"Who are these people? Are they all Japanese?"

"We have several foreign customers here. But most are Japanese."

"Aping the hairy barbarians like a bunch of monkeys!" shouted the man. "What's wrong with you people? What kind of music is this? What kind of filthy dancing is this? Are you adults or children?"

"If we upset you, I apologize. At midnight it'll be all over, for good."

The customers followed the exchange intently. The committee had no actual authority to shut the place down, but nobody wanted trouble. Still, Blue Max hadn't been ordered to shut down until midnight; it could operate freely until then, committee or not.

"Look at those women! Every woman in here is wearing jewelry. Shame on you! All of you!" shouted the elderly man in gaiters. "The Moral Committee is dedicated to preventing civilian extravagance! And the corruption of standards of public decency! We support the government by ensuring that all citizens adhere to national policy!"

"We are all aware of that," replied the owner, the politeness of his tone not wavering for an instant. "And, in keeping with national policy, we are closing down at midnight."

"Look at the men in here!" said the woman with the sash. "Every one of them in a suit and tie! How can you dress like this when our soldiers in China are covered in mud and blood? You call yourselves Japanese?"

"I didn't choose to be born Japanese," murmured someone in the back. The committee woman's head spun in the direction of the voice. Her eyebrows arched. Nobody said another word.

The woman with the sash signaled to the women behind her. Each held a deck of white cards. Each card was the size of a business card.

Part Two

Warning cards, thought Ando. He remembered Yuki telling him that she'd received one on several occasions. The committee members handed them out to women on the street that they felt didn't live according to public standards. The cards contained warnings like "Tone down your attire" or "Now is your chance to get rid of ornaments."

The women from the committee strode into the crowd and thrust cards into the faces of women. Heads cast downwards, they accepted the cards and placed them on their tables.

"You had your hair permed, didn't you? Look at the lipstick on your mouth! You look like you've been feasting on human flesh. How dare you wear jewelry when we're at war?" spat the committee women as they made their way to each female customer.

The atmosphere had been completely poisoned. The band members stared off in different directions. The customers kept their mouths shut, their expressions blank. The waiters stood perfectly still. Blue Max was dead quiet save for the voices of the committee women echoing through the hall.

The woman in the sash had finished giving out cards to the female customers closest to the dance floor. She tried to wade further into the crowd, but chairs filled every bit of available space.

"May I have one, too?" said Mariko, suddenly standing up. Her voice was bright and innocent, the voice of a child begging for candy from her mother.

Ando and others looked up at her, alarmed. Mariko winked at her brother. Her eyes were sparkling with mischief. The patrons parted to make way for her.

The sash woman's eyes opened wide.

Mariko, a bright smile on her face, walked up to her. The woman hesitated slightly before giving Mariko the warning card. Mariko quickly pinned the card to her chest. It looked like a white flower on her red dress. The women from the committee couldn't believe it.

"Are you Japanese?" asked the sash woman dubiously.

"Of course," answered Mariko. "And I think moderation is important."

Ando stood up and caught the band members' eyes. He spun a finger to signal them to start playing again. They nodded at each other and resumed, somewhat hesitantly, the jitterbug that had been playing when the

153

committee arrived.

Ando stepped forth and took long strides to where Mariko stood. He approached the woman with the sash, snatched a card from her hand, and stuck it halfway-in into his pocket as if it were a handkerchief.

Then he extended both hands toward Mariko, who accepted them with a smile. Ando nodded to the band. The music kicked up a notch, and brother and sister began dancing.

The members of the committee looked around uncomfortably. The young man with the wooden sword cast nervous glances about him.

Yuki took Yamawaki's hand and walked out to the dance floor. Yamawaki seemed to be enjoying the scene. The old man in the gaiters caught a glimpse of Yuki's exposed thigh. He gulped uncomfortably as she plucked a warning card from his fingers.

She said, "You wouldn't believe how extravagant I am. I'm wearing silk panties right now!" She gave her behind a sexy wriggle for the old man to see, and then touched his mustache with her card.

"You…you whore!" yelled the old man, stepping backward.

"Right on!" cried Yuki, pulling up her dress to expose both her thighs. "Oh, please scold me! I'm so naughty!"

Yamawaki took Yuki's hand and spun her. She threw a kiss to the young man with his wooden sword as she glided past him.

Couples began returning to the dance floor. The pair of amazing dancers also took to the floor.

The committee ended up being pushed off the dance floor by the growing number of couples. They moved farther and farther back until finally they were at the exit. The band was playing louder than ever. Clamoring conversations resumed. Waiters began serving drinks again. The owner flashed a smirk at the old man in the gaiters.

The sash-woman opened her mouth. She shouted something, pretty short it was, just a word or two, perhaps "Traitors!" Whatever it was, it was drowned in the din of music, dancing feet, and laughter. Defeated, the members of the National Moral Mobilization Committee retreated from the club, returning to the shadows from where they had come.

CHAPTER 24

Less than ten days after Ryojiro Shibata returned to Delhi from Eastern Bengal, he was already preparing for another trip. Gaj Singh, lord of Kamanipur, had invited Shibata to visit his palace. The meeting concerned Shibata's request for a refueling stop for aircraft. Gaj Singh seemed intrigued, and offered to discuss the matter in further detail. *Sounds friendly enough,* thought Shibata, *but I'd better go and make sure.*

Shibata boarded a trans-Indian express at Delhi station bound for Jodhpur and arrived on the morning of November 7th. Jodhpur was located at the tip of the Thar Desert, which strethced across northwest India. The city was some 600 kilometers from Delhi. The old city in Jodhpur was surrounded by castle-like walls. Fort Meherangarh, in the center of town, was particularly impressive. It was clear that this place had endured more than its share of wars. Jodhpur was a tough-looking fortress of a city.

Kamanipur was roughly 100 kilometers southwest of Jodhpur. Normally, to get there, one had to take a train from Jodhpur to Hyderabad in Baluchistan, then switch to another line. But Gaj Singh had told Shibata to head to the airport in Jodhpur instead, where a private plane would be waiting for him.

As soon as Shibata arrived in Jodhpur, he left the station and found a hotel. First things first, he ordered a cup of coffee. His hemp pants and jacket had been heavily wrinkled during the overnight trip. He had wanted to appear clean and pressed before the Maharaja, who followed Western customs, but there wasn't time to launder his clothes now. Instead he went to a restroom to wash and shave his face.

The airport in Jodhpur was located near the edge of the city. He could see the walls of the old city in the distance. Two dome-shaped hangars stood side by side on the hard yellow earth of the airport. Several single-engine biplanes and a double-engine transport, scorched and faded by the blistering desert sun, sat in front of the hangars.

As Shibata climbed down from the rickshaw he had taken, a short Caucasian man approached him. He wore a pair of loose tweed pants and a short leather jacket, and his face was covered with blonde stubble.

"Are you a Japanese man named Shibata?" asked the man in American English.

"Yes, I am," nodded Shibata. "Were you sent by Lord Singh to pick me up?"

"I'm Jim Parvis," said the man. "But you can call me Jim. I'm an American. I work for the Maharaja. He asked me to take you to him."

An American! Shibata could barely hide his discomfort. Jim may have been a civilian, but Shibata didn't want any Americans or Brits, least of all pilots, getting involved in this project.

Jim took off his white gloves and extended his right hand to Shibata. Shibata shook it. *Better keep an eye on this one.*

"Bring any luggage?" asked Jim.

"Just this," said Shibata, pointing at his leather bag.

Jim turned toward an Indian boy who stood waiting in the shade of one of the hangars. The boy ran to take Shibata's bag.

"Do you like airplanes?" asked Jim.

"I can't fly them," answered Shibata, "but I like flying in them."

"Truth be told, the plane's pretty long in the tooth. The other day, when I brought it to pick up another guest of the Maharaja, the guy turned around and left as soon as he set eyes on it. I'm wondering how you'll react."

"Is it really that old?"

"It's a 'Jenny.' Ever heard of one?"

Shibata shook his head.

Jim began walking. Shibata walked alongside him.

"It's a Curtiss." Jim pointed at a two-seat biplane painted in bright orange. "A Curtiss JN4D."

Shibata remembered the name. The Curtiss JN4D had been used to train pilots in the U.S. during World War I. That made the model at least twenty years old. Considering the developments in aviation technology since then, by all rights the JN4D ought to have been encountered in a museum. *If the planes that Gaj Singh boasted about are JN4Ds, what's his private airfield going to be like?*

Shibata recalled his disappointment at seeing the polo field in Eastern Bengal. *Are they going to show me some kind of dirt road? Is that going to be Gaj Singh's idea of aviation...?*

"What's wrong? " asked Jim. "You look pale."

"I'm fine," replied Shibata, trying to conceal his disappointment. "I like airplanes that have two sets of wings. I still have a hard time believing that monoplanes can fly."

Jim laughed and slapped Shibata on the shoulder.

"The Maharaja also owns a Junkers F13 that can carry four, but unfortunately it had already left for Bombay. So I had to pick you up in this trainer here."

Junkers F13? Shibata didn't have any idea what that plane looked like, but he assumed anything that could carry four passengers wouldn't be a toy. That meant Gaj Singh's airfield could be a decent one. Shibata started feeling better.

Shibata walked up and began studying the Curtiss JN4D. Actually, the biplane didn't appear to be in bad shape. It obviously hadn't been left exposed to the elements for twenty years or pushed through aerobatics day after day. Quite a few parts of the plane had worn out and lost their original hue, but all of the exposed metal and wood had been polished to a sheen. Some sort of skilled repair work had been done on the wings. Whatever else it might turn out to be, Shibata could tell the aircraft was, at least, well-maintained.

"It's an old model," said Jim. "But it's in pretty good shape because I've been swapping out parts with other Jennys. I've overhauled the engine three times. I'm telling you, this is the best Jenny in the skies today."

"What do you mean?" asked Shibata.

"Over the last ten years, I've bought up every Jenny I could, taking them apart and salvaging the best parts. Of course, I bought new ones, too, when I could. The wings and the chain on the steering column, they're all new. This baby doesn't have many original parts left."

"You like it that much?"

"I learned to fly on it. It's like my first woman."

"Ah, so you're being faithful. A lot of men hop around, you know."

For a moment, Jim looked mildly embarrassed despite himself. Then he smiled and stroked the plane's orange skin gently.

"My first flight was with the Army Air Corps. I was eighteen. The war ended twenty hours later, so I didn't get the chance to try anything more! Maybe if I'd been born a year earlier, I could've been in a dogfight. I could've gotten the chance to take on Richthofen!"

"So you haven't flown anything else?"

"Eh, I've flown others. A few British and German planes."

Jim mentioned the handful of planes he had flown, the Standard J1,

Thomas Morse S-4 and SE-5, the Fokker D VII. Shibata knew all of them were biplanes that had last seen use during World War I.

Shibata asked Jim how he'd gotten by his unique experience. It turned out the Yankee had worked as a barnstormer in an air circus in 1925-26. The marketplace had been flooded with skilled pilots fresh out of the war; it could not have been easy for Jim to get in with the circus. Of course, he said, he started as an apprentice. He worked his way up from wing-walking to the aerobatic team as other pilot-performers died in one accident after another. The circus used old surplus from the war in Europe, giving Jim the opportunity to fly some of the most famous aircraft that Germany and Britain had produced.

"Soon enough, though, airplanes just weren't as interesting as they'd once been in America," said Jim. "After the circus split up, I bought a Jenny myself. I flew her solo, to Canada and South America. I eventually even made it out to Australia. I scraped together a living wherever I could, and finally found myself here in India."

Jim pointed to the little flags painted on the tail of his plane.

"You've shot down that many?" asked Shibata. There were more than twenty different flags.

"No!" laughed Jim. "Those are the flags of the countries that my Jenny and I've been to. Haven't had the good fortune to fly to Japan yet, though. Think they'd be interested in seeing some aerobatics out there?"

"Maybe in the countryside."

"I remember the first time I flew in Java. That was ten years ago. The villagers surrounded my plane, they were so excited. The girls just couldn't get enough of me. I felt like an angel descended upon Earth!"

I suppose I could do worse than this scruffy-looking angel, thought Shibata.

Jim walked up to his plane and pulled a flight helmet and goggles from a haversack under the wing. He tossed them to Shibata. Shibata strapped on the helmet.

"Just say the word," said Jim.

"Anytime's good for me."

"Don't worry, okay," said Jim, patting Shibata on the shoulder. "We're not flying to the moon. It's just a half-hour trip."

The Jenny taxied to the dirt runway and roared into the sky. To

Shibata, the takeoff felt nearly vertical; there was a tremendous weight on his body for a few moments, followed by a disorienting feeling of lightness. He felt the airframe tremble and heard the wings squeak and groan. Before he knew it, a vista of yellow earth and blue sky spread before his eyes.

Once the vibrations had subsided, Shibata finally dared to look down. He watched Fort Meherangarh recede in the distance off to the right. Shibata realized that they were still gaining altitude and let out a sigh of relief.

The ride smoothed out considerably once the Jenny began flying horizontally. Jim flew due southwest, keeping the railroad tracks on his left as a landmark. Soon the ground below them turned into a total wasteland, devoid of woods, fields, and farms. Just yellow dirt extending to the horizon. Someone had to be dwelling down there, raising crops or sheep or something. But from Shibata's vantage point of one thousand feet, the area appeared forsaken.

Half an hour later, Shibata spotted a village ahead. Before long it became clear that the "village" was actually a walled city like Jodhpur. In fact, enormous walls encircled the entire city, with what looked like a palace in the dead center of it all. Quite a few houses stood outside of the walls as well. The city seemed to have been built atop a fertile oasis, for the walls were surrounded by plants and vegetation.

The plane began its descent. Shibata could now make out human figures walking along the streets. The city covered about two square kilometers. The population, he guessed, was somewhere around 50,000. The main street leading downtown from the city gate was thronged with people. The palace sat at the end of the street, surrounded by four towers.

Jim circled the downtown area and headed away from the city. Roughly a kilometer away was a compound with a neat row of huts and several parked cars. It appeared to be the Maharaja's training facility.

As Shibata expected, the plane descended sharply towards the area. They came in for a landing, bounced once, and rolled to a stop.

Jim cut the plane's engine. Shibata unstrapped his flight helmet. Several young Indians ran toward the plane. Each of them wore khaki pants and shirts with orange insignia. After being helped down from the plane by one of the Indians, Shibata looked around at the training facility.

The runway was nothing more than packed dirt. In fact, aside from a pair of windsocks, there wasn't any particular way to tell where the runway ended and where the desert began. If they called the area between the windsocks their runway, it was a good 800 meters long. At any rate, it looked better than the runway that Das had shown him the other day. There wasn't much risk of running out of room. Shibata also noticed, a short distance away from the other buildings, a brick warehouse that looked like it might be a hangar.

The buildings that Shibata had thought were huts from the air turned out to be barracks. Five stood in a neat row. Each was as large as a Japanese public school building, and they appeared to be totally identical. Did each one house a company, perhaps? A small but sturdy-looking brick edifice behind the barracks seemed to be a depot for either weapons or ammunition. Another brick house, some way off from the barracks and depot, appeared to be either the headquarters or the officers' billet. An orange flag fluttered in the wind atop a tall flagpole. Orange seemed to be the official color of the Kingdom of Kamanipur.

An elderly man wearing a yellow striped turban stepped out from behind a car parked next to the pole. He wore a jacket with a vertical collar and a thick, striped belt.

"Welcome, Mr. Shibata. I will take you to the lord," said the man in perfect, British-inflected English.

Shibata shot Jim a glance.

"He's a steward," said Jim. "He'll take you to the palace. My job's done."

CHAPTER 25

The car passed through the gate and headed down the main street towards downtown. The road was wide, some fifteen meters across, and lined on both sides with similar-looking two-story buildings. They appeared to be shops. Shibata was somewhat surprised to see the variety of merchandise on display. The street was full of people in bright clothing, camels, and horse-drawn wagons. If this street was any indication, Gaj Singh was quite successful at managing his property.

The street ended in a public square with a stone well in the center. The pavement around the well was dark with spilled water. A group of ten camels rested nearby.

The palace stood directly in front of the square. A pair of guards in blue uniforms flanked the gate, behind which was a large building with a domed roof. It appeared to be made out of some sort of brown stone, with watchtowers on both sides. A plethora of turrets and observation slits watched over the square and main street. The strong sunlight of the Thar Desert threw the complex design of the walls into sharp relief.

The car passed through the palace gate, into a paved garden, and parked by the front veranda of the palace. A statue of a warrior on camelback stood on either side of the porch. More guards in blue uniforms were stationed next to the pedestals of the statues. A young man dressed in black appeared and opened the door of the car. Shibata stepped out and handed his bag to him.

Shibata climbed the stone steps of the veranda into the entrance hall. A huge pair of double doors stood at the end of the hall, and two men in red turbans and black uniforms flanked the doors. Black probably meant the Maharaja's servants, blue his guards. The men in black pushed the doors open as soon as Shibata and the old steward approached.

They entered a large hall with a dome-shaped roof. The doors closed behind them. They took a central staircase to a corridor that extended along a wall beneath the dome. They followed the corridor to another long straight hallway that was covered with traditional paintings in the West Indian style. The handrails and columns in the hallway were intricately carved and detailed. The interior was indescribably luxurious, decorated in tones of orange and gold. Sculptures, some carved from ivory and others from ebony wood, were displayed along the length of the hallway. In contrast to the scorching heat outside, the interior of the palace was cool and refreshing.

Shibata followed the steward down the hallway and through an arch guarded by another man in a blue uniform. They seemed to have entered the left wing of the palace.

"This is the Chamber of the Lion," said the steward, pointing at a door in the middle of the hallway.

The room had a high ceiling and was decorated entirely in yellows. It was large enough to have swallowed a pair of Jenny-sized planes with ease. An enormous tapestry hung on one wall. A lion-skin rug covered the floor in front of the tapestry. A low table surrounded by floor-cushions woven from gold thread sat in the center of the room, topped by a glass bowl filled with various kinds of fruits. One wall featured a large window. Shibata could see a pond in the courtyard outside.

The steward opened the door opposite the tapestry to reveal a bedroom. Shibata saw a huge bed with a canopy inside.

"There is a western-style bathroom over there. I assume you must be very tired from the long trip. Please make yourself at home," said the steward.

"Would you mind ironing my clothes? I'd like to freshen up a bit," asked Shibata.

"The bell on the desk will call the maid. Feel free to ask for anything you like."

"When might I be able to meet with the lord? How much free time do I have?"

"Dinner will be served at seven o'clock. Please feel free to rest until then."

Shibata took a leisurely bath in the large bathroom. The clock had just struck two. Shibata began to feel that he had a little too much free time on his hands. *I can fit in two or three long baths before dinner, I guess.*

Shibata realized that he was quite hungry after stepping out of his bath. *Should I ring the bell and have them bring something, or head into town instead?* Shibata considered his lunch options as he walked into the Chamber of the Lion. He was somewhat surprised to see a prepared meal and chilled bottle of wine sitting atop the table. Shibata shrugged, pulled the cork, and sat down to eat.

Part Two

After he finished his late lunch, he realized that he had absolutely nothing to do until dinner. He knew it would be a mistake to continue drinking the wine until evening fell, so he decided to take a stroll around the palace grounds instead. If there was anything they didn't want Shibata to see, no doubt a guard or steward would stop him. Shibata decided to have a look around until someone hollered.

The palace reminded Shibata of nothing so much as a museum. He went up and down many different staircases. At last he reached a garden behind the left wing of the palace. The garden had been arranged in the French manner, with various grasses and shrubbery arranged in a geometric pattern. The sound of something being hit, and of bouncing, echoed through the air. Shibata also heard a woman's voice.

Shibata followed the sound around a large hedge to find a tennis court. A white man and an Indian woman appeared to be in the middle of a match. The man looked about sixty years old. He wore white pants with a matching white shirt and vest. Even his mustache was white. The Indian girl was about fifteen years old. She was dressed in white as well. Judging from the presence of a maid-like woman on either end of the net, the girl was likely one of the Maharaja's daughters.

The Indian girl noticed Shibata, swung her racket, and missed the ball. It bounced and rolled toward his foot.

Shibata picked up the ball. The girl flashed a shy smile.

"Let's stop for now, Mr. Haywood," she said.

"That's fine, Miss Dia. That's game set," said the man.

As the girl walked off the tennis court, a servant rushed over with a parasol to shade her.

Shibata bounced the ball. The Caucasian man daubed his forehead with a handkerchief as he approached Shibata. He was breathing heavily. He was a tall man, with an oval face and blue eyes. His hair was thinning and white.

"You must be a guest," said the man. "Japanese, am I right?"

"Yes, I was invited here by the Maharaja. My name is Shibata."

"My name is Haywood. I'm English. A tutor," said the man, extending his right hand. Shibata shook it.

"You teach tennis?"

"Oh no, not at all. I teach English, geography, history, and western culture. Tennis is simply one aspect of that. To be honest, I prefer sitting behind a desk."

"Is she the Maharaja's daughter?"

"Indeed she is. His second daughter, to be precise."

"How many children does the Maharaja have?"

"Five. His eldest son is studying abroad, in the United States, at the moment. Another son attends a boarding school in Delhi. The rest live here in the palace. Are you here on business, pray tell?"

"Yes. I'm here to discuss the Maharaja's copper mine."

"You came all the way from Delhi?"

"Yes. I arrived in Jodhpur just this morning. Jim and his airplane brought me the rest of the way. You know Jim, I take it?"

"Not very well, I'm afraid. He spends most of his time at the airfield. I, on the other hand, spend nearly all my time inside the palace with the Maharaja's family."

When he said this, Haywood didn't sound particularly warm. Perhaps he and Jim had had a falling out. Or perhaps Haywood just didn't like Americans, Shibata couldn't tell. In any event, he wasn't surprised at all to find someone like Haywood here. With his flashy, Oxford-cadenced English, Haywood seemed like yet another of the British intellectuals that Shibata had encountered so often in Kuala Lumpur and Delhi.

Shibata tossed the tennis ball back to Haywood.

"We shall meet again at dinner tonight," said the tutor. "Do enjoy your stay."

The old man gave his racket a little swing as he walked back toward the girl.

CHAPTER 26

Gaj Singh, thirty-seventh Maharaja of the Kingdom of Kamanipur, was born in Delhi in 1901, at the turn of the twentieth century. His father Ahmed was only twenty-two years old at the time.

Gaj Singh, Ahmed's first son, was raised in the royal quarters until he was ten, at which time, following the custom of contemporary Maharajas, he was sent to study in England. Ahmed expected nothing more or less from his son than to maintain their thousand-year-old kingdom and pass it on to the next generation. Ahmed's only fear was that his son would become an ambitious Maharaja. For Ahmed was so conservative that he believed no true Maharaja had any need to aim for greatness. In fact, if anything, he strongly believed that a real leader should be rather timid.

Alas, Ahmed's beliefs and way of life had become all but untenable in Gaj Singh's era. Gone were the days when the prince of a small desert kingdom could spend his days in an idyll of horseback riding and sitar playing. The increasingly tumultuous events of the twentieth century dictated otherwise. The Great War broke out while Gaj Singh was studying at Eton. By the time he entered Oxford, the Romanovs and the Kaiser's regime had disappeared from the face of the earth. Gaj Singh witnessed the falls of these great imperial establishments at an impressionable time in his life and hungered to learn more about the world around him.

In 1919, he received word of the Amritsar Massacre in Punjab. British mercenaries, led by General Reginald Dyer, had opened fire on an assembly of unarmed Indian protesters that included many women and children. A subsequent British investigation found that some four hundred had been killed and more than a thousand injured. The British exercised strict control over the press to cover up the incident. Several months later, however, Indians living in England began hearing about it from tourists returning from India.

Trembling with anger upon hearing the news, Gaj Singh swore revenge. He dedicated himself to pushing the British Empire down the path of the Romanovs. He would see to it himself that they did. Gaj Singh was descended from a tribe of honorable warriors called the Rajput. When the time came, he knew, he would be on the front lines.

When Gaj Singh turned twenty-two, he spent six months on a

"grand tour" across Europe and in the Mediterranean before returning to his father's kingdom in Rajasthan. He brought two cars, a thousand history books, and a quarter share in the Barnes & Patterson Mining Company with him. At the age of twenty-five, Gaj Singh succeeded his father as the thirty-seventh Maharaja of Rajasthan.

Over the next fourteen years, Gaj Singh dedicated himself to supporting the Indian nationalist movement and to steadily increasing his holdings in the mines. He was a pragmatic and eminently practical man who harbored no misconceptions about how bloody the battle against England would be. He knew that Indian victory would be achieved only after a long and arduous battle.

Gaj Singh knew that in order to fight the British forces, Indians would need guns and ammunition. But with the exception of the feudal lords scattered throughout the country, India remained incredibly poor; England had systematically plundered the nation of its wealth. Singh knew that many Indians would join a nationalist army when the time came, but they would need weapons to fight. Thus, he reasoned, procuring weapons and ammunition was nothing less than a duty for the lords of the Indian kingdoms, who could use their special privileges to obtain the needed supplies.

Gaj Singh had fully developed the commercial aspects of his kingdom, fostering successful sheep breeding and wool spinning industries in his realm. At the same time, he sank large amounts of money into outside concerns in an attempt to build his various interests into a single conglomerate. He invested heavily in railroads and public transport systems, warehouses and spinning industries, and purchased a whole mountain with a copper mine. He converted his quarters in Delhi into a hotel, and purchased several tea farms in Assam as well. By 1936, Gaj Singh had become the major stockholder in the second largest bank in Bombay. Fortunately, he had never wanted for money. The combined value of the interior decorations in just one room of his palace was enough to purchase a company. If Ahmed were still alive, there would have been no way for Gaj Singh to do what he was doing. But Ahmed was no longer among the living; and Gaj Singh was the rightful Maharaja of his kingdom. His father's servants remained, but none dared speak out against their new lord.

Gaj Singh also worked hard to strengthen his relationships with neighboring kingdoms. India contained some five hundred native kingdoms. Gaj Singh harbored no misconceptions about the weakness of his kingdom compared to many others. He had his sister marry the prince of Jodhpur. He had his younger brother wed the second daughter of Jaipur. And Gaj Singh himself married a beautiful girl from a powerful kingdom in Kashmir, a descendant of the royal family of Nepal. Gaj Singh rose to become the supreme Maharaja in Rajasthan, a man with unrivalled political power, financial assets, and connections via his in-laws and relatives.

Shibata shook himself back to attention. Gaj Singh had stopped talking. It seemed that Shibata had missed the end of the story. Singh peered into Shibata's face. Shibata nodded quickly in an attempt to conceal embarrassment.

Gaj Singh had been relating the story of his life to Shibata on a palace balcony overlooking a courtyard. They sat on thick cushions. Ten or so musicians sat behind a pond playing traditional songs. The melody that rose through the air of the desert perfectly matched the lord's subdued tone. Even the flame of the torches near the pond flickered as if in time with the music.

"Unfortunately," resumed Gaj Singh, "many of the Maharajas are complacent, satisfied with the privileges that they have been granted by the British. They refuse to open their eyes to the reality, the poverty and misery, of their fellow Indians. They do not care about the humiliation that our country has suffered. Many Maharajas live as decadently as their predecessors during the Mughal Empire, holding banquets night after night while those who work their lands die of hunger. They spend a thousand pounds simply to celebrate a daughter's third birthday. You could build a small clinic with that amount of money!"

Shibata remained silent. The lord continued.

"Most of the other Maharajas see their armies as mere decorations. Can you believe it? They make their soldiers wear flashy costumes and ride on camels to liven up their parades. That's their only use. There are many kingdoms with three hundred servants and only thirty soldiers. I believe those numbers should be reversed. What do you say?" asked Gaj Singh expectantly.

"Lord, I suspect your kingdom is an exception," was Shibata's careful reply.

"You are correct. As I told you the other day, my army has grown large enough to form a battalion now. I have some five hundred men armed with modern weapons. I have ninety servants. The grand chamberlain wouldn't agree, but I think we still have too many of them."

"I suppose you need to spend money to maintain the facade of the kingdom, even if it does feel like a waste."

"It's nonsense! I've never held a banquet with more than forty-eight guests, and I never waste even a single dish then. I keep telling my family that anyone I catch spending foolishly, spending vainly, will be exiled at once. I've said again and again that we can have our parties once India obtains its freedom and independence. We'll sell some of our treasures and use the proceeds for an entire week of singing, dancing, and cheering with my subjects. But until that day, I don't have a single rupee to waste."

"May I ask you something, my lord," asked Shibata. The matter had been nagging at Shibata ever since first meeting Gaj Singh in Delhi. He needed to clear it up.

"What is your view of the Indian independence movement? The Indian National Congress seems ambivalent, to say the least, about the existence of feudal kingdoms such as yours. You are a staunch supporter of Chandra Bose, yet his stated intention is to create an Indian republic. Once that day comes, won't your kingdom be dissolved as well? Or am I misunderstanding the situation?"

"The republic is but one possibility," nodded Gaj Singh with something of a bitter expression on his face. "Judging from the history of other countries, short of a Bolshevik revolution, powerful nobles will survive the transformation of their nations into republics. Were the title of Maharaja to become trivial, I would yet remain the richest and most powerful man in Rajasthan. My clan will continue to dominate business interests in many industries. In the same way, we will send our people to gain control of the new congress, and hence the core of the new republic's bureaucracy. I am not afraid of republicanism."

"You said that a republic is only one possibility. What are others?"

"The system of your country is one," replied Gaj Singh. "Another possibility would be a parliament in the style of England. Maharajas would then become members of the House of Lords, while people from society at large would be selected for the House of Commons."

"You mean a constitutional monarchy. Who would become head of state, then?"

"A Maharaja, of course. The most popular Maharaja. The one who supported the independence movement most bravely."

The ambition in Gaj Singh's eyes was unmistakable. He looked out over the musicians in the courtyard and continued.

"I learned from your nation about the restoration of imperial rule. When Japan faced the threat of being colonized by Western powers, didn't Japan's imperial faction gather feudal lords on the western tip of Japan and send them in an attack to topple the Shogunate?"

That's one way to summarize that history, I guess.

"That is correct, Lord Singh," replied Shibata.

"During the time of the Restoration, the Meiji Emperor was still a child. Later in life, however, he led the nation to prosperity and glory. The Emperor proved himself to be a brilliant leader and consolidated the totality of Japan under his command. Am I remembering this correctly?"

"Your memory serves you well, lord."

"I shouldn't be disappointed if the same thing happened here in India. When the Indian Army of Liberation marches on Delhi, they'll need a leader who can give them orders. Will this man be one of the worthless Maharaja who wasted his money and blinded himself to the realities of our country? I think not."

Shibata stared at Gaj Singh's profile in silent shock. *Is he planning to become the first head of state of an independent India? The Meiji Emperor of India?*

"I know what's on your mind, Mr. Shibata," said Gaj Singh. "You worry that an army of four or five hundred isn't enough to overwhelm the British forces. But if I gather soldiers from every kingdom in Rajasthan, my army's ranks will swell to twenty thousand strong. When that many soldiers rise against England, I believe the forces of other kingdoms will join us as well. The kingdoms of Hyderabad and Mysore, for instance. Do you still think I'm talking nonsense? Do you still think my dream is but a delusion?"

"My lord, I don't think it's a delusion," said Shibata. In fact, Shibata had never worried about the size of Gaj Singh's forces. "My question would be: how do you plan to gather these soldiers? Do the other Maharajas agree with your plan?"

"When the time comes, they will have no choice," said Gaj Singh darkly. "Any Maharaja foolish enough to turn his back on a cause as noble as this deserves to be sent into the darkness for good. I'll build a kingdom here in Rajasthan first if I must. It will be the first kingdom of Rajasthan ruled by a single Maharaja."

A single Maharaja...? Gaj Singh's ambitions were now completely clear to Shibata. It was a dangerous plan. *His fellow Maharajas won't be happy about this, that's for sure. And if the British caught wind...*

Four servants stood nearby on the balcony. They showed no signs of having heard anything that Gaj Singh had just said. Perhaps they were simply used to hearing it. Shibata idly wondered if the man could be trusted with a secret.

Shibata picked up his porcelain cup and took a sip of tea.

"When, exactly, is the 'right time'? When do you plan to give the order?"

"There are several possible answers to that question," replied Gaj Singh, nodding thoughtfully. "One scenario would begin with an English surrender to Germany. If England surrenders, India will be thrown into chaos, as happened in the Dutch-controlled East Indies and French-controlled Indochina. I don't know what Germany might have in store for the British colonies, and I don't really care. Because that is the time for us to cast off our chains. When our army advances from Rajasthan to Delhi, the British Indian army will fall, company by company. The Indians among them will take up arms against their British masters. Our advance to Delhi would trigger their revolt."

"And the other possibilities?"

"Another scenario," said Gaj Singh with obvious relish, "involves your country declaring war on England. If that happens, England will attempt to send Indian troops to fight the Japanese. During the last battle fought by the British Indian Army, Indian troops suffered the heaviest losses. Anti-British sentiment among the armed forces is ready to boil over; at this rate, England may well be unable to successfully mobilize Indian troops again. Mark my words, Mr. Shibata. Revolution is coming. In Malaya, Singapore, anywhere England fights the Japanese, the Indian forces will lay down their arms and surrender. While England deals with trouble in the Far East, the true revolution will begin, here in western India. Our army will advance on Delhi with the force of a tidal wave."

Gaj Singh paused for a moment, gathering his thoughts. Then he leaned over, looked into Shibata's eyes, and continued: "A situation where Indian soldiers fight the Japanese must be avoided at all costs. I don't want to see Asians kill fellow Asians. The British Empire is our common enemy.

We shall not spill Asian blood for England's sake!"

"I agree with you completely, my lord," said Shibata. "I can't discuss this mission in detail, but I assure you this is why we are approaching friendly Indian forces about it directly. We want to avoid such situations."

"Chandra Bose will begin a fast in Calcutta soon," said Gaj Singh. "England knows that there will be a riot if Bose dies in their custody. And so they will undoubtedly remove him from the prison and place him under house arrest instead. At any rate, his fate will have a definite impact on my decision. If India becomes a republic, Bose will undoubtedly become its first president. And so I'm keeping a close eye on him. If he and I can reach an agreement, if he and I can see eye-to-eye over the direction of the Indian independence movement, I'm thinking to offer my army to him."

Gaj Singh looked out at the musicians in the courtyard again. The torch was burning quite low now. *Was the song ending as well?*

"Each of the scenarios I just described are deeply intertwined with international affairs," noted Gaj Singh.

Shibata adjusted himself on the cushion and focused more intently. Gaj Singh added, "But there is yet another scenario in which my soldiers will spring to action, Mr. Shibata."

Shibata examined his host's face. The flame from the torch was reflected in Gaj Singh's eyes.

"Amritsar. If there is another Amritsar, if the Royal Army begins butchering Indians again, I'll give the order regardless of what's going on in the world around us. We will annihilate the British forces so brutally, so mercilessly, that the entire world will shudder. I am descended from a famed tribe of brave warriors. I yearn to show them our brutal traditions of war. This soil is ours and I swear by all that is holy to me that my sword will drip with British blood. I shall make a mountain of the severed heads of British officers."

The song drew to a close. The final chords traveled across the pond, echoed through the corridors of the palace, and disappeared. The musicians quietly stood up from their rug and began to leave. Soon the courtyard was filled with nothing but silence.

Shibata looked out over the empty courtyard. The musky smell of incense filled the air.

Suddenly, a steward appeared and whispered something in Gaj Singh's ear. The hate and sadness drained from the Maharaja's face. His expression returned to that of an ambitious Sikh.

After the steward left, Gaj Singh turned to Shibata again.

"Unfortunately, I must attend to an unforeseen visitor now."

Shibata thanked Gaj Singh for the meal and entertainment. He also mentioned his growing interest in the lord's broader plans.

"Please feel free to use my airfield. I'll coordinate the supply of fuel, maintenance service, a rest area, and anything else that might be required. I shall place one of my top commanders, Karmajit Singh, in charge."

"I have one final request, my lord."

"What is it?"

"Is your American pilot trustworthy? We are extremely sensitive about the British and Americans at the moment."

"He is an aerobatic performer, a pure pilot, with no government or military connections," assured Gaj Singh. "You need not worry about him."

Gaj Singh stood up and prepared to leave.

"By the way, my servants have made preparations in your room, as a consolation for your lengthy trip. Good night, Mr. Shibata."

Somewhat puzzled, Shibata returned to his room. Opening the door, he immediately understood. A young woman in light clothing lay across his bed. Her hair was thick and dark; her eyes reminded him of a deep spring. She was very young. In fact, to judge by her skin, she was more a girl than a woman. Her breasts and hips weren't fully developed yet.

She may have had the guileless expression of an innocent child, but her amorous skills were unlike anything Shibata had ever experienced before. The smell of incense filled the room. Enveloped in the scent, Shibata learned the true meaning of pleasure in Rajasthan, tasting the final and most exquisite dish on the menu of a Maharaja's banquet.

When Shibata woke up the next morning, there wasn't a single trace of the girl in his room.

CHAPTER 27

While Ryojiro Shibata was visiting Rajasthan, Lieutenant Commander Ohnuki visited the Yokosuka Air Corps base again. Ando and Inui had begun their flight training only eight days before. Ohnuki was alone.

Ando climbed down from his Type Zero and spoke briefly to the ground crew before approaching Ohnuki and saluting. *No secretary today,* thought Ando.

"By yourself today?" he asked.

Ohnuki nodded. "He's at the Foreign Ministry. But there's something I wanted to give you. So I came on my own."

"What is it?"

"To tell the truth," said Ohnuki, smiling almost shyly, "it isn't all that important. It's a report on the RAF presence in India. But I wanted to see how the training was coming along with my own eyes."

"We're working our tails off, sir," smiled Ando. "We've been putting in more than four hours of flight time a day."

"Don't push yourselves too hard. I don't want you two taking to bed. If you can't fly, we won't have any choice but to call this whole thing off."

"We're taking next Sunday off."

"How is it going otherwise?" asked Ohnuki. "Have you encountered any problems yet?"

"We've flown the Zero before. We're done familiarizing ourselves with the planes for the most part. The only thing remaining is trying to reduce fuel consumption."

"2,000 kilometers isn't any problem, right?"

"We've been flying thousand-kilometer runs on 300 liters of fuel. That means we could have made 3,000 kilometers if we'd continued flying."

"Really? The Aviation Headquarters didn't promise 3,000 kilometers."

"You can't just hop in and do it. It takes some skill and practice to pull it off."

Ando launched into an explanation of the special techniques that he

173

and Inui had developed for the flight. They had learned that fuel consumption was most efficient at an engine speed of between 1,700 and 1,900 RPM. This speed could only be attained by flying at an altitude of 4,000 meters at an airspeed of 210 kilometers or 120 nautical miles per hour. Keeping the engine speed at 1,800 RPM required holding the injector valve at a setting so low that the fuel-air mixture only barely achieved combustion. It was delicate work that required tremendous skill. But once you managed to pull it off, you could reduce fuel consumption to roughly 60 liters an hour. The Type Zero Carrier Fighter, Model 11 was capable of carrying 800 liters of fuel, which included 330 liters stored in drop tanks. That would give an operational time of 14 hours, which translated into a range of 2,900 kilometers.

Ando also explained that that the longer an aircraft flies, the lighter it becomes, as fuel is consumed. This meant the longer the flight, the lower the average fuel consumption. Ando theorized that it might even be possible to reduce fuel consumption to almost 50 liters an hour for the flight. That raised the possibility of extending flight time to between 15 and 16 hours, so that the Type Zero Carrier Fighter could potentially fly over 3,000 kilometers at a stretch. Ando and Inui were aiming for that range.

"That means the Type Zero actually has far more range than detailed in the report from Aviation Headquarters. I've got to tell the Air Corps about this. So far as you know, you're the first to come up with these numbers?"

"It's possible that someone else has figured it out as well. But it wouldn't be a bad idea to spread the word."

"With a little more practice," cut in Inui, "it might be possible to lower it to 70 liters an hour at 300 kph and an altitude of 4,000 meters."

"That would mean," said Ohnuki, looking up at the sky as he ran the figures in his head, "a range of 3,400 kilometers."

"It's a new model, you know?" said Ando. "It may have more potential than anyone's given it credit for."

"Maybe we should have placed the refueling stops at 2,500 kilometers instead."

"That's too risky, sir. There's no guarantee that we'll be flying straight and level the whole time. You made the right decision in setting the stops at 2,000 kilometer intervals."

The three men walked to the front of the hangar. Ando still felt stiff from the six-hour flight. He moved his arms and neck in circles to try and relax his muscles.

Suddenly the sound of dozens of aircraft engines began to fill the air. The three men watched as a squadron of Type 96 Carrier Fighters began to land, one after the other. Another large aircraft could be seen in the air beyond the east hangar as well. It appeared to be a Type 97 Seaplane on final approach for a water landing.

It was early evening, the time when planes homed in from their sorties. A spiral-shaped cloud, glowing faintly red, hung in the air far above the base. The light of the setting sun reflected off another plane still at high altitude.

Inui brought over a wooden bench from inside the hangar. The three men sat down and watched the Type 97 gradually reduce altitude and touch down with a splash in Yokosuka harbor. The wake gradually reduced as the plane slowed down, turned, and began heading for a dock.

"I suspect there's something else you wanted to discuss, sir," said Ando, his eyes fixed on the taxiing seaplane.

Ohnuki cleared his throat uncomfortably. "I don't know if I'd call it a discussion. But you're right. I've come because there's something I'd like to ask you."

"What is it, sir?"

Ohnuki tightened his lips and looked out over the sky. He saw a shadow to the east. It appeared to be another seaplane. Finally, having found the right words, Ohnuki spoke again.

"I want to know why you took the mission. I'd like to know the truth."

"My answer the other day wasn't good enough?"

"No. 'Because you're a pilot'? I don't buy that. No other pilot in the navy would have accepted the mission willingly. And not just because it's dangerous."

"I don't know who you talked to before us, sir," said Ando. "What the pilots want most right now is to go to China. They want to win medals and awards. Flying to Berlin wouldn't interest them at all. It must seem to them as boring as a transport run."

"But you didn't see it that way. Even though you called it pointless and stupid."

"I can't speak for my wingman," said Ando, giving Inui a quick glance, "but I know why I took the mission. Given the choice between stupidity and savagery, I'll take stupidity every time."

"Are you calling our operations in China 'savage'?"

Ando heard the rebuke in Ohnuki's voice. But it was too late to take back what he'd said.

"If I call our Chinese policy 'savage,'" said Ando calmly, "it's only logical to say that the execution of that policy is also barbaric. We discussed Nanking the other day. How about Chungking? Are you aware of what we did to Chungking, sir?"

"I heard we reduced it to ashes."

"Horrible," said Ando, shaking his head.

Right before the attack on Chengdu, Ando was ordered out to survey the extent of damage inflicted by the bombing raids on Chungking. He had flown low and slow over the path of the barrage until he reached what was left of the downtown area. The scene was one of utter devastation. The bombings and strafing runs had reduced the entire city to scorched, smoking debris. There was no sign of life at all. Reading Ando's report, headquarters called the bombing a "tremendous success."

Ando grimaced as he recalled the sight.

"I was ordered to scout Chungking once. It was after we'd destroyed the Chinese Air Force in September. I flew it alone. There was nothing left. I'm not talking just military facilities. The markets, schools, hospitals, civilian houses... Gone. All gone. I didn't see anything untouched, not even a single post or pole. Everything had been incinerated. I can't even begin to estimate how many Chinese died there."

Ohnuki listened in silence. He watched Ando's face intently.

"Unfortunately," continued Ando, "that's the face of the Imperial Army's campaign. In spite of their stated ideals, their republic of the five peoples of Asia, co-prosperity and all of that. They didn't distinguish between soldiers and civilians. This is the twentieth century! It was a massacre. If you don't call that savage, what is, sir?"

Ohnuki shook his head slightly. Ando couldn't tell what that meant. Did he disagree? Or did he not understand?

"Going to Berlin is my only way out of that savagery, the only way I can refuse to participate in it. I can leave it all behind. I'll even get to do it with my beloved Zero. So now you know why I jumped at the mission, sir," said Ando, twisting his flight helmet as he spoke.

"Ando," said Ohnuki quietly. "Do you always talk like this?"

"I've never made a speech at the barracks, if that's what you mean. But my feelings aren't secret, either."

"How about you, Inui? What do you think?" said Ohnuki, looking over at the sergeant.

Inui shrugged. "I'm not as good at talking as Lieutenant Ando."

"I don't care. Just be yourself, and answer my question."

"Well," Inui stroked his chin thoughtfully, "I think I've got a pretty good sense of people. Who's stupid, who's smart, all that. To be honest, I didn't see a smart face on any of the officers and commanders I met in China. The more a man was called 'courageous' or 'high caliber,' or whatever, the stupider he looked to me. People like that only know how to be stupid. That's all things were about, sir."

"I don't think you answered my question."

"It's like this, sir. When I fly, the sky's all mine. It's out of the hands of stupid commanders. It's not even in Lieutenant Ando's hands. When I'm up there, I'm free."

Another Type 96 Carrier Fighter touched down on the runway. It hit hard, bounced once, and appeared to lose balance for a second, but recovered quickly and scooted down the runway. The flaps deployed and the engine revved briefly as the plane reduced speed. The pilot in the open cockpit began signaling the ground crew, who guided it into a hardstand near the center of the runway.

Is he going to hit me with that iron fist of his again? thought Ando, spying Ohnuki from the corner of his eyes. Ohnuki was thin and wore silver-framed glasses. He looked like a typical "brick," but he had proven otherwise that day at Blue Max. Ohnuki didn't boast or stand on ceremony. Ando could tell he was a fearless man; he wasn't to be underestimated. Ando wondered if he and Inui had crossed the line.

But Ohnuki's reaction was nothing like Ando had expected.

"Well," said Ohnuki, standing up. "I'm glad we had an honest talk today, unlike our first meeting. But now I'd better get going."

Ando looked up at Ohnuki.

"What is it?" said Ohnuki.

"Th-the radio," stuttered Ando. "Please don't forget your promise about the radio, sir."

Ohnuki nodded. There was a somewhat mischievous expression on his face. He avoided Ando's quizzing gaze.

Ohnuki raised his hand and walked towards base headquarters without looking back. Ando and Inui continued to stare until he disappeared into the building.

CHAPTER 28

On the day after Shibata's arrival in Kamanipur, Gaj Singh invited him to inspect a parade of his soldiers and their training.

Shibata was at the base located by the airfield. There were some five hundred soldiers altogether, and all of them appeared disciplined, full of fight. It was obvious at a glance that they were fiercely dedicated to the idea of Indian independence.

Watching the soliders, Shibata was convinced that each could become an officer when the time came. That meant that the Kamanipur kingdom's army had the potential to expand to ten times its size within a very short period of time. Shibata was surprised to see Gurkha troops as well. He was told that they were instructing the other soldiers in fighting techniques. Each of the Gurkhas carried a crescent-shaped knife on their waists.

Most of the army's equipment was British, but some of the light machine guns were German, while the armored vehicles were American. There were also two fairly large airplanes. Apparently the Maharaja intended to convert them into bombers. There were ten trucks on the field that day, but Gaj Singh told Shibata that he owned an additional thirty. They were being rented out for public use at the time, but upon orders the army would retrieve them for use as troop transports.

The inspection lasted until evening. As things were wrapping up, Shibata realized that he'd begun to regard Gaj Singh's army with a certain amount of affection. He saw them as something akin to the samurai who pulled off the Meiji Restoration. Shibata even found himself wistfully considering becoming a battlefield officer again.

It was dusk by the time Shibata finally met with Colonel Karmajit Singh.

Like his master, Karmajit Singh was a Sikh. He was a former soldier in the British-controlled Indian Army. The Maharaja had already briefed him, so the meeting with Shibata didn't last too long.

"How much and what quality of fuel is required? Will you require lubricant? What kind of parts or supplies will you need?"

Singh peppered Shibata with such specific questions, and Shibata answered each of them.

"And a final question," said Karmajit Singh. "When will the aircraft take off? When exactly are they due to arrive?"

"I'm embarrassed to tell you this, but I don't know," replied Shibata. "I anticipate that the planes will depart at the beginning of December."

"Can you contact us several days in advance?"

"I'll send a telegram from Delhi. Where should I send it? Base headquarters?"

"Please send it to Lord Singh. It will be treated as being of the highest priority."

"The telegram will say: 'The bird is in flight.' The aircraft will arrive within a few days of the message."

"I assume I'm not supposed to ask which direction the planes will be coming from."

"Actually, I don't know the answer to that myself. By the way—I assume the lord already told you—this is highly confidential."

"This airfield's very existence is confidential," replied Karmajit Singh. "So there is no need to worry."

"But it's so impressive," said Shibata, recalling everything he'd seen that day. "I can't imagine the British government doesn't know about all this."

"They sent a reconnaissance plane once before. But no British have come to investigate on foot yet. We may attract more flies once the state of world affairs changes."

"I've gotten the impression that the lord actually wouldn't mind showing off his army."

"Perhaps you're right."

With that, Shibata and Karmajit Singh shook hands and went their separate ways.

By the time Shibata left base headquarters, the sun was about to disappear over the horizon of the desert. The clouds were lighted in gold. The sky was as beautifully and richly hued as the tapestry Shibata had seen inside the palace. He stopped to watch the dazzling colors of the sunset for a long moment.

Over the last two weeks, Shibata had traversed nearly the entire width of the Indian subcontinent. His efforts had secured refueling bases in Eastern Bengal and Rajasthan. Shibata was looking forward to returning to

Part Two

Delhi, where he would send an urgent telegram to Tokyo containing the single word "Assured." With the arrival of the telegram, Shibata knew, the Eighth Section, Army Division of the Imperial General Headquarters would know that sending a spy to Delhi was the right thing to have done. In fact, they were getting more than they'd expected. Shibata, bathed in the glow of twilight, was enjoying the satisfaction of a job well done.

Suddenly he caught the strains of a harmonica. He turned and followed the sound to a Curtiss parked in front of a hangar. By its wings stood Jim, his hands cupped around the harmonica held to his mouth, his eyes closed and his head moving from side to side. Shibata listened to the melody for a while. The tune was vaguely familiar; it sounded like it might be an American folk song. Musical appreciation wasn't a prerequisite for joining the army. Shibata walked towards Jim.

Jim's face appeared bright red in the sunset. His unshaven face looked rather forlorn.

As Jim finished his song, he looked up and smiled at Shibata. It was an innocent and youthful expression, one Shibata hadn't anticipated seeing on the grizzled face.

"Done with business?" asked Jim pleasantly.

"Yes. I'm leaving tomorrow," answered Shibata. "Would you mind giving me a ride to Jodhpur?"

"I'll take you there before the train leaves in the afternoon," said Jim. Then, sneakily, "Hey, you want a drink?"

"Drink?"

"The Indians don't like drinking, so I can't say it too loudly. But I have a bottle of Bushmill's. Want some?"

"Bushmill's?"

"Irish whisky."

Not a bad idea, thought Shibata. His chauffeur stood next to base headquarters watching the two of them. *It'll be fine, I suppose. I'm a guest here, after all.*

"Yes. Thank you."

Jim nodded, disappeared into the hangar, and returned with a bottle and two tin cups.

"It's been almost two years since the Maharaja hired me," said Jim after a sip. "I'm getting bored here, to be honest. It's about time for Jenny here to retire, too. I'm thinking to leave Rajasthan."

Jim and Shibata sat on a wooden crate in front of the hangar. The sun had dipped below the horizon and the colors were gradually fading from the sky. The clouds in the west had turned from a rich gold to a dull orange. The soldiers seemed to have returned to their barracks. The orange-colored flag of the kingdom had been lowered from the flagpole.

"Going to look for another job as a pilot?" asked Shibata, taking a sip from his cup.

"You got it," nodded Jim. "All I know is flying. I've always flown old planes, but I don't think the technology's all that different with the new ones. Just based on my flight time alone, I'd say I qualify as an experienced pilot."

"What would you like to fly?"

"A mail plane, maybe, or a transport. But if I ever get the chance, I'd like to fly a fighter."

"So you're going to rejoin the military?"

"No. I'm thinking to volunteer."

"Where?"

"In England, maybe. I heard there's a squadron of Poles or Czechs there. Some Americans, too, from what I hear. I'm kind of old, though. I don't know if they'll take me."

"You want to fight the Germans?"

"Well, I don't have any love for that German guy with the mustache. But I don't want to fly a fighter because I want to fight Germans. It's not even because of the war."

"But if you fly a fighter, it'll be combat for sure."

"I know. War is war. But air combat is a little different. I mean, battles in the sky aren't like the mess on the ground. There's still some kind of dignity."

"Why is that?"

"Pilots aren't like common soldiers. We're the chosen few. A knighthood."

"Maybe that's how it was during the last war," said Shibata pensively. "But I don't know if that holds true anymore."

"Well, I think it does. I couldn't make it to that war, but I think I can do it this time around."

"How old are you?"

"Forty-one," answered Jim. "Why?"

Part Two

"You're forty-one years old. You're a heavy drinker. You'll pardon me for saying this, but you're a little shabby for a knight."

"No argument there," said Jim, laughing. "I'm a fallen knight, maybe."

"Tactics have changed drastically over the last twenty years. Maybe too much for you. There's no room for knights or heroes today."

"I know all of that," said Jim. "War is getting more and more brutal as time goes on. Now we've got tanks, poison gas, machine guns, bombers. All of them evil. But fighter aircraft are different. At least, that's how I feel. I felt that way when I heard about Spain and Dover. Oh—did anyone tell you about what they did in China?"

Jim stared off at the horizon in the west as he related the story to Shibata. He had heard it in Calcutta two years ago.

It was the fall of 1938. A "Flying Tiger," or an American volunteer, and a Japanese pilot had duked it out in the skies over China. The American was a Lieutenant Conrad. He had been trained by the United States Army Air Corps.

It had all begun that summer, when the fresh volunteer Conrad was shot down in his Curtiss Hawk in an engagement with a Japanese Navy squadron. Conrad bailed out from his burning fighter, but he'd given up any hope of returning alive. The word among his fellow pilots was that the Japanese did not follow the rules of engagement agreed upon during World War I. He himself had witnessed Japanese aircraft firing at pilots who'd parachuted from their damaged fighters. Some Japanese pilots even sliced through parachutes with their wings. Others flew close to parachutes to collapse them so the hapless freight would plop straight to the ground.

But this Japanese pilot was different. He must have seen Conrad bail out, but he held his fire. He passed by and climbed back into the sky. Conrad even caught the man saluting him from the cockpit as he went by. The aircraft featured not only the typical rising suns, but also the "sash" of a wing commander.

It was the Mensch!

Every Flying Tiger knew this particular Japanese pilot. They called him "the Mensch," the decent man.

He was a constant source of discussion among the American pilots. His flight technique and marksmanship were legendary. In a dogfight, he was untouchable. He had a knack for getting behind an opponent and taking him down with a single short burst of his guns. Unlike his fellow Japanese pilots, however, he never attacked anyone who'd bailed out. That was just the Mensch's style. Conrad had heard that the Mensch had shot down more than ten American pilots. They all assumed he was leader from the red sash painted on his tail, and theorized that he belonged to the squadron stationed at Kunda airbase in Shanghai. Every Flying Tiger wanted his shot at taking down the Mensch.

When Conrad happened to meet an employee of the American government—in plain English, an intelligence agent—in Chungking one day, he asked if it was possible to dig up the Mensch's real name. The agent made some inquiries with his counterpart in Shanghai. Four weeks later, he came through. It turned out that the pilot was a lieutenant junior grade in the Imperial Japanese Navy and belonged to the Second Joint Air Corps. The agent even uncovered the pilot's favorite hangout, a dance hall in the joint protectorate, which he visited every time he was on leave.

Conrad wrote a letter and asked the agent to get it to the Japanese pilot. Two weeks later, the agent succeeded. He had hired a Chinese boy to deliver it to him in the dance hall.

I propose a duel, began Conrad's letter. *The rules are as follows. You and I will engage one another, man to man; any other aircraft in the area will remain on stand-by, with no other combat until the end of our duel; we shall fly straight towards one another, and the duel will begin the moment our planes cross paths; if either party wishes to give up, he will wave a white cloth; and all shooting will stop the moment the white cloth is displayed.*

Conrad wondered if the Japanese pilot would accept his terms. And there was also the worry, of course, that the Mensch's commander might not allow it, or that his wingmen would refuse to hold fire.

On a sunny October afternoon in 1938, two weeks after the letter had been delivered, Conrad's flight of six Curtiss Hawks encountered five Japanese Type 96 Carrier Fighters over Anqing, southwest of Nanking. The Japanese aircraft circled for a moment before climbing high into the sky. But one remained behind. It seemed that Conrad's challenge had been met.

Conrad had issued standing orders to his fellow pilots to climb and wait at altitude if ever this situation came to pass. He confirmed that the enemy aircraft bore the Mensch's sash as the two planes screamed past each other. The duel had begun in the skies over Anqing.

As a pilot, the Mensch was everything Conrad had expected him to be. The Flying Tiger quickly realized that his being shot down hadn't been a fluke. No matter how many times he tried to shake him off, the Japanese stuck to his tail like glue. In fact, the Mensch never even gave him a single opening. Fifteen minutes later, the Mensch finally fired a short burst into the back of Conrad's aircraft. Conrad felt the impact and saw tracers spraying past the cockpit glass. It was time to concede defeat. Conrad waved a white scarf.

The Type 96 Carrier Fighter pulled in alongside Conrad, executed a right turn, and disappeared. Back at the base, Conrad inspected his aircraft for damage: eight bullet holes drilled neatly through his wing and fuselage.

"So as you can see, things are a little different with aerial combat. They still fight that way, even today," said Jim in conclusion.

Shibata shook his head. It couldn't possibly be true. He couldn't think of a single man in the Japanese military who would consent to engage in such a duel. He couldn't imagine anyone ignoring official rules of engagement to stand by and observe, either.

"That has to be a myth," Shibata objected. "No Japanese military pilot is like that."

"What, are you saying none of them is decent?"

"No, what I mean is that no Japanese soldier would confound a duel with actual operations."

"I believe it happened."

"You're too optimistic. A typical American."

"I hate to say this in front of a Japanese," said Jim, lowering his head slightly as if in apology, "but that's why I want to go to China."

"You want to fight the Japanese?"

"Not really. I'm not a Chiang Kai-Shek supporter, either. I let the governments deal with war. I just want to fly. Hell, you must feel the same way I do. The war's got nothing to do with you personally, right?"

Shibata raised the tin cup and took another gulp of Jim's Irish whisky. It burned pleasantly as it slid down his throat. Shibata wiped his lips with the back of his hand.

"Is that really why you want to go to China?"

"That and I'll get paid 600 bucks a week. Plus, Chiang Kai-Shek gives out a bonus for every plane shot down. It's a pretty attractive deal for a dirt-poor pilot like me."

"Why are you telling me this?" asked Shibata suddenly. He really and truly wanted to know. "Did you think your story would make me happy?"

"Why wouldn't you want to hear it? I'm not talking about the war. Just relating a story that may happen to be true. It tells us that there's at least one pilot out there who still respects his fellow man in this hopeless war. A man with real samurai spirit. Which part upset you? I thought you were a civilian. You're not a government employee, are you?"

Shibata fell silent for a moment. Looked at a different way, it was actually something of a touching story. Shibata had heard nothing but vicious rumor after vicious rumor lately: 10,000 P.O.W.s slaughtered, the raping and pillaging of Nanking. They were disgusting enough to make Shibata shudder, but still he believed them, based on his own experience with the army. Jim's story was welcome and refreshing in this light. Private battle or no, it didn't have a negative impact on the Japanese campaign in China.

He's probably right. I should just relax.

The sky had become a rich and dark blue. The stars were beginning to come out. They shone so brightly that they reminded Shibata of diamonds.

The chauffeur still stood at attention next to the car, waiting for Shibata. Shibata finished the rest of his whisky in a single gulp.

"I'd better be getting back to the palace."

"I'm sorry if I upset you," said Jim. "But I meant no disrespect towards the Japanese, nothing like that. I just like airplanes. I want to experience what I missed out on the last time. That's why I want to go to China."

"Understood. Thanks for the drink."

Shibata stood up from the crate, waved at Jim, and headed towards the car and his chauffeur. As he walked, he heard the strains of the harmonica again. Shibata finally remembered the title of the song: "My Old Kentucky Home."

He should forget about China, thought Shibata, *and go home. His old Kentucky home, or wherever. Somewhere peaceful. Back to his hometown, where they'll welcome him back as a hero. Back to the house where his old parents are waiting for their son to return.*

CHAPTER 29

The wind was strong that day. Ando checked the weather map at the base and learned that a front was on the way. Long-range flight training was out of the question, then; he decided to spend the day on navigational training instead. Two weeks had passed since they'd started training on the new Zeros.

Ando and Inui took off from Yokosuka at ten in the morning and headed for Miyake, one of the seven islands in the Izu chain. They flew low above the ocean to practice over-water navigation, studying the waves and using the Beaufort wind scale to calculate the direction and force of the wind. Fighter aircraft weren't equipped to inform pilots when they drifted off course. Thus fighter pilots used a navigational calculator called the "fan" to determine their flight path, flight speed, and flight time. If the actual path appeared to be deviating from the planned course, a pilot would need to compensate. Mission Ibis required Ando and Inui to fly over water from Japan to Kaohsiung in Taiwan, and then again from Kaohsiung to Hanoi. Ando and Inui practiced the technique on the flight from Miyake Island back to Yokosuka. In the end, it took several tries before they got the hang of it.

Rain had begun to fall by the time Ando and Inui returned to Yokosuka. The wind had picked up as well, blowing strong to the southeast. The two pilots climbed out of their cockpits and handed off the aircraft to their ground crews. Holding their helmets on with one hand, they dashed for the Experimental Flight Division's hangar.

Once inside, Ando turned to see that Warrant Officer Marugame from Aviation Maintenance was coming running after him. Squad leader Marugame was known as a perfectionist not above using a wrench to discipline his underlings when necessary. He was about forty years old.

"The fighters are in great shape," Ando told Marugame. "Not even a hint of trouble. Perfect, as usual. Good job."

"Thank you, sir," said Marugame, his round face breaking into a smile. "Everybody's talking about how you managed to fly 2,100 kilometers on just 500 liters of fuel."

"We think we can do even better. Inui and I are starting to think you put something special in there!"

"The youngsters can hardly control themselves. Every time you come back from a practice flight, you've broken a new record."

"Glad to hear it. But don't let them get swollen heads, you hear me?"

"Aye, sir!" said Marugame, nodding vigorously. "By the way, I've been meaning to tell you. The hours you put in can start taking a toll on the aircraft."

"You telling me to give it a rest?"

"To tell you the truth, we'd like to have them for a day. Aviation Headquarters just told us that they've gotten two new radio sets. Any chance we can borrow your aircraft for a day to put them in?"

"New radios? Are they German?" asked Ando.

"I don't know, lieutenant. But they called them 'new,' so I assume they're Japanese."

"I hope they work better than those toys they've been giving us."

"Does that mean you're taking the day off tomorrow?"

Ando looked at Inui. Normally robust, Inui was looking a little haggard lately. He must have been exhausted. The two had only taken a single day off over the last two weeks. And they'd been putting in more than four hours of flight time a day.

Inui spread his arms. It seemed the decision was up to Ando.

"All right. We'll take tomorrow off," said Ando, looking out of the open hangar door. "I'd better give the maintenance guys a break. I've been pushing them pretty hard over the last two weeks. And the weather isn't on our side, at all. "

"I'll give everyone except the radio guys the day off, too." Marugame turned to leave. Ando stopped him.

"Marugame, I apologize for this, seeing as I just told you to get some rest. But would you mind doing something for me?"

"What is it, sir?"

"Remove the radio homing devices. We don't need them."

"It'll be a problem if you need to land on a carrier at some point," warned Marugame, his eyes questioning.

"I'll ask for them again when we need them. Right now, I want the aircraft as light as possible."

"Consider it removed, sir."

Later, in the locker room, Inui removed his helmet and turned to

Part Two

Ando.

"I'm thinking to go to Hamamatsu tonight. To see my parents."

"Hamamatsu?"

"Yeah. Otherwise, I don't know when I'll get another chance before we go."

"You should go, then."

Ando glanced at a calendar on the wall. *November 16th. Down to two weeks. I wonder how the negotiations for refueling stops are coming along?*

"How about you, lieutenant? What are you going to do tonight?"

"I'm getting some sleep. Dunno what I'll do tomorrow, though. I'll play it by ear."

That night, Ando called Yuki's apartment in Yokohama.

"Drop by anytime," she said.

Ando promised to do just that the next day.

CHAPTER 30

Yuki's apartment was in Yamashita ward, Yokohama, close to Chinatown.

It was a red-brick two-story building, originally built as a store-house. Each floor had been divided into three rooms. In an attempt to cut costs, however, the landlord had only provided the first floor rooms with woven *tatami* mat flooring. The second floor rooms used rough-hewn boards as flooring instead. The building's tenants shared a group kitchen and toilet located outside of the building.

Ten years ago, when the building was still being used as a store-house, there had been a fire. The original owner, an old man, had died in the blaze. The burnt, skeletal remains of the structure stood untouched for more than a year before being rebuilt and converted into apartments.

Yuki had moved in three years back. A little before that, she had met a married clarinet player, a graduate of prestigious Keio University, at a dance hall in the Ginza. They fell in love, and ran off together to the Philippines. Her happiness lasted eight short weeks, at which point she discovered that the clarinet player had been cheating on her with yet another woman. Yuki exploded and returned to Japan, taking all of his money with her. She'd lived in the remodeled storehouse ever since.

Ando came by to see her on a rainy Sunday afternoon. He was dressed in civilian clothes. He didn't need to ask for directions. He had escorted her home after the final party at Blue Max. She'd rested her cheek on his shoulder the entire way. But today marked the first time he'd ever stepped inside.

Yuki regaled Ando with tales of her neighbors. Six people lived in the building. Two were common-law wives of foreign sailors. The others were a hooker, a dancer, an artists' model, and Yuki.

"We're all out of work, thanks to the war," laughed Yuki. "The landlord better get ready for some late payments."

Yuki's room faced the rear of the second floor. It had a single window. An old rug covered the rough flooring. A steel-framed bed sat in one corner, near the curtains. A mirror, as tall as Yuki, stood against another wall. A wicker basket next to the mirror overflowed with dirty laundry. The place looked desperately cheap. The one exception was a magnificent, box-shaped gramophone that seemed oddly out of place.

"Too bad for you, Mr. Lieutenant," said Yuki, offering Ando a seat on a small sofa. "You finally get a day off, and it rains."

Yuki wore a black sweater and a dark brown skirt. It was an unusually conservative choice for her. If she walked outside, she might not even receive a warning card. That being said, not even a funeral dress could put a damper on the provocation in her eyes. *Was that her fault? Surely not*, thought Ando. *Blame her parents' genes.*

Yuki filled a small glass with Scotch whisky for Ando and handed it to him on the sofa. Her drink was larger than his.

"I don't have much in the way of glasses and tableware," she apologized. "But don't worry, the drink'll taste good regardless."

Ando and Yuki toasted. It was good Scotch, hard to come by during wartime. Yuki must have had a reliable supplier. Someone rich, with connections to foreigners, Ando guessed. A band member, maybe? Ando noticed a pile of empty bottles in one corner.

Yuki kneeled and lifted the arm of the gramophone. She began to flip through her record collection.

"Do you like Fumiko Kawabata?" asked Yuki. "When I started out I used to copy her style."

There was a screech and hiss as the needle dropped onto the record. But soon, the sultry voice of a female vocalist filled the room. She had an odd accent and intonation, almost like a foreigner speaking Japanese. Yuki stood up and began singing along with the record in a low voice.

Outside, the rain was pouring down. It was a cold rain, a late fall rain, and it seemed to be a turning point. Winter was coming. The rain streaked down the window in tiny rivulets. It drummed endlessly against the galvanized tin roof.

Gazing at the window, Ando thought about the climate of the places he'd be flying through. Hanoi and Eastern Bengal would be hot and humid. Iran and Iraq saw huge temperature swings between day and night. Berlin would probably be cloudy. Halfway around the globe. So much weather, in so short a time. *Rajasthan and Turkey are another deal still. What kind of underwear do I bring on a trip like this?*

Yuki sat down on the sofa and leaned against Ando. Ando put his arm around her. Fumiko Kawabata continued her crooning on the gramophone.

With you I'd suffer
Any pain, any sadness

Yuki took sips of Scotch between the songs. Ando looked at her face. Whether it was too much makeup or too much booze, her skin was rough. Her face couldn't hide her fatigue. But her eyes were different. They shone bright, filled with hope; and they flirted none too subtly with Ando.

He looked into her eyes for a while. She smiled shyly. Ando brought his face close to hers. Yuki closed her eyes. He kissed her on her forehead.

Yuki quietly opened her eyes. Her eyelids and cheeks were flushed.

"What made you come here?" asked Yuki. "What made you want to see me today? You never wanted to before. What happened to you?"

"I'm going away again." Ando looked deep into her eyes.

"China? You're sure making your share of trips there."

"Good fighter pilots are always in short supply."

"So you took pity on me, huh? Going to be there long this time?"

"I don't know."

"I'm thinking to go to Shanghai. By ship. The *Kamakura* sets sail next month. Will I see you there?"

"No. I won't be anywhere near Shanghai."

"That's right. Said you were going to Berlin..."

"I did? Anyway, I'll be far away."

"When are you leaving?"

"Soon. But the date's a secret, too. So don't ask."

"Will I see you again before you leave?"

"I can't tell you that, either."

"I guess...I should take advantage of this while it lasts, then."

"I thought you said you'd make me something to eat."

"What the hell are you talking about?" Yuki broke into a wry smile. "You saying you want dinner before me?"

"No. You first. Meal second. I like that order."

"Hold me."

Ando plucked the glass from Yuki's hand and placed it on the floor. He took Yuki in his arms. Ando didn't have to find her lips; she devoured his. Her long fingers traced along his back and neck. Ando slipped his hands under Yuki's sweater. He found, without much surprise, that she wasn't wearing a bra. Her nipples hardened right away when he took her breasts in his hands.

The rain showed no sign of letting up. In fact, it was getting even stronger. The window glass was being pounded so hard it was on the verge of rattling. The water cascading from the gutters was like a brook or a stream. The room had begun to cool. Or was it just because their sweat had dried?

Ando gazed over Yuki's body. Her thin back and well-shaped behind stuck out from under the covers. Yuki dozed, her face resting on Ando's chest. He pulled the blanket over her exposed rear end.

She woke up.

"What is it?" she asked, her voice hoarse. She sounded like she was half-asleep.

"Aren't you cold?"

"Uh-uh."

Still, she moved her naked body under the blankets to press against Ando.

She looked into his eyes. "Tell me why a good-looking guy like you doesn't want a girlfriend. Why won't you go steady with anyone?"

"There's no way a fighter pilot can keep up a relationship," replied Ando, staring at the white frame of the window.

"Somebody told me you've never paid for sex."

"He or she was right."

"That's odd for a soldier. You didn't in China?"

"Nope."

"Why not?"

"I don't want to sleep with someone I pity," replied Ando, choosing his words carefully. But he knew his answer wasn't the full truth.

"But you're a healthy man. How can you handle it?"

"I've never paid for a woman. That doesn't mean I've never made a move on one."

Yuki raised her head from Ando's chest to look at him.

"So you pick up amateurs?"

"'Amateurs'? I don't know if I'd use that term. But the women I go for aren't the type I could sleep with for money. Paying money to have sex, it just isn't my thing. If I want a woman, I just go straight up to her and ask her. And I don't head for the cathouse just because I couldn't find anyone to spend the night with."

"Sounds like you're a real player."

"Sure, maybe it's a game. But I've had affairs with some amazing women, you know. I may not have been in love, but I was honestly interested in them. I gave my all to get close to them."

"Were they all one-night stands?"

"What's this all about?" Ando shot back. "I'm not some womanizer. Look, I don't like to talk about this stuff."

"All right, all right." Yuki flicked Ando's chest. "I know you pretty well, don't I? I know you're more interested in the game than the prize. You're always shooting straight ahead. And you never ask for a discount when you buy something. Even though you know it's your loss. You pay the full price, no matter what."

"It doesn't matter if I win or lose," Ando agreed. He had to hand it to Yuki. She seemed to draw something out of him. "I guess you're right. I'm more interested in the game than the prize. If you can't stand the way you get something, it won't be worth shit. That's true not just about women. That's how I deal with life."

"Do other people accept it? I mean, you're a soldier, you know? You can act that way? When there's a war on?"

"No. That's why I always end up on the outside, no matter which Air Corps I'm assigned to. Who knows, maybe I'll even get kicked out of the Navy one of these days."

Yuki sat up, and looked at Ando.

"How about me? How does that apply to me?"

"I think I've been fair to you."

"Fair? Oh, yes. You never tell me that you love me. You don't ask me to go together. You never sweet-talk me at all. Sure, you asked to come over, but the words you used weren't anything special. So it's all the woman's fault if she feels like she's getting nothing from you. It's all her fault. She was stupid enough to believe there was maybe something special behind your words. It's her fault if she expected something more than you said, when you didn't even imply it!"

Ando recoiled. "Hey, don't invite me over if you're gonna ask for something I can't give."

"You cold bastard!"

"Look, I like you. I like the way you sing. I like the way you drink. You were real pretty that night at Blue Max. I mean it."

"But you'll never ask me to marry you. Never."

"We had a great time in bed. We had a wonderful time today. What's wrong with that? You sing songs and live by yourself. And I'm on my way to another military base somewhere. It's pointless for us to exchange promises about the future. You know damn well we can't."

"What about your sister? Is that how you want her to feel about men?"

"My sister..." began Ando, but grasped for words in vain. He had to hand it to Yuki again. *I do have a double standard.* "My sister isn't as strong as you are. She doesn't know how to choose men. She can't control herself when she falls in love with somebody. She might destroy herself," said Ando, a little uncomfortably.

Yuki pulled away and grabbed a cigarette. Her back to Ando, she said: "How strong do you think I am? What kind of trash do you take me for?"

The wind rattled the building, disturbing the regular patter of the rain for a moment. The tin roof rang and the window shook with the impact of large raindrops.

Ando sat up, quietly, and kissed Yuki's thin, soft back.

CHAPTER 31

That same rainy Sunday, Yamawaki left his home in Azabu, Tokyo, for Yokohama. He was going to see Ando's sister, Mariko. Several days ago, Yamawaki had called the hospital where she worked to inquire about her schedule. Unlike Yamawaki, nurses worked irregular hours: nights, weekends, and even holidays. He knew he'd never see her if he just sat around waiting for her to get a day off. And so he took the train to Sakuragi ward in Yokohama that afternoon to ask her out in person.

A sign painted on a large drop cloth dangled from the building in front of the station. It read: *The festivities are over! It is time to work!*

A festival celebrating the 2,600th anniversary of the Imperial family's reign had commenced on November 10th. People had drunk, danced, and played music for six days straight. The party had ended two days ago. The drop cloth was a reminder to those on the home front to focus anew on work. Perhaps because of the bad weather, everyone on the street was dressed in conservative clothes of khaki or gray. The colorless pedestrians only made the dreary weather and cold rain more depressing. Yamawaki looked for a taxi, without any luck. There was nothing but trucks in front of the station.

He opened his umbrella and began walking briskly, clutching a paper bag to his chest. He walked toward Iseyama Shrine for ten minutes. The Yokohama Rising Sun Society Hospital was just beyond the shrine. Yamawaki cursed the war that prevented him from finding a taxi. *Damned Imperial Japan... Can't they even make an exception for a poor guy trying to look his best for an attractive young lady?*

Yamawaki arrived at the hospital just after four. His suit was damp from the rain. The front lobby was filled with Sunday afternoon visitors.

Yamawaki slid his umbrella into a stand and headed towards the front desk.

The nurse behind the counter raised her head. She looked quite young.

"And who are you calling on today?" asked the young nurse.

"I'd like to see Miss Ando," answered Yamawaki.

"May I have her first name too, please?"

"Mariko."

"Miss Mariko Ando," the nurse repeated the name under her breath as she flipped through the patient lists. After a long while, she finally raised her head again.

"Is she a patient here?"

"No. She works here. She's a nurse."

The young nurse visibly stiffened in her chair.

"And may I ask what this is regarding?"

"I came to see her. That's what this is regarding."

"I'm afraid she's on duty right now, sir."

"Is she in the middle of an operation or something? If not, I'd like to see her."

Another nurse standing nearby overheard the exchange and fixed Yamawaki with a stare.

"Head nurse," said the young woman, asking for help.

The head nurse was a plump woman in her fifties. Her cheeks were flushed and her expression stern.

"Sir, I'm afraid meeting a man while on duty is…" She trailed off.

"Is what?"

"Is prohibited."

"I'll tell you what. I'm her brother. I'm Mariko's brother."

"But she's a half-breed…" The head nurse quickly corrected herself. "You don't look like her at all. I'm afraid I don't believe you."

"Wait, did I say 'brother'? I meant stepbrother. Would you tell her Keiichi Ando is here to see her? We need to discuss the thirteenth anniversary of our father's death."

"It doesn't matter who you are. She is on duty."

Yamawaki fumed. *Can Sundays really be that busy?* Yamawaki had to admit he didn't have a clue about hospital schedules. *Perhaps this won't be as easy as visiting a college buddy at the Ministry of the Navy.*

"I guess I'll just wait for her, then," said Yamawaki, backing down. "Her shift ends at five o'clock, right? Could you just let her know that I'm here, and that I'll be waiting?"

"We have a responsibility, in lieu of parents, to look after the girls who work here," the head nurse stated coolly. "I can't take a message from a total stranger to one of my girls. Certainly not from someone who pretends to be her brother."

"Girl? I'm afraid there's been a misunderstanding. The Miss Ando

I need to see is an adult."

"She works under me. I am responsible for her private life as well."

"Are you saying she isn't allowed to talk to any men *at all*?"

"Certainly not to strange men who appear out of nowhere and demand to see her. I keep a strict eye on wolves that come sniffing around for our nurses."

"Are you calling me a wolf?"

"Indeed I am. You certainly seem to be a man of leisure."

"What? A man of leisure! What makes you say that?"

"Real Japanese men don't wear suits in this day and age."

Yamawaki couldn't believe it. There was no good reason for her escalating antagonism. No reason for this narrow-minded woman to be attacking his lifestyle.

"I suggest you don't judge people by their appearance," said Yamawaki, lowering his voice and injecting as much venom into it as he could muster. "Take yourself for example. Are you really comfortable being called an angel in white? I'm sure the things you do after hours would make the devil blush."

The color drained from the head nurse's face. Muscles bulged and twitched dangerously in her neck.

"Get out!" she shouted. "This is a hospital, not a waiting room!"

"Wonderful discipline. A model for imperial society."

Yamawaki quickly checked the map of the hospital hanging behind the woman. The patients' rooms were all located on the second floor of the two wings. The nurse's station wasn't far from the entrance. Yamawaki figured that he would find Mariko there unless she was making her rounds.

Grabbing his umbrella, Yamawaki stalked out of the front door, keeping a wary eye on the receptionists the entire time. He turned left at the garden in front of the hospital and headed nonchalantly to the side entrance. This part of the building felt deserted; he didn't see any men carrying boxes of equipment, no patients walking around. Yamawaki slipped through the entrance, removed his shoes, and grabbed a pair of hospital slippers from a nearby slipper box. He left his umbrella leaning against the box.

He padded down the hallway, looking for the staircase. The smell of disinfectant hung thick in the air, but Yamawaki got used to it and soon put it out of his mind. He found the staircase in the corner where the two wings met. He spotted the back of the reception desk to his left. The head nurse was talking to Army personnel who wore some sort of armband. Yamawaki clambered up the stairs. The doors of patients' rooms lined both sides of the hallway on the second floor.

One of the rooms had a large glass window facing the hall. A small sign stuck out of the wall above the door. *That must be it.*

Yamawaki peered into this room from around the doorjamb. It was long and narrow, with several desks and shelves lined with patient records. Some sort of nutrition chart hung on one wall. A nurse sat at one of the desks, filling out some paperwork. It wasn't Mariko.

Yamawaki silently continued down the hallway, looking into each room as he passed. Each door had a small glass observation window. The third door on the right was wide open. The room was large, with four beds on each side. All of the patients were men. There were several visitors too. A nurse was speaking softly to one of the patients. Mariko!

"If you're feeling so well," Mariko was saying in a mock-scold, "I'll have to tell the doctor to send you home! Do you really want me to tell him that you're faking?"

Yamawaki knocked on the door.

Mariko raised her head. Her eyes widened in surprise when she saw Yamawaki. And then her face positively glowed. For Yamawaki, her expression was like warm spring sunlight. He flushed. He could hardly contain himself. The unpleasant memories from just a few minutes past dissipated in an instant.

"Hello," said Yamawaki thickly.

Mariko made a slight bow to the patient, and headed straight for Yamawaki. She wore a long white uniform, with her hair tucked underneath a round white cap. It seemed almost deliberately designed to cover and obscure her femininity. But Mariko was attractive enough that even the nurse's uniform couldn't hide her essential beauty.

"What brings you here?" asked Mariko, without lowering her voice. Her eyes were filled with the same excitement Yamawaki remembered from Blue Max. "Are you visiting somebody?"

"Actually, I am," answered Yamawaki brightly. "I came to give some words of encouragement to a hard-working nurse."

"Are you talking about me?"

"I don't know anyone else here."

The patients stared at Mariko and Yamawaki. Some of the men

appeared somewhat uncomfortable. Mariko was popular with the patients, too.

Mariko indicated the hallway with her eyes. Yamawaki stepped outside, and she followed him. She closed the door behind her. They began walking side by side toward the nurse station.

"The truth is," said Yamawaki, "I came here to ask you out. I'd like you to dine with me. Even if you've already made other plans."

"Tonight?" Mariko's voice rose half in surprise and half in excitement. "Oh, I'd cancel anything! But can you wait until five?"

"May I wait for you here?"

"Would you mind? Oh, but I'd be terrible to ask you to wait out here in the hallway."

Mariko looked into the nurse station. The nurse that had been filling out the paperwork exited, glanced at them, and headed down the hall, apparently in response to a patient call.

"Mind waiting in here? I'm sorry it's such a mess."

"Not at all. I hope I'm not being too much of a bother."

"I'll have to answer immediately if a patient calls, but if not… Just make yourself comfortable!"

"Sure beats standing in the rain."

Yamawaki followed Mariko into the nurse station. Mariko offered him a chair.

"Oh, by the way," said Yamawaki, pulling a record out of his paper bag. "I brought you something I bought in Berlin. A recording of the Berlin Philharmonic. We discussed it the other day. The conductor is Karajan, a rising star."

"You're lending me this? *Thank* you!"

"Please, I want you to have it. It's a waltz by Johann Strauss called 'Artist's Life.' I hope you'll like it."

"Oh, I love waltzes, especially from that period."

"It was recorded just last February. I don't think it's even officially on sale yet. Consider it a present from one music lover to another."

"But this is too valuable."

"Like I said, your brother has done me a big favor."

"I know, but still…I'm just his sister."

"What if I told you it was just a token of my appreciation for your agreeing to dance with me the other night?"

"Thank you very much," said Mariko, putting her hand on Yamawaki's. "I'll play it at the dormitory. Everybody will love it."

Mariko served Yamawaki a cup of tea. They chatted at length about the record and Blue Max's last night. Mariko seemed to have been hoping to see Yamawaki again. Sometimes they got so excited that they talked over one another. Soon they reached a certain level of understanding about each other, became comfortable, and began sharing their true thoughts. Mariko wasn't like the other women Yamawaki knew, who nodded blindly at whatever men said to them. She had her own views on subjects that Yamawaki brought up; she expressed her opinions, logically and with conviction, but she wasn't stubbornly opinionated either. *A rare jewel among Japanese women*, thought Yamawaki. *The legacy of an early education abroad?*

The sound of rain against the glass window never let up, but the patient call buzzers remained thankfully silent. The nurse who had stepped out earlier had yet to return. Yamawaki and Mariko sat close enough for their knees to touch, and enjoyed a good twenty minutes of uninterrupted conversation.

Just as the rain began to pick up, they heard footsteps just outside of the room. They stopped talking and looked toward the hallway in time to find a nurse and a man in a white coat open the door.

Startled, Mariko leapt to her feet.

"Dr. Kurihara!"

The man, tall, appeared to be about forty years old. His graying hair was neatly parted in the middle and slicked back. Bewildered, he looked from Mariko to Yamawaki and back again. Standing behind him was the head nurse who had confronted Yamawaki at the front desk.

"Miss Ando, what are you doing here? Have you forgotten that you're on duty? Dragging a man into your office during your shift! How could you?" cried the head nurse.

Yamawaki stood up.

"She didn't 'drag' me in. I came here unannounced and on my own. There's absolutely no need to insult her."

"You! Didn't I ask you to leave? What are you doing in here?" said the nurse, glaring furiously at Yamawaki.

"I thought her shift would end soon, so I was waiting for her here."

The doctor said, "You aren't permitted to walk around this hospital without permission. Who are you?"

"Are you asking for my name? Or my job title?"

"Your relationship to this woman."

"He claimed to be her brother at the front desk," the head nurse cut in. "A bald-faced lie to force his way in. I think he's some kind of hoodlum! I can just imagine the loose women he associates with."

"Look, this is a special place," said the doctor. "We're charged with taking care of human lives here. If you want to visit, you must clear it with the front desk. That's the rule. And what's more, Miss Ando is on duty. Whatever were you two doing in this little room all by yourselves?"

"As I said," answered Yamawaki, "we were chatting between patient calls. You're talking about a lady. I would ask you to drop the insinuations."

"For the last time, who are you?" asked the head nurse again.

"My fiancé," said Mariko, stepping forward.

The doctor's jaw dropped, and Yamawaki, too, hardly managed to conceal his shock. He looked at Mariko. She seemed to be serious. Her eyes were fixed on the doctor's.

"Did you say f-fiancé?" stuttered the doctor.

"Yes, I did. His name is Junzo Yamawaki. And we're engaged to be married."

The doctor looked at Yamawaki in amazement, his expression practically begging Yamawaki to deny it.

"Who are you?"

In response, Yamawaki withdrew a business card from his front pocket and handed it to the doctor.

In an era of special provisions for all military personnel, a secretary to the Ministry of the Navy was entitled to the degree of respect accorded to a commissioned officer. Although technically a civilian, Yamawaki's status was equivalent to that of an army lieutenant. *That ought to shut them up*, thought Yamawaki. The head nurse peered at the card over the doctor's shoulder.

"Secretary to the Ministry of the Navy," read the doctor slowly. The head nurse appeared transfixed, her eyes glued to the card.

"I apologize for my breach of etiquette and protocol. I didn't mean to interrupt Miss Ando's work. But when the head nurse refused to even bring a message to her, I was forced to take matters into my own hands. I hope you can see that I'm neither the 'hoodlum' nor the 'wolf' that this woman has accused me of being."

"You're a liar!" screamed the head nurse. "Her fiancé? Preposterous! You claimed to be her brother only a while ago!"

The doctor and Mariko continued to stare at one other. The doctor still appeared to be in shock. Mariko remained at attention, but Yamawaki detected some subtle provocation in her eyes.

"I didn't know you were engaged," said the doctor, blinking.

"I should have told you earlier." Mariko's voice was cold as ice.

"This all appears to be a misunderstanding," continued the doctor lamely.

"I'll ask him to wait at the entrance. I apologize for deviating from regulations."

"Well," said the doctor, glancing at his watch. "It's about time for your shift to end, anyway. Go ahead. It's all right."

That there was something beyond the professional between Mariko and the doctor was clear to Yamawaki by now. Yamawaki wasn't a student of psychology or of literature, but he had had his share of relationships. In the present case, at any rate, not even an Ohnuki could have missed what was going on.

Yamawaki looked at the head nurse. She looked just as confused about the situation as the doctor. She, too, saw that there'd been things going on behind the scenes.

"Mr. Yamawaki, would you mind waiting for me downstairs? I'll go and change," said Mariko.

"Certainly."

Yamawaki bowed to the doctor and head nurse and left the nurse station.

That evening, Yamawaki and Mariko had dinner at a Western-style restaurant near the port of Yokohama. After that scene at the hospital, however, they couldn't manage to shake the awkwardness between them. Yamawaki attempted, with surprising success, to forget what Mariko had said to the doctor. She, on the other hand, seemed to feel worse than necessary, ashamed at the trouble she had caused for Yamawaki. They stayed together until eight, but Mariko never recaptured the brightness Yamawaki had so relished in her back at the nurse station.

The two walked back to the nurses' dormitory in silence. Arriving at the door, Mariko turned to Yamawaki.

"I did really put you on the spot back there. I can't tell you how sorry I am."

"Oh, don't worry about me," Yamawaki was quick to respond, as if he'd never heard what she'd uttered to the doctor. "There really wasn't anything else you could have done. If anything, the fault is mine for showing up unannounced like that."

"I probably sound like an idiot asking this, but can we see each other again?"

"You know, I was going to ask you the same thing. Let me know what you think about the record," said Yamawaki. "Oh, and make sure to let me know what they're saying about me. 'A preposterous wolf of a hoodlum' for starters, but I'm looking forward to hearing whatever else they come up with."

This managed to extract a faint smile from Mariko.

Yamawaki took out his schedule book. They decided to meet again on the first Sunday of December. It would be after Ando's departure. It was the earliest break in both their schedules that they could find.

And with that, Yamawaki and Mariko stood in silence for a few moments. It was a strange date for Yamawaki. He wasn't quite sure how to end it. Perhaps Mariko felt the same way. He had acted awkwardly all evening long, when he was usually such a smooth talker; whatever the reason, he felt as though he'd suddenly lost his gift.

The rain picked up again. Finally, Mariko said goodbye in a tone that suggested that she meant to forget the events of the afternoon and evening. She turned around and practically ran back into her dorm.

CHAPTER 32

Ando returned to his hangar at the Yokosuka Air Corps to find an unfamiliar face. The man was engaged in an intense discussion with maintenance chief Marugame. He appeared to be in his mid-20s, and wore glasses. His body seemed almost too thin. He wore a white coat, like an engineer.

Marugame introduced the man in white as Morita, an engineer for the Naval Aviation Technology Development Center. Morita's position was equivalent to that of a junior-grade lieutenant.

"I'm here to explain how to use the radio," Morita said to Ando. He didn't seem particularly fond of dealing with people. "Try it out. If you find any problems with it, I'll make you another one."

"I used a Sora 1 in China, but it just didn't work. Why was that?"

"It could have been a blown vacuum tube, the poor-quality capacitors and resistors, or the primitive antenna."

"In short, the whole thing's junk," Inui commented with a laugh.

Morita's face colored, but he kept his cool and stayed polite. "The problem was our inexperience with mass production. We couldn't manage to produce large numbers of radios of a uniform quality. Each one came out a little differently, and in the end none of them worked. A chain is only as strong as its weakest link."

"Meaning if there's even one bad part, the quality of the whole product drops to that level, right?" asked Ando.

"Precisely. The same rule can be applied to an individual machine or an entire mechanical system. If we had spent the extra attention we should have on the components, the Sora 1 wouldn't have been such a disaster."

"Really? Would you care to elaborate?"

"The circuitry was a copy," said Morita. "It was based on circuits found in American and European radios."

"That doesn't exactly instill us with confidence."

"We didn't have any other choice. To be honest, that's our level of technology at the moment."

"How are these new radios different from the old ones?"

"We redesigned the circuitry and assembled them ourselves at HQ.

We selected each part carefully. They've tested favorably, too."

"And they're already in the aircraft. We saw to that yesterday," added Marugame.

"I'd like to explain how to use these new radios," said Morita. "You'll find them quite different from the Sora 1."

Marugame handed brand new flight helmets to Ando and Inui. They differed markedly from the standard issues. The ears projected outward and featured earmuff-like covers on the inside.

"What's this?" asked Inui, flicking an ear-cup with a finger.

"A flight helmet with a built-in receiver," answered Morita. "We created them based on a study of similar German and British products."

"It's heavy."

"I think you'll get used to it."

Ando and Inui put on the flight helmets. They fit like gloves. Perhaps the engineers had measured their old flight helmets. The new-leather smell was almost overwhelming.

Ando, Inui, Morita, and Marugame approached the Zero fighters. The aircraft had already been moved out to the front of the hangar. Ando climbed up and slid his body into the cockpit. A brand new metal radio, the size of a lunchbox, had been attached under the tail hook deployment lever. The box had been painted a dark gray and featured numerous dials, switches, and indicator needles. It appeared similar to the Sora 1, but the controls were laid out somewhat differently. As Ando had requested, the radio homing device seemed to have been removed; there was no sign of its directional lever. The wireless transmitter and receiver units on the left side of the cockpit had been replaced with shiny new metal boxes as well.

Morita stood on the right wing, stretching his neck to peer into the cockpit. Inui and Marugame watched from the left wing.

"The controls look similar to the old model, but mark my words, this is an all-new unit," boasted Morita. He proceeded to point out and explain each control. "That's the switch for turning it on and off. There's the main frequency adjustment knob and the fine-tuning dial. That's the frequency gauge, that's the volume control…"

There was a switch for the aerial in front of the control board. There was a telegraph-style key atop the board as well, but Ando didn't have high hopes about its practicality. Looking things over and with some help from his experience with the Sora 1, Ando began to feel comfortable about the controls of the new radio.

"Now let me explain the substantial differences between this and the older model," said Morita. "There is a cable connected to the power box below. Can you see it?"

Ando located a coil of cable on the right side of his seat and pulled. It had a thickness of seven or eight millimeters, and was coated in a black material. It reminded Ando of a water hose. The very end had been stripped to expose bare wire. Morita took the cable from Ando and inserted the bare portion into a jack on the flight helmet.

Morita also produced what looked like a gas mask. He explained that it was a microphone. Ando took the canvas device and strapped it around his head. It covered his mouth completely. Another black wire extended from the microphone into the power box.

"Please keep the power on while you're flying. That will allow you to hear orders from base and to converse with your wingman. The channel is fixed, but if you get too much noise or the volume is too low, you can adjust it manually by turning this," said Morita.

"It's hard to breathe," said Ando, pulling the microphone down to his chin.

"You'll be able to hear incoming transmissions so long as you're wearing your flight helmet. So if you want, you can leave the microphone off while you're flying, and only put it on when you need to speak."

"Mind if I take it for a test run?"

"By all means. Actually, I was going to ask you to do just that. That's my main reason for coming here."

Ando and Inui made preparations and took off almost at once. They returned to base a half hour later. Morita was waiting for them.

"It works," said Ando. "It's nice to be able to communicate with your wingman."

Morita was overjoyed. "I kept telling them, but nobody would listen!" he said excitedly. "Will you please let the admirals know that the Sora 1 radios need to be replaced?"

Ando wasn't sure how much pull he had with the higher-ups, but he nodded anyway. He knew that once they saw the radio in action, they'd immediately recognize its importance. He suspected that, before long, a fighter plane without a radio would be considered obsolete. It was a matter of time.

CHAPTER 33

On Tuesday, November 19th, Rear Admiral Tadao Yokoi was finally able to assure Major Graf that the Japanese government had secured a flight route. Tokyo had cabled Yokoi that they had managed to find a string of refueling bases leading between Japan and Germany. Colonel Hussein of the Iraqi Army would be providing one of them.

Yokoi made his report in Graf's office at Luftwaffe Headquarters.

"We can assure delivery of the Type Zero Carrier Fighters on or around December 8th," said Yokoi.

"I look forward to it," said Graf. "I'm very interested in this Japanese fighter aircraft, not just as the coordinator for this project, but as a former pilot. It's a matter of intense personal interest for me."

"Were you a fighter pilot, major?"

"I was a member of the 2nd Fighter Wing until last May," answered Graf. "I was shot down by a Spitfire at Dunkirk. After recuperating from my injuries, I received a transfer to headquarters."

"I assume that was the battle in which you were awarded the Knight's Cross to the Iron Cross?"

"Indeed. The Knight's Cross to the Iron Cross and my scar are mementos of the time I spent in France."

"I heard that the Knight's Cross to the Iron Cross is only granted for a soldier's third military exploit. Did you distinguish yourself elsewhere in France as well? Or in Poland, perhaps?" Yokoi resisted the urge to avert his eyes from the horrendous scar on Graf's face.

"I received my Iron Cross First Class just before the push into France. The British called it the 'Phony War.' But I can assure you that our fighter squadrons were anything but."

"And the Iron Cross Second Class?"

"Spain. I flew with the 'Condor Legion.' Of course, like everyone else, I was flying as a volunteer. After the end of the Spanish Civil War, the Führer honored me with the Iron Cross Second Class in recognition of my service."

Graf seemed mildly embarrassed at the boastful turn of the conversation. He made a show of closing his file loudly to end it.

"Rear Admiral Yokoi, would you mind accompanying me to

Alexander Square? I'd like to have a beer to celebrate your success in securing the air route."

"Certainly, Major Graf."

Graf took Yokoi to a small beer hall located on a side street off of the west side of Alexander Square. The sign read "Zeppelin." Yokoi could not tell if the beer hall was named after the famous airship, or the count, and Graf didn't explain. Inside, a large model of the German aircraft known as the Albatross hung from the ceiling. More than a few of the customers sported Luftwaffe uniforms.

Yokoi accepted a beer stein from the waitress.

"A toast to the Tripartite Pact."

"To the Tripartite Pact," agreed Graf.

"And to the success of our transport mission," said Yokoi.

"To our transport mission," the major concurred.

"But perhaps I made a mistake in the order of my toasts. Allow me to propose another: to the Führer's health."

To this, Graf did not respond. He had a quiet sip from his beer. Yokoi wondered what that meant. Graf remained impassive, betraying nothing one way or the other. He simply sat and drank his beer. Yokoi decided not to press the matter. *It takes all kinds. Even in the officer corps of the Luftwaffe...*

Once Graf had finished half of his beer, he turned to Yokoi again.

"I know next to nothing about Japanese aircraft, but I've met several Japanese pilots. One of them, in fact, was quite skilled."

"Where did you meet them?"

"At the flight school in Braunschweig. I studied advanced flight techniques there in 1936. It was the year after the Luftwaffe dropped pretenses and stopped calling it a 'private flying club.' Several Japanese pilots studied there as well. We staged daily mock dogfights with Heinkel He51s."

According to Graf, one of the Japanese pilots happened to be exceptionally good. He was a fighter pilot, of course, and belonged to the Imperial Naval Air Corps. He was only in his twenties. He was a lieutenant, junior grade. His forte was one-on-one air combat.

"In the Luftwaffe," said Graf, "the most difficult aerial technique is considered to be the Immelman."

The Immelman was a special turn used when being chased by an enemy. The pilot climbed rapidly through the vertical in a half loop, then executed a quick roll back into the upright to attack his pursuer from above. The Immelman required a pilot to carefully control the rudder and elevator at the same time to spin the aircraft around to bear on the enemy target. Needless to say, it was necessary to keep absolute control of the aircraft at all times during the spin to aim properly. Only a scant few Luftwaffe pilots had managed to perfect their Immelman turns. To hear Graf tell it, natural aptitude was just as much a necessity as practice to pull it off.

"We have something similar in our Air Corps as well," said Yokoi. "I believe the pilots call it 'the Twist.' I've also heard it called the 'Reverse Whirlwind.' It may be the same as your Immelman."

"Can every Japanese pilot do it?"

"Oh no, no. Only a few pilots. Very few."

Graf continued his story about Braunschweig. One day, the Immelman turn came up as a subject while German and Japanese pilots were unwinding over beers in the canteen.

"I can do one," said a Japanese pilot.

Everyone laughed, dismissing it as childish bragging.

"I have mastered the technique," repeated the Japanese. His face was pale, his pride apparently hurt.

The Germans broke out in laughter again. Nobody believed him. At the time, none of the Luftwaffe pilots were actually capable of pulling off an Immelman. The technique had slipped into legend; it was known only by name and description among the German pilots at Braunschweig. That some random pilot from the Far East could have managed to perfect this most advanced of flight techniques was impossible for them to believe.

"You're calling me a liar?" said the Japanese, looking at each of the German pilots in turn. "You think I'm just bragging?"

The laughter stopped at once. A frost descended over the friendly atmosphere. It was Graf who broke the silence.

"Tell you what, Japanese. Let's try it tomorrow. In one-on-one mock combat."

"All right," answered the Japanese. "If I can show you an Immelman, you'll pay for all my drinks from now on."

"And if you fail?"

"Drinks for every pilot in the school. As much as you want for three days."

"It's a deal."

Moments after the deal had been sealed, the other pilots began passing around a flight helmet to make bets. The odds were decided at seven to one against the Japanese pilot at first. But several pilots had misgivings, seeing how confident he was. In the end, they settled on four to one.

The following day, the Japanese pilot and Graf climbed into their Heinkel He51s and took off before the watchful eyes of their fellow pilots.

The battle commenced. The Japanese left himself wide open to Graf, as if he were a rank amateur. Graf seized the opportunity and immediately fell in behind him. The match seemed to be over before it had even begun. Graf was appalled.

So, what was he boasting about? He's practically begging to be shot down!

Chuckling, Graf closed in on his opponent. He could almost hear the shouts of victory from his fellow pilots on the ground. The Japanese began to jink, hard, swinging several times from right to left. Graf stuck to him like glue. Suddenly, the Japanese climbed steeply in what appeared to be a curve. Anticipating that his opponent would end up behind him, Graf immediately raised the nose of his aircraft to follow.

But a split second later, the Japanese aircraft cut the loop short with a quick roll, spun, and pitched his aircraft into a steep dive. Now Graf was still climbing, but the Japanese fighter had him in his sights from above. And before Graf could react, the Japanese had already streaked past his tail.

It was an Immelman. A superb, perfectly executed Immelman. The realization filled Graf with an odd combination of admiration and fear.

Accepting defeat, Graf returned his aircraft to the horizontal. The Japanese fell in alongside and slightly below. The match had ended in less than a minute. Graf hadn't even been able to show off any of his own techniques. The Japanese had lulled him into a false sense of confidence. A split second after gloating over his impending victory, Graf had been nailed. He was left speechless by the skill with which he had been manipulated.

"I respect that Japanese pilot to this very day," concluded Graf.

"As an officer of the Imperial Navy, your story fills me with pride. Do you remember his name, by any chance?"

"It was... And..."

"Ando?"

"Yes, Ando! That's the pronunciation. I remember him being somewhat standoffish."

Graf stared off into the distance, perhaps recalling his past. He finished his beer in silence. His scar looked slightly flushed.

CHAPTER 34

In the twenty days that had passed since Ando and Inui began their intense flight-training regimen, several special modifications had been made to their Type Zero Carrier Fighters. The special radios were one. The mechanics had also swapped the original oil coolers with larger ones.

Ando and Inui's training was proceeding smoothly. Just as Inui had predicted, they managed to achieve a range of 3,000 kilometers at an altitude of 4,000 meters and a speed of 180 knots. The Zeros were ready to leave for Berlin at any time.

On December 20th, Ohnuki summoned Ando and Inui to the Ministry of the Navy in Tokyo for a briefing regarding the flight route, the location of refueling bases, and the schedule. Ando and Inui put on their dress uniforms and headed to the Kasumigaseki section of Tokyo.

They had been told that Ohnuki and Yamawaki's office was located in the south wing of Aviation Headquarters. Aviation HQ itself was located in a new five-story building facing Gaisen Street behind the Ministry of the Navy. Although it had its own entrance, visitors generally reported to the reception for the main building. Ando and Inui appeared at the main building at five minutes to three, just as Ohnuki had requested, and gave Yamawaki's name at the reception desk.

"So this is where the 'bricks' work," said Inui, looking around the entrance hall. "Given our past with that Curtiss, I expected our first visit to be a court-martial."

"Just think about the files they must have on us here," said Ando.

"Maybe we ought to find them and do a little re-writing."

Yamawaki arrived to pick Ando and Inui up. As they had expected, he showed up wearing a suit. It stuck out like a sore thumb in the ministry's sea of military uniforms. It was probably even more conspicuous out on the street, where the average citizen dressed in a drab national uniform. Yamawaki didn't seem to care.

"How is flight training coming along?" asked Yamawaki. "How are the aircraft doing?"

"We're doing fine. So are the aircraft," answered Ando.

"Just don't go overboard. You've got your work cut out for you."

"Not to worry. We'll get some rest before departure."

Ando and Inui followed Yamawaki upstairs, taking a hallway from the main building straight into Aviation Headquarters. They took another staircase down from the Bureau of Legal Affairs and arrived at a door with a sign that read: *Office of Procurement*. Yamawaki opened the door to reveal his and Ohnuki's office. *So this was where the "Ibis" had been planned out*, thought Ando. Behind a large table in the center of the room stood Ohnuki.

Ohnuki skipped the small talk and launched directly into the briefing. A large map of Asia had been spread across the table. It had been marked in several places with tiny navy flags, representing the locations of the refueling bases.

"We have secured eight airstrips altogether," said Ohnuki. "If we include Kanoya, that's a total of nine stops for you to land and refuel at."

Ando and Inui were instructed to take off from Yokosuka and head for Kanoya base in Kagoshima prefecture. The next day, they were to head southwest over the East China Sea and make for Kaohsiung base in Taiwan. From Kaohsiung, they would fly west-southwest over the South China Sea to Gia Lam, a base located on the outskirts of Hanoi in French Indochina. Ohnuki explained that official orders had been prepared stating that Ando and Inui were flying to Gia Lam to join the 14th Air Corps there.

Immediately upon arriving in Gia Lam, Ando and Inui would receive new orders from Japan ordering them to Hankow base in China. The next day, Ando and Inui would take off to the north, but immediately change course to head west instead.

In other words, the second set of orders was nothing but a cover. The whole mission was being kept secret, even within the military. Perhaps it would be announced once the Germans actually signed the contract to produce their own Type Zero Carrier Fighters.

Rather than head to Hankow, the two planes would fly across the Indochina peninsula, over British-controlled Burma, into Eastern Bengal, and head for Sirajganj on the northern outskirts of Dhaka. A refueling stop awaited them there.

The next day, Ando and Inui would head west again. They would cross the Indian subcontinent and land in Kamanipur in the desert of Rajasthan. A friendly Maharaja had promised fuel, oil, and a place for them to stay. Most of the territory between Hanoi and Rajasthan was controlled by the British. The pilots could expect to encounter the RAF at any time;

Ando and Inui had to be particularly careful while flying near Rangoon. The bright side was that the route was far enough to the north that the RAF stationed in Singapore would not give them any trouble, nor for that matter the Australian and New Zealand Air Forces.

"The real headache is India," remarked Ohnuki.

The Indian headquarters for the RAF were located in Ambala. The cities of Kohat, Quetta, Peshawar, Lahore, and Karachi hosted RAF airbases as well. Quetta would be particularly dangerous, as it was home to the No. 5 and No. 31 Fighter Squadrons.

If the RAF spotted Ando and Inui, they would fire at them without hesitation. Each of the Zeros had been painted with the Japanese flag. Japan was now unambiguously part of the Axis. There was no way to expect a friendly reception. Ando and Inui would have to fly as fast and high as possible during the run from Hanoi to Rajasthan.

Roughly 1,900 kilometers separated Hanoi and Dhaka. Another 2,000 lay between Dhaka and Kamanipur. Those two legs would be the most difficult of the entire journey. Speed, altitude, and the careful planning of detour routes were the only ways to survive discovery by the RAF. The pilots would have to keep a close watch on fuel consumption during these legs.

After Rajasthan came Iran. Ando and Inui would use the runway at a test well site some 150 kilometers from Bandar Abbas. It was owned and operated by a Japanese petroleum company.

From Bandar Abbas, Ando and Inui would fly northwest over the Persian Gulf into Iraq. Once in Iraq, they would make for an Iraqi Army base in Imam Hamid, northeast of Baghdad. The RAF maintained a potent presence in Iraq as well. They had set up their headquarters in Habbaniya, on the western outskirts of Baghdad. Bomber squadrons were stationed at bases in Hinaidi, Mosul, Shuaiba, and Basra. There were additional reports of a new airfield in Musalla as well, but they remained unconfirmed.

"Once you leave Baghdad," said Ohnuki, his voice betraying premature relief, "you'll enter a neutral country, Turkey. From there on, you won't have to worry about any military obstacles. The Turks don't seem to have any problems with us. You'll be able to relax a little."

Ohnuki said that the Minister of Foreign Affairs had already contacted the Turkish government. They had obtained permission for Ando and Inui to land at an army base on the outskirts of Ankara. In fact, said Ohnuki,

Ando and Inui could expect to receive a warm welcome there.

The next destination after Ankara would be Italy. The Italians offered the use of the Cerveteri airbase, just outside of Rome. But if Ando and Inui had to make an emergency landing farther south, the Italians wouldn't mind in the least.

After Rome, there was only the final destination, Berlin, some 1,200 kilometers to the north. It required Ando and Inui to fly over the Alps; still, that leg would be child's play compared to what they'd have accomplished by then. The Germans had requested that the aircraft land at Gatow airfield in western Berlin.

The flight route to Baghdad was to be kept fully confidential, the number of people involved restricted to an absolute minimum. Everyone involved along the way had only been told that a pair of courier aircraft would be landing. They knew nothing about the types of planes, the mission objective, or the route they were taking. The Turks and Italians had been kept in the dark about the details as well, but unlike with the other airfields, negotiations had been carried out through normal diplomatic routes. Japanese Embassy officials were set to meet with Ando and Inui as soon as they arrived in those countries. They'd be treated as important guests.

All flights were to take place during the day. Single-seat fighters were simply not equipped for night use. Normally, a flight of fighters was accompanied by a long-range scout aircraft, but that wasn't an option for this mission. Ando and Inui would have to spot enemy aircraft without the help of reconnaissance.

Ohnuki cautioned Ando and Inui not to leave any trace of their mission behind. If they encountered the RAF, confrontation was to be avoided if at all possible. If they had no choice but to engage, they were to attempt a hit and run. Each Type Zero Carrier Fighter was equipped with twenty-millimeter machine cannons and a pair of 7.7-millimeter machine guns, but the less they opened fire, the better. Ando and Inui's mission was to get to Berlin as quickly as possible.

"I guess that's about it," said Ohnuki, and looked at Ando and Inui. "Any questions?"

"This says that the RAF is using only old Gladiators and Gauntlets in India and Iraq," said Ando, looking over an intelligence report. "Are you positive they haven't deployed any Hurricanes or Spitfires there?"

"The Germans assure us that the British have committed all of their

Part Two

Hurricanes and Spitfires to defending their home isles. The air war over England won't be letting up any time soon. It seems that they can't spare any of their best fighters."

"Not even one?" asked Ando skeptically.

"The only Hurricanes and Spitfires outside of the British Isles are stationed in Malta and Cairo. I don't think you need to worry about them for this mission."

Ando crossed his arms. "We'll be flying five or six hours straight for ten consecutive days," he observed.

"If at all possible, try not to rest until you make it past Baghdad," said Yamawaki.

"How about feeding us more meat until we take off?" Inui jested.

"You'll get a special allowance. Twenty yen. Do whatever you want with it."

There was a knock at the door. Cups of tea had been brought for them. Yamawaki stepped out to receive the tray. Ohnuki, Yamawaki, Ando and Inui sipped tea and continued discussing the flight schedule and course. Ohnuki provided general climate information for each area as well.

Ohnuki and Yamawaki acknowledged that flying for ten days straight would be a heavy burden on the pilots. They wanted to give Ando and Inui a day off after flying the first half of the journey.

But the Japanese government had promised to provide two Type Zero Carrier Fighters by December 8th. Because of the great distance, the Germans weren't being particularly strict about the date; at the same time, they had originally requested that the planes arrive on November 15th. As the actual delivery date had been delayed once already, Ohnuki didn't want to push it back any further.

What was more, the Imperial Japanese Army was about to send a military technology observation group, led by Lieutenant General Tomoyuki Yamashita, to Germany in early January. Despite heavy opposition from several admirals, the Ministry of the Navy had decided to organize an inspection tour, too, and were busy compiling a roster; the group would probably be headed by Vice Admiral Naokuni Nomura and include twenty or so others. Simply put, thanks to the secret articles pertaining to cooperation over military technology in the Tripartite Pact, Japan was in the enviable position of enjoying the fruits of German engineering. Ohnuki was reluctant to do anything to displease the Germans when Japan was clearly the greater beneficiary of the technical exchange.

"I originally thought we'd need four weeks for flight training, but I think we've attained a satisfactory level already," said Ando. "We can cut training short by a week."

"Can you leave earlier? Is that what you're saying?" Ohnuki demanded.

"Would that mean changing the entire flight plan?" asked Ando. "Have you contacted the refueling bases with specific dates?"

"No. We just told them it would be around the beginning of December. We're supposed to cable each of them just before your arrival."

"That means we can hasten the departure date, then."

"How about leaving a day earlier? The new departure date will be the 27th. That means you're leaving in seven days," said Ohnuki, glancing at a calendar on the wall.

"No problem for us," said Ando. "How do you feel about it?"

"I don't see any problems on our end. Let's see… All I have to do is whip up a few transfer orders for you two before you leave."

"We'll continue our training for the next four days, and if you have no objections, take two days off. We'll leave for Hanoi on the 27th."

The meeting ended. It was a quarter past five.

Just before getting up to leave, Ando turned to Yamawaki.

"Mr. Yamawaki, can I have a word with you?"

Yamawaki cast Ando a questioning look.

"It's not about the mission. It's a private matter."

Now Ohnuki and Inui looked puzzled as well. But Ando didn't explain. He stood up and left, followed by Yamawaki.

Ando walked down a dark staircase, and turned around once he reached the lower floor. The Ministry was closed. They were surrounded by bookcases. No one else was around. Yamawaki began to feel nervous.

"Mariko told me that she met you after work the other day," said Ando, staring directly into Yamawaki's eyes.

Yamawaki started. Somehow, he hadn't expected Mariko to tell Ando about their meeting.

"How serious are you?"

Yamawaki blinked once. "What's that supposed to mean?"

"Mariko's a 'half-breed.'"

"So?"

Part Two

"So she's had a hard time both in the U.S. and over here. Mariko doesn't know much about our father, and we lost our mother when she was little. She was raised by a totally different family. She's been through a lot. She's suffered more than her fair share of unhappiness."

Yamawaki said nothing. Ando continued:

"She's getting older. She's twenty-seven."

"I know."

"She's a grown woman, of course. But she's never had luck with men. I don't want to see her go through it anymore. I don't want anybody to play games with her."

"I'm not playing any games with her."

"You went all the way to Yokohama to see her. In a downpour. She'd get the wrong idea."

"I went to Yokohama to give her a record that I bought in Berlin. And we had dinner together. What did she say?"

"That you gave her a record and bought her dinner. She seemed to want to see you again."

"We promised to meet again."

"If you aren't serious about her, I want you to knock it off. I want you to stay away from her. I don't want you encouraging her to expect something you can't give her. You're a civil officer, a graduate of Tokyo Imperial University. Hell, I hear your whole family's full of officers. If you want to play around, you don't have to do it with a half-breed woman from a humble family who's past her marrying age. She's made it this far by not having false expectations. If you build them up for her, she'll be the one who suffers in the end. That's what I mean."

Ando stopped to watch Yamawaki's reaction. *Is he going to talk back? Or is he just going to agree and back off?* To be honest, Ando did not know what he wanted to hear.

"I'm serious about your sister," said Yamawaki, without hesitation.

Ando gauged Yamawaki's response, wondering if he was serious. *Well, he seems honest enough; he didn't try to give excuses or dodge the question. Smooth talker or not, maybe I can trust him.*

"I hope you mean it."

"I can't speak for Miss Ando, but I'm serious about her."

"Let me make one thing crystal clear before I leave," said Ando, pointing a finger at Yamawaki. "If you make her sad, or give her a hard time, I'll come back for you. I'm serious. I don't care where I'll be. India, Berlin, it won't matter. I'll come back here and kick your ass."

"I assure you, my intentions are honorable."

"That's all I have to say, secretary."

"Duly acknowledged, lieutenant."

CHAPTER 35

It was already dark by the time Ando and Inui left the Ministry of the Navy. Ando paused momentarily on the stairs leading from the entrance and gazed into the sky above the office buildings in Kasumigaseki.

During training, Ando hadn't paid a tremendous amount of attention to the details of his mission. But after the meeting, he'd begun to realize just how incredibly far it was to Berlin. Not only did he have to worry about the technological and military aspects of the journey, but also the complicated formalities within the ministry and negotiations for support for the flight as well. Ando began to wonder if he'd been too cavalier about accepting the mission. He didn't particularly want to quit, and he knew that he was still happy to leave Japan, no matter what obstacles lay ahead. But he realized he should have tempered his excitement when he didn't know the full extent of what lay ahead.

A cold wind blew through Tokyo that night. Many of those leaving the Ministry of the Navy wore heavy winter coats. Several American-made cars were parked in front of the building. Perhaps they were for the top staff.

Ando and Inui continued down the stairs, crossed the yard, and exited through the main gate of the Ministry of the Navy. They headed to a streetcar stop. To get back to Yokosuka, they needed to head to Shinbashi station and take a train. Ando stopped to check which streetcar they needed to take.

Suddenly, a car appeared from inside the ministry and pulled directly in front of Ando and Inui. An officer stepped out the car as soon as it came to a halt. He wore a winter uniform with an adjutant sash identical to Ohnuki's.

"Are you Lieutenant Ando and Flight Sergeant Inui?" asked the man.

"Yes," answered Ando. He'd never seen this lieutenant commander before. Was he one of Ohnuki's colleagues?

"I'd like to talk to you. Would you mind riding with me?"

"Is than an order?"

"Does it have to be one?"

"No, sir. But I'd like to know what this is about."

"It's about two birds," answered the lieutenant commander. "A pair of ibis."

Ando and Inui exchanged glances. Ohnuki had told them that the mission was highly classified. It was under the direct supervision of Minister-Admiral Oikawa, and only a handful of people in the Ministry of the Navy knew about it. Did the man's uttering "ibis" mean that he was involved? Neither Ohnuki nor Yamawaki had said anything about him during the meeting.

Ando and Inui remained where they stood.

"Get in the car, Lieutenant Ando," said the man. "You too, Sergeant Inui. That's an order."

Ando shrugged. It seemed they had no other choice. At any rate, it might be better to find out what this was all about rather than insist on seeing official orders. Ando and Inui got in the back seat of the car. The car pulled away from the gate the moment the lieutenant commander took his seat next to the driver.

"This won't take long," he said, his eyes never leaving the road ahead, Sakurada Street. "I'll even drop you off at the train station when we're done."

The car crossed the intersection at Toranomon Gate and continued straight. Ando wasn't very familiar with Tokyo. He had no idea where they were being taken.

From that point on, neither the officer nor the chauffeur said a single word. In fact, if anything, Ando and Inui detected subdued hostility. It was clear that the officer didn't intend to roll out the welcome mat for them. Ando nervously watched the scenery roll past his window.

"Reminds me of when those M.P.s took us in Shanghai," whispered Inui. "I hate life on the ground."

The car turned off of Sakurada Street and began climbing a steep side street. An open gate stood at the top of the slope, and the car passed through. It appeared that they had entered the front yard of a private mansion. Ando heard gravel under the wheels. The car pulled up near a porch. The officer got out and opened the back door for Ando and Inui. Ando stepped out and took a good look at the garden. It was dark, with no lamps save for one on the porch; it wasn't particularly bright, but enough for Ando to discern his surroundings. The garden was large and well-tended. A garage stood on one corner of the lot. The two-story mansion had been built from dark-colored stones. Ando thought it had to be owned either by an aristocrat or someone very, very wealthy.

The officer led Ando and Inui into the entryway. An old man, apparently a butler, appeared, approached the lieutenant commander, and whispered something in his ear. The younger man nodded, and ushered Ando and Inui into the foyer. Yellowish, indirect lighting highlighted the patterns of an antique carpet on the floor.

The officer stopped in front of a pair of heavy-looking wooden doors and pushed them open. A piano could be heard in the next room.

The three men entered. The room was large, with a high ceiling. There wasn't much furniture. The floor was polished linoleum, and a luxurious chandelier hung from the ceiling. The room appeared to have been designed for holding receptions of some kind. There was a grand piano in one corner, on which a girl was playing a piece.

An admiral sat in a straight-backed chair next to the piano, listening to the girl's playing. Ando saw the man's profile, but couldn't tell who it was. The admiral showed no sign of having noticed the three men entering the room. The lieutenant commander didn't say a word. Following his lead, Ando and Inui remained silent as well.

Ando recognized the song the girl was playing. Mozart's Piano Sonata No. 15 in C Major. The piece was one of Mariko's favorites; in fact, it was the only Mozart tune she knew how to play.

Ando stared at the girl. She was about fourteen or fifteen and wore a dark red velvet dress. Her long hair had been tied back with a white ribbon. Even from across the room, Ando could see the determination on her face.

The music ended. The girl looked up at the admiral shyly. He gave a faint nod and gestured a few claps.

The girl noticed Ando and the other two men. The admiral swiveled his head to regard his visitors as well. The lieutenant commander saluted sharply.

The girl, suddenly nervous, stood up and shut the keyboard cover. She wore black shoes that sent echoes across the room every time she took a step.

"Thank you, dear," said the admiral affectionately. "You've improved quite a bit while I was away in China. You played that piece beautifully. I feel so relaxed."

The girl smiled shyly again. She looked very innocent. She picked up her sheet music, bowed towards Ando and the other two men, and left hurriedly.

"Here they are," the officer announced. "Lieutenant Ando and Sergeant Inui."

The admiral looked at Ando and Inui.

"This is Vice Admiral Shigeyoshi Inoue, head of Military Aviation Headquarters," the officer introduced the admiral.

Inoue motioned to a pair of chairs and Ando and Inui sat down. The admiral moved to the bench in front of the piano, placing one hand casually on the keyboard cover. Inoue sported a mustache and closely cropped hair; he had a good posture, though he appeared to be in his early fifties. His mouth was firmly shut, and his sharp eyes hinted at self-confidence and a profound intellect. Ando was reminded of the prim and proper headmaster whose strictness they had always joked about at the private school he'd attended in America.

"When is your departure?" asked Inoue.

Ando hesitated. *Is he asking about Ibis? Am I allowed to tell?*

Ando remained silent.

"Relax. I understand that your mission is highly confidential. So much so, that it was planned completely behind my back." Inoue's voice was gentle. "But I want you to understand that this mission should have been under my control from the beginning. I've been in charge of Aviation HQ since October. Overseeing missions like this is one of my duties. You don't have to worry about Lieutenant Commander Ohnuki right now. Just answer my question."

"I'm just a fighter pilot, sir," said a perplexed Ando. "I understand about duties, but only about my own. If it's at all possible, would you mind discussing this with Lieutenant Commander Ohnuki directly?"

"I'm simply asking about your orders. I'm not going to stir anything up by asking how the mission was organized. When are you going to be transferred to the 14th Air Corps? That's what you discussed at headquarters today, correct?"

He seemed to know everything already.

"The 27th of this month, sir," answered Ando.

"Have you managed to secure the necessary refueling bases?"

"We have one roughly every 2,000 kilometers along the way, sir."

"When will you arrive in Berlin?"

"On December 7th, sir."

"It'll be a tough job, flying all by yourselves."

"I'm confident about our training, sir."

"I heard you're the top pilots of our Navy."

Ando let the last comment slide without a reply. Had it been Ohnuki, he would have immediately agreed. But this was an admiral. Ando stayed quiet as a matter of courtesy.

"I wish you luck, gentlemen," said Inoue.

Ando and Inui blinked. They hadn't expected the meeting to turn out this way. Vice Admiral Inoue was known as a staunch opponent of the Tripartite Pact. It was seen as a given that he would oppose their mission as well. Yet here he was wishing them godspeed. Perhaps he'd spoken the words only formulaically?

"Thank you, sir," said Ando suspiciously. "But I was under the impression that you wouldn't support this mission at all. May I ask why you're wishing us good luck, sir?"

"Because the fate of our country may well hinge on your success," replied Inoue.

"What do you mean, sir?"

"Your success may change the very atmosphere of the Navy. Don't you think so?"

"I believe it could prompt the Navy to work more closely with the Germans, sir."

"That's one possibility," agreed Inoue. "But more importantly, I believe it will draw attention to the importance of air power." Then, turning to Inui, the admiral asked, "Do you think the war in China will be over soon?"

Inui was flustered. "I don't think it'll end soon, sir. Even if we keep it up for another ten years, I don't think we'll be able to lick them."

"And what about the United States?"

"I think we're going to war with them if things keep up the way they've been, sir."

"And do you think we'll win that war?"

"Even a kid could answer that one for you. America's too damn big and strong," said Inui, forgetting himself and beginning to chuckle.

"Precisely," said Inoue. He didn't seem to mind Inui's manners.

"Merely because Japan has won a few important battles and signed a treaty with Germany, the Japanese people are under the illusion that we can solve any political problem by force. In particular, I'm referring to our air war in China, and the growing political tension with America. Soon, I fear, Japan will abandon the diplomatic solution for all-out war against the United States. It's preposterous. It's idiotic."

Inoue gave his views on the coming war with the United States. Japan was inferior to the United States in almost every respect. There would be no way to overwhelm them through sheer force or to wear them down until they surrendered. And the idea of invading the American mainland, or of totally annihilating its military forces, was simply out of the question.

The United States, on the other hand, had the wherewithal to occupy not only Tokyo, but all of Japan. That the Japanese military would be totally annihilated in the process was a distinct possibility. War against the United States would end in tragedy. It was a foregone conclusion.

The only way to avoid total destruction was diplomacy, Inoue declared. If war did break out, Japan would find itself in a drawn-out quagmire of a battle even if they did manage to gain temporary control of the Pacific. Once Japan committed its forces, the United States would target Japanese supply routes and impose a blockade. The way Inoue saw it, the Imperial Japanese Army and Navy would be systematically starved and destroyed, and the war would likely end with the United States occupying Tokyo and the rest of Japan.

"Once it begins, there will be no easy way out," said Inoue, shaking his head. "If Japan allows itself to become intoxicated by a few triumphs in the Pacific, the chance for a diplomatic solution will slide through our fingers. Imperial Japan will be reduced to ash before it surrenders. Our Army and Navy will be wiped out, our cities and towns will be burned, our civilians will be killed, the survivors turned adrift. I cannot shake this vision. Mark my words: tragedy, misery, and loss for Japan, the likes of which the world has never seen. That's where this will end."

Inoue finished his speech. A deep silence descended upon the room. Ando had never heard such a high-ranking officer speak so bluntly about Japan's prospects.

Imperial Japan cannot defeat the United States. A war with them will end in our total destruction. The rumors were true, then. Inoue's "vision" was so bold that it bordered on treason, but his chilling logic was so sound that it left no room for disagreement. In fact, there was no other sensible conclusion. Ando, Inui, and the lieutenant commander remained silent.

Suddenly, Inoue turned to face the piano's keyboard and lifted the lid. He began to play. Ando immediately recognized the piece as *Umi Yukaba*, the funeral dirge for sailors who have given their lives in combat. It was a sorrowful, baleful tune.

Inoue stopped almost as quickly as he had begun. He stared straight ahead, the frustration and sadness over his country's path etched deeply in his face. After a while, Inoue composed himself and turned back to face Ando and the other men once more.

"We cannot win, that is for sure. But we can avoid that tragic fate," said Inoue, closing the keyboard cover.

Ando waited intently for the admiral to continue.

"We must endeavor in whatever way we can to maintain the possibility of a diplomatic solution. And I believe I know the way to do just that."

Inoue believed that Japan's first priority should be to create a dedicated air force using naval aviators. Next, they would build up coastal defenses and increase the number of submarine groups.

"Listen carefully. If Japan and the United States go to war, it will take the form of island-to-island fighting in the interests of securing airfields throughout the Pacific. You can bet that battles will be won or lost with air power. The most important showdowns won't be between fleets on the sea. We will see air combat waged on a far greater scale than seen in England and Europe over last summer and this fall. The Navy needs to be able to dominate the skies as well as the seas. We must stop wasting money on building more useless battleships.

"As head of Aviation HQ, I'm in the middle of writing a proposal to increase our air capabilities on a dramatic scale. The coming war will be fought in the air. The number of aircraft will determine loss or victory for each side. No matter how much of our production capacity we devote to building aircraft, we won't ever catch up with the United States. But we can, at least, create an air force that is large enough to ensure our security for a certain period of time. If we are to prepare for the coming war, we must fully embrace the tactics of the future."

Inoue paused for a moment to clear his throat before continuing. "If the Germans take an interest in our Type Zero Carrier Fighters and license them for production, it will have a major impact on the Imperial Navy. It will force a shift away from our current blind worship of ever-larger ships and cannons to an air-focused strategy. And that, Lieutenant Ando, is why I pray for your success with all my heart."

"An interesting theory, sir. But I'm afraid there's a fatal weakness in your plan," said Ando.

Inoue's eyes widened.

Ando could sense the utter shock of the lieutenant commander sitting next to him. He clearly hadn't imagined that Ando would disagree with the vice admiral. Ando ignored him and plunged ahead.

"You talked about building up Japan's air combat capability. But are you aware how many pilots there are in Japan at the moment, sir?"

"Some three thousand in the navy alone."

"Yes, sir. But only sixty percent of them are really capable of flying an aircraft."

"I'll grant you that."

"Next, you'll have to consider how an air force can be organized with so few pilots. Who will fly the fighters? Do you know how few fighter pilots come out of Kasumi-ga-ura every year, sir?"

"You're right. The current training program must be overhauled as well. That is just as important as increasing aircraft production."

"As you're undoubtedly already aware, sir," continued Ando, "most young men in America know how to drive a automobile before they even apply for flight school. They already have a basic grasp of engines. Quite a few of them even own cars. It may be difficult for us to believe, but even the children of farmers in America know how to drive. In fact, it's uncommon to find a farmer who can't. I was sent to flight school in Germany several years ago, and I can report their situation is similar. In my class at Kasumi-ga-ura flight school, on the other hand, only one other person besides myself knew how to drive a car. I suspect things haven't changed since then. That means that even if we do reorganize the program, we've still got to start from zero: the basic principles of an internal combustion engine, how they work in vehicles, things like that. Even if we increase the number of aircraft, we'll still be short of men to fly them. It's going to be difficult to cull an air force from a population of young men who've never even driven a car. "

"Are you saying my plan is wishful thinking?"

"What I'm saying is that increasing the number of aircraft we produce doesn't address the woeful shortage of pilots."

Inoue looked down and exhaled heavily through his nose. "You've got a point," he murmured. "A country full of farmers who still rely on hoes, declaring war against the United States! Those glory-craving idiots, that moron of a major general..."

"Vice admiral, it's time," cut in the lieutenant commander. Inoue looked up, apparently realizing that he had gone too far. Certainly there was nothing attractive about an admiral complaining about his colleagues in front of lower-ranking men.

"You're right. It's about time to head back to Suikosha. Can you give these men a ride?"

"And you, sir?"

"I'll walk. It's just the right distance for a walk."

Inoue stood up and put on his hat. Ando and Inui stood and saluted.

"Shall I tell Lieutenant Commander Ohnuki about our meeting tonight?" asked Ando. "Should I let him know that you're aware of the mission?"

"No," said Inoue, shaking his head. "We should keep up the charade of my knowing nothing about it. It will make it easier for him to do his job. Keep this meeting to yourselves."

Inoue walked up to Ando and Inui and looked at each man in turn.

"Let me reiterate that I wish you luck."

"We'll do our best, sir," Ando replied respectfully.

Inoue's footsteps echoed as he walked out of the room.

Training ended on November 24th, four days after the meeting with Inoue. They would be departing for Berlin in just three days. That night, Ando went to Yuki's apartment in Yokohama.

Ando had tried calling the common phone at Yuki's apartment building, but nobody answered. So he decided to drop by unannounced. There weren't any job openings for a club singer like Yuki these days. All of the dance halls had been shut down, and strict regulations applied to the performance of foreign music. Yuki would probably be at her apartment listening to records, like the Sunday before.

Ando arrived at the converted warehouse and headed to the second floor. He knocked on Yuki's door. There was no response. He tried the doorknob. It wasn't locked, and the door swung open. Yuki's room was completely empty.

Ando went inside and turned on the light. The furniture was gone. There was no sign of Yuki's gramophone, sofa, mirror, or bed. The only sign of her presence was a white mark on the wall where she had hung a calendar or a painting. It appeared she had moved.

But she said she was going to Shanghai next month, recalled Ando in his confusion.

Suddenly, he sensed someone approaching from behind and spun around. He found a tiny woman, perhaps thirty years old. Ando remembered how Yuki had described her neighbors: the mistresses of foreign sailors, a hooker, an artists' model, and a dancer. She could have been any one of them. Her skin was fair and her lips full, sensual. Ando bowed in greeting.

"Did the tenant who used to live here move out?" asked Ando.

"Yes," nodded the woman. "The day before yesterday."

"Do you happen to know where she might have gone?"

"She said something about Shanghai. She sold her furniture to a secondhand shop and left with just three suitcases."

Ando felt more disappointed than he'd care to admit. He hadn't expected Yuki to leave without saying goodbye. He may well have done it to her, but hadn't expected it to happen the other way around. In spite of having told Yuki he might not be able to see her before he left, Ando still couldn't believe it.

"Hey, soldier. Were you close to her?"

Ando smiled at the straightforwardness of her question. "Yeah. We were pretty close."

"Because if I were her, I sure would've chosen you over him."

"Him?"

"Yuki took off for Shanghai with some musician. A trumpet player. But you know, you look a lot better than he did. I live next door—wanna have a drink?"

Ando thanked her but declined the invitation.

Ando returned to Yokosuka, and then decided to head for a small inn on Okusu mountain on the Miura peninsula. It was a secluded getaway known for its excellent hot springs. Inui was already there.

Ando arrived late at night. Inui, clad in a *yukata* robe, met him at the entrance.

"Didn't expect to see you tonight," Inui said. "I'm kinda surprised."

"Same here... My destination just disappeared," Ando explained with a bitter smile. "Figured I might as well join you."

Ando changed into a *yukata* and headed to the open-air bath for a midnight dip.

Part Three

CHAPTER 1

Ohnuki and Yamawaki arrived at Yokosuka Airbase in a government limousine at six in the morning. There was still some time until dawn; the sky had only just begun to brighten. A thick cloud layer hung over the area. If one strained one's eyes, the clouds could be seen gliding from west to east. The wind was cold and there was a fine mist in the air. Ohnuki and Yamawaki couldn't tell if it was rain or the wind whipping moisture in from the ocean. Whatever the case, a storm front appeared to be on the way.

Their car took them down a paved road to a hangar. The two Zeros were parked inside. Some ten maintenance men swarmed over the aircraft, performing pre-flight checks and topping off the tanks. A maintenance man sat inside each cockpit making final adjustments. Powerful lights on the ceiling of the hangar illuminated both aircrafts and the crew around them.

A truck sat next to the hangar door. Ando and Inui, in full flight uniform, stood next to the truck talking to ground crew. Their expressions appeared serious, and they nodded frequently in response to what the mechanics were telling them. A haversack and a sword each sat on the ground next to Ando and Inui's feet.

Yamawaki spotted a trumpet case next to one of the haversacks. He remembered Mariko mentioning that Ando always took it with him, even into battle. Ando and Inui noticed Ohnuki and Yamawaki and headed towards their car.

Yamawaki and Ohnuki got out. Yamawaki shivered as the cold wind stung his cheeks. It was about five degrees Celsius below freezing. His exhaled breath turned white and mingled with the cold Yokosuka air.

Ando and Inui saluted Ohnuki and Yamawaki separately. Ohnuki returned the salute. Yamawaki, still unused to the military style of greeting, bowed slightly instead.

"Did you sleep well?" asked Ohnuki.

"Very well," replied Ando. "With those two days off I'm in tip-top shape."

Yamawaki agreed that Ando looked vigorous, nothing like the harried man that he and Ohnuki had first seen in Yokohama. He didn't appear to be stressed or showing his age. Ando had restrained his cynical air, but the desperation Yamawaki had seen in the lieutenant's drunken eyes at Blue

234

Max was gone.

"How about you?" said Ohnuki to Inui.

"Never felt better," replied Inui.

"I heard a low pressure front is on the way."

"Not a problem," said Inui. "Even if it were sunny today, it doesn't mean we'd have good weather for the next ten days."

"We're ready," said Ando. "No sign of trouble with the engine, fuselage, weapons, or other equipment."

"We're fully prepared as well," said Ohnuki. "Everyone is standing by. You can take off as planned."

"We're ready anytime. Any particular time you want us to take off?"

"Don't ask us. Go ahead and take off whenever you feel ready."

"Then we're taking off now."

"We're looking forward to hearing your reports."

"Understood, sir. You won't regret selecting us for this mission."

"Confident as ever."

"Sir, it's just that I know how good I am."

Ando turned to look at Yamawaki; he seemed to want to say something. Yamawaki could tell it was something Ando didn't want to discuss in Ohnuki's presence.

"There is no need for you to worry about your family," said Yamawaki.

Ohnuki gave Yamawaki a strange look. He had no idea what Yamawaki was talking about. Yamawaki shrugged, and Ohnuki didn't press the issue.

Ando came to attention and saluted. "Sir! Lieutenant Ando and Sergeant Inui, departing to join the 14th Air Corps."

Inui snapped a salute too.

The two fighter pilots turned and walked away without looking back. Their brisk boot-steps were audible over the wind.

"Soon enough..." said Ohnuki, turning to look at Yamawaki. "Soon enough, we're going to learn if we chose the right men."

"And those same men will find out if we two are any good at organizing missions," Yamawaki pointed out.

Ando, standing next to his fighter, signaled to the maintenance man sitting in his cockpit to turn on the engine. Another man began turning a crank near the bottom of the aircraft. Yamawaki and Ohnuki heard a series of small explosions. Soon the propeller began spinning smoothly. Inui's engine was also doing just fine.

The two fighter pilots climbed onto the wings of their aircraft. Ando and Inui accepted their haversacks from their crews and tossed them into their cockpits. The maintenance men climbed out of each cockpit, and Ando and Inui took their places. Their seats seemed higher than usual; the top of their heads seemed to peek out over the side windshields. The pilots put on their flight helmets and tightened the chinstraps. The ground crew removed the wheel chocks.

Ando saluted Ohnuki and Yamawaki again from his cockpit. Ohnuki saluted back. This time, Yamawaki managed a salute as well.

Ando and Inui revved their engines. The bodies of their brand-new aircraft were vibrating. The two Zero fighters nosed out of the parking area. Yamawaki and Ohnuki stepped back to avoid the wash from the propellers.

The aircraft headed to the runway and positioned for takeoff. Soon they began to roll down the runway, with their tails facing Ohnuki and Yamawaki. The ground crew members had removed their hats and were waving them at Ando and Inui's departing fighters. Ando's Zero rumbled down the right side of the runway, with Inui following slightly behind and to the left. The two aircraft lifted off the runway and raised their noses. Once the planes were airborne, their landing gear folded slowly into their bellies. The two planes drew a wide arc westward and continued to climb. Soon they had disappeared into the thick clouds. By the time the aircraft had disappeared from Ohnuki and Yamawaki's sight, the roar of their engines had faded as well.

Yamawaki looked at Ohnuki, who was still standing next to him. Ohnuki's eyes remained fixed on the patch of sky into which the two fighters had disappeared. He looked somewhat sad.

"What's the matter?" asked Yamawaki. "Something on your mind?"

"No, not really," replied Ohnuki, his eyes never leaving the sky. "I'm being transferred. I just received the orders."

"Transferred? Where to?" asked Yamawaki.

"I've been named Staff Officer of the Combined Fleet. I'm being promoted to commander."

"Commander? Congratulations!"

"My duties won't really change, so there isn't anything to congratulate me about. It's just…"

"What?"

"Doesn't it feel like the end of an era?" said Ohnuki, turning to look straight into Yamawaki's eyes.

Yamawaki didn't understand. He quietly waited for Ohnuki to continue.

"The Manchurian Incident, the Army uprising, the Sino-Japanese Incident, and now the Tripartite Pact. It feels like too much to bear right now, but soon we'll look back on these as better days. I can hear it already: 'Boy, it sure was quiet back then.'"

"Are you worried about war with the United States?"

"It's inevitable. There isn't an officer in the Imperial Navy who thinks otherwise. But don't expect it to be pretty. I foresee tragedy, even mass slaughter. Soon enough we'll envy those old-fashioned pilots who had the good sense to kiss Japan goodbye."

Ohnuki turned back toward the sky the two fighters had vanished into. That sky was dark, and it was rainy and windy, in what almost seemed a bad omen for Japan's future. It was late November of 1940.

CHAPTER 2

It was two in the afternoon on November 28th when Ryojiro Shibata returned from the New Delhi telegram office to his hotel near Connaught Place.

He had sent three telegrams, all related to Mission Ibis. Shibata had received word in the morning that the mission was under way. That meant that he needed to notify the men at the airfields he'd arranged for. Two telegrams were sent to those who were supporting the mission within India, but the third one was an extra. It was something like insurance, designed to make sure the mission proceeded smoothly.

Shibata retrieved his room key from the front desk, and took the stairs from the lobby. His room was on the second floor of the Hotel Shankar, facing a back alley. In addition to being Shibata's temporary quarters, the room also served as the branch office for the Union News Service. His room even had a phone line, but he only used it to file occasional (and entirely phony) stories with the Calcutta office for appearance's sake.

Shibata pushed open the door to his room. He immediately sensed something wrong, but before he could react, the door slammed shut behind him and he felt the pressure of cold steel against the base of his neck.

Another man emerged from the closet. He was Caucasian and appeared to be about fifty. He carried a large submachine gun. Shibata recognized it as being of Belgian manufacture.

"Don't move, please," said the man politely. "I abhor violence."

The man holding the pistol against Shibata's neck quickly frisked him for weapons. Shibata didn't move a muscle. There were two armed men inside his room, and Shibata wasn't eager to put his hand-to-hand combat skills to the test.

The man behind him finished checking Shibata. He drove his gun harder into Shibata's neck.

"Move over there," said the man. He sounded young.

"We're paying you this little visit because we have something important to discuss," said the middle-aged man.

"Who are you?" asked Shibata. "What are you doing here?"

"Oh, just who you'd expect. We're British, and we work for the government. For your information, that metal thing you're feeling right now happens to be a gun. It's fully loaded, I can assure you."

"Does the British military make a habit of pointing guns at foreign journalists?"

"A journalist!" laughed older the man. "Do you really expect me to believe that you're a correspondent for the Union News Service? According to my report, you're an Imperial Army officer, stationed in Singapore until two years ago. Am I wrong?"

"I have a journalist visa."

"Ah, well, immigration officials aren't perfect. Don't waste your breath. We already know you're a spy." He motioned toward a chair. "Why don't you sit down?"

Shibata did as he was told. The young man moved from behind Shibata to stand next to him. He appeared to be in his mid-twenties. He kept his gun, a snub-nosed revolver, trained on Shibata. It looked like an Enfield No. 2.

The middle-aged Caucasian moved to stand over Shibata. He was a stout man with broad shoulders. The striped tie he wore indicated that he belonged to the Royal Army, but perhaps he was a retired officer. The man's cold, blue eyes drilled into Shibata.

"Your recent activities have attracted our attention, and so we decided to have a chat with you," he said.

"What activities?"

"Your meeting with the Maharaja Gaj Singh. Several meetings with Pritam Singh. A trip to Calcutta. Another trip to Rajasthan. Those activities."

"I'm a journalist. It's my job to travel around and meet people."

"Suspicious people. We keep Gaj Singh and Pritam Singh under special surveillance. They're dangerous men. One supports an organization of extremists who insist on full independence for India. The other is an ambitious dreamer who'd have been better off born two hundred years ago. Calcutta is a political hotbed. And something's brewing in Rajasthan. I don't think you chose such interviewees by accident."

"So?"

"So I'm telling you this marks the end of your waltzing around undisturbed. You've been far too busy since the signing of the Tripartite Pact. I want to know why. I want you to tell me what's going on."

"Get out of my room. I don't have anything to say. I have absolutely no obligation to inform you about my activities here."

"By the way, we found something in your closet," the middle-aged man said motioning towards the table. A holstered gun, its magazine removed, sat atop it. "A Nambu, correct? It's illegal for foreigners to carry guns here. Do you have a special permit? If you don't, I'm afraid I'm going to have to place you under arrest."

"Can you prove that's my gun?"

"Of course! If you'd like, I can also 'find' stolen jewelry and blood-stained sheets."

"Blackmail. This is false arrest!"

"Let me remind you that we happen to be at war. Your country signed a pact to formally join the Axis. That means Japan is a de facto enemy of the crown. I'm afraid the usual laws don't apply."

"You're wasting your time if you think you're going to get anything out of me."

"Oh, I'm sure. But I have one simple question for you. If you answer promptly and honestly, I may even let you go."

"What is it?"

"Tell us about the telegram."

"Which telegram are you talking about? I've sent and received dozens. It's part of my job."

"I'm talking about the telegram that you received from the Japanese consulate that said, 'The ibis flew on the 27th.'"

"Are you even aware of the concept of a confidential communiqué?"

"I'm going to ask you again. Remember, we're at war. I'm convinced that the telegram will tell me something very critical. I don't have time to deal with formalities at the moment. To be honest, I'm feeling quite jumpy right now."

"I have nothing to tell you. If you want to arrest me, bring an arrest warrant. Contact the Japanese Consulate in Bombay or Calcutta. As a foreign visitor I believe I have that right."

"You're a military officer who entered the country under false pretenses. Believe me, my 'ignoring your rights' wouldn't strain diplomatic relationships between England and Japan any further."

"I'm warning you that this could indeed make things worse."

"I understand. And now I have a warning for you. Actually, choices, two of them. One is to tell us everything and be deported in three days. I highly recommend this choice, incidentally. You will be arrested right here for a petty crime and taken into police custody first."

"What's the other choice?"

"Too horrible even to contemplate," said the man, making a show of frowning and shivering. "People will think you just disappeared."

The man walked to the window and opened the curtains. He looked down into the alley and whistled. Shibata heard a car door being opened. The footsteps of several pairs of feet sounded in the alley. Riveted boots.

How much do they know? wondered Shibata. *And what do they want to know? Whatever it is, they'll try and find out over the next few days. I've got to keep my mouth shut for that long...for as long as my body and mind can take.*

The middle-aged man turned to face Shibata again, tilting his head. He seemed to be waiting for an answer.

Shibata only smirked.

CHAPTER 3

Ando and Inui arrived at Gia Lam airfield near Hanoi at one in the afternoon on November 29th.

Some 900 kilometers lay between Yokosuka and Kanoya base in Kagoshima prefecture. The weather hadn't been favorable, but Ando and Inui didn't need to worry about fuel consumption while flying over Japan. They had to take a detour around northern Kyushu to avoid a low-pressure area. It took them two and half hours to make it to Kanoya, all said and done.

The next day, Ando and Inui waited until noon for the weather to clear. They left Kanoya shortly after noon. The distance to the next destination, Kaohsiung base in southwestern Taiwan, was 1,400 kilometers. Given the relatively short distance, Ando and Inui lowered their flight speed. They landed at six in the afternoon on the same day.

They left Kaohsiung at seven in the morning on the 29th. Flown straight and level, the distance between Kaohsiung and Hanoi was only 1,500 kilometers. However, the RAF maintained a strong presence in Hong Kong. To avoid the area, Ando and Inui had to fly south over the Dongsha Islands and then west, adding two hundred kilometers to their flight plan. Furthermore, unlike the flight between Kanoya and Kaohsiung, this wasn't a trip across the safe skies over the Empire of Japan. They paid extra attention to their gauges until reaching the airspace over Haikou base in Hainan.

The heat of Indochina wrapped Ando as soon as he opened his cockpit in Gia Lam. The humidity was so high it felt like it might condense into rain at any moment. Ando felt sweat gushing out under his winter flight suit. A hazy cloud layer hung above in the still, stagnant air.

Ten brand new Type Zero Carrier Fighters sat in a parking area near the runway. They were intended for the 14th Air Corps, which would soon head out to assault the enemy air force in Kunming, Yunnan. The 14th Air Corps had just been deployed to Gia Lam in September.

Navy Captain Michio Uematsu, base commander, arrived to greet Ando and Inui.

"You may be surprised to hear this, seeing as you've only just arrived, but you've received new orders to transfer," said Uematsu.

"What's that, sir?" asked Ando, pretending not to know what was going on. "Does that mean we're not staying here?"

"Correct. You're off to rejoin the 12th Air Corps," said Uematsu, the relief evident on his face.

"When?"

"Orders say you're supposed to leave tomorrow." Uematsu looked at Ando and Inui's Zero fighters. "I wonder why they made you take such a roundabout route? They could have sent you directly to the 12th."

"Who knows, sir? Bet they have some good reason for it. Maybe there's been a change in plans. At any rate, it's a pleasure to be here. Even if it's only for a night."

"That was a long flight for you. I'll have them prepare a bath. Make yourselves at home."

"Sir. If it's possible, I'd like to have the engines checked out and the oil changed."

"I'll tell the crew."

Ando and Inui were introduced to the pilots of the 14th Air Corps in a meeting room that evening. Although they were leaving the next day, they had flown all the way from Japan. Had the new orders not arrived, Ando and Inui would have served under Uematsu, and so the captain introduced them to the other pilots according to etiquette.

Uematsu had Ando and Inui stand in front of the other pilots. Then, he told the group that the two were from the squadron that had shot down twenty-seven enemy aircraft in Chungking. He also informed them that Ando and Inui were originally supposed to join the 14th but had just received new orders to transfer immediately to the 12th Air Corps.

The other pilots exchanged looks at the sight of Ando and Inui. Some stifled laughter. A few showed open contempt. None showed any sign of admiration.

Ando knew the reason. He and Inui had gotten a reputation as troublemakers. The pilots of the 14th no doubt saw them as the "Ando and Inui" pair who caused a stir wherever they went. Perhaps, too, rumors of the Army investigation in Shanghai that had gotten them transferred back home had already reached these pilots.

Naval pilots were as close to one another as members of any exclusive club. Rumors traveled at the speed of fighter aircraft, particularly rumors about Ando, who'd shot down more enemy fighters than any other pilot in the Japanese military. Ando looked around the room; none of the faces were familiar to him.

"Have they fixed those guns yet, lieutenant?" called a voice from the back of the room.

Someone else snickered.

"Some reception," whispered Inui, the smile never leaving his face. "I can hardly wait to have dinner with them."

"Just remember, this is nothing compared to what the 12th would give us if we really went back to them," Ando whispered back, keeping a smile on his face as well.

Ignoring the comments, Ando and Inui introduced themselves.

After they had dinner separately, they met up and headed out to a veranda attached to the flight control office. There just wasn't enough time to talk to the other pilots and set them right. The Ibis pilots didn't even have the desire to, given that they were leaving for Berlin the day after. They simply shrugged off the matter.

The two men sat down on a pair of wicker chairs. They had been hoping for a cool evening breeze, but the air remained stagnant and muggy, covering greater Hanoi like the dregs at the bottom of a barrel. Silent for a while, both men peered into the western sky, where the clouds showed no sign of lifting. There was a fair chance they'd be hitting a thundercloud the next day.

"So this is it," said Inui, his eyes still on the sky.

"Yep. Time to kick off," said Ando.

The trip so far had simply been hopping from one friendly base to another. Although they'd flown over the open sea twice, those legs of the journey were through areas dominated by Japan. The flight from Gia Lam would be different; they were closer to the front lines. And once they left the base, they'd be heading directly into enemy territory. The British and Chinese controlled an enormous amount of land along the way. Though their Zeros were capable of flying long distances, it was a lot of enemy territory to cover in a single leap.

"I wonder if the British pilots are any good?" said Inui.

"They're superior pilots," Ando assured his buddy.

"You sound pretty sure."

"Think about it. They managed to drive away the Germans last summer. The British pilots were confident enough to call Goering's bluff. They can't be bad."

Part Three

Ando and Inui heard footsteps behind them. They turned to find a young officer accosting them hesitantly. "Lieutenant Ando, may I speak with you?" he said. Perhaps twenty-three or twenty-four, he was a junior-grade lieutenant, and appeared to be a pilot.

"How can I help you?" asked Ando, sitting up straight in his bamboo chair. "I must say I was deeply moved by our warm reception by your colleagues today."

The young officer blushed.

"You know," continued Ando, "I've noticed that we've become pretty famous. No matter where we go, everyone seems to know our names and military records. Come to think of it, they even take a step back when they hear our names."

"Unfortunately, lieutenant," answered the young officer, "there are people out there who take foolish rumors about you too seriously. It upset me to see how they treated you. They should have been honored that Lieutenant Ando and Flight Sergeant Inui had come all the way down to our base."

"There's no need to tell us what they've been saying about us, if that's why you're here. I've heard it all before."

The young man took a seat on the edge of the chair next to Ando's. He seemed as nervous as a novice seaman addressing an admiral. Ando didn't like it.

Inui, on the other hand, appeared to be enjoying it. He stuck a cigarette in the corner of his mouth and watched the young man with open amusement.

"I've heard a lot of rumors about you, lieutenant," said the officer, his face still flushed. "Some are so stupid that I don't believe they're true. But the story about your duel with the Curtiss... That really made me proud to be a member of the Air Corps."

Not again, groaned Ando inwardly. Any time Ando was introduced to a pilot who had flown with the 13th Air Corps, the subject inevitably came up. Even Ohnuki had asked about it, and he wasn't even a pilot. *Why is it such a big deal to these people?*

"Yeah, I've heard those rumors, too. They haven't got anything to do with me," replied Ando.

"They say you took a Type 96 into a one-on-one duel with an American Curtiss. They talk about it back in Kasumi-ga-ura, too. Some

245

people get angry when they hear about it, but I think it's the only attitude for a combat pilot. You're the samurai of the air, sir."

"Hey. I'm telling you, this 'duel' thing never happened."

"Officially, sure, that's what they say. But I'm convinced that's not the truth. Please, lieutenant. I'd love to hear about it. Wasn't it a real duel? If the rumor's true, it's as though the Baron von Richthofen's days aren't history. I think all combat pilots should be like you, sir."

"Okay, listen," said Ando, who was quickly tiring of the conversation. "Just think about it. I served under a commander in the 13th, just like anyone else. How the hell could I manage to fly a 'duel'?"

"Word is, your maintenance men were in on it. You got a note from a Chinese boy in Shanghai. It turned out to be a challenge to a duel from an American pilot you'd spared out of your noble warrior spirit. The ground crew heard about it and cut corners on your blockhead commander's fighter. On the day of the duel, he bellied in and broke his leg. Which permitted you, lieutenant, to take over as next in command and fly to Anqing. I heard all of your wingmen were in on it, too."

"Wow, is that the story? Too bad it never happened. But if your story were even half true, I'd be in the brig right now."

"The only ones who know the truth are the men who were directly involved. So that's five of our pilots including you, lieutenant, and the enemy pilots, and a few maintenance men. I bet you all got your story straight beforehand. But people can't keep a secret forever. Somebody had to tell, and word got around."

"Look. The flight record tells it all. Nothing more happened, nothing less. And I don't have any funny stories for you," said Ando coldly.

"I guess one of the rumors was true," said the disappointed young officer.

"Which one?"

"The one about your being incredibly stubborn and unreasonable, Lieutenant Ando."

"How long have you flown the Type Zero?" asked Ando, changing the subject.

"I just picked mine up in Shanghai the other day. I guess I've put in about twenty hours."

"How many enemy planes have you shot down?"

"I, uh, haven't encountered any enemy aircraft yet," confessed the young officer. He looked down at the floor.

"You aiming to be an ace? Looking for the highest number of kills?"

"No. Nothing like that," said the young officer, raising his head suddenly. "I just want to give my best as an Imperial Japanese soldier. I want to destroy the enemy for the sake of our country."

Ando snickered at the novice serviceman's naiveté.

"Kid, as a lieutenant with a little more experience than yourself, I have something to tell you."

The young officer's eyes shone with excitement. He leaned forward in his chair, eager, making sure he wouldn't miss a word. Ando shot a look at Inui, who was enjoying this very much.

"My advice for you is very simple," said Ando. "Watch your ass up there. If you encounter the enemy, don't engage them. There is no such thing as 'the samurai spirit' in the skies of 1940. If you want to live, stay timid. Don't be brave, don't even dream about it."

The young officer's eyes widened in shock.

"Be timid... I didn't expect to hear that from you, lieutenant," said the young officer. He shook his head.

"I'm just misunderstood. Commanders tell me I lack fighting spirit. Greenhorns think I'm the bravest pilot in aviation history. Both of them are wrong. It's just people seeing me through some lens. They don't understand the real me at all."

The young officer studied Ando's face, as if trying to detect a joke at his own expense. Soon, total disappointment spread across his face. The young officer stood up.

"Thank you for your advice, lieutenant," he said, snapping a salute. He looked pale.

"Watch your ass up there, all right?"

The young officer left without saying another word. Ando and Inui were alone again.

"Looks like you were his hero," said Inui.

"Maybe I overdid it, huh? Well, I gave him the best advice that kid's ever heard."

Inui tossed his cigarette to the ground.

The two pilots stared into the western sky until dusk fell and moths took to the air.

Nobody visited them again that evening.

CHAPTER 4

At 7:30 the next morning, Ando and Inui climbed into their Zeros and began their pre-flight checks. The sky was still just as cloudy, but the coolness was already gone from the morning air. The sweet smell of some sort of tropical flower or fruit filled the airfield instead. A red-headed bird about the size of a pigeon flew over the tarmac. One of the ground crew handed Ando and Inui their boxed lunches.

Sitting in his cockpit, Ando buckled his harness to his parachute, and checked his fuel gauges. Both the main fuel tank and the wing tanks were full. Including the drop tank, that meant 800 liters of fuel.

Ando set his fuel switch to the wing tanks for takeoff. Once he was at cruising altitude, he would switch to the drop tank. Then, when the drop tank was empty, he would switch back to the wing tanks, and then finally use the main tank.

Ando checked his ailerons, elevators, and rudder. The steps of the pre-flight check were second nature to him. Ando looked to his left to check on Inui, who was also in the process of checking his equipment. Ando watched Inui's ailerons wiggle up and down.

Ando glanced at his power switch to make sure it was off and shouted down to the ground crew.

"Away in front! Main switch off! Start the engine!"

Ando wrapped his right leg around the control stick and pulled it toward himself. When the engine was started, the control stick needed to be pulled all the way back or the aircraft's nose would tilt into the ground. The take-off procedure required a lot of work on the part of the pilot. Ando used his leg to hold the stick to free his hands for other tasks. Ando watched as the ground crew inserted a crank into the cowl of his aircraft. Presently the inertial starter began to hum at full speed.

"Contact!"

Ando switched the power on and pulled a lever to connect the inertial starter with the engine's transmission. The propeller began to turn. He quickly moved his left hand to the throttle and opened it slightly. A cough and a series of small explosions could be heard from within the fourteen cylinders of his Nakajima Sakae engine, which began to rotate in time with the propeller and backfired, loudly, several times. Exhaust fumes wafted into the cockpit. To Ando, nothing smelled sweeter. It was the sweat of his aircraft.

Ando put on his flight mask and goggles. Suddenly he noticed a talisman sitting atop his dashboard. The characters on it read, *Eternal Fortune in War*. Ando didn't believe in talismans or amulets. He never put them in his cockpit even when they were gifts. He had no idea where this particular one had come from.

He ran a fingertip over his gauges as he checked them: hydraulic gauge, oil temperature gauge, air intake pressure gauge, fuel pressure indicator, tachometer, cylinder temperature gauge, others. All systems appeared normal. He shifted from the pre-flight warm-up to the engine check, watching the tachometer and boost gauge all the while. Then he checked his right and left onboard electrical generators, the movement of his flaps, and the oil pressure for his landing gear without finding any problems.

Ando reached for his new radio set and turned it on.

"How's your aircraft?" said Ando into his mask.

"Excellent. No problems at all," replied Inui at once.

"I found something strange inside my cockpit," said Ando, flicking the talisman with his fingers. "'Eternal Fortune in War.' Any idea where it came from?"

"I got the same thing," said Inui. "Guess we were a little more popular than we thought."

"I wonder if that kid did it who came to see us?"

"No. It has to be from the ground crew."

"How do you know?"

"Don't forget, I was a common marine before I went to flight school. I may not have scored as many kills as you, lieutenant, but I'm a hero to these guys all said. They stayed up all night taking care of my aircraft. I hate to tell you this, but they took care of yours second."

"Fine by me," laughed Ando. "I may have come second, but that doesn't mean they were slacking off. Ready for take off?"

"Ready to go."

Ando adjusted his engine and signaled the ground crew. A young maintenance man removed the wheel chocks. Paying attention to his surroundings, Ando slowly guided his aircraft to the edge of the runway.

Ando glanced at the flight control office with its galvanized tin roof. Several men sat inside, watching Ando and Inui. Ando saw the windsock; it appeared the wind was blowing from the northwest. That meant that the winds were blowing from upstream the Song Hong River.

Ando opened his cowl flaps to full, pressed hard on the brakes, and raced the engine to "boost zero." The thrumming of the engine kicked up a notch. The propeller turned faster and faster, to the point where it appeared to be spinning in reverse. He then opened the throttle as he loosened the brakes and his aircraft nosed onto the runway.

The wind beat past both sides of his cockpit. He could feel the subtle ups and downs of the runway through to his legs. The aircraft rolled down the runway, faster and faster, until the vibration of the airframe became almost unbearable. Ando tugged lightly on the control stick. The wheels left the runway and the aircraft climbed swiftly and eagerly into the air.

Ando pulled the landing gear retraction lever as he gained altitude. The indicator lamp turned from blue to yellow and finally to red, signifying that the gear had finished the process of folding away beneath the wings. The vibrations stopped as the air resistance disappeared from the bottom of his aircraft. Everything felt lighter. Ando placed the control stick into a neutral position and reached up to close the canopy.

Ando and Inui planned to fly at an altitude of 3,200 meters for this leg of the journey. It would take a half hour to reach it. They also had to pretend that they were flying north. Ando raised his goggles and glanced over his left shoulder just in time to catch sight of Inui's landing gear folding away beneath his aircraft. He looked down to see the spread of Gia Lam airfield beneath them. A row of ten brand new Type Zero Carrier Fighters sat parked in an orderly line in front of a trench.

About twenty minutes after Ando and Inui's departure, Captain Uematsu received a telegram from the signal corps. It said: *Mission secrecy likely compromised. Advise extra caution regarding RAF.*

The coded telegram was for Ando. It had been sent by the Yokosuka Air Corps command.

Uematsu read the message again, thoroughly confused. The two pilots of the Type Zeros had been ordered to join the 12th Air Corps in Hankow instead of the 14th Air Corps in Hanoi. For one thing, they were en route to China, to a base on the banks of the Yangtze River. And for another, calling such a routine flight a "mission" was odd, to say the least. Not to mention the comment about the RAF. Why would they need to worry about the RAF? The closest bases were in Hong Kong, Singapore, and Rangoon. None of them were anywhere near Hankow.

"Are you sure this is right?" said Uematsu to the man who had taken the telegram. "It just doesn't make sense for those two pilots."

"We checked it three times," replied the soldier. "There isn't any mistake."

"But they're flying to China! Why should they be cautious about the RAF? It would make more sense to warn them about Chinese forces, or the Flying Tigers."

Uematsu studied the northern sky for a while, pondering the telegram he still held in his hand. It had arrived only ten minutes earlier. Even if they had managed to decipher it sooner, it still wouldn't have reached the pilots in time. *In other words*, thought Uematsu with some relief, *it was through no fault of the 14*[th] *Air Corps that they hadn't received the message.*

"Cable Yokosuka: 'Two took off 0730.' That should say it."

Ando and Inui's Zero fighters turned west-northwest once they had taken off from Gia Lam. Their route took them over the northern part of the Indochina peninsula, mountainous terrain with ever-shifting political borders. They cut across the Wuliang Shan mountain range to reach the Shan highlands in Burma. Ando and Inui looked down at what seemed to be an endless sea of clouds for most of the flight. The clouds hung at 2,500 meters in a near-continuous sheet broken only by the occasional Wuliang Shan peak.

The pilots kept a close watch on the mountains through breaks in the clouds. Small tribal villages could be seen scattered throughout the valleys. The mountains appeared brown rather than green; more than a few mountain faces seemed to have been stripped bare by slash-and-burn farming. White smoke rose in lazy curls from some of the slopes.

Once they passed the Wanding River, the border between China and Burma, they spotted enormous purple clouds looming ahead. Storm clouds. The squall line extended across the entire sky from north to south. The pilots had been told that this was the dry season in Indochina, but perhaps the mountainous area was a different story. Whatever the case, turbulence began buffeting their aircraft.

Ando and Inui tried to climb over the clouds, but the magnificent peaks were completely enshrouded, meaning that Ando and Inui needed to reach at least 7,000 meters if they wanted to pass over them. Flying at that altitude would consume an enormous amount of fuel and supplementary oxygen. The only way to maintain their altitude and also avoid the mountains was to detour around the cloud mass. Ando and Inui banked just before entering it.

"Inui," radioed Ando. "Let's head south for a little. I think we can avoid the storm if we get over to the plains. We'll head west again once we get there."

"Roger," said Inui.

"The river below us is the Irrawaddy. We'll follow it down south. We'll be going low, through a narrow valley. Read me?"

"Roger that."

As luck would have it, the storm happened to be moving far faster than Ando and Inui thought. The rain clouds swallowed the aircraft before they managed to reach the plains. A strong gust jerked Ando's aircraft upwards through the sky. It took all of his strength on the stick to keep the aircraft in trim. The sky outside his cockpit window quickly darkened as large raindrops began to smash against the windshield. The temperature inside the cockpit dropped noticeably.

Soon Ando spotted a break in the clouds. He banked hard and punched his aircraft in between them. The river came into view, meandering through the valley. The farther Ando and Inui flew along the river, the lower came the cloud ceiling. Before long they found themselves flying low enough to make out the churning on the river's surface.

The valley narrowed quickly into a steep canyon, the cliff faces drawing in ever closer. Certain stretches were narrow enough to have accommodated a suspension bridge. It was a gorge carved deep into the Earth, and covered with a close-fitting lid of thick clouds. Ando and Inui flew the canyon as though they were driving cars down a narrow and winding mountain road. Ando swerved to avoid a rock face, encountered another directly in front of him, and banked hard again, his wingtip nearly scratching the wall. He jerked his aircraft's nose upwards and came face-to-face with another outcropping of rock to evade. The flight through the canyon lasted only ten minutes, but contained enough hair-thin escapes to last a lifetime. Ando and Inui focused on their controls, brows furrowed, neither cracking any jokes along the way.

Finally the canyon opened up into a broad valley. Ando managed to pull a hand off the stick and thumb the radio.

"Inui. Hope you're still with me."

"Right behind you," came the reply. "Reminded me of the time I flew the Three Gorges in China. The weather then was nasty enough to make me break out into a cold sweat. But this was worse. I nearly pissed myself a couple times."

"I almost caught a wingtip on some branches. If I had the choice, I'd take a showdown against a wing of Spitfires over going through that obstacle course again."

An hour later, Ando and Inui reached the Patkai mountains at the border between Burma and India.

The Patkai range extended over a hundred kilometers through the Naga region of India, with peaks averaging some 3,000 meters. It acted as a natural barrier for both Indochina and India. Ando and Inui began looking for their most important landmark for the leg: Loktak Lake, which lay in a broad, basin-like valley south of the mountain range. The lake was supposed to be large enough that no other body of water could be mistaken for it. Ando had figured that Loktak Lake represented the halfway point of that day's flight.

The sprawling plains of Hindostan awaited them once they passed over the Patkai mountains, and it was there that the real test of their terrestrial navigation skills began. The flatlands teemed with swamps, curving rivers, and villages. There would be no mountains, or even hills, to serve as visual references. Finding the refueling stop under such conditions was going to be a challenge, to put it mildly.

Ando glanced at his watch. It was close to noon. The cloud cover had largely dispersed. Now the skies were clear, offering good visibility. Ando, who was beginning to tire, radioed Inui that he would eat his lunch. He ate the rice ball that had been prepared for him at Gia Lam base and drank from a flask of water. He had also brought a single piece of sugar candy from Japan, which he popped into his mouth to ease his fatigue. He had only savored the sweetness for a few moments when the radio crackled with Inui's voice.

"Lieutenant. Can we speed up a little?"

"Why?" asked Ando. "Is something wrong?"

"No. Not yet. But I think there's a good chance our engines could start overheating, the way we've been keeping down the RPMs. They're probably pretty gummed up right now. We need to open the throttles."

Ando spread his map on his knees to check their current location. They were approaching Loktak Lake. The city of Imphal lay on the north shore. Compared to the sparsely inhabited mountains of the northern Indochina peninsula, flying through this area meant, Ando knew, a far higher chance of being seen by people on the ground. It would be best to cover the distance as quickly as possible. Furthermore, Ando completely trusted Inui about things mechanical.

"All right, let's up the speed," said Ando. "Maintain present course and an altitude of 4,000 meters. We'll try to get through here as quick as we can."

Ando pulled back on the control stick and opened the throttle. The Type Zero Carrier Fighter, its fuselage glinting in the sunlight, quickly began to climb. Inui's aircraft followed about fifty meters behind and to the left.

CHAPTER 5

An hour had passed since entering Hindostan. Ando and Inui flew over river after river. Some moved sluggishly from east to west. Others flowed down from Kashi in the north to join with those in the plains. Several described enormous curves across the landscape, eventually branching into smaller tributaries to the north and east.

Swamps, marshlands, and villages appeared in front and disappeared behind them one after another. Occasionally, Ando and Inui found themselves flying over rice paddies large enough to take five or even ten minutes to cross even by air. They also flew over what appeared to be plantation fields for growing tea. At one point, they saw a decrepit temple, its tower and dome close to collapse.

Soon they caught sight of a relatively large river ahead. Ando spotted railroad tracks along its south bank. The Zeros kept the river on their right until a large city loomed on the horizon. *Mymensingh? Jamalpur?* Ando couldn't tell, but it had to be one or the other: there weren't any other cities large enough to have a rail line on that side of the river. They had been told that if they maintained a course due west from Loktak Lake, they would encounter one of the cities with a margin of error of less than one degree.

Ando checked the map. Their next landmark was a tributary of the Ganges River called the Jamuna. Though a tributary, it was quite large in places, swelling to twenty kilometers wide at one point. The refueling stop was roughly halfway down the river, just outside of a town by the name of Sirajganj. According to the flight plan, Ando and Inui would pick up the Jamuna River near its source in the western Kashi mountains and head south from there.

According to the map, a river called the Brahmaputra ran to the east of the Jamuna, flowing northwest to southeast over the plains of Hindostan. It was smaller than the Jamuna, but relatively wide. The towns of Jamalpur and Mymensingh were located on the banks of the Brahmaputra. Even after consulting the map again, however, Ando couldn't figure out which of the two cities lay in front of them.

He opened the throttle. Whatever the case, it made sense to get past large population centers as quickly as possible.

Immediately after passing the city, Ando spotted another large river in front of them. It appeared to be a good 200 meters wide. *Larger than the Brahmaputra. Is this the Jamuna?* But on second thought, Ando felt the river lay too close to the city to be the Jamuna. If Ando and Inui had just passed over Mymensingh, it would be sixty kilometers to the Jamuna. *We've only gone about thirty. It can't be that close to the city.*

Ando focused his attention on the horizon. He spied a glimmering line in the distance: another river! *Could that be the Jamuna?* Ando stayed his course with high hopes, but the river turned out to be far too small. *Guess that must've been it, back there.*

"I think we've come too far," radioed Ando. "That large river we passed a while back has to be the Jamuna. We'd better turn around."

"Roger," Inui responded.

Ando banked into a tight turn to the right and began heading back. When he reached the river, he followed it south. Soon enough it became clear that it wasn't a river after all, but an enormous swamp.

"Inui," radioed Ando again sheepishly. "I misidentified the landmark. It appears we've got to fly a bit further to the Jamuna."

"I leave the navigation up to you, lieutenant," came the reply. "Lead on, I follow."

"Okay. Turn around and head west again."

Ando and Inui flew west from the swamp. Ten minutes later, another large river came into view ahead of them. It ran from right to left.

Ando looked down at his compass. His expression turned to one of shock when the needle kept jiggling and wouldn't stop. Now he'd lost his orientation. There was no way to determine in which direction they were flying.

"Inui. My compass is acting strange. Check yours and tell me which way we're going."

"Mine's acting up, too, lieutenant," replied Inui anxiously. "It keeps spinning."

"Did we lose our bearings when we went back and forth? I thought we were heading west, but maybe we weren't?"

"You're making me nervous, lieutenant," replied Inui. "Maybe that gigantic river over there is the Jamuna?"

"Could be," said Ando, peering at the river in front of them. It was full of sandbars, and it was at least several kilometers wide. "If it is, 9 o'clock should be due south, and we're heading west."

"The airfield is to the south, right?"

"That's right. We'll follow the river."

Ando and Inui banked left over a sandbar. Ando dropped to a lower altitude and began scanning the surface of the river. There were no visible disturbances on its mirroring surface. It appeared to be almost dead calm. It was a typically outsize continental river, reminding Ando of the downstream section of the Yangtze. He caught sight of a light barge on the surface. A small town appeared on the left bank. The two fighters flew in formation at 1,000 meters over the river.

Ando confirmed the location of the airfield on the map. The town he just saw was probably Baghon. According to the map, the river would widen and contract several times, with several major sand bars visible along the way. But Eastern Bengal was a land of many floods, and it was more than possible that the shape of the river had drastically changed since the map was made. It was too risky to base a decision simply on how the river appeared from the aircraft. *Maybe we should keep going until we hit Sirajganj?*

"Something just occurred to me, lieutenant," Inui radioed.

"What is it?" asked Ando.

"What if we're heading upstream, instead of down?"

"Your compass start working?"

"No. But I can't tell which direction the water is flowing. Think we might be heading the wrong way?"

"We're heading downstream, Inui."

"Are you positive? Do you see something ahead?"

"Look down at the sandbars. Find a small one in the middle of the river."

"Okay. What am I looking for?"

"The sharper end. It always points downstream. The upstream side should be more rounded. I learned that from flying over the Yangtze."

"Got it."

The two fighters followed the ever-widening and -narrowing Jamuna south. A ferry crossed the river at one point, leaving a white trail behind. Ando thought he noticed a few men looking up at the sky from the deck. The chance that anyone would see the rising sun markings on their aircraft was remote, but he prayed that there weren't any military officers or British people aboard.

Ando glanced at his watch and noted that a good six hours had passed since takeoff. He started getting anxious. Ando and Inui were trying to find an airfield that they had never seen before. In fact, even though they kept calling it an "airfield," it was merely a substitute. There wouldn't be an official installation, nor any aviation lamps or markings that would indicate the end of the runway. In fact, there wouldn't even be any of the internationally recognized icons of airfields: a control tower, a main building, some kind of hangar. *How the hell are we going to pick this place out of a bunch of rice fields? Maybe I ought to be searching the ground for aircraft. If I happen to spot one out in the open, that'll be the place.*

Another ten minutes passed. Inui's voice crackled over the radio.

"Lieutenant, do you see that at 2 o'clock?"

"What is it?" asked Ando, looking in the direction.

"Looks like a white arrow. I mean, a white pattern that looks like an arrow."

Ando didn't see anything but dull green fields stretching to the horizon. It reminded him of the Japanese countryside in the summer. He could practically feel the humidity on the ground. Were those bamboo trees that were swaying in the wind?

Suddenly Ando caught sight of a white line drawn on a flat area of ground ahead and to the right. Judging from the distance, the white line had to be huge. It appeared to be pointing towards a runway.

"Great eyes, Inui!" cried Ando in admiration.

"Do me a favor and don't spread the word, lieutenant. I wouldn't want to be transferred to a spotter crew."

"Let's take it low and slow over the arrow for confirmation. If it looks right, we'll turn around and land from the side facing upstream."

Ando lowered his altitude and headed for the arrow. Soon it became apparent that the arrow had been drawn on a large, grassy field. It seemed to have been created with countless white stones.

The "runway" appeared to be either a park or a football field. It was surrounded by low scrub brush and appeared slightly domed. Ando noticed a few people standing near a truck at one corner of the field. A man was swinging his arm in a big circle. Ando didn't know anything about the customs of Eastern Bengal, but the signal certainly didn't appear to express danger or rejection. He made a slow pass over the field at an altitude of about twenty meters.

Two men had unfurled a large white cloth. In the middle was a crudely drawn red circle. The Japanese flag? *This is it,* Ando saw with sudden clarity. *The "airfield" we've been looking for.*

The runway afforded roughly 400 meters for landing. The ends were thankfully clear of any trees or other tall obstacles. It was rough, but definitely looked good enough for Type Zero Carrier Fighters to attempt a landing.

Flying to the end of the runway, Ando pulled up a bit and turned towards the northern corner of the grass field.

"Inui. What do you think?" asked Ando. "At least, it's a bit longer than the deck of an aircraft carrier. Think we can do it?"

"If I knew of a better place, I'd go there instead," Ando's wingman responded. "I'd like to see you land first, lieutenant. Then maybe I'll give it a try."

Ando gained some altitude and pulled on the landing gear lever. The pilot lamps for both legs cycled from red to yellow and then to blue. Ando sensed the increased drag even before the gear locked into place.

"Inui, gear check. Everything clear?"

"Yes," confirmed Inui.

Inui gunned ahead and to the right of Ando's plane. Ando watched Inui's landing gear deploy slowly.

"You're looking good, too."

After the gear check, Ando adjusted his flight path to match the direction of the arrow. He reduced his speed to the brink of a stall. Ando managed it so that his tail wheel made contact with the ground the moment the white arrow disappeared under the fuselage. He guided his nose downward to bring the front wheels into contact as well. The aircraft bounced once, skidded slightly sideways, and came to a fairly rapid stop on the grass.

Ando quickly slid his canopy back and raised his seat. He saw a small British-style house at the edge of the field. Ando had to move his aircraft away for Inui to land. He taxied the aircraft towards the house, intending to leave it there for the time being. Ando cut the power as soon as the aircraft rolled to a stop next to the house.

An Indian man ran toward the Zero fighter. He looked to be about thirty years old, with a high forehead. He looked up at the Japanese pilot in

Part Three

the cockpit and said:

"Welcome to Eastern Bengal."

Ando heard the sound of an engine rev as Inui's aircraft touched down moments later.

CHAPTER 6

His name was Das. He spoke perfect, almost painfully formal English. He introduced himself as the member of an organization fighting for Indian independence. Das said that he had prepared fuel and oil for the aircraft, and meals and beds for Ando and Inui. Ando gave his family name and nothing else. Whatever the case, this so-called airfield had been prepared for by the Japanese government. Even without telling the man his title or military affiliation, Ando was confident he and Inui would receive everything they needed.

"Would those happen to be fighters?" asked Das, peering at the two parked aircraft with obvious interest.

"They can be used as fighters," answered Ando in English. *But not on this mission.*

"Might you be planning an attack on a British base?"

"No. We're just couriers. Look, is there a hangar around here? I'd like to keep the aircraft out of sight," replied Ando, quickly changing the subject.

Yamawaki had said that the airfield had some sort of hangar. But the only buildings visible to Ando were the suburban-style British house, and a barn-like structure. Even if they threw the barn doors fully open, the doorframe itself didn't seem to be more than about three and a half meters wide. A Type Zero Carrier Fighter had a twelve-meter wingspan. There would be no way to fit them in. Behind the barn was a fenced-in run for horses with a huge pile of straw.

"I do apologize that we lack a hangar here, but we have prepared a place suitable for hiding your aircraft," said Das.

"Where is it?" asked Ando.

"Right over there."

"Over there? All I see is a fence."

"May I ask you to move your aircraft inside the fence? We will pull a large sheet across the fence to hide the bulk of the aircraft. We shall then cover the higher parts, such as the windshield and propellers, with bamboo. You shan't have anything to worry about until tomorrow morning."

Ando and Inui looked at each other. There must have been a misunderstanding somewhere along the line, but there wasn't much of a choice.

If their airstrip was nothing but an open field, there wasn't anything else to do but to park their beautiful Type Zeros inside the horse pasture. They'd already been made to park them in a glorified ditch at Gia Lam anyway. Ando and Inui couldn't realistically expect better conditions here.

Ando noticed a group of seven or eight men approaching the aircraft. They all appeared deeply curious about the planes and their pilots.

"Will you fill the tanks right away? This man here, Inui, will oversee the process. Do you want to do it here, or inside the fence?"

"Let us move the aircraft inside the fence," replied Das. "That way we shan't have to worry about being seen."

Das separated his men into two groups. Each group waited behind a wing of Ando's aircraft for further instructions.

It took an hour to finish refueling and concealing the aircraft. Ando and Inui took off their flight suits and directed the men. Most of them did not understand English, and needless to say, Ando and Inui didn't speak a word of Hindu or Bengali. The process of giving orders and explaining things through Das took far longer than expected. Complicating the situation was the fact that while Das' men could be trusted with a secret, none had even a remote clue about servicing aviation equipment. Ando saw Inui's expression darken in frustration at their lack of expertise, and the distinct possibility that one of them might accidentally break something important. Ando and Inui saw it as a minor miracle that the worst thing that happened during the entire process was twenty liters of oil being spilled on the ground.

"Be patient, Inui," said Ando in an attempt to calm down his partner. "We're inside enemy territory. We can't expect any better."

Inui shrugged.

Ando and Inui, completely exhausted from the flight, refueling, and camouflaging, collapsed into the crude beds that had been prepared for them inside the British building. Das explained that it had once been used as a clubhouse. They slept for four hours, waking up around eight that evening.

They walked to the main room to find dinner waiting. A single dim lamp illuminated the chipped surface of an old table. All of the windows had been boarded up from the inside.

Das joined Ando and Inui for dinner. The rest of the men had bedded down in the barn and were taking turns guarding the aircraft. A young girl, no more than twelve or thirteen, with eyes as deep as black pearls, brought dinner to them. She worked efficiently and in total silence.

After finishing, Inui tried speaking to the girl in his broken English. "Cook this?"

Das immediately interpreted this into Bengali. The girl looked into Inui's eyes and nodded.

"Very good," said Inui. "Good cook."

Das interpreted again. The girl blushed.

"What is your name?"

"Sufia," answered the girl immediately upon hearing the interpretation.

"Sufia. What a pretty name. It sounds like some gemstone," said Inui, slipping back into Japanese. The girl smiled as though she understood his remark. It was a charming, innocent smile, and looking at her, Ando felt the urge to smile himself.

"Shh!" Das suddenly blew out the lamp, plunging the room into darkness.

The girl's smile was gone.

"Keep quiet, please," came Das' strained voice from the dark. "Someone is coming."

Ando strained to listen. He heard footsteps approaching the house. It seemed to be a single person. The footsteps sounded cautious.

Ando pulled his revolver from its holster. He felt Inui stand up next to him and heard him move to the doorway.

It was just after nine in the evening. The people in the barn had undoubtedly masked their light as well. An intruder wouldn't be able to see inside.

The footsteps stopped in front of the entrance. Whoever it was, he (Ando had decided it was a he) seemed to hesitate. *Is the guy going to try the knob, say something, or what? Is he listening through the door?* Ando prepared to cock his gun. If anything happened, he had to shoot first.

A squeak. Was it the doorknob turning? Ando held his breath; the room remained shrouded in total darkness. Inui, Das, and the girl had melted into the shadows. They appeared to be holding their breaths, too.

There was another squeak. The door seemed to have been opened. A gust of wind blew into the room.

Part Three

Suddenly there came a muffled sound, like a punch to a sandbag. Someone groaned. Then Ando heard the door being flung open, and something heavy dropped to the floor. There was the sharp sound of metal on metal, and a spark in the darkness.

Somebody said something, but Ando couldn't understand the words.

"Kahn! " screamed the girl somewhere in the darkness.

"Kahn!" said Das.

Das lit a match at once. A flame flickered to life in the darkness. The tiny light showed two men, their arms locked around one another, wrestling on the floor in front of the door. Ando quickly racked the slide on his gun and dropped into a shooting stance. The match flame blew out.

"Kahn!" the girl shrieked again.

"Don't shoot! It's our friend!" shouted Das.

The lamp was re-lit. The girl seemed to have done it. The room was filled with its dim light once again.

A well-built man sat astride Inui. He held down Inui's arms with his foot and left hand, and held a knife against Inui's neck. A monkey wrench that Inui always carried around for protection sat on the floor next to Inui's head. Inui was pale. Ando kept his Nambu automatic trained on the intruder. *Who is this guy?*

"Kahn!" said Das. "He is our guest. Get off him at once!"

The man looked at Das with dissatisfaction. He appeared ferocious. He reluctantly removed the knife from Inui's neck and stood up.

"What happened? I thought you were in Calcutta," asked Das in English.

"I was ordered here to tell you something," answered Kahn.

"By them?"

"Yes."

"There was no need to have you sent here. You are a wanted man. There is a warrant for your arrest."

"They're watching everyone in Calcutta now. Warrant or not, I'm the only one who can still travel freely," said the man, sliding the knife under his shirt. "Chinese?" he asked.

"Japanese. Pilots. I shall explain the details later."

"I had no idea. They told me you'd be here, but it was completely dark. So I became...cautious."

Inui stood up and rubbed his neck. He seemed surprised that his neck was still attached to his body.

"Kahn is invincible as long as he has his knife. You should have waited three more seconds before jumping," said Das to Inui, after seeing the look on his face.

Ando interpreted.

"I saw the tip of his knife. I didn't have any other choice. If he was a friend, he sure could have entered the room a bit more cheerfully," said Inui.

"So. What is the message?" Das asked Kahn.

"It's about Bose," said Kahn. "He has begun to fast."

"Fast? That means—"

"That's right," Kahn cut in and lowered his voice. "It's only a matter of time before the uprising begins."

"But—"

"If Bose dies in prison," interrupted Kahn again, "there won't be any stopping it."

"The British will not let Bose die in prison," said Das. "They know best the impact his death will have."

Das sighed, and turned at Ando.

"I have something to discuss, so I must move to the barn. Please make yourselves at home. You are leaving at six tomorrow morning, correct?"

"We'd like to depart at dawn."

"The girl will prepare a breakfast for you. Good night."

At Das' signal, Sufia quietly left the room, followed by Das and Kahn.

Ando glanced at this watch. It was 9:15. It had been a long day, and it was time to get some sleep. Apparently, something very serious had just happened for Das and his men. For the moment, at least, it appeared to be an internal matter, nothing concerning Ando and Inui's flight. Nothing to do with the Ibis mission.

"I don't know what the hell is going on, but things sure seem to be getting dangerous these days," said Inui. "Shanghai, Bengal, it doesn't matter where."

"I guess that's just how it is," said Ando, his eyes not leaving the door through which the three had walked out. "Nowhere safe anymore.

Doesn't matter if it's Rajasthan or Baghdad."

"Or Tokyo, or Berlin."

Ando looked at Inui and tapped his watch. Inui nodded and began rubbing his neck again.

CHAPTER 7

The first thing next morning, Ando and Inui went to the horse pasture to check their aircraft. Fortunately, there didn't seem to be any evidence of damage, intentional or otherwise. Since the planes had been refueled the night before, Ando figured on doing a quick pre-flight check and taking off after breakfast. Ando asked Das to remove the bamboo from the aircraft. It appeared Das hadn't slept much. Ando remembered the discussion. Perhaps it had continued all night.

Ando and Inui walked back to the clubhouse to eat the meal that Sufia had prepared for them. By the time they returned to the pasture, Das' men were almost finished removing the bamboo from the aircraft. Upon seeing the two pilots again, Das and Kahn halted their work and approached Ando with serious faces.

Das stood directly in front of Ando. "Is it possible for each of your aircraft to carry two?"

"These are single-seat aircraft," said Ando, shaking his head. "They can't carry two people."

Das looked disappointed. "Do you think a two-seat aircraft could land and take off again from this grass field?"

"Ideally, it'd need to be a little longer, but it isn't out of the question. Why?"

"Do you know of Chandra Bose?"

"No."

"He is a famous man, an advocate for Indian independence." Das described Bose as a politician with an enormous base of support among citizens who supported Indian independence. Bose was far more radical than Gandhi, and because of that, he had become public enemy number one as far as the British government was concerned.

Last July, when England was preparing for a possible German invasion of the British Isles, there were fears that Bose would use the opportunity to incite a large-scale riot in India. And so the C.I.D. trumped up some false charges and arrested him. Bose had been incarcerated at Presidency Prison in Calcutta ever since. It had been five months now.

"Bose has begun to fast. He has entered battle by rejecting all nourishment," said Das.

Part Three

"And what does this have to do with our aircraft?"

"If Bose dies in prison, there will be riots across India. Needless to say, we plan to join them. Bose is ready to die for his beliefs. He is fully committed. The fast is but the beginning of the battle."

"We don't want him to die in prison," added Kahn. "The British government doesn't want him to, either."

"Kahn is right," said Das. "The British know that if Bose dies in their custody, they'll have a riot on their hands. We believe that the British government may reduce the sentence to house arrest in the near future. At least, we assume that is their only alternative to letting him die of hunger."

"If he is placed under house arrest, the British will relax their guard," said Kahn. "He can escape. In fact, he must."

"All right. But what does this man's escape have to do with our aircraft?"

"Bose wishes to go to Berlin," said Das simply.

Berlin! Ando hadn't expected to hear that. But he managed to conceal his surprise. Ando and Inui had deliberately kept Das and his men in the dark about the flight route and destination. But now he began to wonder if whoever had negotiated the use of the airfield had let the information slip.

"Bose has completely parted ways with Gandhi. Bose firmly believes that Indians cannot rely on British mercy to win our independence. It will never happen. Instead, he wishes to go to Europe, to gather Indian activists and funds, to establish a government in exile. The entire world is in the process of establishing a new order. It is no different for us Indians," said Das.

"And so he's got to get to Berlin," said Ando, as casually as possible.

"Precisely. I do not know where you came from or where you are going. But you must have started out from Japanese territory, and you are most definitely passing through British territory. Your aircraft prove that this field can support other types of planes as well. Such as passenger aircraft."

"Are you saying that you want Bose to take a passenger aircraft to Berlin?"

"It is just an idea, nothing more. What do you think? Do you think your government will help Bose escape Calcutta? Do you think they might arrange another aircraft for us? If this field proves too difficult, perhaps we can find a better one near Calcutta."

"I don't know the answer to that. I'm just a pilot. I'm not authorized to represent my country."

"If that is the case, would you mind carrying our request to your government, at least?"

Ando was silent.

"Just think about the effort we have put into providing fuel, preparing the runway, and covering up," said Das. "It was so ordered by our organization, and as such we had to obey. Still, it was risky work gathering enough men to carry it out. We converted this meadow into an airfield. We did all that for a pair of aircraft from the land of the rising sun."

It was risky work. Ando thought about Sufia and the food she had prepared for them. If Inui hadn't spoken up first, he would have praised her skill with Bengali spices himself. How much did she understand about the dangerous dreams of the men around her?

"We're only pilots. It's difficult for us to meet high-ranking officials. I'll be happy to pass along what you said to any officers that we meet. But I strongly suggest trying to get word to the Japanese government in other ways."

"I plan to contact the Japanese man who arranged things for you in India. But I had hoped that speaking to you would be a faster, more concrete method of explaining our situation to your government."

Das asked Ando to tell the Japanese government to contact the Federation for Indian Independence. The Federation had active chapters in Delhi, Calcutta, and even Bangkok in Thailand. Das assured Ando that the Japanese government would know how to contact the federation. Ando promised to deliver the message.

Five minutes later, the two Zero fighters had been moved from the pasture to the field that served as a runway. Ando and Inui began their usual pre-flight checks. The quality of the fuel and oil seemed adequate; the engines didn't knock at all during the warm-up process. The rotation of the propellers sounded smooth and even.

Just as Ando looked out of his cockpit to give the take-off signal, he caught sight of a man on a bicycle approaching from the road behind the former clubhouse. The man was pumping furiously, standing on the pedals, pushing the bicycle as fast as it would go. Das noticed the man as well. All eyes nervously watched him approach.

The man threw his bicycle to the ground and ran for the planes. Das and Kahn intercepted him halfway. Something seemed to be bothering the man; he spoke excitedly, gesticulating and pointing urgently at the road from where he'd come. Even from his vantage point in the cockpit, Ando could see spittle fly from the man's mouth. No sooner had the man finished than Das sprinted to the wing of Ando's aircraft.

"Please take off now! Immediately!" shouted Das.

"What is it? Is it the RAF?" yelled Ando over the engine.

"It's the police! They're looking for Kahn! He is leaving immediately, but—"

"What about you? How are you going to hide the fact that we were here?"

"We are planning to play football today. We are all team members. We merely came here to prepare the field," answered Das.

"Better erase that big white arrow before they come!"

"Don't worry. A minute with a broom and it shall be gone. Now, please, you must go! Now!"

"Thanks for everything," said Ando, waving. He gunned the throttle and rolled to the strip of field that served as a runway.

Ando's aircraft rolled down the field and took off at once. As his wheels lifted off the grass, Ando spotted Sufia standing at the far edge of the field, silent, neither waving nor even smiling. She just watched the Zero, her dark hair blowing in the breeze.

Soon the girl disappeared behind him. Ando continued to climb. Some 2,000 kilometers lay between them and their next destination. This leg would take Ando and Inui across central India. The weather was clear, the visibility perfect. Ando expected navigation to be easier on this leg, but the possibility of encountering the RAF would be far higher. The flight plan called for an altitude of 4,000 meters. Ando banked widely to the left and continued to climb.

CHAPTER 8

Jim Parvis stopped in front of the hotel and took a deep breath. It was one o'clock in the afternoon on the first day of December. He was on a large thoroughfare near Connaught Place in New Delhi. Jim had asked the Maharaja for a four-day vacation. He had taken the train from Kamanipur, changed in Jodhpur, and finally arrived in Delhi late that morning.

He was dressed in a white shirt, a pair of hemp pants, and flight boots. He carried his well-worn leather jacket on one arm. He hadn't bothered to shave. It was not as though he was going to meet the board of directors of some large firm; he figured he would be excused.

Jim pulled a creased telegram from his shirt pocket and read it again before entering the building.

Job opening at Chennault Air Company. Meeting to explain details on 1 and 2 December. Contact Edward Kutchnik Hotel Dynasty New Delhi if interested.

C.A.C. at the Hotel Dynasty

Jim had screamed for joy when he had received the telegram three days earlier. He figured Chennault had to be the famed former U.S. Army Air Corp Captain Chennault. Jim had heard rumors that Chennault was in China serving as commander of the American Volunteer Group, a.k.a. the Flying Tigers; and also, that he had the full backing of Uncle Sam. Perhaps The volunteers weren't exactly a group of volunteers. Jim had never heard of any other Chennault besides the captain, nor had he ever heard of a Chennault Air Company. *The Flying Tigers. It has to be!*

Jim knew that he could contact a Flying Tiger recruiter in Calcutta. But it seemed that they had come to Delhi themselves. And whatever the case, they seemed to know Jim well enough to find him in his remote spot in western India.

At forty-one, Jim had been hesitant about contacting a recruiter. But the telegram had bolstered his confidence enough to shake his worries. Old or not, he had been trained to fly biplanes by the U.S. military. He may not have been old enough to see any combat during World War I, but he'd been flying ever since. *Maybe this telegram means age isn't an issue. I don't know if I'll get the job, but it can't hurt to go talk to these people.*

Jim thought about Conrad's famed duel with the Japanese ace again and again during the trip to Delhi. It had been the ultimate dogfight, the type of combat that required the highest degree of skill and finesse and that coaxed the maximum out of aircraft. The smell of gunpowder mixed with exhaust fumes. Spent cartridges popping out and tumbling through the air. Tracer fire arcing from one aircraft to the other, illuminating the marks on the fuselages indicating the pilots' respective kills. It didn't take long for Jim to find himself in Conrad's role in the fantasy.

I don't need any reward, thought Jim. *I don't care about titles, either. Salary? A secondary issue. All I want is to fly a fighter. Air combat, man to man! I want my name carved alongside the legends of aviation, next to Immelman and Rickenbacker. If the recruiter asks about my age, I'll hit the floor and do fifty push-ups on the spot. Hell, I don't even care if they prohibit drinking! I'll still sign my name on the bottom line. If they don't pay me as well as the younger pilots, I'll take it anyway. I'll go as low as three hundred dollars a month. I'll insist on a bonus of five hundred dollars a Japanese plane, though.*

It took a full day and night and two train changes to make it to Delhi, but Jim was so excited that he hardly felt the fatigue. It was like the time his father had taken him on a trip to Washington, D.C., when he was twelve. Jim had earned the trip by winning "best of show" in handicrafts at the state fair. A journalist for the local newspaper had said that he might even get a chance to meet the President. Jim spent the entire train ride to D.C. dreaming about meeting the President. This trip to Delhi reminded him of the excitement he'd felt back then; it was as if he had a fever. The young Jim, however, had never quite gotten his chance to meet the President.

In the afternoon, on the second day of his journey, Jim finally arrived at the Hotel Dynasty in New Delhi. A ceiling fan spun lazily in the hotel lobby. The other customers were all well-to-do Caucasians in sport coats. Jim began to feel increasingly insecure about his rumpled clothes and three-day stubble. The Sikh bellboy greeted Jim courteously enough, but Jim Parvis thought he detected a flicker of disdain in the man's polite salutations. No question about it: this was an upper-crust place. The Chinese government must have been paying the American volunteers handsomely if they could afford staying here. Jim immediately decided to raise his minimum to three hundred and fifty dollars a month.

"I'm here to see Mr. Kutchnik," said Jim to the white-suited receptionist.

"Mr. Kutchnik," answered the young man, tilting his head to one side. "Would you happen to know his room number, sir?"

"No, I don't. But I have an appointment to see him here today."

"And you believe this Mr. Kutchnik is staying with us?"

"I do. He told me to meet him here."

The receptionist shuffled through a stack of guest cards.

"I'm afraid I don't show anyone by the name of Kutchnik on today's guest list, sir."

"Perhaps he made the reservation under his company name. Can you try Chennault Air Company instead?"

"Chennault Air Company, Mr. Kutchnik," the receptionist recited under his breath. This time, he flipped through the guest register book.

Jim put an elbow on the counter and looked around the lobby. *Well, well. Should I salute Kutchnik when I see him, like a soldier? Then again, I don't want to seem out of date, either. Don't want to give him the impression that I'm an old fart. I got it. I'll walk straight in, chewing gum, and start right in with pilot slang. And I'd better put on the old jacket. It's damned hot in here, but I'd better look like a pro. And maybe I'd better smoke, too.*

"Sir," said the receptionist, startling Jim out of his reverie. "I'm afraid we don't have any reservations for either Mr. Kutchnik or the Chennault Air Company."

"That can't be!" said Jim, almost shouting. He whipped the telegram out of his pocket. "Here, take a look at this. He's got to be staying here. Or he's using one of the rooms for meetings. Look, I have urgent business with him. I've got to see him today or tomorrow!"

"But I cannot find any record of those names, sir."

"Perhaps he hasn't checked in yet? He must have made a reservation, at least."

"I'm afraid not, sir. We have very specific records..."

"What about 'C.A.C'? Maybe he used the abbreviation, or..." Jim trailed off and took a breath.

"Do you have any other possible names, sir?" asked the receptionist, tilting his head slightly to the side again.

Part Three

"What about the Chinese government?"

"I'm terribly sorry, sir, but we don't have any guests from the Chinese government staying with us today, either," answered the receptionist. He appeared aggrieved at being unable to help. He had probably taken some harrowing lessons in etiquette from the British.

"Damn, what the hell is going on?" mumbled Jim in utter confusion.

Kutchnik must have gotten hung up somewhere along the way. I came here just like it said in the telegram. Hell, they contacted me first! Otherwise, I wouldn't have come all the way out here from Rajasthan. He'd better have a real good reason for standing me up like this...

He couldn't have misconstrued the telegram. It clearly stated that meetings would be held today and tomorrow. Jim began to wonder if Mr. Kutchnik might show up the next day. He decided that staying in the hotel would make it easier for Kutchnik to contact him when he did arrive.

"All right," said a resigned Jim. "I'll wait here. Can I have a room?"

"Certainly, sir."

"What's the rate?"

"We have a room available for thirty dollars per night."

"You know, it doesn't have to be a suite."

"How about a single room, sir? They're quite cozy."

Jim silently cursed Kutchnik. *If they decide to hire me, they're footing the bill, that's for sure. I'll throw the damn room-service charge slip in his face!*

"I'll take it. Show me the room. And do me a favor and send up a bottle of whisky, a bucket of ice, and some soda right away."

Jim almost asked for a girl as well, but held his tongue. *Bet I can find a cathouse in this city easy enough.*

"Certainly, sir," replied the receptionist, the polite smile never leaving his face.

CHAPTER 9

At one in the afternoon, roughly the same time Jim was speaking with the hotel receptionist in New Delhi, Ando and Inui touched down on the airfield in the Thar Desert just outside of Kamanipur.

Ando taxied to the hangar and looked around from his cockpit. The door of the hangar stood wide open. A group of ten or so men stood inside. Ando saw a couple of single-engine Junkers transports and an old American biplane lined up on a hardstand alongside the tarmac. The airfield had sandbags, barbed wire fences, an observation tower, and even a barracks. It was like an actual military base. The men approached Ando's Zero as soon as he stopped rolling. It was obvious from the confident way they approached the aircraft that they had received some serious military training.

Ando switched the main power off, hoisted himself out of his cockpit, and began to climb down to the ground. Halfway down, he nearly lost his balance and desperately grabbed hold of the fuselage to steady himself. Flying for so long in such cramped quarters without a break had taken its toll. He realized that he felt far more tired than after the previous day's flight.

Ando lied down on the firm red ground to stretch his back. He felt swallowed by the intense, dry sunlight. The weather was completely different from the concentrated humidity of Indochina and Eastern Bengal. He loosened his scarf.

"Whoa! I feel dizzy," said Inui, walking over to Ando. "Guess I'm too hungry."

A man sporting a turban and an impressive beard approached them. He wore a military-looking shirt and pants. There was an orange sash slung diagonally across his chest, and a pair of binoculars dangling from a strap around his neck. He appeared to be the base commander.

"I am Colonel Karmajit Singh," he said. But no sooner had Ando saluted than Singh dropped the formalities.

"Let us move your aircraft into the hangar first. We'll have plenty of time for introductions later."

The ground crew had already taken up position behind the wings of Ando's Type Zero. Another man sat inside his cockpit. They seemed more than familiar with aircraft.

The colonel signaled and the men began to push Ando's plane skillfully into the hangar. They repeated the process for Inui's aircraft. The hangar appeared to have been designed to house the Junkers transport planes, and there was more than enough space for the two Japanese fighters. The men draped a large olive-drab tarp over the cowls of the aircraft. The door remained open, but the strong sunlight and the tarp were sufficient to obscure the sight from a distance. The two aircraft were as completely hidden as if the door had been closed.

In the shade of the hangar, Ando and Inui saluted Karmajit Singh once again.

"I'm Lieutenant Ando of the Imperial Japanese Navy," said Ando, using his full title as a courtesy to a fellow serviceman. "This is Flight Sergeant Inui."

"I've heard about you. The Royal Army of Kamanipur welcomes you," said Karmajit Singh.

"Thank you, sir. May I request maintenance and refueling for our aircraft? Sergeant Inui would be happy to supervise."

"Would you like a bite first? We've prepared a meal for you in the mess, behind the hangar."

"I'd like to wash my hands, first," said Inui in Japanese.

Karmajit Singh understood the request from the body language.

"There is a bathroom behind the barracks. Let us go there first."

Ando and Inui took lunch alone in a large mess hall attached to the barracks. Sufia hadn't prepared a portable lunch for them, and not wishing to give any hint as to their destination or flight duration, the two pilots had not asked. So they had eaten nothing but emergency rations, hard biscuits and water, during the flight. Ando and Inui ate in silence until they had regained some of their strength.

They were done eating and were sipping cold tea when Karmajit Singh reappeared.

"An RAF reconnaissance plane flew over our base at noon. It's quite unusual. Have you encountered any RAF aircraft during your flight?" he asked.

"Actually, we did," said Ando, recalling his latest flight. "We ran into a formation of six fighters, an hour before landing."

"Where was this?"

"Due south of the town of Khota."

"Did you engage them?"

"No, we did not. We were at 4,000 meters, while they were at roughly 3,000. We climbed immediately to evade them. I don't think they noticed us."

"Could you identify what kind of aircraft they were?"

"Biplanes. Gloucester Gladiators, I believe."

"The RAF is very active today."

"Is that unusual?"

"We've only had a single reconnaissance flight over our base before this. Two years ago, when our army purchased the two Junkers transports."

Ando wondered if the mission had been compromised. Had one of the higher-ups leaked word? Had the police in Eastern Bengal figured out that two foreign planes had landed there? If the RAF knew about the mission, knew that Ando and Inui were in Rajasthan, it was an enormous headache. Then again, perhaps they only knew part of the story, and were simply on the lookout for unidentified aircraft violating their airspace. A single group of Gladiators didn't really tell Ando anything one way or the other.

"How many people were informed of our arrival, sir?" asked Ando.

"Only my lord and I knew until yesterday. This morning, I told the maintenance crew that we would have guests. Even then, they only just realized that you were Japanese, and even I didn't know that you would arrive in fighters. "

"Do you think it's possible any of the crew leaked the information?"

"They didn't know the visitors would be foreign, and what's more, I can assure you that all of my men are true patriots. They hate the British. None would sell out their country to England."

"Are there any Americans or Europeans here?"

"There is one," answered Karmajit Singh. "An American biplane pilot in the employ of the Maharaja."

"Does he know about us?"

"I don't think so. He took several days off beginning yesterday. He must be in Delhi by now. He told me that he planned to look for another job, as his contract would expire soon. He won't be back for another two or three days."

"Maybe the reconnaissance flight was just a coincidence, then."

"I am quite sure that the information did not leak from this base. But it's true that the British see our royal army as something of a thorn in their side. It's possible that the RAF has heightened their surveillance of us in light of recent international events."

"What do you mean, a thorn in their side?"

"If civil war breaks out in India, it is common knowledge that our army will take the lead. The lord makes no secret of it, either. Perhaps England has finally begun to take us more seriously," said Karmajit Singh with pride.

Ando had a bad feeling. *Hold on, now. Like we were saying, the world's getting to be a dangerous place and it's not surprising that the RAF's on high alert. Still...*

"Should we prepare for an attack from the RAF?" asked Ando tensely.

"Our presence may make the RAF uncomfortable, but we aren't at war. I find it hard to believe that they would attack us. But your country has signed a pact with their sworn enemy. I can't guarantee that they'll tolerate Japanese military aircraft within their territory. And this is why we want to keep your aircraft out of sight."

"If the base is attacked, can you defend yourselves?"

"Unfortunately, we don't have either anti-aircraft guns or cannons. If the RAF attacks from the air, there is nothing we can do."

"And your ground defenses?"

"We are located in the middle of the desert. There aren't any British bases within 300 kilometers of here. If the British decide to attack us on the ground, we'll know about it two days ahead."

"Lieutenant, I'd better go and check our aircraft," said Inui standing up from the table. "I heard a little knocking during the flight. I think it's the carburetors. I want to take care of it."

"Dinner will be served at seven in the palace. The lord will join us," said Karmajit Singh. Ando nodded.

Inui walked to the exit. Suddenly he paused in the open door and turned back to face Ando.

"Lieutenant, could you ask the colonel if they have any high-wing monoplanes here?"

"What's going on?" asked Ando.

"A plane's approaching. It's a monoplane with fixed landing gear."

Ando and Karmajit Singh walked to the door. They stayed inside and peered into the sky where Inui pointed. He was right. A plane was approaching the base. Now they could hear the sound of its engine.

"What is that?" asked Ando.

"It has to be the RAF," said Singh, his binoculars pressed to his eyes. "I think that's the same reconnaissance plane that flew over at noon. This is a historic event, a reconnaissance plane flying over us twice in the same day. It's a first for our kingdom. Nothing of the kind has happened in the last thousand years!"

"It could be another coincidence," reasoned Ando. "It doesn't look like they have any specific intelligence on us. They're probably just doing a survey of all the strategic points in the area."

"What makes you think so?"

"If they had been sure, they would have dispatched a fighter from the very beginning."

"I think that's a Lysander Mk. II," remarked Inui, without taking his eyes off the plane.

"We did right to stow the aircraft in the hangar right away," Ando observed.

Singh lowered his binoculars. "I agree. It appears we need to reconsider our anti-aircraft defenses. I must take this up with the lord at once."

The noise of the incoming aircraft engine grew louder. The plane flew straight over the base at 2,000 meters, neither turning nor changing altitude. Before long it had disappeared into the western sky.

CHAPTER 10

That evening, Ando and Inui were brought to a small dining room deep within the Maharaja's palace. Seven or eight other men sat at the table, all except one relatives of the Maharaja. The exception was a British man, introduced as a tutor. His name was Haywood.

The Maharaja's steward had provided Ando and Inui with new clothes, outfits featuring Indian jackets with standing collars, for the banquet. After having been cooped up in the tiny cockpits of their fighters for so long, Ando and Inui welcomed the opportunity to wear something other than their uniforms. The steward hadn't insisted that they wear turbans, but the Indian clothes were strange enough to them as it was. Ando and Inui felt as if they had stumbled into some fairytale kingdom.

Only the British tutor wore Western clothes, a dark blue suit and a bow tie, to the banquet. He appeared to relish his role as a bastion of British culture in this far-flung desert kingdom.

"Two Japanese gentlemen will be joining us tonight," said the Maharaja Gaj Singh in introduction to the rest of the guests. "Lieutenant Ando and Sergeant Inui are both pilots with the Imperial Japanese Navy. They've just arrived today."

Ando and Inui lowered their head in greeting to the Maharaja's relatives, who regarded the pair with unbridled curiosity. Gaj Singh continued:

"I hear they have flown across India on some important mission. They will be leaving us tomorrow for an unknown destination. Theirs is a brief and busy visit, but I believe that is how men of consequence travel. I wish they could stay longer; I cannot ask them to do so simply for my sake. Tonight, I'd like these gentlemen to enjoy our kingdom's full hospitality, and let us all pray for the best of luck and safety for the rest of their journey."

One of the guests immediately turned towards Ando. "What kind of aircraft do you fly? Is it British-made?"

"Their aircraft are Japanese fighters," answered Gaj Singh for Ando.

Ando stared at Gaj Singh, alarmed. Guests of the Maharaja or not, Ando had no desire to discuss their mission in front of anyone, let alone a British intellectual. Besides, the guest had asked him, Ando. Gaj Singh may have been the host, but it was not his place to answer questions posed to guests.

Gaj Singh continued, unconcerned. "I went to the airfield and saw their aircraft myself. They are beautiful, brand-new, metal, single-seat monoplanes. They seem to represent the cutting edge of the Imperial Japanese Navy's aviation technology. I believe they will prove more than a match for Spitfires and Hurricanes."

Ando snuck a glance at Haywood. The tutor made no effort to conceal his interest.

"I would love to purchase some of those aircraft for my kingdom! It is about time to retire the Curtiss. The Jenny is twenty years old! The owner and aircraft alike are showing their age. My kingdom needs real fighters, the latest ones, instead of the old practice model we currently have," burbled Gaj Singh happily.

"I'm amazed the British government gave you permission to fly over their territory," remarked another guest.

"Who would be stupid enough to ask the British government for a permit? These two brave men flew as freely as the telegram described them, as freely as two birds!" laughed Gaj Singh.

Ando loosened his collar, unable to hide his growing discomfort. *Didn't Japanese intelligence tell him to keep the mission secret?*

"So, where is this 'unknown' destination?" asked the same guest. "Baluchistan? Afghanistan? I'd imagine you must be heading somewhere in the Persian Gulf."

"I'm afraid our mission is highly confidential," said Ando. "I'm not at liberty to say anything at all. I beg your understanding when I say that I cannot agree or refute what the Maharaja has just said."

"Ah, that's right! This is a highly confidential mission!" said Gaj Singh, tilting his head back and laughing merrily. "Lieutenant, I must beg your pardon. The other guests are all close to me that my tongue has loosened too far. Let us turn the conversation away from the lieutenant's mission and aircraft. On my word, you shan't be asked anything again. I believe my guests understand your situation and will keep to themselves what they have heard and seen here. Will you forgive me?"

"Of course, my lord."

"Just one more question, lieutenant," said Haywood. "I am an aficionado of airplanes myself. What kind of fighters are you flying? I recall someone mentioning that they were of the latest type."

"Please, Mr. Haywood," said Gaj Singh. "We have just promised not to touch on the subject. Let us turn instead to the matter at hand: dinner."

Heeding Gaj Singh's request, nobody asked about the flight again. Instead, the guests launched into a furious and passionate discussion about the neighboring kingdoms and their lords. One told a story about a lord who gave his mistress a carriage coated in gold. Another told of a young secretary who had been beheaded for having an affair with a princess. Yet another spoke of a lord who surveyed his assets for the first time in ten years, only to discover that his vaults contained a mere third of the treasure that they were supposed to.

Soon Ando realized that only Gaj Singh's relatives seemed to take part in the gossip. For his part, Gaj Singh kept silent, merely nodding here and there to keep the conversation flowing. Gaj Singh pretended to enjoy the stories, but it was obvious to anyone who cared to know that he was totally bored by them.

Another man didn't seem to take any particular interest in the conversation, either: Haywood the tutor. His forced smile couldn't hide the fact that he was preoccupied with something else. Ando watched him roll up his napkin and unfold it, over and over again.

Soon enough, the servants brought the final course. The guests seemed to have run out of gossip as well. Once the meal was over, servants removed the empty plates and the table lapsed into silence.

"I must excuse myself, my lord," said Haywood, standing and coughing nervously.

"Have a pleasant evening, Mr. Haywood," said one of Gaj Singh's brother-in-laws. The rest of the table burst into laughter. Haywood seemed to visibly shrink in embarrassment, looking down at the floor as he left the dining room. Since Haywood's had been a totally inconspicuous comment, Ando surmised that he was missing the background. The rest of the guests stood up and moved to another room as well. Only Ando, Inui, and Gaj Singh remained seated at the table.

"May I ask you two to spare some time for me?" asked Gaj Singh.

"I'm afraid we only have a little while," answered Ando.

"I must apologize again for my...outburst at the dinner table. My introduction must have shocked you."

"I thought you had been made aware of the secrecy of our mission when you agreed to provide the airfield."

"Of course. I shared the secret on purpose."

"On purpose? Why, my lord?"

"I think everything will become clear shortly. Please wait for a moment."

An old steward entered the room. He stated softly, by Gaj Singh's ear, "He just left, my lord."

At this, the Maharaja stood up. "How would you like to see my city, Lieutenant Ando?" he offered.

"The city? Not the airfield?"

"The city. I'll introduce you to some of Kamanipur's ladies of the night."

The three climbed into a limousine that exited the palace from a rear gate. A motorcycle with an armed sidecar rode point ahead of the car.

By this time of evening, most of the stores had called it the day and the main street had emptied of most pedestrian traffic. Ando and Inui had seen many camels and horse-drawn carriages on their way to the palace. Now only a handful plied the streets. *If this is anything like a Japanese town,* thought Ando, *it's time for the show to move to the back alleys.*

"Are there any nightclubs in town?" asked Ando.

"Just like any other city, we have…a special district," answered Gaj Singh. "We have a variety of facilities, ranging from the enjoyable to those lurid enough to make one avert his eyes."

"And which side of the spectrum are we visiting?"

"I don't know yet. To be honest, this is my first time as well."

"Are you making a special trip just for us?"

"Not exactly. But I thought you'd enjoy coming along yourselves."

"I'm afraid I don't quite understand," said Ando. "Where are we going, and what are we doing?"

"We're heading to a whorehouse, to ascertain something."

"Ascertain?"

"I want to see if Haywood the Brit is as much of a dog as they say."

Soon the motorcycle turned into a narrow side street, followed by the limousine. Pedestrians scattered as the car barreled down the narrow street without slowing down. Before long they came to a stop in front of an old building.

Part Three

A group of men sat on the curb, gambling with dice. A woman, her arms crossed on her chest, stood near them watching the street. She looked to be Arab, possibly Persian. Her eyes widened when the car and motorcycle parked in front of her. Ando heard the twang of a string instrument and female laughter from the building. A middle-aged man in a Turkish hat walked through the front door with a woman on his arm.

A figure appeared from the shadows. He wore a shirt with a standing collar and an orange sash across his chest. He seemed to be a soldier of the kingdom. Probably a non-commissioned officer.

"Is this it?" said the Maharaja to the soldier as soon as he got out of the car. "What a lewd little establishment!"

The soldier led Gaj Singh, Ando, and Inui into a dark alley that ran along the building. Another two soldiers stood at the back entrance. It seemed that they had been guarding it for some time.

"Are you ready?" asked Gaj Singh.

The N.C.O. withdrew a small pistol, took a step backwards, and kicked the door in. A woman screamed. The soldiers went in. More screaming. Now a man could be heard shouting as well.

Gaj Singh walked through the shattered doorway first, followed by Ando and Inui. A young man standing next to the door with his hands raised looked at the Maharaja in shock.

"Maharaja…M-Maharaja," mumbled the man over and over, as if he still couldn't believe his eyes.

The Maharaja had been right. The place was a brothel. The soldiers had herded a group of women in provocative clothing into one corner. Inui whistled.

The second floor was in even more of an uproar. Ando heard someone battering a door fiercely, the sound of many footsteps, shattering glass.

A soldier led Gaj Singh upstairs. Ando and Inui followed. The door at the end of the hallway upstairs had been opened, spilling light into the darkness. A middle-aged woman, apparently the owner, screamed at the soldier blocking her door. Ignoring the woman, Gaj Singh pushed into the room.

The scent of incense was overpowering. The walls and windows had been covered in pink and red cloth. A canopy bed stood in the center.

Haywood kneeled on the floor next to the bed, his arms pinned behind his back by a soldier. Another held a gun to Haywood's chest.

Haywood looked up angrily as Gaj Singh walked over.

Ando noticed a machine sitting atop a dresser. It had a button-like contraption of the sort used on telegraphs. It appeared to be a wireless communication device. The window next to the dresser was broken.

"Ah, using the whore as cover to send coded messages? Very clever, Mr. Haywood, very clever. Unfortunately for you, we've known for quite some time. In fact, from all indications, it is not women that interest you. Am I right?"

Haywood stayed silent. Gaj Singh continued:

"According to your resume, you received a bachelor's degree from Cambridge University. You are a member of the Royal Academic Society of Topography. You worked as a teacher. Your hobbies are traveling and photography. But you left off the best part, didn't you? You are a full-time agent of the British intelligence service. Unfortunately for you, Haywood, I hate the British government and all its organs. You'll regret having taken this assignment, I assure you."

Haywood seemed to have pulled himself together. He took a deep breath and then, suddenly tried to break free. The Maharaja ordered the soldiers to stand back. Once released, Haywood stood up proudly and adjusted his bow tie.

"Are you accusing me of something illegal? Is gossiping with my friends about your kingdom a criminal act? Is that what you're trying to tell me?" Haywood demanded.

"Stop your babbling. You are in the Kingdom of Kamanipur. I am the law and the judge. And your activity is a threat to our very existence."

"I'm English," said Haywood in an arrogant tone.

"What of it?"

"If you arrest me or take me to court, my government won't stand idle. The RAF will come down on your tiny kingdom like a hammer."

"You think we can't do anything to you?"

"In fact, the only thing you can do is to deport me. That's all."

"How interesting! I like that! How about leaving this kingdom by crossing the Thar Desert on foot? I'll keep your silly hat as a keepsake. In fact, it's a wonderful time for a walk on the desert. I suspect you'll be a shriveled corpse within three hours."

"You barbarian!"

"Barbarian? Did you call me a barbarian?"

"Let me remind you that I was the one who civilized those nigger daughters of yours! I taught them the English language, proper manners, and tennis. And don't forget that it was England who taught you to act like a normal man! Yet here you were, ready to betray us. In spite of the privileges we generously granted you and your fellow relics, you've built an army with the express purpose of fighting us! A civilized man would know better than to bite the hand that feeds him."

"Civilized?" said Gaj Singh, real anger flashing in his eyes. "You civilized my daughters? England taught me how to act like a 'normal man'?"

"That's right. It was England who showed you a civilized society. Who wouldn't be satisfied with such a gift?"

Gaj Singh took a step towards Haywood, his body trembling with anger.

"Haywood, I am the one who taught the true meaning of civilization to my daughters. You merely showed them a few European customs. In a backwater language from a tiny island of limestone!" spat Gaj Singh, his finger pointed at the Englishman. "Listen to me closely, Haywood. While British still lived in caves to hide from wolves, the people of India pondered the mysteries of the universe in homes with complete sewage systems. While you busied yourselves counting to ten, Indians created the concept of zero to work on algebraic problems! India is civilization, you imperialistic bastard, not your pathetic little island!"

"Is that so? Then tell me why your wonderful civilization is a colony now? Why else would Indians look up to the King of England as their own?"

"Because you are the true barbarians, shameless and greedy!" Gaj Singh turned to his soldiers. "Take him! Throw him in the dungeon! If I have to hear another word out of his lips, I swear I'll gouge out his heart with my bare hands!"

"Stay away from me!" yelled Haywood as the soldiers moved closer. The soldiers hesitated. Haywood adjusted his bow tie and smoothed the wrinkles from his jacket. "If I fail to report, the RAF will swarm your kingdom looking for me. And if I am hurt in any way, they will turn your toy of a palace into a smoking heap of rubble!" said Haywood, glaring straight into Gaj Singh's eyes.

"Take him! Now!" screamed Gaj Singh, his voice filled with hate and disgust. "Don't let him open his mouth in front of me again. Ever!"

A pair of soldiers took Haywood's arms. He maintained as proud of an expression as he could as they led him out of the room and downstairs.

Gaj Singh leaned on the wall and exhaled heavily. He looked truly shaken and furious with his eyes wide open and bulging, almost ready to pop out of their sockets. Inui jogged up the staircase as Haywood was being brought down. Ando thought Inui had been standing behind him the entire time.

"Where were you?" asked Ando.

"I saw a man trying to escape from a back window," answered Inui, holding up a black notebook. "I took this from him."

Inui handed the notebook to Ando. Ando passed it to Gaj Singh.

Singh flipped through the pages. "This appears to contain a list of British collaborators," he said quietly. "This is a very good thing for us to have. What happened to the man?"

"What happened to the man?" repeated Ando in Japanese.

"He's out like a light, upside down in the side car of his motorcycle," answered Inui.

Ando interpreted for the Maharaja, who smiled at Inui in response.

"I didn't expect you to participate. I very much appreciate your help," said Gaj Singh.

"My lord, if you're done here, we'd like to go back to the airfield," said Ando.

"You shall be taken there at once," said Gaj Singh. "We believe Haywood didn't finish his transmission. They may not know that you are here."

"But if he was in the middle of sending a message, they will be aware that something has happened. I wouldn't be surprised if another reconnaissance plane flew over your base tomorrow. They may send another agent, too. We'll leave before dawn tomorrow."

Gaj Singh nodded to Ando. Then he turned to his soldiers. "Close this place down, and arrest the owner," he said. "Contact the police and tell them to keep a close watch on any Westerners, particularly Americans and British!"

"Yes, sir!" answered the soldiers at once, their heels clicking together in unison.

CHAPTER 11

Ando and Inui took off into the cool desert air before dawn the next day. Ando ascended to 3,000 meters in three minutes, but Inui's plane took an additional twenty seconds to reach the same altitude. They hadn't been able to spare the time for a proper warm-up. The Thar Desert spread below their aircraft like a flat, yellow ocean. Ando spotted a caravan route extending from the city of Kamanipur to the horizon.

Ando and Inui turned south. The sun had just risen and soon a golden morning glow crept over Kamanipur and the surrounding desert. Ando and Inui saw the towers and domes glitter as they flew overhead, the sunrise casting long shadows behind the buildings. The city looked like a stack of gemstones rising from the desert floor. One dome glowed brighter than the rest; it had to be the Maharaja's palace. Under the morning sunlight, the walled city looked like some mirage, a mysterious wonderland. Ando wondered idly if it might melt under the light of day.

The Zero fighters headed towards the Kachi wetlands on the southern border of the Thar Desert. The original plan had been to fly over two major cites as they made their way west, Hyderabad, in Baluchistan, and Karachi. But now, cities were the last places the pilots wanted to be near. To avoid detection, they decided to detour over the Kachi wetlands and make for the Arabian Sea. Once they reached the water, Ando and Inui would head to the Jebel Akhdar Mountains a thousand kilometers to the west. They would fly over the Gulf of Oman to find their next stop, a runway at an oil camp. The revised flight plan called for them to fly some 1,700 kilometers, all said and done.

"Gaj Singh was an interesting man," said Inui over the radio. "Dignified. Proud of his kingdom. It must really be something when he puts on his armor and rides on his horse!"

"The Maharajas are all descended from tribes of warriors," answered Ando. "They're like living fossils. Relics of an era when heroes fought hand to hand."

"Wish I could have met the American pilot who was working under him during our stay. Wonder if he's being paid just like a *ronin*? Based on the number of heads he's collected, or something like that?"

"The American flies a Jenny. It's a practice plane. I don't think it's capable of combat."

"Did the Maharaja say anything to you?"

"About what?"

"About hiring the two of us and our fighters. He sure seemed to hate England."

"I think he sees the bigger picture," said Ando, pondering for a few moments before continuing. "I think he wants the whole Imperial Navy on his side. That's why he offered the use of his airfield."

"Makes sense."

Inui increased his speed and passed on Ando's left, raising a hand in signal as he flew by. It looked like he wanted to open his throttle. Ando followed Inui's lead. The two Type Zeros pirouetted through the skies over the Thar like the ibis for which they were code-named.

Presently the Jebel Akhdar Mountains appeared on the horizon, signifying that they had nearly reached the eastern tip of the Arabian peninsula. Once there, the fighters banked northwest to cut across the Gulf of Oman.

Several oil tankers could be seen plying the gulf, either heading towards or away from oil sites around Abadan. In fact, the maritime traffic appeared quite heavy, and Ando decided to adjust the next day's flight route accordingly. In light of the number of tankers in the gulf, he thought it'd actually be safer to fly overland to Baghdad instead. There was some danger in violating Iranian airspace so flagrantly, but the far lower chance of being seen was worth it.

Ando and Inui followed the Iranian coast of the Gulf of Oman. Just after passing the small town of Ra's-al Kuh, they caught sight of an isolated oil camp, a dingy oasis in a vast and barren vista of sand. Even from the sky it was obvious that the camp had fallen into disrepair. They could make out the shapes of several scrapped cars and the remains of a collapsing building. Only a pair of roughly built barracks still appeared to be in use. Ando and Inui had been told that the runway was about a thousand meters long, but a good portion of the strip appeared to be buried in sand. Ando made a quick pass first to scout the condition of the runway before touching down.

When the wheels of his Zero made contact with the ground, a cloud of sand sprayed into the air.

He waited in his plane for a moment for the visibility to improve, craning his neck out of his cockpit to get a better look of the area. Rusting pipes, discarded electrical generators, and oil drums had been piled on the left side of the runway. The two barracks, shanty-like huts, could be seen behind the pile. Both of them were falling apart. The rusty galvanized tin sheet used as roofing material rattled angrily in the desert wind.

Behind the huts stood a test well, a twenty- or thirty-meter-high tower of rusty scaffolding. Some large piece of mechanical equipment, no longer working by the looks of it, lay next to the scaffold. Ando taxied to a free spot near a storage shed by the barracks. Once Ando had moved out of the way, Inui's aircraft came in for a landing, trailed by a cloud of sand.

Seven, eight men ran for Ando's aircraft from the barracks. They were Japanese, sunburned, the brims of their hats pulled down close over their eyes. They appeared overjoyed to see Ando, treating him with the reverence accorded a warrior returned from a victorious campaign. Several of the men appeared transfixed by the rising sun markings on his aircraft's wings and fuselage.

Ando cut the engine and clambered down from his fighter.

"Finally! Our Navy has arrived in this godforsaken land! Finally!" cried a middle-aged man, who had removed his hat.

"We've come a long way," said Ando in reply. The man appeared to be in charge of the site. "Everyone Japanese here?"

"Yes. There are ten of us. It's been two months since we've seen any other Japanese. You of all people should know how far we are from the motherland. It's a forgotten place, a deserted place…"

"It looked like a ruin from the sky."

"It'll become one in a week."

"Yeah?"

"We just got orders from back home. We'll start wrapping things up here tomorrow."

"Guess we made it just in time."

"I'm afraid we don't have much of anything to offer you, but please make yourselves at home."

"We'll stay until tomorrow. May I ask you to refuel the aircraft and check the engines right away?"

"Fuel we've got, but we don't have a mechanic, unfortunately."

"Get the wheel chocks in and pull a sheet over the cowls immediately!" Inui directed the minute he'd climbed down from his aircraft.

"Engines and sand don't mix! Cover them tightly, especially the oil-coolers!"

The wind picked up. Everyone turned downwind and instinctively covered their mouths with their hands.

"Understood," said the man once the wind died down again. "I guess times have changed. The Imperial Navy has made it to the Persian Gulf after all. We're a bit behind, sure, but now Japan'll get its chance."

"What do you mean?" asked Ando.

"With the Japanese Navy in the Persian Gulf, we won't have to settle for leftovers anymore," said the man. "We'll be able to try better areas. The reason Tokyo instructed us to pack it in is that they've found a better site. Good to know you're scouting things out here in the gulf, but you've only got a week before this camp closes down."

Ando and Inui left their aircraft to the men and headed for the barracks. They wanted nothing more than to wash their hands and to drink some water. Their muscles were completely stiff; they felt exhausted. Ando desperately wanted a long soak in a hot bath, but, knowing he was in the middle of a desert, forced the thought out of his mind.

What day is it today? wondered Ando. *December 1st? 2nd maybe?* Ando's nerves were frayed from the tension of flying so many long-distance flights in a row. Just talking to Inui over the radio had tired him out during the last leg. He realized he was losing his appetite as well. What they really needed was a break.

"I don't think they get it," said Inui as he walked alongside Ando. He sounded unusually annoyed.

"Have we met anyone so far who does? We'll put it out of our minds and keep our chins up," said Ando, struggling to control his tone of voice as well.

Another gust of wind shook the tin roofs. Ando and Inui held down their flight helmets and ran for the nearest barracks.

CHAPTER 12

Ando and Inui began their preparations before dawn the next morning. Like the day before, intermittent gusts of wind threw clouds of sand into the air. A thin layer of it covered their entire planes; some had even worked its way under the tarps covering the cowls. Looking things over, Ando figured Inui had his work cut out for him at the next destination.

With the help of the other men, Ando and Inui removed the sheets from their aircraft, climbed into their cockpits, and began their pre-flight checks. The aircraft had been refueled the night before. Inui gave the planes another visual once-over. Ando didn't see any abnormalities in any of the cockpit readouts. He started his engine. It surged to life with a cough and a cloud of thick black smoke.

The workers removed the wheel chocks. Ando looked out to the right. The sun was just about to come over the horizon, and Ando could barely make out the peaks of a mountain ridge in the distance.

He rolled his plane onto the runway. The propeller kicked sand behind the aircraft. The foreman had removed his hat and was waving it at Ando from in front of the barracks. He was watching the departure with open pride; judging from the smile on his face, he still didn't have a clue about the true purpose of their visit.

The two fighters took off and climbed steeply, banking left as they gained altitude. The oil camp dwindled to a speck below them, dry and worthless despite the blood, sweat, and tears lavished on it. The isolated desert worksite was all that remained of a once-pulsing dream, the wreckage of a bold business venture that had, in the end, amounted to absolutely nothing. It was a dark omen for the future of Japanese industry.

The two fighters ascended to 3,500 meters and turned north-northwest. The original plan would have taken them up through the middle of the Persian Gulf, but Ando and Inui had decided to fly along the Iranian coastline instead. That way, there would be a far lower chance of encountering RAF patrols from the 203rd Air Corps base in Basra, Iraq, or the 84th Air Corps base in Shuaiba, west of Basra. Their new flight plan took them into Iranian airspace, but it seemed worth the risk to avoid the RAF.

Two hours later, while flying over Kharg Island, their fears took physical form. Inui spotted the incoming aircraft.

"Four at 10 o'clock," reported Inui over the radio. "They're at our altitude and heading towards us."

Ando peered out his windscreen. Inui was right. He saw a black smudge in the distance ahead.

Inui radioed in again. "Make that five, no, six aircraft."

Ando had continued to watch the smudge. Now that Inui had said it, he could just barely make out six spots. There was no way civilians could fly in formation, unless they were trained in aerobatics. That meant the incoming aircraft had to be military. And considering where they were, that meant the RAF.

"They're biplanes," came Inui's voice. "Gladiators, I think."

"We can shake them," said Ando. "Let's climb, Inui."

"Direction?"

"Due north," said Ando, pulling back on his control stick. "Let's make a little foray into Iranian territory."

"I kind of wanted to tease these guys a little."

"Leave them alone. Better get out of here before they see our markings."

Ando twisted the stopcock for his oxygen supply.

The six aircraft seemed to take notice of Ando and Inui, changing course and climbing to intercept.

The Zeros ascended swiftly, punching through the sky like a needle through silk. Ando felt as though a weight had descended over his entire body, pressing him deeply into his seat. It was difficult to move at all. Ando watched the sky darken as the aircraft climbed. Before long, Ando reached the 6,000 meter mark. The sky had become a rich ultramarine. Ando slowly moved his control stick back to a neutral position.

He dipped his left wing to look for the RAF planes below. They were far behind him and much lower than he had expected. Ando didn't have any trouble spotting them because the RAF aircraft had been painted a desert camouflage pattern that stuck out almost comically against the perfect blue ocean beneath them.

Inui's aircraft fell in behind Ando's.

"You've been lagging on the ascents the last few days," said Ando.

"The supercharger may need a little work," agreed Inui. "But don't worry, I'm still fast enough to shake off a Gladiator."

Ten minutes later, Ando and Inui turned deeper into Iranian territory over a town by the name of Ganaveh. The RAF aircraft had disappeared; they'd either given up the chase or were still desperately trying to climb. In any case, there was no way for them to catch up with Ando and Inui. The only thing that worried the two pilots now was the thought that the Gladiators may have radioed back to base for back-up. There was a distinct possibility that a reconnaissance plane had been dispatched from Habbaniya or Hinaidi. Ando made a snap decision to penetrate deep into Iran and approach Baghdad from the east.

"There's something that's bothering me, lieutenant," came Inui's voice over the radio. "We saw those Gladiators two days ago. Then that recon plane over the kingdom. And today we've encountered more Gladiators. I'm starting to think they know about our mission."

"I don't like it either," said Ando. "But if they knew the whole story, you can bet they'd have hit the oil camp yesterday. They didn't. So we know they don't know our exact flight route or the locations of our refueling stops."

"They must have something, though. Two groups of fighters in three days. What are the chances of running into a six-fighter formation twice in a row? That's like winning the lottery! I don't think we should consider it a coincidence."

"Remember, though, the RAF is probably still on alert from Haywood's transmission yesterday. I don't know what's going on, but there's no question the RAF's acting up in India and the Middle East."

Ando and Inui maintained course along the edge of what had once been the plains of Mesopotamia. The visibility was excellent. Through the clear skies, Ando saw a mountain range, a river, a village, and a stone tower that looked ready to collapse. The land below was far more green and fertile than Ando had expected.

Ando nervously scanned the skies around him during the entire flight, never relaxing his guard for a second. Before long Ando's eyes had begun to ache and well with tears. He raised his flight goggles and massaged his eyes over and over again.

Fortunately, they didn't encounter any other aircraft during the flight, RAF or Iranian Air Force. The Zeros came in for a landing at an Iraqi Army base in the vicinity of Imam Hamid.

"I am Colonel Mohammed Hussein," the uniformed officer said in welcome to Ando and Inui. The colonel had well-defined facial features and a meticulously groomed moustache that rivaled that of the Maharaja of Kamanipur. "I've heard all about you. Please, do not hesitate to ask for anything you need."

Ando and Inui returned the greeting.

The Iraqi base was located in the middle of a large, flat plain about fifty kilometers northeast of Baghdad. It consisted of several barracks and huts arranged around a large open lot. Judging from the size, the base appeared to house a single regiment. Ando saw several trucks and armored cars, but no tanks or artillery. Two biplanes, apparently used for reconnaissance, sat in front of a stone hangar.

A large contingent of Iraqi soldiers had gathered around Ando and Inui's fighters.

"I was shocked to see you arrive in fighters, as I had only been told of a courier flight headed for Berlin," said Hussein, his curious eyes never leaving the aircraft.

"We had to fly through RAF territory," said Ando. "We couldn't have made it this far without high-speed fighters."

"Are those bombs under the wings?" asked Hussein. He sounded hopeful.

"No. They're extra fuel tanks to help us stay in the air longer."

"Are they detachable?"

"Of course. We can even drop them during flight if we need to lighten the aircraft."

"That means, you can use these aircraft as bombers as well. All you would need to do is attach bombs instead of fuel tanks," said Hussein thoughtfully. He made a slow circle around Ando's fighter and paused before its right wing. "This must be a gun. What is its caliber?"

Is that confidential info? Ando hesitated for a moment before deciding to answer. "It's a cannon. Twenty millimeter."

Hussein's mouth opened in shock. Ando detected a flicker of something in the colonel's eyes.

"How much ammunition can it carry?"

"Sixty rounds for each cannon."

"And those openings in the nose. Those must be guns too?"

"Yes. 7.7-millimeter machine guns."

Hussein looked at the fighter again and nodded, thoroughly impressed.

Part Three

"I suppose these must be Japan's latest fighters. They look fast and sharp, like our stallions. Your country has truly impressive weapons. With aircraft like this, I would suspect Japan is by no means inferior to Germany."

Ando smiled but didn't say anything. He actually agreed, but didn't particularly want to discuss it.

"Please make yourselves at home. We have prepared everything that was requested: food, fuel, a place to rest. If you'd like, I'd be happy to arrange a banquet in your honor tomorrow night."

"I'm afraid we must decline your kind invitation. We must leave early tomorrow morning. But we thank you for your gracious hospitality."

"Oh, no, please. Please stay with us a while longer," Hussein pleaded rather earnestly. "You look exhausted. And that makes your flight more difficult, I should think? If you're too tired, you may not be able to make the appropriate decisions or take prompt action when necessary. Why don't you stay a whole day? You aren't in any hurry, are you?"

Judging from the Gladiators that Ando and Inui had encountered today, it didn't seem a good idea to stay in Iraq any longer than necessary. Ando and Inui had promised Ohnuki to make it to Turkey as quickly as possible, no matter how exhausted they were. *Better not take a break until we get past hostile territory. We're still in the middle of RAF country here.*

"I am touched by your kindness and have no words to express my gratitude, colonel. But we have noticed increased RAF activity in India and the Middle East over the last few days. Extending our stay may cause unnecessary problems for the Iraqi Army. I believe we must leave tomorrow. I humbly request that you refuel our aircraft and have your mechanics look over them as quickly as possible."

Hussein's face clouded in obvious frustration. Ando wondered if he'd made some breach of Muslim or Arab etiquette. Hussein waved a sergeant over and growled an order in a low voice. The sergeant dashed for the hangar.

Hussein turned back to Ando. "I understand. Let us exchange information about the RAF later. At any rate, this officer will take you to your tent."

Ando and Inui followed the young officer to the tent that the Iraqi Army had prepared for them.

CHAPTER 13

Two hours later, Hussein appeared at their tent with a soldier in tow. The soldier quickly set up a table and prepared three cups of coffee.

"It's Turkish coffee. I hope you'll like it," said Hussein, proffering a cup to Ando.

"I've never had it before," admitted Ando, taking the cup. "Is it common here?"

"For some reason, westerners call this coffee 'Turkish' in spite of it being common to Arabia. A relic of the Ottoman Empire's previous control over the entire region, perhaps."

"It's very strong. I hope this doesn't keep me awake tonight."

"We simmer ground coffee, water, and honey together in a pot. What we're drinking right now is the top layer, the clear liquid skimmed off the top."

Ando spoke with Hussein over their coffees. Inui sipped his in silence. Hussein was quite familiar with Asian culture and Japanese politics. He even knew about the Tokugawa Shogunate, and had heard about Admiral Isoroku Yamamoto's exploits in the Imperial Navy. Hussein even surprised Ando and Inui with his knowledge of the great haiku poet Basho. He was a well-educated, well-informed man.

When they had finished their small talk, Ando told the colonel of the six Gladiators that they had encountered over the island of Kharg.

"Is it common to see the RAF over open water?" asked Ando.

"The situation between England and the Middle East is tense at the moment. The RAF has held back up to now, afraid of our reprisals. They're quite nervous about Arab nationalism," Hussein explained.

"Is war imminent?"

"England sees it as a crisis. But for the Arabs, it will be a glorious day of independence. We are poised on the brink of war; it could break out at any time, particularly here in Iraq. It could be tonight. It could be tomorrow."

Hussein's expression turned very solemn. "To tell you the truth, Lieutenant Ando, I came here to ask a very important favor of you. I hope you will give me a positive answer."

"What is it?" asked Ando nervously. It sounded like the sort of

298

favor that inevitably resulted in trouble for the person asked to do it.

"I'd like you to help us attack a British base."

Ando stared at Hussein. He couldn't comprehend the statement; it was too absurd. He blinked. "Did you just say 'attack a British base'?"

"Yes, I did. You can deal some serious damage with your twenty-millimeter cannons. You could even destroy a Victoria bomber!"

"I'm afraid that our mission is to fly to our destination," said Ando levelly.

"Yes, I'm fully aware of that. Rear Admiral Yokoi told me all about your mission in Berlin. In spite of that, I'm asking you. Iraq requests the assistance of the Imperial Japanese Navy in our battle for independence."

"I'm not authorized to do anything outside of orders. Please forward your request to a higher-ranking officer or to a government official."

"There is no time for that, lieutenant. The clock is ticking."

"Absolutely not," said Ando, finally turning down the request in plain terms. "We must leave tomorrow morning and head north. Anything other than that would be against orders."

"So you are sure you cannot do this for me?"

"It's impossible. We can't simply start a war against England on our own."

"But your country has signed the Tripartite Pact with Germany. You're a de facto enemy of England."

"Japan hasn't officially declared war against them. And there haven't been any serious altercations between Japan and England yet."

"Please hear me out, lieutenant," said Hussein, standing up.

Ando put his cup on the table.

Hussein launched into an explanation of the political and military tensions between Iraq and England. It was less an explanation than a speech. Hussein gesticulated broadly and spittle flew from his mouth as he desperately tried to change Ando's mind through sheer rhetoric. Yet, before long, Ando found himself captivated by the colonel's passionate delivery. There was no way Ando could help the Iraqi Army, of course, but Hussein's speech was impressive nonetheless.

To hear Hussein tell it, Germany had secretly pledged to provide material support to the Iraqi independence movement. Iraqi independence from England was close at hand. Over the last few months, Hussein and his core group of officers had carefully plotted their triumphant return to

Baghdad. Their plan involved surrounding the British Embassy and military bases to force a total withdrawal of British forces, and deposing the current king, a Saudi royal who had been installed by the British as a puppet. Hussein and his men felt ready to take action any day, any time, as soon as tomorrow or the day after.

"The morale of the Iraqi forces is on par with the British. The only difference between us is their bombers. I have no doubt they'll use those barbaric machines to tilt the odds in their favor! The bombers are truly the only obstacles between us and independence. If only we could manage to get rid of them, somehow, we could proceed without a worry in the world!"

"And so you're asking two fighter pilots to destroy every British bomber stationed in Iraq?"

"I don't expect you to destroy them all. All I'm asking is for you to turn your cannons on the six deployed at the base closest to Baghdad. Germany has promised to send us twelve fighters. I hear they're preparing them for shipment as we speak."

"Well, if twelve fighters aren't enough, two isn't realistic, either. I'm afraid there are too many holes in the plan, colonel."

"I disagree," said Hussein, shaking his head vigorously. "It is just as it was when I managed to escape from the Ottoman Army twenty years ago: one must take action immediately when one is able to. Gathering officers and holding meetings, it's all a waste of time. The time for meetings is when we are strong, when our military and political position is established. What we require at the moment is a breakthrough. Once it happens, the rest of the pieces will fall into place. The divisions will turn against the British, one after the other, with the inevitability of a tidal wave."

"But you don't have your outside support in hand yet," Ando countered. "I would caution against expecting support to arrive without incident after such a surprise attack. England's military forces are already ensconced throughout Asia and the Middle East. They could easily bring them to bear on Iraq. Is the Iraqi Army ready to deal with that? You shouldn't underestimate British resolve. Remember, not long ago, they quashed Hitler's plan to invade their islands."

"Oh, I'm fully aware of what England is capable of," said Hussein. "They may indeed be the world's strongest empire, but they are teetering on the brink of collapse. That's how I see England."

Ando said nothing. Hussein continued:

"Fortunately, several divisions of the Iraqi Army have already agreed to our plan. We haven't convinced everyone yet, but our base of support isn't small, either. We've been biding our time, waiting for Germany's aid. But things have changed. We have two fighter planes now. If you'll stay for a week, our plan can commence. We are ready to coordinate everything with the other divisions."

"You can't throw out your timetable on the account of having just two fighters! That, colonel, is overly optimistic."

"Will you contact your country and request more fighters for assistance, then?"

"I'm not authorized to do that. Anyway, if you have the time to wait for more Japanese fighters, you're better off staying put and waiting for the German planes to arrive."

"I don't think it would be such a bad thing, Japan and Germany cooperating over the Iraqi situation. After all, you signed the Tripartite Pact. You are part of the Axis."

"As I said before, you'll have to negotiate that directly with the government or the Japanese Navy. We're only pilots." Upon speaking the words, Ando suddenly recalled, with some regret, that he had described himself and Inui as "special pilots" to Hussein.

Ando continued to resist. Hussein continued to beg. This went on for a while.

"I suppose there's nothing I can say to convince you," Hussein relented, but his cheeks were flushed.

"Our hands are tied," said Ando. "I beg your understanding."

"How about leaving one fighter behind for a week?"

"We can't do that, either."

Hussein's eyes glared darkly. Finally, he said, "I suppose this is my mistake, expecting too much from the Japanese. I thought you would give something in return for our hospitality." With this, he angrily swatted the tent flap open and stormed out.

Ando sighed. Having been quite stirred by Hussein's speech, he wondered if he hadn't been too direct in his refusals. There must have been a more delicate way for a guest to reject a host's plea. Ando picked up his cup of coffee and took a pensive sip.

"That was quite the argument you were having, lieutenant. What's up?" asked Inui.

"Could you make out what he was saying?"

"Something to do with the fighters."

Inui's English may have been poor, but he had managed to figure out the gist of the discussion. Ando filled in the details.

"Seems like the only reason anyone's welcomed us is because they wanted something for themselves," said Inui after hearing Ando's explanation.

"We need to get out of here as early as possible tomorrow," said Ando. "I have the feeling that the longer we stay, the deeper we'll get pulled into this mess."

Ando and Inui left their tent. Ando needed to borrow a map from the Iraqi Army for the next leg of the flight, while Inui wanted to supervise the maintenance work. The two stopped to watch a two-seater biplane take off under the strong Mesopotamian sun, and to marvel at how far they'd come.

CHAPTER 14

After dinner, Ando and Inui carried a bench out of their tent to enjoy the cool desert air. The sun had passed below the horizon in the west. The temperature had dropped remarkably; it was cold enough to wear a winter flight uniform. It could drop below freezing by the time they took off tomorrow. Ando and Inui built a small fire and stared at the nighttime sky over Iraq.

Inui stretched his legs and smoked a cigarette. Ando thought about some of the songs he'd played with his friends at Blue Max. The pilots' faces reddened as the fire grew, and the stars brightened as the sky continued to darken. The two men didn't say anything, but they didn't need to. Each simply enjoyed the quiet and relaxing moment for himself. There was no one to ask them difficult questions, nothing that demanded their attention. It was a brief but precious break for the two. Ando realized how tired he was; he felt it in his bones. The fire popped.

"We'll be in Turkey, tomorrow," said Inui.

"Finally getting out of British territory," agreed Ando, his eyes fixed on the fire.

"Think we can drink beer there?"

"Turkey's a Muslim country, but I heard they're pretty open-minded about drinking. It'll be our first break. Let's find a good place, when we get there."

"I'm going to order five or six bottles just for myself. I won't need any snacks. Just beer."

The firewood continued to pop and send up sparks. Ando grabbed a stick to stir the fire. Ingesting oxygen, the flames roared up.

While Ando and Inui relaxed around their campfire, back in Delhi Jim was climbing onto a night train bound for Jodhpur. In the end, he'd never gotten a chance to meet Mr. Kutchnik, the Flying Tigers recruiter. The man had simply never shown up. Jim felt like an actor who had just memorized all his lines only to jump onto the wrong stage. His desperate efforts to play along had ended in vain, and now he took his cue to exit. In the end, the only thing he'd accomplished in Delhi was to settle a ridiculously expensive room charge when he checked out.

Jim took his seat on the train. *My contract with Gaj Singh is up this month. It's almost 1941. I should take the Jenny to Calcutta and approach the Chennault Air Company myself. I've already decided once to try and join the Flying Tigers, and I'm not giving up without a fight. Hell, I've been thinking about nothing else for months. I may have missed the interview, but my mind's set and I can't do anything about it.*

The train moved out of the station. Jim took a bottle of whisky from his bag. The Sikh sitting across from him frowned, but Jim didn't care. He opened the cap and took a good swig from the bottle, remembering the young hooker he'd been serviced by in Old Delhi. A mixed-blood, half Indian, half Chinese. *At least I got to spend the night with that girl. That wasn't nothing. Got my chance to enjoy the mysteries of the Orient. Nice break from the daily grind.* He wiped his lips with the back of his hand.

Later the same night, Ando and Inui dropped in to watch the maintenance work being performed on their aircraft. Their two Zeros rested side by side in the high-ceilinged hangar. Bright lamps illuminated the ten or so men who were working on the planes.

The cowling of Ando's aircraft had been removed to expose the Nakajima Sakae engine. Several curious workers stood on the wings or stepladders to get a better view of this or that part. Several men were cleaning out the oil coolers, while others peered into a detached exhaust pipe. The pieces of what looked like a carburetor lay spread across a clean sheet on the floor. Only a few of the workers appeared to have been trained as maintenance men. Some even lazily leaned against the fuselages.

Inui spotted the sergeant that Hussein had ordered into the hangar earlier. He seemed to be supervising the operation. Inui strode over and began gesticulating at him. The sergeant regarded Inui with obvious dislike and annoyance. The mustachoed man, who appeared to be around forty, had a scar running next to his right eye.

"What's wrong?" asked Ando, catching up with the two.

"They're handling the parts too roughly," replied Inui. "I told him to pay more attention. He and his workers need to be more careful with the components. Can't stand watching amateurs mess around with machines!"

"Did you say that in Arabic?"

"I think he got the point from my tone. Are they really going to be done by tomorrow morning?"

"Think the Japanese engines are giving them trouble?"

"Engines are engines. The principles are the same all over the world. To be honest, lieutenant, I don't think they care that we're in a hurry."

Suddenly, the sound of metal hitting the floor echoed through the hangar. Ando and Inui turned to see a man pick up a part from the floor under Ando's fighter.

"What did I just tell you, idiot!" yelled Inui.

Inui's holler sounded shockingly loud inside the hangar. The workers stopped to stare at him. They were dead silent. They didn't even appear to be breathing.

The sound of Inui's boots on the concrete floor broke the silence. He strode over and snatched the component from the worker's hands.

Ando looked around carefully and made his way over to Inui. Every man in the hangar stared at them. The atmosphere had become undeniably hostile. Ando felt the angry stares piercing his body.

"This is a bolt for a cylinder head," said Inui, pointing at the part. "If you crack the tip, it's all over!" Inui thrust the bolt into the sergeant's face. "I told you to be careful. If you break even one, you've destroyed everything. These are fighters, not trucks!" he yelled in Japanese.

The officer spat on the ground without taking his eyes off Inui.

Ando tugged on his partner's sleeve.

"Inui, calm down. Don't forget, we're asking them to do us a favor."

Finally noticing the atmosphere in the hangar, Inui looked around sheepishly and lowered his head in embarrassment.

"I didn't mean to raise my voice. I was just worried," he said.

Inui handed the bolt back to the worker, who accepted it with a stiff look.

"So what are you going to do? Stay here until they finish?" asked Ando.

"No, I'd better leave them alone after this. In the morning pre-flight, I'll get to see how they did anyway."

Ando walked up to the Iraqi sergeant, who was still smoldering with anger.

"Sergeant, we thank you for everything. We deeply appreciate your working late into the night for us," said Ando. The sergeant's cheeks twitched. The scar next to his eye burned fiery red. "But we're in the middle of a very important mission right now. We must leave early tomorrow morning. Can we expect everything to be done by then?"

"I can't guarantee anything," the sergeant answered. "It's up to the will of Allah." He smiled cynically.

CHAPTER 15

Ando and Inui's worst fears came true the next morning when they climbed into their fighters. No sooner had they begun the warm-up process than Inui radioed Ando that he had an engine malfunction.

"This isn't good," said Inui. "The tachometer doesn't read normal, and I'm getting some vibration."

"Think you can take off?" asked Ando. *Sometimes he's too obsessive about the engines. Maybe he's just overreacting.* "Is it too bad to fly?"

"Lieutenant, I can't take off like this."

Can't take off! Ando tried to recall the flight manual that he had studied for the Type Zero Carrier Fighters. *Vibrations, vibrations... Isn't that a problem with the exhaust gas temperature? Or was it the oil temperature, or the AC? Had he accidentally set the air-supply temperature lever to its original position? The manual said changing the RPM could shake off the vibrations... But we're talking about Inui here. He must have tried everything before contacting me.*

"I think I've got a couple of dead cylinders. I'm afraid I'm going to have to overhaul the engine by myself," said Inui.

Ando looked up at the pre-dawn sky. It was a deep, dark blue, and the stars were still visible. It was still nighttime on the desert plain. *Merchants preferred traveling at night in ancient times because the stars were their only guides. We're just the opposite: we need the sun to fly. Judging from the color of the sky over east, sunrise won't be for another half hour. Taking off a few hours later than we'd planned shouldn't cause any major problem.*

Ando looked down to the floor of the hangar. The maintenance workers had gathered around the fighters. The sergeant was there, too, his arms crossed on his chest as he regarded Inui's aircraft. There was a smile on his face, a cool smile.

"Let's get down," said Ando to Inui over the radio. "We'll postpone takeoff for a few hours. Ankara isn't that far. We have time."

Ando stopped the engine, turned all the switches off, and climbed down from the cockpit. Inui did so as well.

"Inui's engine isn't operating properly," Ando told the sergeant. "We think some of the cylinders aren't working. Would you take a look at them right away?"

"We worked all night on your aircraft."

"We appreciate that. But the engine isn't working right. Please check it again."

"Are you saying it's our fault?"

"No. I'm just telling you that it isn't working. We can't take off. We need you to check it again, please."

"Listen, Japanese," said the sergeant, his chin thrust forward. "You gave my men a pair of aircraft they'd never seen before. We took out the engines, cleaned them to remove the carbon, put them back together, and tightened the bolts. We checked the entire fuselages, cleaned out the sand, tightened up the wires, and topped off the oil. Without a proper manual, it took us fourteen hours. The crew is exhausted."

"We appreciate all that," said Ando patiently. "But we can't take off. The engine isn't working."

"My men are excellent. We are the best maintenance group in Iraq!"

Light flashed across the sergeant's face. It appeared to be the head-lights of a car approaching the tarmac. Ando and the sergeant stopped arguing for a moment.

A four-wheeled military vehicle with a camouflage paint job pulled up next to them. Colonel Hussein stepped out. He greeted Ando warmly.

"I'm glad I was able to make it," said Hussein in a friendly manner. "You're taking off in a moment, correct?"

Hussein seemed to have forgiven his guest's discourtesy, as Ando noted with some relief.

"Colonel Hussein. Unfortunately, we can't take off. One of our aircraft isn't working properly."

"It can't fly?"

"No. I was in the middle of asking the sergeant to do some more work on the engine."

Hussein said something to the sergeant. The sergeant stood up straighter and answered in rapid Arabic. Ando couldn't understand a thing. Hussein turned back to Ando.

"The maintenance men are exhausted. I must let them have sleep and food."

"How long do they need?"

"Five or six hours, perhaps."

Part Three

Ando did a quick mental calculation. It was 1,300 or 1,400 kilometers to Ankara. *With the drop tanks, it shouldn't be too hard. With the throttles open, we should be able to get to the Turkish base in four hours. There's a good chance we'll run into the RAF, but what else can we do? Waiting until noon to take off won't mean the end of the world.*

"We'd like to take off by noon. Can it be done by then?"

"That's quite a difficult request," said Hussein, looking at Ando and Inui. "Why don't you leave one of them behind?"

"Come again?"

"I suggest that one of you go ahead to the next destination. As soon as the necessary maintenance work is done, the second plane will follow. What do you think?"

Ando hadn't seen the suggestion coming and was plunged into confused thoughts. He and Inui had agreed that if either plane experienced problems, the other would fly by itself to Berlin. But the situation here in Iraq didn't appear particularly serious to Ando.

Suddenly, Ando recalled his verbal tug-of-war with Hussein the night before. *Didn't he want us here for a week?*

"The sergeant will make every effort," assured Hussein, "to repair your aircraft once his men have had some rest. In the meantime, as we speak, one plane is ready to fly."

"We take off together," Ando stated firmly, shaking his head.

"Are you sure?"

"Yes. Even if it means a change in plans, we will take off together."

Hussein looked disappointed. He turned and said something to the sergeant. The sergeant saluted.

"The mechanics are taking a rest," said Hussein bluntly. "Maintenance will resume once they are ready. I hope you understand."

Ando nodded in agreement, realizing there was nothing he could do.

CHAPTER 16

Maintenance work resumed at eleven o'clock. Both Zeros were wheeled back into the hangar. This time, Inui stayed to supervise. The maintenance men did not appear to have gotten enough sleep. To a man, they appeared weary and irritable. The sergeant in particular regarded Inui's presence with manifest displeasure.

Ando decided to just watch from a corner of the hangar. He wasn't anywhere near as knowledgeable as Inui about aviation maintenance, and had next to zero hands-on experience when it came to repairs.

The Iraqi mechanics had surrounded Inui's aircraft. A stand for the engine and a box for parts that had been removed sat immediately underneath the fuselage. A ceiling chain-hoist had been moved over the fighter as well. The sergeant pointed to various parts of the engine as he gave a steady stream of orders to the mechanics.

One of the men slipped into the cockpit and started the engine. The propellers began to spin, but it was immediately clear the engine wasn't turning over as smoothly as it should. In fact, it rattled like something was stuck inside. The man in the cockpit seemed to be checking the throttle or the lever for regulating the fuel-air mixture. He also appeared to be testing the air-supply temperature. Every time the man in the cockpit moved, the engine's pitch shifted. Inui listened intently.

Perhaps they'll be done in a couple of hours? Ando glanced at a clock. He was already giving up on taking off at noon. *Even if we can't take off by noon, we'll make it to Ankara before dusk if we can leave by one past.*

At noon, Hussein appeared at the entrance to the hangar and approached Ando.

"How are things going?" he asked. Ando thought he detected a hint of trickiness in the man's question. "The maintenance work, I mean?"

"They've really just started," answered Ando. "This is a fourteen-cylinder engine. It'll take a lot of work to find the one with the problem."

"Oh, they'll find it soon. Everyone here is a professional. The sergeant in particular is a great mechanic. He's been working on my cars ever since we first fought together in Syria. He is a trustworthy man. You can rely on him."

"Inui is quite familiar with engines himself. He was an auto mechanic before he joined the Imperial Navy."

"Lieutenant," said Hussein, studying Ando, "if we encounter a problem so severe that it can't be fixed without new parts from Japan, what will you do? Will you still insist on flying in tandem?"

Ando thought it over.

"We don't have much time. If it comes to that, one of us will head to Berlin alone."

"One of the planes will stay behind?"

"We wouldn't have any other choice."

Inui walked up to Ando, frowned, and shook his head. "This isn't looking good at all. It's going to take a lot more than just a couple of hours. Me, I think it's either the air intake or the spark-ignition system, but they're convinced otherwise." He completely ignored Hussein as he said this.

"How long do you think it'll take?"

"If they skip that afternoon prayer break of theirs? Four hours or so."

"Then we can't leave today. Guess we can have those beers tomorrow."

"I have to apologize, sir," Inui said. "Keeping the aircraft in working condition was one of my responsibilities."

"Don't worry, this is exactly why we left Tokyo a day early."

"Won't somebody from the Japanese Embassy be waiting for us in Ankara?"

"Yeah. I'll ask these guys to send a telegram. But we'll be there tomorrow afternoon, anyway."

A military car pulled up in front of the hangar. Ando, Inui, and Hussein turned to see a young man step out of the car. He appeared to be an officer.

"Colonel Hussein!" called the man from the entrance. "I must speak to Colonel Hussein!"

"I'm here!" Hussein yelled back.

The officer hurried towards Hussein and handed him a piece of paper. The colonel took it, read it over, and frowned. The young officer walked away.

"Is there something wrong?" asked Ando.

Hussein nodded. His cheeks were flushed.

"Those imperialist bastards. There has been another incident," answered Hussein through clenched teeth.

"What happened?"

"An Iraqi police officer has been shot by a British soldier," replied Hussein, tearing the paper into pieces. "Last night, an Iraqi civilian was injured in a melee at an illegal British bar by a freshly appointed British officer. The officer locked himself inside a hotel room afterwards. The British attempted to bypass the Iraqi police to take the man into their own custody. There was an argument between the British troops and the Iraqi police, who wanted to arrest the man themselves. It escalated, and one of the Iraqi police officers got shot. He's in very serious condition."

"And so what is the Iraqi Army going to do?"

"What do you mean?"

"You're going to do something about it, aren't you? I assume that's what that piece of paper was all about. Orders of some kind?"

"No," said Hussein flatly. "In fact, it's the exact opposite. Headquarters has ordered us to do nothing. Nothing!"

Ando mulled over the unexpected answer. Hussein continued:

"Personally, I don't care what the other officers think. I want to charge into Baghdad and make the British pay for their vandalism of the city. At the very least I want to see that man in court." Hussein took a breath. "And if I can't do that, I want to bomb the hell out of their bases. I don't care what happens. If I have my way, I'll see their base under a hail of bullets tonight."

Throwing the torn memo to the ground, Hussein stomped towards the exit. His footsteps echoed through the hangar.

"What did he say?" asked Inui.

"Says he could use a fighter plane," replied Ando, his eyes still on Hussein.

Maintenance work was interrupted for lunch and prayer. It was already past three by the time the men returned to Inui's fighter.

Ando cabled the Japanese Embassy in Ankara. The telegram was simple, stating only that they would arrive the next day in the afternoon. *That's all they need to know. We're just postponing things by one day. It's not like we've lost Inui's bird or botched the mission. At any rate, they're not expecting us to show up like clockwork.*

Ando took a seat on a bench and leaned back against the wall. He felt the tension ebb from his body before he was even aware of it. His eyelids drooped as he began to drift off to sleep. Suddenly he heard someone shout. Inui.

"What the hell?" Inui yelled again. "So this is why!"

Ando heard the sound of metal hitting metal. Then something hard hit the floor of the hangar.

Ando snapped back to full awareness and looked toward the source of the commotion. An Iraqi mechanic stood atop a ladder against the side of the plane. It tottered and began to slowly tip over. The man waved his arms in a desperate attempt to stay upright, but the whole thing came crashing to the ground, throwing the maintenance man towards the fighter's landing gear. His tools clanged like a string of firecrackers onto the floor.

Inui jumped down from the right wing of his plane and approached the mechanic. Ando stood up from his bench.

"Inui!" he shouted.

The mechanic climbed to his feet again. Inui grabbed him by the lapels and slapped his face hard, twice. The man's eyes opened wide. Inui threw him back onto the floor.

"Japanese!" shouted the sergeant as he rushed in from the side. He spun Inui around by the shoulder and landed a solid punch in the face. Ando saw blood spray from Inui's nose.

The blow didn't faze Inui, who proceeded to drive his knee into the sergeant's solar plexus, followed up with an uppercut to the jaw. The sergeant dropped like a sack of potatoes next to the Zero's tire.

"Sabotaging my fighter!" screamed Inui. "You bastards!"

The sergeant got up. He had a rod-like metal tool in one hand. Inui instinctively dropped into a fighter's crouch. Ando saw a flash of metal in Inui's hand as well. It looked like the monkey wrench that he always carried around.

Inui and the sergeant squared off against each other, their weapons gripped tightly in their hands. Their eyes locked, they cautiously began circling and reducing the distance between them.

"Inui! Stop it!" shouted Ando, sprinting for the two men.

A mechanic rushed to block Ando's way. He brandished a long and narrow tool in his hand and appeared more than willing to use it. Ando stopped in his tracks and peered anxiously beyond the man.

The sergeant made the first move, jabbing his metal rod at Inui's face. Inui swayed backward to dodge the blow. The sergeant tried again, swinging the rod in a lateral arc, but, in one fluid motion, Inui ducked and lunged forward with his wrench, successfully knocking the rod from the sergeant's hand. He took another step forward and swung his wrench. The sergeant jumped out of the way, disappeared under the fighter's wing, and popped up again behind the aircraft.

"Inui, cut it out!" shouted Ando.

The rest of the mechanics were more than ready to join in the fracas. They surrounded Inui and the sergeant, their tools held tightly in their clenched fists. *No way for a pair of Japanese to win on an Iraqi base! How the hell did we get into this mess?*

The sergeant circled calmly around the fuselage, his eyes on Inui, arriving at the opposite wing of the plane. He had picked up another weapon along the way, a combat knife with a fifteen-centimeter blade. Undaunted, Inui made his way over to the sergeant.

"Knock it off, Inui!" shouted Ando again.

Inui turned his head slightly towards Ando, perhaps hearing him for the first time. The sergeant took the moment to thrust his blade. Inui slipped under and grabbed the sergeant's knife hand. The two men wrestled over the knife. Inui tried to slam the sergeant into the fuselage of his Zero, but he was outweighed. The sergeant thrust back with all his might, sending the pair away from the plane and smashing into a wall. Oil cans and tools scattered as they both hit the ground. The men rolled over in the tools littering the floor—then, at last, stopped moving.

Inui got up first from the bed of tools, parts, and containers. The sergeant remained on the ground. A pool of oil had begun to spread across the floor. Breathing heavily, Inui looked down at the sergeant's prone form. Inui's shirt was stained red.

The sergeant lay curled on one side, very still. Inui looked around, made his way to his fighter, and turned to face the maintenance workers. Each raised a tool menacingly. They began to close in on Inui.

The mechanic who was blocking Ando's way looked towards them for a moment. Ando took the opportunity to unholster his Nambu automatic, release the safety, and rack the action in one rapid motion. The mechanic took a nervous step backward.

Raising his arm, Ando fired once into the ceiling. The mechanics all halted their advance and turned to face the source of the report. Ando pushed his way through the group to get to Inui.

"Inui, what's wrong with you?" barked Ando, keeping his Nambu automatic trained on the mechanics. "You're out of control!"

"It was them! They did it on purpose, to keep us here on the ground," Inui answered, heaving for breath.

"What did they do?"

"They sabotaged my engine so I wouldn't be able to fly. Stuck some sort of insulator into a spark gap. The guy I knocked off the ladder was try-ing to cover it up."

"That must be why the sergeant attacked you."

"Guess so. He didn't like my prying from the start. And when I knocked that torque wrench out of his hand, he went straight for his com-bat knife."

"He looks hurt."

"I'm so sorry, lieutenant, I didn't intend things to go this far," Inui conceded in a pained voice.

The maintenance crew closed in on the pilots as though they didn't see Ando's pistol. The Iraqis' eyes were full of murderous hatred.

Eight men, thought Ando. *We're surrounded by eight men who aren't afraid of getting shot.* Ando regretted having wasted a bullet on the ceiling.

Suddenly, another gunshot broke the tense silence, and two more came in rapid succession. Everyone turned to the entrance. It was Colonel Hussein. He lowered his gun, shouted something in Arabic, and ran toward them. The mechanics stepped back to make room. He strode into the pile of oil cans and tools, and kneeled down next to the fallen sergeant. When Hussein lifted the body, the man's head lolled lifelessly. It reminded Ando of a sunflower drooping down after a heavy rain. The neck was covered in blood.

"He's dead," said Hussein, looking up at Ando. Hussein's face was pale.

The maintenance men stiffened.

Several soldiers ran into the hangar. It was only natural, after four gunshots. The troops rushed towards the fighter.

Hussein screamed at the maintenance men. They exchanged glances and lowered their arms. They appeared disappointed; one even threw down his tool angrily. Some others walked over to kneel beside the dead sergeant.

Hussein shouted an order at the soldiers. They stepped toward Ando and Inui and pointed their rifles at the two; the sound, almost absurdly loud, of the weapons being cocked echoed in the quiet hangar.

"The British officer may have gotten away from us, but you're different, Japanese. Hand over your man right now," said Hussein.

"Your men sabotaged the aircraft," Ando replied angrily. "The argument began when Inui found out. The knife was your sergeant's. My friend didn't intend to kill anybody."

"Tell it to the judge. He will determine the appropriate punishment."

"It was self-defense."

"The man is dead! That's a fact. Given the humiliation we have just suffered at the hands of the British, I don't expect our courts to be lenient."

"Lieutenant," Inui muttered, "just hand me over to them. Let them punish me."

"Don't be a fool," Ando rebuked him sharply. "Do you have any idea how severe Islamic law is? No way. We're leaving this country tomorrow. Together."

"But I killed somebody."

"It wasn't your fault, Inui."

"I did kill him."

"We're flying together to Berlin."

The soldiers took another step forward. Ando put out an arm to hold Inui back, and realized he hadn't lowered his gun the entire time. Hussein gave another order in Arabic from behind the soldiers.

"Wait, colonel," Ando said, re-aiming his pistol.

"Why?"

"We can make a deal. My plane will take off tomorrow, for Berlin, and Inui's coming with me."

"Tell me why you call that a deal, lieutenant?"

"Before we set ourselves on course, we'll attack the British base as you requested."

CHAPTER 17

Early the next morning, two Type Zero Carrier Fighters descended through a misty sky. It was just before dawn.

The white line of the Euphrates River stretched across the horizon ahead of the planes. The pilots had been told that a paved road lay beyond it. The RAF's Musalla base was to be found ten kilometers down the road.

Musalla happened to be where the British officer from the Baghdad incident was posted. Lieutenant Ando had been told that Musalla was the smallest RAF base in Iraq, home to a small detachment of the No. 70 Bomber Squadron stationed in Hinaidi. The base flew Victorias, twin-engine biplane bombers that were rapidly approaching obsolescence. Without any air force of their own to oppose the aircraft, however, Middle Easterners saw the aging Victorias as the invincible tools of the devil. There would be a total of six on the base.

The sky began to brighten. According to what the lieutenant had been told, the base should be coming into view fairly soon. He and his wingman would have the bright morning sun behind them.

According to Colonel Hussein, Musalla featured a single runway and two hangars. The six Victoria bombers were usually parked in a line on a hardstand in front of the control tower. The base had no fighters of any kind; the Victorias were the only combat aircraft.

In the strategy meeting the night before, Lieutenant Ando and Flight Sergeant Inui had been told to strafe the line of bombers with their cannons and machine guns. *We'll drop to ten meters,* thought Ando as he looked over the maps. *With the bombers that close to one another, even a short run should cause a lot of damage. The Victorias are big, but our twenty millimeters'll make easy work of them. Some of the shells will hit the fuel tanks, and the secondary explosions should damage the fuel depot, hangar, and control tower. That should keep the base out of commission for the next few weeks. That ought to satisfy Hussein.*

"I have the base in sight," came Inui's voice from the radio. He sounded nervous, or in some kind of pain. "11 o'clock. I see the runway."

Ando focused his eyes ahead. He could just barely make out a thin white line in the scrub brush ahead. As they approached, he saw two large buildings to the right of the runway. What appeared to be barracks stood on the left. The bombers were indeed parked in a neat line along the right side of the runway.

"We'll commence the attack. Are you ready?" said Ando, flipping the switch atop the throttle lever to activate the machine guns and 20mm cannons. The Type Zero Carrier Fighter allowed a pilot to arm and fire the cannons and machine guns separately, but Ando and Inui planned to use them both on this mission. Ando released the safety for the machine guns, and threw the main switch to arm the cannons.

"Aim for the Victorias, the hangars, and the fuel depot. Only go for the aircraft and their support structures. Avoid the barracks, or any people on the ground," Ando commanded.

"Copy. Ready to fire," replied Inui.

The two adjusted their approach as they descended, moving parallel to the runway in order to approach the bombers on their sides. At two kilometers from the target, the Zeros had descended to 100 meters.

Ando could practically see the telegram in his head: *RAF base attacked by Imperial Japanese Navy fighters*. It may have been early in the morning, but tensions were high in Iraq; the guard tower and anti-aircraft artillery emplacements were undoubtedly manned around the clock.

Still, this was a surprise attack. There was almost no chance of failure, but there was no way to hide the rising sun markings on their aircraft, either. The RAF would probably see it as a huge step for the Axis powers. Ando didn't even want to think about how Ohnuki and Yamawaki would react once the news reached Tokyo.

This could well trigger war between England and Japan. The idea was as comfortable as a stone swallowed by mistake. This wasn't just disobeying orders; there'd be no way for Ando and Inui to make up for this. It was utterly irresponsible. *But how else could I save Inui? Was there any other way? We were told to fire only when absolutely necessary. I wonder if they'll accept this as that kind of emergency?*

Ando swallowed hard and tried to endure the pain in his stomach. *Inui, I'm doing this for Inui. I got him off the hook with the Islamic court. I'll always be able to tell myself that, at least. I brought him into this, after all*. Ando saw protecting Inui as his duty, as a mission of its own. Even if it meant changing the world, for the worse.

The fighters dropped to twenty meters. The base loomed ahead, drawing closer and closer. The control tower was in clear view, its glass windows reflecting the early morning sunlight. Ando saw the silver-tinted bombers lined up along the runway.

The Zeros descended to an altitude of just ten meters above the desert floor. Now Ando had the line of bombers in his Type 98 gunsight. They were no more than five hundred meters from the target.

"Fire!" called Ando, and pulled the lever for his weapon. The airframe shook from the recoil of the 20mm auto-cannons. A tracer bullet curved gracefully through the air. Smoke began to rise from the concrete tarmac, followed by a cloud from the line of bombers. Ando caught sight of metal leaping into the air. The roar of the cannons and the smell of gunpowder filled his cockpit.

Ando's pass lasted only a fraction of a second. He saw an anti-aircraft machine gun at the edge of the runway. A man watched Ando's fighter in silent astonishment in the control tower.

Ando pulled up at once, banked hard right, and checked his rear. Inui's fighter followed Ando's path over the bombers as if on rails. Explosion after explosion erupted from the tarmac as Inui's shells perforated the Victorias. By this point, soldiers had begun streaming from the barracks.

Keeping the base on his right, Ando headed back to the point where he had commenced the attack. A sandbagged anti-aircraft emplacement began firing in a totally misguided direction. The attempt was so futile it seemed almost that they were trying to warn Ando and Inui rather than shoot them down. Ando spotted what appeared to be a refueling truck slinking across the runway toward the hangars.

Ando banked to face the end of the runway. Several of the bombers were completely aflame. There was a flash as an explosion threw one bomber's wing into the sky; it was trailed by a comet-like cloud of thick black smoke and glittering bits of metal.

"Next target, hangars and fuel depot," stated Ando. "Location is behind the bombers. Watch distance."

"Roger."

Ando adjusted his course towards the hangar and dropped his altitude. The soldiers below were in a panic, not yet realizing what was going on, running in every direction. Perhaps they were still half asleep. A car drove into a wall of sandbags and rolled onto its side. One soldier stood his ground and fired his sidearm three times at Ando's aircraft. Ando was close enough to make out each wisp of smoke as the pistol fired.

The hangar swung into view in Ando's gunsight, and he pulled the trigger on the machine guns. A sheet of dust lifted free from a hangar wall as a stream of Ando's bullets riddled it and continued onto the roof. The air was getting thick with the soot from multiple fires. Ando winced as the concussion from another explosion buffeted his fighter.

Ando punched through a plume of smoke to find the fuel depot squarely in his sights. The fuel tank was guarded by sandbags that proved absolutely defenseless against the stream of shells from the Zero's 20mm cannons. Ando passed directly over the depot and pulled up in a steep ascent, catching sight of a squad rushing to the gun at the end of the runway.

Ando kept the throttle full open and banked right, turning his head to watch the base over his shoulder. The bombers appeared completely destroyed. Some were aflame, while others lay askew on broken wings. Smaller secondary explosions continued to rock the shattered remains of the Victorias. The fuel supply truck had stopped and was on fire as well, hit by either stray bullets or shrapnel.

A large hole had been opened in the hangar's roof by repeated strafing runs. Ando couldn't see, but there was probably either a patrol aircraft or a Victoria under repair parked inside. Whatever it was, Ando figured, it'd be as full of holes as the rest of the building. The fuel tank at the depot continued to flash and shudder amidst a growing plume of thick, black smoke.

More than enough, thought Ando. *That should satisfy Hussein for letting Inui go. The rest is between Hussein and the British Army. He can attack them, make an official statement, whatever; it's out of our hands.*

"Time to head for Ankara, Inui," said Ando, his aircraft finally climbing back to cruising altitude. "Hope everything's okay."

Ando could hardly believe his ears when Inui replied, "I'm hit. I think I got hit by that anti-aircraft gun."

"Hit! Are you okay?"

"I'm fine. And the engine sounds okay. For now, at least."

"How's she handling?"

Inui remained quiet for a long moment. "I'm having some difficulty with the ailerons."

"Talk to me, Inui. We can go back to Imam Hamid if we have to."

"I'm going to try to climb. Let's put some distance between us and the base."

Ando looked over his shoulder to confirm that his wingman was behind him. Inui was lagging by a good 300 meters. Ando descended and eased back on the throttle. When Inui's aircraft finally pulled alongside, Ando flew closer to inspect the damage. Several bullet holes were visible on the rear of Inui's fuselage and in his vertical stabilizer. The left wing appeared to have been holed in several places as well.

"It isn't too bad," radioed Ando. "Check your fuel gauge. Did your tank take a hit?"

"That's a negative."

"Then you're fine. Let's ascend to 4,000."

"Wait!"

"What's wrong?" asked Ando, passing Inui's aircraft.

"Formation ahead. Above us, 2 o'clock," said Inui. Ando thought he heard Inui sigh.

He looked up. Inui was right. A formation was swooping down on them. Six aircraft. Enemy planes were closing in.

It was only a few minutes after dawn. Ando knew there was only one way the RAF could have found them so quickly: there'd been a leak. Somehow or other, the RAF had learned that Ando and Inui had just taken off for their next destination. Perhaps they'd even known about the surprise attack.

Be that as it may, there was no doubt that word of the surprise attack had been passed to all RAF bases in Iraq by now. The formation bearing in on Ando and Inui was likely only the first of many they'd encounter on the way to Ankara. Off the top of his head, Ando knew that the No. 30 Squadron of the RAF happened to be stationed in Mosul, 350 kilometers north of Baghdad. This leg would not be an easy one.

Ando climbed and opened the throttle. It was only a half-hour since takeoff, so their main and drop tanks were still full. The weight of the tanks severely hampered the Zero's maneuverability. *This isn't good. We're going to have to climb higher if we want to run!*

"Engine trouble," came Inui's tense voice.

"What?" cried Ando.

"I can't squeeze any more RPMs out of her. She's turning over too slowly."

"How about the boost gauge?"

"I'm on max. It's in the red."

Ando eased back on the throttle to wait for Inui to catch up. It took longer than Ando expected for him to pull alongside.

"You're fine. We can still shake them off. Just follow me," said Ando, looking directly at Inui's face as he spoke over the radio.

"I can't," replied Inui, pointing to the front. "Those aren't old fighters."

Ando peered through the windshield. Three fighters with a low-slung wing configuration were approaching rapidly. They weren't the old Gladiator biplanes that Ando and Inui had encountered in the last few days. *Spitfires? Hurricanes? Whatever they are, the RAF wasn't supposed to have anything but biplane fighters here in Iraq…*

Ando watched as the three fighters entered a steep nose-dive in formation, apparently intending to intercept Ando and Inui's flight path. The three remaining fighters stayed at altitude. Ando figured those three would try to flank them from the left.

"Lieutenant, please go on ahead to Ankara. I'll take care of this," said Inui. Ando watched in horror as the drop tank detached from the bottom of Inui's plane.

"What 'take care of this'? Inui! What are you doing?"

You dropped the tank! It spun end over end in a graceful curve through the air and quickly vanished out of sight. *You can't make it to Ankara without the tank!*

Freed of that burden, Inui's aircraft surged forward smoothly and lightly.

"I'm too damaged to make it to Ankara, anyway. The supercharger's shot, too. I'll head back to Imam Hamid once I get the attention of these fighters."

"Inui!"

"I messed up, lieutenant. Please go on without me. Goodbye!"

Inui's aircraft climbed rapidly to meet the incoming RAF fighters. He obviously intended to engage them in combat to distract them and facilitate Ando's escape.

Ando hesitated for a split second before he made the decision. It was the hardest of his entire career.

"Thank you, Inui," said Ando, putting his Zero into a half roll. "It's in your hands now."

"Have a beer for me in Turkey, lieutenant." Inui's reply came through a sudden burst of static.

"Inui? Inui!"

There was no reply. Ando looked in the direction his wingman was headed. The three attacking fighters had spread out to intercept him. Ando got his first clear look at them: Hawker Hurricanes. They had been painted in a desert camouflage, and now Ando could clearly make out the RAF insignia on their wings and fuselages.

Inui's Type Zero Carrier Fighter rolled as it climbed, the morning sunlight sparkling on its beautiful metallic hide. Tracer bullets arced through the sky.

CHAPTER 18

Lieutenant Colonel Ilhan Ozgu of the General Staff Office of the Turkish Army stood outside the base's control tower, ready to greet the Japanese pilot. It was just before eleven in the morning. *Much earlier than I expected,* thought Ozgu. *He must have left Baghdad at dawn.*

The lieutenant colonel had been told to expect two Japanese aircraft, but only one had landed. He saw no sign of any other aircraft making an approach, either. Ozgu watched the lone fighter's landing with trepidation.

Yoshihiro Nagano, a secretary from the Japanese Embassy, stood next to Ozgu. He was a young diplomat who had only been assigned to his post in Ankara three months ago. He had arrived at the base at nine that morning. With his thick overcoat and constant shivering, it was obvious that he had not yet acclimated to the chilly weather of the Turkish highlands.

Following the directions of the ground crew, the fighter changed direction towards the tower as it taxied down the runway. *So this is Japan's newest fighter,* thought Ozgu. *All metal, low wings, single seat, enclosed cockpit, retractable landing gear. That's a lot of new technology to pack into one little fighter.*

The aircraft obviously represented the cutting edge of military aviation, but it looked strangely dilapidated to Ozgu. The dented fuselage was covered with dirt and soot. If Ozgu had seen any bullet holes, he would have assumed it had flown through an anti-aircraft barrage. Nagano seemed surprised by the appearance of the plane as well.

The propeller spun to a stop, followed by the engine. Ozgu watched as the pilot climbed out of the plane's cockpit looking totally exhausted, moving slowly, awkwardly, as though something weighed as heavily on his mind as his body. The pilot didn't glance around with curiosity, Ozgu noticed, though this must have been a completely unfamiliar environment for him. Even the ground crew failed to attract his attention.

Ozgu and Nagano walked out to greet Ando.

"I'm Lieutenant Ando of the Imperial Japanese Navy," the pilot said in English, snapping a salute.

"I'm Lieutenant Colonel Ozgu, Army of the Republic of Turkey," replied Ozgu, returning the salute. "I had been told that two aircraft would arrive..."

"The other plane's been delayed," replied Ando. "It should arrive tomorrow or the day after."

Then Nagano spoke to Ando in Japanese. Ozgu didn't understand a thing, but noted that Ando answered with few words and with less expression. When he sensed that the conversation had ended, Ozgu handed a telegram to Ando.

"This is for you. It was routed through the German Embassy."

Ando looked down and read the telegram. It said, *I hail your courage and send my gratitude. May Allah guide the remainder of your flight, 10:00 Dec. 5, Colonel Mohammed Hussein.*

Ando turned pale. His eyes bored into Ozgu's, practically begging him to reveal that it was some kind of mistake.

It took only a moment for Ando to pull himself together. "I must revise my initial report. The second aircraft has had an accident."

This time, it was Nagano who turned pale.

"What happened, lieutenant?" asked Ozgu. "What kind of accident was this?"

"We encountered the RAF while the second aircraft was having engine trouble," replied Ando. "The pilot said he would return to Imam Hamid, but now it appears...he didn't make it."

"You mean the aircraft was shot down?"

"I can only assume."

"We receive comprehensive intelligence reports concerning anything having to do with the Iraqi Army and the RAF. I'll check for any report of a Japanese military aircraft going down."

"Thank you, sir."

"Please let me show you to the barracks. We've prepared a room for you. Lunch will be served in the dining room of our officers' club."

After Ozgu took Ando to the barracks, he returned to the command room to look through that day's and the previous day's reports. Iraqi intelligence was categorized in a folder of its own. According to the report, the Iraqi police and the British military had scuffled in Baghdad, resulting in the serious injury of an Iraqi policeman. The young British RAF officer responsible for the incident had been arrested by the British and was promptly being sent back to England. Iraqi Army HQ had issued strict orders to all Iraqi servicemen to stay put. There had been an incident involving angry Iraqi civilians throwing stones at the British Embassy, but otherwise the situation appeared stable.

Ozgu flipped to that day's report. At nine that morning, all British servicemen in Iraq had been restricted to their bases. R&R leave had been cancelled as well. The British military seemed to be taking the previous day's incident quite seriously. In addition, an explosion had been reported in Musalla, outpost of the No. 70 Bomber Squadron of the RAF. It said that at least one of the Victoria twin-engine bomber deployed there had been completely destroyed. In other news, two Gloucester Gladiators deployed to Hinaidi base had suffered a minor collision during a routine patrol flight. Both had made emergency landings, and no injuries were reported. And finally, at eleven, a radical cadre of Iraqi Army officers had issued a statement claiming responsibility for attacking Musalla. It appeared to Ozgu that the Iraqis were behind the explosion in some way.

Ozgu skimmed through the rest of the report, but found no mention of a fighter, Japanese or otherwise, being shot down. It appeared that the Iraqi and British forces had their hands full, but there was nothing about any Japanese fighters. Perhaps, thought Ozgu, the missing fighter had made an emergency landing somewhere. He made a mental note to check the reports again later that day.

Ozgu visited Ando before dinner and conveyed the content of the reports to him. Ozgu had hoped to cheer Ando up, but the pilot's expression remained dark, dismayed.

The Turkish officer had hoped to discuss Japanese military aviation strategy and equipment with Ando that evening. But seeing the exhaustion on Ando's face, Ozgu decided to cut his visit short. Ando simply didn't appear strong enough, physically or emotionally, to have any kind of discussion at the moment.

"Please feel free to ask for anything you might need, lieutenant. We'll do our best to get you what you need," said Ozgu as he prepared to leave Ando's room.

"I'd like to have dinner alone tonight," replied Ando quietly. "I'd like a candle placed on the other side of the table."

As Ozgu was getting ready for bed that evening, he heard the strains of a trumpet being played somewhere on the base. Ozgu had never heard the mournful tune before. He stepped outside to listen.

Part Three

The base rested in silence beneath a sky full of stars. The runway was empty, and there was no sign of any activity. The bombers and courier planes sat on the hardstand, their noses gently facing the stars like gargoyles protecting the base. The trumpet came from the direction of a structure that was no longer being used, a mooring tower for airships. The sound seemed to tremble slightly in the cold, still air. Ozgu almost felt as if he could see the crisp notes etching a silver line across the nighttime sky.

Ozgu noticed that Nagano had appeared as well, apparently lured by the sound of the trumpet.

"It's Lieutenant Ando," said Nagano.

"It's such a sad tune. A Japanese song?" asked Ozgu.

"It's a requiem. It's played for navymen who've lost their lives."

"In other words..."

Nagano nodded. "It seems that Lieutenant Ando believes that his wingman is dead."

The requiem reached a crescendo and ended, leaving only dead silence. It was quiet enough for Ozgu to hear his own heartbeat. The song must have captivated the entire base. Touched, Ozgu stood and watched the stars for quite some time before going to bed.

CHAPTER 19

Yamawaki caught sight of Mariko and waved as she ran across the bridge towards him. It was just after 5:30 on December 7th. The sun had set and the skies over Yokohama had turned to dusk. There were only a few other people on the bridge.

As Mariko approached, she stopped running and placed a finger to her lips. She was winded. She seemed to be asking Yamawaki not to say anything until she caught her breath again. A cold wind blew across the bridge from the north, but her forehead was beaded with sweat. Finally, she took a deep breath, looked into Yamawaki's eyes, and said, "It's today! Today is the day, isn't it?"

"That's right. Your brother should be arriving in Berlin today," Yamawaki said, nodding.

"Is he all right? Do you know how he's doing?"

"We received a report from the naval attaché in Rome a little while ago," said Yamawaki, nodding again. "Lieutenant Ando left Rome at eight sharp, local time. That's to say, just an hour ago."

Mariko smiled. Yamawaki thought her teeth looked beautiful. Her cheeks were flushed and her expression so innocent Yamawaki couldn't help but smile too.

"Flying between Rome and Berlin is as safe as flying over Japan," he noted. "I can assure you that your brother is out of danger."

Yamawaki did not tell Mariko that an army intelligence officer had gone missing in Delhi, and that word of the mission might have leaked to the RAF. Yamawaki and Ohnuki had worried constantly about Ando and Inui's safety, but Yamawaki saw no need to burden Mariko with the information. *The only news she needs to hear,* thought Yamawaki, *is good news at the end.*

"Do you know when my brother will be coming back?"

"Well, given the current state of affairs in Europe, I assume he'll stay in Berlin for a while. The officer in charge of this mission said that Lieutenant Ando might be posted there as a special assistant to the naval attaché."

"Did my brother fly alone from Rome? Or was Mr. Inui with him?" asked Mariko, tilting her head.

"You knew?"

"My brother made me promise first to keep it a secret, and then he told me. He told me, saying I shouldn't worry because Mr. Inui would be flying with him."

"Lieutenant Ando was accompanied by Flight Sergeant Inui," replied Yamawaki, "for part of the mission."

"Part of... Why not all the way?"

"Sergeant Inui's aircraft was lost to the mission. He and your brother took off together from Baghdad, but parted ways. His aircraft still hasn't been located."

"Hasn't been located..." echoed Mariko.

"The Japanese Embassy in Iraq has been investigating, but they haven't found anything solid yet. Lieutenant Ando reported that they ran into the RAF, but that's all we know. The RAF hasn't reported shooting down any Japanese fighters."

"How long has Mr. Inui been missing?"

"It's been three days now."

Mariko's face clouded. She looked at the ground.

"My brother always talked to me about Mr. Inui. I know there was a big difference between their ranks, but Mr. Inui was his best friend."

"He was always smiling when he was with Lieutenant Ando. That's what I remember best. That and the fact that he was an excellent pilot."

"It's hard to believe Mr. Inui's gone missing. My brother must be..." Yamawaki waited for her to continue, but she looked away to gaze at the breakwater in the harbor. She seemed to be trying to pull herself together. She remained silent for a while before she spoke again. "My brother must feel devastated. He's not good with people, so I know what Mr. Inui must've meant to him."

"I noticed that, too," agreed Yamawaki. "But they knew from the beginning that chances were only one of them would make it to Berlin. In fact, it was your brother who suggested that something like this would happen."

When Mariko looked into Yamawaki's face, her eyes were rimmed with tears. The early winter wind picked up again. Keeping her hair down with one hand, she said, "But they went anyway. They were prepared to risk their lives. They were also ready to risk losing a best friend."

"Yes. This may sound trite, but we're talking about servicemen, and

329

they're always aware of the risk."

"But my brother isn't a model soldier. Actually, he barely qualifies. Isn't that so?"

"Your brother is an outstanding soldier. He's a decorated pilot."

"But do you think he's a model for Imperial Japan?"

"The other day, the lieutenant described himself as a pilot who was born too late," replied Yamawaki, somewhat evasively. "He told us that he was descended from those men of old who piloted their ships to the faraway land of America. The sergeant was cut from the same cloth. Your brother must be grieving over his friend, but I believe, very strongly, that he does not regret taking the mission."

Mariko fixed her hair, turned up the collar of her winter coat, and looked out over the harbor again. A skiff was crossing it, the engine's rumble seemingly lagging behind the boat. The surface of the water reflected the darkening sky like a mirror. The stars would be coming out before long.

"So that's how my brother sees it. I didn't know. That makes me so sad for him," said Mariko, her face still turned toward the harbor. "No matter where he went, my brother never found a place where he felt he belonged. His mixed blood... People rejected him, time and time again. Now he must be feeling he's lost something irreplaceable. He just talks tough to hide his weakness. I feel like I've already said too much about him. But I know I'm right."

Yamawaki recalled how Ando and Inui were the morning of their departure.

"Lieutenant Ando was happy when he was flying with Sergeant Inui. He wasn't playing tough that day he took off," said Yamawaki.

"My brother is a lonely man," repeated Mariko. "He doesn't belong anywhere in the world, anywhere."

The wind had grown stronger. Yamawaki turned up his collar and hunched his shoulders to keep warm. Mariko held her lapels tightly together and began walking back across the bridge. Yamawaki followed, and their footsteps sounded a monotonous beat.

Mariko was silent for a long time. As they approached the Mizukami police station, Yamazaki finally stopped and said, "Miss Ando, I must go. I'm expecting a telegram from Berlin to arrive in the next few hours. It will tell me that the lieutenant's mission is complete. I'm thinking to wait for it at my office."

Part Three

Mariko looked up in confusion. She'd almost forgotten that she was with Yamawaki.

"Thank you for filling me in about my brother," she said simply.

"I'll call you at the hospital dorm tonight to tell you that the lieutenant has arrived safely."

"...Let me please walk with you to the station, Mr. Yamawaki."

The couple walked side by side toward Sakuragi station—slowly, savoring the last few moments in the other's company.

CHAPTER 20

Major Graf spread the reports over the desk in his office on the second floor of Luftwaffe Headquarters. First, he selected a report from the Luftwaffe attaché in Rome. It said that a single Japanese A6M2 Type Zero Carrier Fighter had departed on schedule at eight o'clock that morning from Cerveteri airbase outside Rome. The report confirmed that two A6M2s had left Imam Hamid airbase but that one had an accident of some kind and was lost.

It can't be helped, thought Graf. *Two would have been ideal for flight testing and reverse engineering, but one should suffice. It won't hinder the feasibility study for licensed production. Hell, we're at war. The plane made it all the way to Berlin from the Far East nonetheless. It flew right through Burma, India, and Iraq, all RAF territory. Certainly a commendable achievement, even if they did lose one of the fighters.*

Graf received a similar telegram from the Office of the Imperial Japanese Naval Attaché in Berlin. It said the fighter had departed Cerveteri airbase at eight o'clock, with an estimated arrival time at Gatow of 11:30. Rear Admiral Yokoi would meet the pilot at the airbase. The telegram did not mention the pilot's name or rank.

There was another report, from the German Embassy in Iraq, stating that the explosion at Musalla base in the early morning hours of the fifth may have been the result of an air raid. According to several RAF officers, the base had been attacked by several fighters of an unknown type, resulting in the total loss of every Victoria bomber on the base. The RAF's Habbaniya HQ had yet to officially confirm the attack as having been an air raid. A group of nationalist Iraqi Army officers had issued a statement claiming responsibility for the attack. However, as the statement lacked any specific information as to how the attack had been carried out, there was no way to confirm its authenticity.

That same day, according to an official RAF report, two Gloucester Gladiators from Hinaidi base had made emergency landings during their patrol. The German Embassy's report noted that the emergency landings may have been connected to the incident at Musalla. Some RAF officials were saying at first that two Hawker Hurricanes had been shot down by an unidentified aircraft, though Hawker Hurricanes were not known to be deployed in Iraq.

According to a separate Abwehr report, however, the No. 94 Hurricane Squadron had been forwarded from Cairo to Iraq on the first of December. A follow-up report stated that Hurricanes had been spotted on the RAF's base in Habbaniya, Iraq, on the third of December.

Without specific knowledge of Mission Ibis, these bits of information would seem unconnected. But Graf, who had been involved from the very beginning, easily pieced together the full picture. The pilots had certainly been busy on their way from the Far East.

Graf glanced at the wall clock. It was five past ten. Time to phone General Udet, Chief of the Luftwaffe Technical Office. Udet was supposed to accompany Reich Marshal Goering to Gatow to welcome the Zero and its pilot. The general had told Graf that Goering was astonished to hear that even a single Japanese fighter had made it as far as Rome. Goering wanted to award the pilot a Knight's Cross to the Iron Cross. It seemed that he had already privately cleared the matter with the Führer. Because of that, the day's schedule included not only the official delivery of the aircraft but Goering's awarding the medal.

Graf rang the Luftwaffe Technical Office. Udet answered the phone at once.

"The Japanese fighter left Rome at eight this morning," said Graf.

"So it'll finally be delivered." Udet didn't sound particularly happy. "What time will it arrive?"

"They say 11:30, at Gatow."

"I'll make sure to be there. I assume there must be some paperwork on your end as well. I'm counting on you, Major Graf."

"Would you like me to contact Reich Marshal Goering?"

"No, I'll contact him. I suppose he'll head there directly from his private residence. Have you prepared a Knight's Cross to the Iron Cross?"

"I have, sir."

"We promised the Japanese that we would keep everything confidential. Although the Reich Marshal will be meeting this pilot, a ceremony won't be necessary. We won't need honor guards or a band."

"I'm aware of the need for secrecy, sir. Only a few officers will be there."

"I'll see you at Gatow."

Graf continued to hold the phone after Udet hung up. Graf understood why Udet wasn't enthusiastic. Actual licensed production of the Type Zero Carrier Fighter would mean more pressure from their head-in-the-clouds Führer. Because it was a direct order from Hitler, Udet made a show of devoting his entire effort to the project, but the truth, Graf knew, was that the general had next to no interest in the Japanese fighter. In fact, General Udet firmly supported continuing the intensive development of Germany's own dive-bombers.

Graf made several calls to arrange for the day's events, and looked at the clock again. It showed 10:40. *The Japanese fighter is probably crossing the Bohemian Forest, or the Ore Mountains.* Graf had already contacted the Luftwaffe squadrons along the flight route to ensure that the Japanese fighter would not be engaged.

Graf stood by his window and looked into the sky. It was a crisp winter day. A thin cloud layer hung over the city, but the weather was otherwise beautiful. *A good day to welcome a brave Japanese fighter pilot.*

Graf's mind turned to the various skies he had seen: the skies over Sachsen, where he had flown a glider; the skies over the Soviet Union, where he had secretly studied combat flight techniques, his group masquerading as a civilian aviation delegation; the skies over Braunschweig, where he had trained openly as a Luftwaffe officer; the skies over Spain, where he had fought as a member of the Condor Legion, and the skies over France where he had been so terribly injured.

Each of those skies held unforgettable memories for Graf. The simple act of flying fascinated him, and he took great pleasure in piloting various types of aircraft. He had flown with passion to restore German air power, and flown with a guilty conscience for carrying out missions without mercy. Sometimes he made friends in the sky. Other times his thoughts turned to his girlfriends. But his last memory of flying was filled with nothing but pure terror. Regarding the skies over Dunkirk, Graf remembered nothing but fear.

The thought of this renewed Graf's frustration. *Will I ever make it into the air again? Will I spend the rest of my career reading the reports of other pilots, barely able to control my envy? Is that how I'll end up despite my Luftwaffe uniform and a Knight's Cross to the Iron Cross? I'm fully recovered. There's no reason for me not to fly now. All that remains is the scar, and what of it? Looks don't matter for piloting a fighter. I could return to a combat squadron any time. Any time at all.*

Part Three

Graf walked back to his desk and gathered up the reports. It was about time for him to head to Gatow. The airfield was located on the west bank of Havel Lake, about twenty minutes by car west of Berlin.

Suddenly, Graf remembered the Messerschmitt Bf109, the one stored in a hangar at Gatow airfield. It had been hauled back from the front lines to Berlin for cadets to study. *An old C type, but it's still a Messerschmitt, by God!* Graf leapt from his chair, grabbed his jacket and hat, and ran out of the office.

The major arrived at Gatow at 11:00. The Swastika and the Rising Sun flapped on flagpoles that had been prepared for the occasion. *Putting up flags is the least we can do,* thought Graf. *We're welcoming the pilot and aircraft of a ten thousand kilometer journey. By all rights he should be getting a gun salute and a glass of champagne.*

Graf climbed from his car and headed straight to the hangar. The Messerschmitt Bf109 already sat on the tarmac. It looked positively intrepid, parked next to a Stortch courier plane and a Junkers triple-engine transport.

The maintenance men noticed Graf and saluted him. Graf knew one of them. His name was Klausen. Corporal Klausen.

"Is the Messerschmitt ready for takeoff?" Graf asked him.

"Anytime, sir," answered Klausen. "The fuel tank is full. No weapons, though. They've all been removed."

"That is fine. Will you get me a flight jacket? I'd like to borrow one."

"Are you going to fly it, sir?" asked Klausen, his eyes widening.

"Why should I not, corporal? I hope you're aware that I was a combat pilot until this May."

"Yes, sir! But where are you going, sir?"

"I assume you've been told already, but a Japanese aircraft will be landing here shortly. I'm thinking to welcome him in the sky."

Graf went to the flight control office and obtained clearance to fly. More precisely, Graf did not ask but rather told them that he would be taking off. As had happened so many times before, none dared disagree with a pilot who wore a Knight's Cross to the Iron Cross and a first-rate scar.

As Graf returned to the Messerschmitt, Klausen handed him a leather jacket and flight helmet. Graf immediately pulled the jacket on over his uniform and slipped into the cockpit. Klausen climbed up on a wing to help Graf buckle his harness.

"This pilot must be an important person. Is that why you're welcoming him yourself, Major Graf?" asked Klausen.

"He is a pilot. That makes him a colleague," the major replied curtly, strapping on his flight helmet.

Not understanding, Klausen gave Graf a quizzical look and climbed down from the Messerschmitt's wing.

Graf closed the canopy and turned on the engine. He was more than familiar with the procedure for preparing an aircraft for takeoff. The Daimler-Benz V-12 began to emit a powerful growl. Graf felt the vibration through his seat, foot pedals, and the control column. The propeller began to spin, sending a powerful gust behind the plane. Graf spoke his pre-flight check of the gauges aloud, as had always been his practice. He checked the intake-pressure gauge, the fuel pressure indicator, the hydraulic gauge, the oil-temperature gauge, and the tachometer. He made a final check of the engine's performance by adjusting the fuel-mix and throttle levers. When Graf, satisfied, looked outside, he saw Klausen finishing up his visual inspection of the exterior of the aircraft. The corporal nodded.

Graf signaled Klausen to remove the blocks from the wheels. Once Klausen had retreated to a safe distance from the aircraft, Graf taxied to the end of the runway, turned onto it, and pushed the throttle fully open. The Messerschmitt rolled down the runway, gathering speed rapidly. Soon the wind blowing past the cockpit took on a higher pitch, and the airframe began to shudder and squeak. The moment the noise stopped, Graf's Messerschmitt Bf109C floated off the runway and climbed smoothly into the sky.

CHAPTER 21

It was just after four o'clock in Delhi, but time didn't really matter in a basement. Men took turns opening the door, stomping into the room, and beating Shibata. He had no way to tell when a day began or ended. All Shibata knew was that they had beaten him just a short while ago, and were beating him again right now.

The basement was a featureless, windowless room. There was no way for Shibata to figure out what was happening outside. Even if he noticed lights, it didn't signify anything except the beginning of another round of torture. Shibata had come completely unglued from his senses of perception. He had been beaten so badly, for so long, that he couldn't even tell if he was lying on a bed or tied to a hard chair.

"If you make us continue," someone said to Shibata in English, "your body will be ripped to pieces." The sheer, unending pain prevented Shibata from opening his eyes. "Why don't you just tell us? It'll be better for you in the end."

But he kept his mouth shut and didn't move a muscle. Even if he'd wanted to sing, it would have taken every ounce of the strength he had left. His entire body burned with pain. Shibata felt like his heart had been smashed to pieces and spread through his entire body, each shattered piece pulsing independently.

"There's only a few things we need to know, at this point," said another man. He sounded younger. "Who is piloting the aircraft? And what are they transporting? That's all we need to know."

"I hope you can still hear us," said the first man. "The courier left Ankara yesterday and managed to break through our cordon! It's gone. At this point, nobody cares if you tell us where it came from or where it stopped to refuel."

"Who is it?" repeated the other man. "And what is it? What could have been worth the trouble? That's all we need to know."

I don't know, thought Shibata. No matter how many times they asked, all Shibata knew was that two Japanese courier planes would fly over India. He had been told nothing about the final destination, who was flying them, or what the planes were transporting. *All I can do is give them the same old answer.*

"What do you say? Should we give up on him?"

Somebody's talking. It sounds so far away.

"I don't think he's refusing to answer us. He just hasn't the strength left to say anything. Look at him. I'm not even sure if he's in his right mind anymore."

"Perhaps you're right," said the older man with a sigh. "It's a miracle he's still breathing, after what he took. Maybe it's about time to show him some mercy."

"Turned out rougher than expected."

"Indeed. But think about what happened in Rajasthan. The Japanese are involved in Haywood's disappearance, that much is certain. His transmission cut off just after keying the letters 'JAP.' Because I think about what poor Haywood must have gone through, I don't see our questioning as all that barbarous. I don't know about the governments, but underground, the war's already begun."

Rajasthan and Haywood, thought Shibata. *Sounds...familiar. Something to do with my mission, but what? Names of places? People? Did I give them up? I can't remember...* As soon as he began thinking, Shibata felt a crushing pain in the back of his head. His back stiffened in a futile attempt to endure it.

"Do you want me to do it?" asked the young man.

"Yes. Do it," instructed the older man.

There was a short moment of silence. Then Shibata heard the sound of metal on metal. *I know that sound! I learned it well when I went through training. I know the sound. The sound of the tool being readied. I know everything about it: its size, weight, use. But what was it called? What was it...*

It was on the tip of his tongue, but Shibata never did manage to recall the word.

CHAPTER 22

Graf leveled off once he reached 4,000 meters. He turned south and peered through the windscreen. The scenery of Havel Lake and Gruenwald Forest spread beneath him. The area south of Potsdam was a large rural district. Graf saw alternating fields of brown grass and plowed farmland stretching like a quilt to the horizon. Here and there were isles of woods, their limbs bare for the winter.

Graf glanced at his watch. It was 11:15. If the Japanese pilot was arriving on time, Graf should catch sight of him in the next five or six minutes. The well-established flight route was a bee line from Rome. *He has no reason to leave the path*, thought Graf.

Graf banked wide right over a western suburb of Berlin to await the Japanese aircraft. Visibility was about twenty kilometers. *The Japanese should see me, too. No clouds to block the view at this altitude.*

After Graf had made several turns, he finally spotted a white dot to the south. It was an aircraft. *A single-engine aircraft, small. Altitude is...3,000 meters, perhaps?* Graf shed some altitude and approached it on his right. Now he could see that the aircraft was painted a light gray. Graf saw the marking on the wing. A red circle. *This is it. This is the Type Zero.* Graf lowered his speed, banked hard around the Type Zero, and pulled to its left.

The Type Zero had a well-balanced and beautiful body. *The flat nose is typical for an aircraft with an air-cooled engine. That must be an external fuel tank, hanging under the fuselage. That's one of the reasons this aircraft can fly for more than 2,000 kilometers.* Because of the long journey, the aircraft's fuselage looked dull. Only the red circles on its main wing and fuselage remained vivid.

Graf took his time to study the aircraft as he flew closer, until the distance between them was about thirty meters. The pilot of the Type Zero looked over at Graf and nodded. Graf saluted to him. The pilot had pulled his scarf to his chin, and his face was shadowed. There was no way for Graf to make out his expression.

Graf also took the opportunity to examine the twenty-millimeter cannons and 7.7-millimeter machine guns. *Four weapons may be a little weak against Spitfires, which have eight. I wonder if it's flexible enough to accommodate more?*

Graf thought it was about time to begin his own personal ceremony to welcome the pilot. *A special greeting that I give to only the best pilots. Worth more than a bottle of champagne, a gun salute, or even a Knight's Cross to the Iron Cross from Goering. A passionate kiss from one pilot to another.*

Graf moved his Bf109 slightly ahead of the Type Zero, and signaled to the pilot. Graf pointed at his face first, then at the other pilot. Then he crossed both hands in front of this face. *You, me, fight.*

At first the Japanese pilot didn't react. Perhaps he didn't understand what Graf meant. Graf pointed at his face again. The other pilot nodded. This time Graf saw the pilot's mouth. He appeared to be smiling a little. Even from this distance, Graf could see the loneliness etched in the pilot's face. For some reason, it made Graf feel a little nostalgic. But he didn't know why. When the Zero pilot faced forward, his plane rolled slightly and then banked hard to the right.

I knew he had something, thought Graf. The pilot had accepted the challenge, confident enough to spar with Graf even after such an arduous mission.

The major responded by banking to the left. Once he felt that he had put enough distance between the two aircraft, he turned to look for his opponent. The Type Zero was approaching him from above. Graf opened the throttle, and they shot past each other at full speed.

Something hot was growing in the major's body. It was as though every cell in his body had awakened from a long slumber and taken a deep breath. *My blood feels absolutely new. I can feel it running hot through my veins!* A new body seemed to be emerging from the old, and Graf knew, once and forever, that he belonged in the sky. Not in a small office filled with the scent of ink and a desk piled with paper. Here, among the clouds.

The two fighters began their mock combat over the south of Berlin. Each pilot tried to anticipate and react more sharply than the other. They flew closer and then split, repeating the process over and over again in their attempts to gain the upper hand. The Type Zero Carrier Fighter certainly outperformed the Messerschmitt Bf109. If Graf had been in a Spitfire, perhaps he could have cornered the Zero. But as it was, the Zero slipped through his fingers, and what was more, never missed an opportunity to take advantage of Graf's tiniest misjudgments. The speed and agility of the

Part Three

Zero didn't even leave Graf room to breathe.

Quick, smart, and sharp, thought Graf. *But is it the pilot or the aircraft?* He could not tell.

The duel lasted for nearly ten minutes. They were evenly matched; it appeared that their dogfight would end without a clear winner.

But suddenly, Graf found himself right behind the Zero. It almost looked bewildered for a moment. Graf hadn't expected the opening at all. Neither, apparently, had the pilot of the Zero.

Graf pressed in to get his quarry in his gunsight. The distance was about 150 meters, well within firing range. Graf instinctively flipped up the trigger guard and imagined the sound of the guns firing. He could practically see the tracer bullets. *This would be it.*

But a split second later, the Zero had jerked out of Graf's gunsight, climbing rapidly to complete a half loop. Graf immediately raised his nose, but only succeeded in making a larger circle around the Zero. It was then that he saw the other aircraft execute a quick roll. He couldn't believe it. *An Immelman!*

The Zero disappeared from Graf's sight. Graf tried a half loop as well, but only moments later, felt the Zero bearing down on him from directly above. Graf froze, the memories of Dunkirk flooding back to him. His Messerschmitt shot, the metal skin shattered, its cockpit completely enveloped in flames. For a moment Graf forgot that this duel was only for show.

The Zero passed behind the Bf109's tail with a roar that seemed to hang in the air, so close, so oppressive, that Graf thought it might crush him. Every muscle in his body shrunk and Graf barely managed to stifle a scream of terror.

I lost, Graf admitted to himself. *If this had been for real, my Bf109 would have been blown across the entire sky. I lost. There's no doubt about that.*

Graf leveled off and reduced speed. The Zero leveled off as well. The pilot seemed to know that the match had ended in victory; he had completely dropped his guard.

Graf exhaled and suddenly remembered. *This isn't the first time. Four years ago at flight school in Braunschweig, during combat training, a Japanese showed me the perfect Immelman. A haughty man, an aloof man, distant with the other pilots...*

"Ando!" shouted Graf. "It's you!"

The Zero wagged its wings, as though he'd been heard. The German sun reflected off the aircraft's metal hide. The red circle painted on the wing pierced Graf's eyes. The Zero accelerated and headed to Gatow. Graf could see Havel Lake glowing in the winter sunlight, and a town of red brick houses nearby. The Type Zero Carrier Fighter headed straight for Berlin and began its approach, making a perfect landing at 11:35 a.m. on December 7, 1940.

Epilogue

Sometime between the end of 1940 and the beginning of the following year, Lieutenant Commander Adolf Galland left his base in France. Christmas leave, he told his colleagues. In reality, however, he was returning to Germany to oversee flight testing of a Mitsubishi A6M2 Type Zero Carrier Fighter, Model 11. After making a series of test flights, Galland handed in his report to General Udet, Chief of the Luftwaffe Technical Office.

The aircraft possesses outstanding endurance and combat maneuverability in comparison to a Messerschmitt Bf109D or E. However, it has the same top speed, and a climb rate that is inferior to the Messerschmitt. In addition, the aircraft's diving and high-altitude flight capabilities are second-class. Its armor is unbelievably poor, far worse than that used on even our courier aircraft. To conclude, the aircraft is unsuitable for deployment in the Luftwaffe.

The report also contained detailed instructions on how best to overcome the Type Zero Carrier Fighter in the event of a hostile encounter.

In the same month, Hitler received the report and comments from Udet. The Führer immediately abandoned the plan for licensed production of the Type Zero Carrier Fighters.

The Imperial Japanese Navy also received Galland's report. They were shocked to read the detailed explanation of the weak points of the Type Zeros. Fearing that the British military would learn of and exploit these shortcomings, the Imperial Navy had Rear Admiral Yokoi request that Galland's report be buried.

The Luftwaffe agreed to the request, assuring the Japanese that not only the report, but all documents relating to the plan would be destroyed. Since precious few records of the flight remain today, it appears that the Luftwaffe must have kept their word. In fact, the Zero fighter that had flown to Berlin left no trace whatsoever after January 1941.

Some details of the supporting players in the saga of the flight to Berlin are in order.

In January of 1941, Chandra Bose, leader of the Indian independence movement, escaped from house arrest in Calcutta and made his way to Berlin. The exact means of his escape and travel remain a mystery even today. In the spring of 1943, Bose moved from Berlin to Tokyo via German and Japanese submarines. He established an Indian government-in-exile in Singapore in October of the same year, assuming leadership duties himself. In 1944, Bose led the Indian National Army in an assault on the city of Imphal. In August 1945, just after the conclusion of the war in the Pacific, Bose died when a Japanese military aircraft crashed in Taiwan.

Gaj Singh, Maharaja of Kamanipur, died when his private airplane crashed in Jodhpur in April 1942, two months after the fall of Singapore. He had been on his way to a conference of the Maharajas of Rajasthan to discuss the war against Japan. The cause of the explosion that sent his aircraft down remains unknown. Hari Singh, Gaj Singh's son, took over his father's title, but the kingdom fell when India declared independence in 1947.

American pilot Jim Parvis joined the Flying Tigers in Burma in July 1941. He became a Curtiss P-40 pilot, transferred to the front lines in mainland China, and participated in more than ten combat missions. In October 1942, he flew from Chengdu to intercept a squadron of Type Zero Carrier Fighters and never returned. By the end, Parvis had earned a total of 6,500 dollars in special bonus pay.

Colonel Mohammed Hussein of the Iraqi Army rose against both the British and their puppets, the Hashemite family. Hussein led a group of like-minded officers to surround the British Embassy in Baghdad. The very next month, however, Hussein would fall in battle, shot while facing British Indian forces under the command of Field Marshal Sir Claude Auchinleck.

Under increasing pressure due to his failure to improve the mass production of military aircraft, Chief of the Luftwaffe Technical Office General Ernst Udet suffered a nervous breakdown. He shot himself dead in Berlin in November 1941.

Luftwaffe Major Gerhart Graf received a promotion to Lieutenant Colonel and served on the Eastern front as deputy commander of the 52nd Fighter Wing until the summer of 1943. In October of that year, Graf was promoted to commander of the 301st Night Fighter Wing. Graf was arrested as a conspirator in the assassination plot against Adolf Hitler. He was executed by firing squad in August 1944.

Lieutenant Commander Seishiro Ohnuki, adjutant to the Ministry of the Navy, had been appointed to the General Staff of the Combined Fleet in December 1940. Under Admiral Isoroku Yamamoto, Ohnuki helped draw up the plans for the attack on Pearl Harbor. Later, he served numerous task forces as chief staff officer. In October 1944, Ohnuki went down with the carrier *Zuikaku* in the Battle off Cape Engano.

Junzo Yamawaki, secretary to the Ministry of the Navy, married Mariko Ando in October 1941. Beginning in the summer of 1944, Yamawaki worked secretly under Deputy Navy Minister Shigeyoshi Inoue to negotiate a peaceful end to the war, to no avail. Yamawaki accompanied the Japanese representatives to the surrender ceremony aboard the USS Missouri in September 1945 as an interpreter. After the war, Yamawaki had two daughters with Mariko and taught international law at Tohoku University and Hitotsubashi University. Mr. Yamawaki passed away in 1972.

In January of 1942, the Naval Memorial Office in Yokosuka issued an official statement that Flight Sergeant First Class Kyohei Inui had died in an accident. British records make no mention of his aircraft. No trace of his body or Zero fighter has ever surfaced.

or just like good books,

DIFFERENT READ

V E R T I C A L.

Comedy of manners
Twinkle Twinkle **by Kaori Ekuni**
"This book is simple. This book is a pearl. This book is like water, clear and loose and natural and fluid." *—BUST magazine*

Ghost story
Strangers **by Taichi Yamada**
"An eerie ghost story written with hypnotic clarity. He is among the best Japanese writers I have read."
—Bret Easton Ellis, author of *American Psycho*

Fantasy epic
The Guin Saga **by Kaoru Kurimoto**
"A swashbuckling fantasy...action is always center stage...intense...dreamlike."
—Seattle Times

THE GUIN SAGA

KAORU KURIMOTO

In a single day and night of fierce
fighting, the Archduchy of Mongaul has
overrun its elegant neighbor, Parros. The lost
priest kingdom's surviving royalty, the young twins
Rinda and Remus, hide in a forest in the forbidding wild
marches. There they are saved by a mysterious creature with
a man's body and a leopard's head, who has just emerged from
a deep sleep and remembers only his name. Guin.

Kaoru Kurimoto's lifework will enthrall readers of all ages with
its universal themes, uncommon richness, and otherworldly
intrigue. New installments of this sterling fantasy series, which
has sold more than twenty-five million copies, routinely make
the bestseller list in Japan.

Visit us at www.vertical-inc.com for a teaser chapter!